SILENCE

D1637134

Books by Zaire Crown

Games Women Play

The Game Never Ends

Silence

SILENCE

ZAIRE CROWN

www.kensingtonbooks.com

DAFINA BOOKS are published by

Kensington Publishing Corp.
119 West 40th Street
New York, NY 10018

All Kensington titles, imprints, and distributed lines are available at special quantity discounts for bulk purchases for sales promotion, premiums, fund-raising, and educational or institutional use.

Special book excerpts or customized printings can also be created to fit specific needs. For details, write or phone the office of the Kensington Sales Manager: Kensington Publishing Corp., 119 West 40th Street, New York, NY 10018. Attn. Sales Department. Phone: 1-800-221-2647.

The Dafina logo is a trademark of Kensington Publishing Corp.

ISBN: 978-1-4967-4190-5
First Trade Paperback Printing: July 2023

ISBN: 978-1-4967-4192-9 (e-book)
First Electronic Edition: July 2023

10 9 8 7 6 5 4 3 2 1

Printed in the United States of America

Shout out to the four kings who helped to shaped me
by lending me their individual strengths:
Steve, the King of Spades, for my intellect and creativity
Rick, the King of Hearts, for my humility and empathy
Matthew, the King of Clubs, for my courage and tenacity
Caesar, the King of Diamonds, for my hustle and game

Chapter One

She was a gangster chick.

In high-pressure situations, people can tell you their life stories with a gesture. She might have been born into money but wasn't some sheltered suburban girl who had spent her childhood in books. She had a few brothers, had seen some things. We had no conversation or shared history. Her response to my presence told me everything I needed to know about her pedigree.

Most women would've screamed. To come out their bathroom and find my big black ass waiting on the other side of the door would've made a few men take a second shit—trust me, it had. But this chick didn't panic. She didn't even flinch when she met the eyes of an intruder.

Without hesitation, she stole me. She threw a stiff right jab that had decent form. Caught me in the nose. Stunned me. She put enough sting on it to water my eyes.

She sprinted for the dining room, where a red ostrich Chanel bag sat on a table of mirrored glass. We both knew what was in that bag, and had I not been so out of practice, I would've thought to search it while she was still on the toilet.

She was quick but couldn't escape my reach. Grabbed her

from the back, a fistful of shirt and good Malaysian weave. I didn't hurt her, just manhandled her in a way to show how easily I could. Shook her up and bounced her off the wall a few times until the fire left her brown eyes.

I searched that purse to find a light-weight Glock 19 and a license to carry registered to Tyeisha Henley. I also found about eight hundred in cash. Both got donated to my revenge fund.

I left Tyeisha on the sofa wearing duct tape. I used her phone to leave Punchy a cryptic message saying: *"Home now!"* That was forty-five minutes ago.

I knew she was alone before I kicked in the back door but went through the house to double check.

I started with the master bedroom upstairs. The lady took her poundings on a king-sized pillow-top with a sturdy headboard in imitation marble. Nearly two hundred pairs of shoes lined the walls—his and hers retro sneakers, heels for all occasions. An avalanche of clothes spilled out the closet with leather, mink, and expensive denim balled up on the floor like it wasn't shit to them. A few icy chains and watches sat on the dresser: the Submariner Rolex and a rose-gold Ulysse Nardin. Life was good.

One of the other two rooms was princess-themed: matching pink lace with flouncing on the drapes and a canopy twin bed. A dream house for the black Barbie dolls along with every pink accessory Mattel ever sold. On the wall, a 56-inch Vizio was connected to PlayStation and Xbox consoles.

I searched every floor, hitting all the likely stash spots, but didn't turn up much. Other than the jewelry, there was a few hundred dollars more in the bedroom. I ran across paraphernalia under the kitchen sink: Saran Wrap, baggies, Ohaus triple-beam, but no dope. All I found in the basement were boxes stacked chest-high with candy bars, snack cakes, cases of canned soda like these people didn't believe in diabetes.

A studio picture hung in the dining room of Punchy holding a girl about eight years old: the princess. She shared her parents' features. Twelve-thirty on a Tuesday would place her at school. I was glad for her sake that she hadn't been sick this day.

I was told that Punchy had come up. The ice upstairs, the Infiniti truck outside, and the eight-thousand square feet in Sherwood Forest offered sufficient proof. I studied the hardwood floors and the coffered ceilings twenty feet above, trying to appraise what the house would go for in a fair real estate market.

Punchy blew up his baby mama, but I had the phone and ignored his calls. I went through his kitchen like I paid bills there, even helped myself to a bowl of cereal. Then I joined the lady in the living room on a butter-soft cream-colored suede sectional with fourteen pieces.

To her credit, Tyeisha handled this like a G. She didn't cry or whimper, just sat on the couch opposite me looking all evil and cute. I could tell she wanted to cuss me out but duct tape covered her juicy DSLs. Pretty doe eyes beamed hatred as I crushed her daughter's Apple Jacks.

Nice little body, too. Petite. One hundred and fifteen pounds. Full C-cups that Punchy had probably cashed out for swelled under a Michigan State T-shirt. White yoga pants with a green splatter print complemented her outfit and toned thighs.

She smelled like hair conditioner and shea butter. The scent was fucking with me and for a moment had me curious as to what she might taste like. My sleeping beast started to stir.

I refocused and put away the temptations a weaker man might have acted on. That wasn't my MO. If I had to kill Tyeisha Henley, she would be left with her dignity.

It took another hour before Punchy finally showed. He pulled up in a new BMW 760Li, burgundy over tan, but fucked it up with some big dumbass twenty-six-inch rims. Just like a nigga not used to having shit.

I watched from the window as three doors opened. Punchy jumped out in an all-white Gucci sweatsuit with the sneakers, chunky chain swinging from the motion.

The other two with him were off-brands. One was a slender

dude in a black Nike shirt and scuffed up LeBrons. The second, thickset, wore a navy-blue Polo shirt and jeans way too tight for a big fella. Neither of them looked like they matched Punchy's hustle, and neither looked threatening.

Punchy was the first through the door to see Wifey tied up on the sofa. She tried to warn him with her eyes, but dude ain't never been too sharp.

The instant the third guy was in the room, I slammed the door shut from where I had hidden behind it. They reeked of a potent strand. All three turned to me with beet-red eyes, slack-jawed like they were waiting for me to explain what was happening.

I had been trained early to capitalize on that split second of surprise or indecision.

Polo Shirt was the closest to me, a full-sized black and stainless-steel Smith & Wesson SR40 tucked into his waistband. I snatched that gun and smashed his partner's nose with the butt. A bloody discharge fired from the nostrils of Nike's broken beak. My left caught his chin, sprawled him on the hallway stairs.

Polo Shirt wrapped me from behind, pinned my arms to neutralize the pistol. This fat muthafucka hid some power under his flab. He locked his arms at the wrists so I couldn't muscle out of the hold.

He tried to lift me but couldn't get my body high enough to leverage it for a slam. He was five-foot-ten, a sloppy-built two hundred and forty pounds. The advantages of my height and weight were due to genetics as much as discipline.

I would go to the ground but only on my own terms. Using my longer legs, I swept his foot, and while he was off-balance, I flopped backwards. Hard. The fall crushed him between the floor and my two hundred and seventy pounds. The impact unlocked his arms and probably knocked the wind out of him.

I scrambled to turn over then pistol-whipped him with his own .40. I thumped the top of fat boy's skull a dozen times like a carpenter trying to hammer a stubborn nail. I left him barely conscious, bloody scalp leaking into his eyes.

By the time I got to one knee, Punchy already had his pistol aimed at my head. My angle caused the bore of his 9mm to loom as large as a battleship cannon.

I looked up to let him get a good view of my face, and watched his eyes swell with recognition. And fear.

He lowered the gun, retreated a few steps as I regained my full six-foot-five-inch height. The expression he wore could've revealed me as Michael Myers or Jason Voorhees.

He mouthed the word: "Silence!"

Chapter Two

More than anything, I had been waiting to see Punchy's reaction to me.

My intrusion made his fear plausible. Punchy knew who I was, knew what the church had done to me. Because of that, I forgave the way his whole body shook. How he looked like he was ready to run and dive straight through the glass of his picture window.

I wanted to know if he had any other cause to fear me.

The skinny one would need his nose reset, and fat boy might require some head staples. Both would be fine after a trip to the hospital. It just as easily could've been the morgue, and Punchy knew fucking with me, it still might be.

That's why his trembling fingers surrendered that Taurus 9 when I held out my hand. I checked Nike Shirt for a weapon, the first one I dropped. He only had a cheap Android with a cracked screen.

I turned back to Punchy, seeing the changes twelve years had put into him. He wore his age in his eyes like most of us—too much liquor and weed, not enough water and sleep. He'd lost about half an inch on his hairline; a few gray strands grew at the temples of his tapered cut.

Punchy used to be the Omega dog in our pack. Every crew has a Punchy. The weak one everybody has to protect. The one who could never maintain his own hustle. On club night, you had to let him rock one of your outfits and might have to pay his cover. You loaned him money knowing you'd never see it back, fronted him dope knowing he'd only fuck up the sack.

I tried to reconcile that bum with the Punchy who stood in front of me dripping in white Gucci, buffalo-horn Cartiers with prescription lenses. The iced-out P hanging from his chain had some weight to it, and the stones had clarity. The same could be said about the platinum Audemar shining on his wrist. It threw me to see the same dude who used to beg to borrow my Regal pushing the flagship Beemer on blades.

And living with a chick who was bad enough to be in the same magazines I was just jacking off to. I saw in Tyeisha a new fear after witnessing the violence I unleashed, violence I kept restrained while we were alone.

I made Punchy join her on the couch while the guns I took from them both joined each other on my hip. Polo Shirt's Ruger rested on my lap when I sat opposite the couple.

Punchy asked, "When the fuck you get out?"

I directed his attention to my attire. I wasn't as fresh as he was. My tan pants were made from polyester so stiff they could stand up without me in them. The matching shirt was a simple V-neck pullover. My shoes were cheap black oxfords made mostly of plastic.

I could pinpoint the exact moment when Punchy realized how serious this visit was. My uniform was what the Michigan Department of Corrections sent prisoners home in when they had no one to pick them up or bring a change of clothes. The fact that I came straight to his house the second they opened the gates—before going to meet my P.O. or getting some ass—proved that I was not bullshitting.

Punchy scratched his cheek, a nervous habit. "Look, man, what happened to Doc was fucked-up. And everybody figured you was gone go ape shit when you got home."

Everybody was right.

"But nigga, you here like I had something to do with that."

My expression said he needed to convince me.

"I bumped into Doc 'bout a year ago at the casino, blowin' stacks at the crap table. We caught up a little bit. That was the last time I saw him."

I adjusted myself on his nice suede sofa, got more comfortable. A novelty wall clock hung in the kitchen with TIME TO EAT above the face, a spoon and fork for the hour and minute hands. My eyes lingered there.

Ninety percent of communication is nonverbal. Punchy had been a longtime friend who knew that a lot was spoken through my subtle gestures. He checked his own watch to confirm that it was after two p.m.

He mouthed, "Whole lotta shit done changed, Sy. It's been about six or seven years since the crew been tight like that. I shook niggas off when I realized Doc, Prime, and Louie wasn't trying to see me shine for real. So I put together my own team, dropped my first blow spot on Fenkell and Griggs—before I knew it, I had six more, along with a hundred of them little four-one hitters ready to shoot for me."

Fenkell Avenue? It ain't nothing but killers over there.

"I had that hood on lock and was ready to drop a rim and detail shop when I got put up on a better move. One that literally let me *change* the game."

I warned Punchy with a glare that he didn't have time for cap or talking in riddles.

He threw a nervous glance to his watch, then started speaking fast, making it hard for me to keep up. "Vending machines—pop, chips, Rice Krispie Treats. And all the change make it easy to clean up the money. I got twenty-three INF5s in office buildings throughout metro right now, and in two years, I'm gone have a few hundred."

That explained all the candy in the basement.

"You know me, Sy. I wouldn't have never threw rocks at the throne."

Coming in, I already knew Punchy didn't possess the mental or testicular fortitude to come for my dude. Had I thought him responsible, there wouldn't have been any need for conversation. He would've come home to find his girl dead; then I would've clapped him and his mans the second they walked through the door.

I was there because Punchy could catch me up and hopefully put me on the right path.

"I ain't even find out about Doc 'til two weeks after it happened. Bands posted something on The Book of her and all her girls wearing RIP T-shirts."

Who the fuck was Bands? He read the question on my face.

Punchy looked at me like I'd been gone too long. "Quianna. She go by Q-Bands now."

Q-Bands? I carried the mental picture of a scrawny twelve-year-old tomboy in braces and braids that the hood used to call Li'l Quay-Quay.

"I felt sick about missing his service," Punchy said, referring to Doc. "Even though we lost touch, I still would've liked to pay my respects to a nigga I went back to elementary with."

The shit had hit me like a gut-shot three months back when I got Mrs. P's card in the mail: *We lost Darius the other day. Try to keep it together.* Those eleven words had been the hardest thing I dealt with on the inside.

The news came four days after my parole board hearing. I was still waiting on a decision: High-Probability on my score sheet and cuts to the state budget, making my release practically a guarantee.

It took everything I had in me not to lose my outdate. I walked around those last ninety days ready to kill anybody who made eye contact.

From the corner of my eye, I saw Nike Shirt's legs start to

move. His black LeBrons scraped back and forth across the floor as if trying to jog his way back to consciousness. I walked to the stairs and dropped a bomb on his chin that stilled his happy feet.

I stepped over fat boy in the Polo shirt to make sure he didn't need a touch-up. He was still fetal, cradling his agony. He gripped his skull as if he feared it would shatter into pieces.

By this time, Tyeisha sat on the sofa squirming, shaking her head like a dog trying to be free of a muzzle. Punchy asked if he could remove her gag, and I nodded my permission. The lady was halfway through a torrent of curses before he peeled off the tape. I couldn't make it all out but felt safe to assume I was the subject.

The spoon was past the two, and the fork was creeping up on the six, damn near two-thirty, almost time for a little girl to come home from school expecting nothing more than a snack and her favorite video game. They didn't want me to meet their daughter.

I found a pen and some scrap paper. I scribbled something quick then passed it along. Punchy looked over the list I had written. He was smart enough to know this was not a request.

Doc was dead. I was home, and the streets was expecting me to go ape shit.

They would get King Kong on laxatives.

Chapter Three

Michigan was so cheap that my state-issue pants didn't even have pockets. After I took all the cash Punchy had on him and added that to what I already took from Tyeisha, my war chest totaled thirty-two hundred. The bills were stuffed down the front of my drawers.

My arsenal currently stood at three pistols. Polo Shirt's SR40 rode on my hip. Punchy's little Taurus 9 and his girl's Glock 19 were stashed under the passenger seat.

My friend was even generous enough to let me borrow his old-school Chevy, told me to keep it as long as I wanted. A clean-ass donked-out '84 Caprice: light-green candy like an apple Jolly Rancher with forest-green interior. I wasn't up on the latest rims, but the thirty-inch chrome monstrosities resembled ninja stars. It looked wired for maximum bass, but the system mattered to me as much as an ashtray to a non-smoker. I did love whatever he had under the hood, because even while idling, the motor sent power-ful vibrations through me.

I had been nice enough not to take the BMW or Wifey's In-finiti truck. Punchy already knew that if I just happened to get pulled over by a cop claiming that the Caprice was reported stolen, I would pay another visit and introduce myself to the entire family.

I drove southbound on Livernois feeling like a tourist in my own city. A lot of new businesses, but a lot more closures. Too many graffiti-covered storefronts with boarded-over windows. The struggle was visible.

From inside, I watched the national news relegate Michigan to a cautionary tale about civic corruption. The proud Motor City, once the literal and figurative driving force behind America's economy, bankrupt and on the verge of collapse. People in Flint drinking sewage when the state is surrounded by the five largest bodies of fresh water on the planet—make that make sense.

I rolled down the window and let air from the free world kiss my face. It was late April but unseasonably warm for the spring. Many of the ladies had already pulled their summer gear out of hibernation: crop tops and short-shorts making an early appearance.

My stomach grumbled a reminder that I had skipped breakfast—couldn't see marching to the chow hall for cold oatmeal and dry toast on my last day. I hit the drive-thru of a KFC/Taco Bell, a restaurant suffering from bipolar disorder. I rejoined traffic with a breast and thigh combo with mashed potatoes and a biscuit. The smell had me unable to wait for a destination.

The very first bite damn near made me spit chicken out the window. I'd spent twelve years fiending for some Original Recipe, so I tried a second bite. That one made me want to gag.

My first thought was that the Colonel had fucked up the secret recipe until I remembered something told to me by one of my old cell mates. He was on his second bit after doing twenty for a body, and he had said that he wasn't able to eat the food when he first got out. Everything on the prison menu is either baked, boiled, or steamed. Decades without fried food leaves us hypersensitive to grease, which explained why each bite seemed like I had just taken a spoonful of Crisco. I dropped the breast and used the biscuit to get the taste out my mouth.

I continued down Livernois, where liquor, cellphones, and fast food seemed to be the only hustles. I hung a right on Davidson Ave and another quick left on a street named Monica.

These were my old stomping grounds, but I barely recognized the area. This quiet little street used to be lined with big brick houses, most of them two-family flats, inherited from the Irish and Polish, who fled during the riotous sixties and maintained by the hardworking black families who still took pride in the properties well into the 2000s. Now over half of those homes were burned-out shells or empty lots the neighbors used for bulk trash. The hood looked like the government did a repeat of Black Wall Street when they flew over and bombed the niggas.

In the middle of the second block, Mrs. P had one of the few remaining structures. The grass was dead, and litter covered the front yard. The red brick façade was cracked, and the trim was paint-chipped. The windows were covered with ripped screens. Shingles slid from the roof. Other than a shiny black-on-black Charger in the driveway, nothing looked like money. I thought it was a trap house, because damn near twenty muthafuckas were out front—kids, hoodrats, and young fellas who look like they gangbang.

I had to park two houses down, but the Caprice had all of their attention by the time I jumped out. Even without the tan uniform, I looked like somebody fresh out the pen. They could see in my face that I ain't had much to smile about the last few years, an animal who ain't did shit but lift weights and brush his hair. My Caesar was low with waves on spin. My beard came down past my neck, full but neatly trimmed.

The adults were perched on stumps, on the steps, and on the concrete railing that lined the porch. A few blunts were in rotation, and nearly everyone sipped from a red plastic cup. The fellas and a butch lesbian all tried their best to intimidate me. I met everybody's grim expression as my trained eyes quickly assessed which of them had pistols tucked.

They looked as if they expected me to acknowledge them. One

of them might have asked who I was looking for. Fuck 'em. I breezed past everybody on the porch and walked straight into the lower flat like I lived there. Because I did once.

The same well-worn brown carpet in the living room was under the same faded leather three-piece sofa set we sat on back in the day. The walls and mantle above the fireplace were covered with old photos of Doc and Quay-Quay along with new flicks of kids I never met.

The smell of fried okra, onions, and Polish sausage told me she was in the kitchen. Nerves soured my stomach more than the KFC.

I cut through the dining room and found her at the stove using her step stool. Her hair was short in a silver bob with bangs. Her oversized gown would drag the floor when she walked.

After a few seconds of me watching her from the doorway, she must've felt my presence. She turned. We locked eyes.

I waved as if to say *Hey!* I even put on a smile for one of the few people in the world who could get that out of me.

She responded by throwing a bottle of vinegar at my head.

Chapter Four

The vinegar came racing towards my head. The fact that she didn't hesitate to throw it, or that I wasn't surprised, should tell you something about what it was like living under Mrs. P's roof. My reflexes were sharp enough for me to duck an instant before the bottle would have caught me in the face.

Before coming to her, I had been raised by savages; by the time I was nine, I knew eight different ways to kill an unarmed combatant with my bare hands. I am six-five, two-seventy, with less than four percent body fat. Yet I was still about to get my ass kicked by a sixty-three-year-old lady who stood five-foot-two and barely weighed ninety-five pounds.

She screwed her face up. "So that's what'cha gone do? After all this muthafuckin' time, you just gone walk in here like it ain't shit, with yo' big Sasquatch-looking ass?" Most of this came from her hands, but her lips added the curses.

I lowered my eyes and stepped forward to accept the punishment I had coming, punishment I deserved. Her small fists beat my chest. I actually had to stoop down to receive the slaps to my head.

"You go dark on my ass for three months, don't write or shit.

And you know what the hell we was going through." Her hands were moving so fast that I could barely keep up with them.

Seeing her tears threatened my own. I used my closed right hand to circle my heart.

"Sorry?! You should be sorry, muthafucka." She scanned the counter. "I need something hard enough to knock some sense into yo' dumb ass."

I handed her the cloth oven mitt hanging from the stove, and that made her smile through the tears. She hugged me, and even with the aid of her step stool, her head only reached my chest.

That I took Doc's passing so hard was a bullshit excuse for shutting out the family. The pain from losing a son had to be ten times worse than the pain from losing a brother. She had every right to beat my ass. Part of me wished she could hit harder.

She pulled back from me and signed, "We tried to get you to the homegoing."

I nodded my understanding. The Michigan Department of Corrections does permit prisoners to attend the funeral service for family members, but the request was denied when the state learned that I wasn't technically related to the Petersons. Living in the same house and being raised as a son didn't matter to the MDOC. I wasn't blood.

Mrs. P looked over me, tugged at my beard. "Supposed to be a goddamned Viking now?"

I stroked my chin hair and gave her a look that said, *Don't hate.*

She frowned at noticing the blood streaked across my shirt, blowback from when I broke dude's nose in the Nike shirt. I offered a guilty shrug.

"Boy, we just got you back. Don't you go doin' nothing stupid."

My hands told lies, but the truth could be read on my face. I was about to fuck up some shit, and the old lady knew it. Convincing me to let it go wasn't a fight neither of us wanted right then, so she just squeezed my arm in a way that said, *Be careful.*

Grief had probably aged her ten years in the last three months.

The dark bags made her hazel eyes appear to sink into her skull, crow's feet pinching them at the corners. Her skin was pale, like she hadn't been outside much, and her dress suggested the same—three in the afternoon, and she was still in a nightgown.

I reached into my drawers to offer her some of the thirty-two hundred.

She lit a Newport off the gas stove. "Nigga, don't nobody want none of yo' sweaty dick-money!" It could have been pride or just her knowing I would need the cash to handle business.

We conversed for a while, her hands so fluid and fast that most of the time I had to cheat by reading her lips. My signing was sloppy, and my old teacher told me so. I was twelve years out of practice.

Then Mrs. P found a wicked smile. She pounded the ceiling with a broomstick, made up something about needing seasoning salt from the store. I was still trying to figure out the game when the old lady hid me in the pantry.

It took about a minute before she appeared in the kitchen. I only had a partial view of her back but could tell by the animated movements she was laying into her mother about not making that trip to the store. I crept up from behind and grabbed her shoulder.

She spun on me, fist raised, face twisted in anger until recognition kicked in. Then Quianna looked sick and stumbled a bit like she was about to faint. When I tried to catch her, she jumped up to wrap me with her arms and legs. She held me around the neck tight enough to choke me out. I felt her tears on my cheek.

I eased her down and looked over Li'l Quay-Quay, now in the form of a grown woman. She still had Doc's light-brown complexion, the hazel eyes they both inherited from Mrs. P, along with the thick, coarse eyebrows I used to tease her about. Other than that, I saw no trace of the skinny tomboy who used to follow me around. Blond hair fell over her shoulder, her head shaved around the left side and back with a fret pattern skillfully cut into the stubble. A sleeve of tattoos covered her right arm that mostly had an Asian theme: Geishas, Kabuki masks, dragons, and Chinese lettering. She was fresh as hell wearing a denim romper over a Chanel T-shirt, gold-colored heels matching a belt with two big Cs on the buckle.

During the same time she was taking in the changes to me. "Look at you. Been in that bitch going hard on the workout."

I wasn't the only one who had added to my physique, but while I had put on muscle, Quianna had packed on those pounds that create feminine curves. She had to be five-foot-four, one fifty-five on the low end.

Then out of nowhere, she punched me in the chest hard as hell. "How the fuck you gone not holla' at nobody nigga!"

Like mother, like daughter.

The three of us stood there for twenty minutes, offering apologies and belated condolences until one the young dudes from the porch intruded on us. He walked in the kitchen, yanked open the refrigerator, and grabbed a juice. He twisted the cap, then leaned against the counter like he had every right to be in the middle of our moment. About nineteen, tall enough to be around six-three but crackhead thin, rocking a bleached nappy afro.

I didn't appreciate him game-tapping and wanted him to know. I mugged the youngster, ready to slap the Tropicana out of his mouth.

Quianna read my hostility. She said, "Silence, that's Trayvion. Your godson."

That immediately thawed my stare. Not until I searched did I see my friend Doc in his oldest boy. Trayvion had been about five or six when I left, so the math added up.

I patted my chest to say *My bad,* offered him a thin smile and my fist.

He dapped me up. "What's up, Unc. I still remember you from back in the day. Never saw my old man unless you was right there with him. Used to think I had two pops."

I recalled the lanky youngster as a toddler. Little Tray, barely able to walk, would stumble up to me and grab hold of my pants leg. This had amazed me, because most kids were afraid of me, like I was afraid of most kids. I never even held a baby before Trayvion. In the UOTA, women take care of the children until they are old enough to start training.

He wasn't that same baby anymore. When I hugged Trayvion, I could smell the fear as much as I could feel it in his embrace. He was old enough to have heard the streets talk. To him I was just a reputation, a name attached to a series of violent stories.

The four of us stood in the kitchen for another hour, catching up as I tried to make my godson feel comfortable around me. In the next couple of days, I had every intention of adding to my reputation.

Chapter Five

Mrs. P wanted to feed me. Quianna wanted to take me shopping. Since I was still nauseated by the taste of greasy chicken and didn't want to offend the woman who took me in by throwing up her fried okra, Quianna won out.

When I told Quianna I could buy my own clothes, she pulled a cash brick from her Birkin that was easily forty stacks, told me not to worry about it. When I asked about the money, she put it back in her bag, told me not to worry about it.

I let her know I wasn't fucking with no skinny jeans.

That loaf she carried should've clued me that the Charger parked in the driveway was hers. Black-on-black Hellcat on black twenty-four-inch Ruccis. It was definitely a woman's car: the leather interior smelled like perfume, hair spray, and premium weed. I watched her from the passenger seat feeling a big brother's pride, even though her driving scared the shit out of me.

Our first stop was to a local cell shop to buy me the latest iPhone. She and the salesman spent twenty minutes teaching me how to send and receive texts. For me, learning all the other features could wait.

Half an hour later, we were out at Somerset Mall with

Quianna dressing me up like she used to do her dolls back in the day. She introduced me to Balmain, Balenciaga, and Fendi denim—only loose fitted. We hit the Gucci store and Louis Vuitton for loafers, shirts, and belts. Quianna sat back, sipping champagne, watching me try on shit I never heard of. It reminded me of Richard Gere and Julia Roberts in *Pretty Woman*, only in this situation, I was the prostitute.

I walked through the mall carrying a dozen bags. I changed in JCPenney and donated that tan prison shit to the trash. Polo shirt with Gucci holding up my Levi's, the shoes matching my belt. I looked like The Man but felt a little like a bitch since it all came on Quianna's dime.

Four guys were walking behind us when we left Foot Action, where I had just got treated to the Jordan 3s, the 9s and a few pair of Air Maxes. Quianna shot back an irritated glare that told me one of them said something disrespectful.

I felt some type of way because they didn't know who she was to me. I turned back, mugged each one, made sure to commit the faces to memory. They were emboldened by their superior numbers, so they looked at me like *Nigga, it's whatever.* I used my phone to ask Quianna what they said, but she just grabbed my arm and led me into another store.

This was a brightly lit boutique filled with women's couture. It was her turn to play Julia.

She tried on a sundress with a purple floral print that I gave a thumbs-up. The next was a sky-blue top and navy tennis skirt that I thought looked good individually but not as a set. I'm a big goon-ass nigga who don't know the first thing about women's fashion, but Quianna seemed to value my opinion.

The fourth outfit was when shit got weird. Quianna came out the dressing room and froze everybody in the store. The yellow baby-T barely fell below her breasts. The matching shorts were so tiny that I first thought they were panties.

The young fellas coming to prison had already gave me the heads-up on some of the new trends in the streets, including the girls wearing tight shit with no underwear to show off their camel toe. Apparently having a fat pussy has become a point of pride for women like having a big dick was for men. I was not ready for Quianna to be so damn proud.

I sent my eyes in every other direction. When she tried for my attention, I played on my handicap.

She modeled the little bit of clothing there was, forcing me to notice that her small upthrust tits were braless under that top, that her stomach had a bit of a pouch that you would expect from a woman missing no meals and was decorated with a navel ring.

She turned to the mirror, revealing to everybody an ass like two pumpkins falling out the bottom of those shorts. I diverted my eyes, but an old head shopping with his wife got caught staring. I watched him get spazzed on then dragged out the store.

I made Quianna flag for my attention again. "I'd do this on a day when it's like ninety outside."

I texted her: *#Thotweather.* She gave me the finger.

She continued to study her reflection, tossing her hair. I looked at those juicy lips, those cat eyes, and had to remind myself this was my best friend's baby sister. I flooded my mind with images of Quianna at eight, the age she was when I spent a year living with her family. I focused on that girl with the braces and braids.

You don't think this look good on me? The question came through my iPhone and felt like a trap. I used a few seconds to think before sending my answer.

Love it on somebody else.

"I'm a grown-ass woman and been wearing what I want for the longest," her lips informed me.

She read my response, then rolled her eyes. I had texted: *It's your money Li'l Quay-Quay.* That made her storm back into the changing room.

My eyes made up for my ears, like a paraplegic whose strong arms had to compensate for his legs. But sometimes my sharp vision was a gift as much as a curse. I had a way of zeroing in and focusing on small things that could turn out later to be important or insignificant.

The hem on those shorts exposed a tattoo high on her inner thigh. It was only an inch long and probably would have been missed at that distance by anybody else.

It was a tiny pair of red lips with a finger in front of them.

Chapter Six

Quianna had the cashier ring up that skanky yellow outfit along with identical ones in white and neon pink, I think just to spite me. She also copped a few other things I didn't have to turn away from when she tried on. We left the boutique adding four bags to our total.

We walked side by side, thoughts connecting through technology. I thanked her for the clothes and promised to pay her back when I got situated. She just cursed me out again for not telling anybody I was coming home, said she could've already had the shit waiting for me.

Quianna was back in the denim romper, but the yellow shorts and tattoo still haunted me. Bony Li'l Quay-Quay with the ashy knees had become a hazel-eyed dimepiece. As much as I tried not to think about it, the world wouldn't let me forget. Some of the guys we walked past made *Damn!* faces, while the more respectful assumed I was the proud owner and offered discreet nods of approval.

I confess to having a fetish for thick chicks. BBW. The first sixteen years of my life was without TV or the Internet. Women in the tribe weren't soft or feminine; they were lean and hard like the men, good for breeding but built for combat. I never saw a D-cup breast until I left the mountains, until I came to Detroit and a girl named T'wanda twisted my mind.

The complexion, the eyes, the brows—there was too much of Doc in his little sister, and that made me check myself. I refocused on the ones who killed her brother. Somebody had left my boy slumped on the wheel of his Bentley with two holes in his skull. I let the images of him refuel my anger and motivate me to stay on task.

When my phone buzzed again, it was Quianna asking me what's up with something to eat. My stomach felt ready to make another attempt.

Riding down the escalator, I saw Quianna make that face again. Her expression let me know that the same guys from earlier were behind us, even before I turned to check. The quartet rode seven stairs back. Two of the bigger dudes were built like bowling pins, while the third looked like he might have seen a gym at least once in his life. The fourth one barely had Quianna by an inch in height. All were giggling like they found something funny about us.

We stepped off the escalator, and I used the shop windows along with every reflective surface to keep track of them. They trailed us at about fifteen feet. The shortest one walking in the middle appeared to be the comedian and the alpha. He did most of the talking, while the three flanking him laughed like trained hyenas. He had on enough ice to be a decent lick to somebody like me.

Quianna led me to a Chipotle stand, and the choice made me nervous. If my system had rejected something as plain as fried chicken, Mexican food would probably fuck me over.

I was hoping little dude and his cronies would continue on past. They entered the food court right behind us. I recognized the look of muthafuckas determined to be on bullshit.

So when they approached, I was already on high alert. The short one came at Quianna like he was trying to holler. I thought he might be some low-level celebrity. He stepped to her, not like somebody trying to make an introduction, but with the brashness of somebody who felt he was already supposed to be recognized and worshipped.

Plus the three with him had the look of security. His boys stood around as if waiting and wanting me to jump. At least two were bonded. Both had Glocks in simple clip-on holsters; not concealing them meant they had licenses to open carry.

And I'm in this bitch naked, feeling like a fool for leaving the SR40 in the car. This was Troy, not Detroit, and I honestly didn't think I would need a gun just to go shopping.

I couldn't read their lips from my angle, but it was clear that Quianna wasn't trying to fuck with this dude. Headshakes and hand gestures indicated that she was politely deflecting his game. I know the phony smile of a woman who's irritated but trying to be diplomatic. Maybe it was because she didn't want to create a scene in front of all these white people.

Only this fool ain't taking hints, steady trying to touch her. I wanted to slap him hard enough to make his little head spin.

He was oblivious, but his bodyguards picked up on my hostile energy. My hands were full: carry straps from six bags fisted in my left, seven bundled in my right. They knew that when I dropped them, it would be time to dance.

We started to hold up the Chipotle line, so I waved the family waiting behind us to go around. The mother escorted her two preteen sons by with a nervous glance. I wasn't the only one who could smell tension in the air mingling with the scent of black beans and seasoned beef.

Quianna jerked her head towards me, then gave my arm a squeeze. I figured she was trying to pass me off as her man, hoping the would-be suitor showed an ounce of decency and respect.

Little Goofy looked me up and down like I was the short one, like he had me by a foot. His smirk was the one you give somebody you clearly feel aren't competition.

I took a step forward in case he couldn't read my face way up here. I didn't see competition, either, but I damn sure wasn't smirking. I frowned to let him know my size ain't just for show, that I want all the smoke.

He turned his back on me like I wasn't even worth considering and kept spitting at Quianna, but his security closed in tighter around me. A mistake. I was looking over these dumb mutha-fuckas to see which of them was going to lend me their gun.

Dude kept tugging at her arm until Quianna finally ran out of patience, loosed that infamous Peterson temper. She snatched away and said something that I guessed was no longer diplomatic. Little Goofy had the face of someone who'd just been slapped, a face I knew all too well. Embarrassment, disbelief, and wounded pride altered his features. I could also see his ego deflate like a balloon.

Then he tried to save face by spazzing back on Quianna. His words came with wildly swinging arms and got attention from everybody surrounding us. I didn't get it all, but I know he called her more than one kind of bitch. He capped it by pulling out a fistful of small bills and throwing them in the air. Quianna stood there mortified as cash drifted down on her.

At this point, everybody's laughing, strangers are recording, and I'm heated. I dropped the bags, got into my fight stance. His security took the stance of men ready to draw weapons.

Quianna looked dead at me, eyes wide. "Silence. No. Please." She mouthed this very slowly to make sure I understood.

My old church has a class on how to snatch pistols out of po-lice holsters, so it ain't shit for me to take a burner right off a per-son's hip, just like I did Punchy's boy. The bodyguard with the funny build was standing way too close to me. His cheap-ass hol-ster was only a nylon sleeve without a strap securing the weapon.

It was about to go down right there in the food court in front of two hundred witnesses. The shootout would lead to a shootout with mall security and would end in a shootout with Troy police.

Quianna saw in my face that I was ready to make all of that happen and begged me not to with her eyes. I saw fury and fear in those hazel-colored irises.

I got into a brief staredown with the bodyguards, scanning which of them had the eyes of real killers and wondering if they could do the same. They waited on me to make a move. I wanted to so bad that my legs shook with the energy.

After a few tense seconds, the short dude mumbled something else slick to Quianna then motioned for his boys to go. I took a deep breath, relaxed my muscles, swallowed my pride and humiliation. I didn't give a fuck about me. I let them walk away with their lives so Quianna could do the same.

I picked up our bags while the two little white boys in front of us scrambled to scoop up the littered bills.

Chapter Seven

Quianna battled traffic on the way back to the city. She treated the Charger as if it had embarrassed her in the mall—yanked the wheel for each turn, stomped the gas and brake pedals. I hadn't even received so much as a glance since the incident. She stared ahead, clearly not seeing the road, jaw muscles working as she ground her teeth. Her body radiated the heat from her rage.

One might expect me to be comfortable with awkward silences, but I had never been good in moments like these. It eventually got to where the tension was thick enough to suffocate me.

I finally texted the question: *Where do you dance?*

The second Quianna read her screen, she turned on me like a pit bull ready to attack. I gave her a few seconds to study my face, to see there was no judgment in my expression. This wasn't a critique of her life choices. I just wanted to know if there was a time and place I would get to bump into Little Goofy and his crew again.

I'm not the sharpest knife but was smart enough to piece together the situation. Dude obviously recognized her from the pole, felt his tips paid for access even outside the club. To him, she was just an object of lust and ridicule dehumanized by his wrinkled dollar bills. That's why he felt he could come at her sideways in a public place, even while walking with somebody like me.

Quianna exclaimed, "I ain't danced in six months, and when I did, I made bank. I'm a boss now. I ain't gotta twerk for no nigga I don't wanna twerk for."

She was still kind of aggressive with it, so I raised my palms in surrender. I tried to tell her that she didn't owe an explanation to me or anybody else, but her phone went ignored. I don't knock nobody for how they have to secure their bag.

"I'm not on that shit no more Sy, I swear." Tears were in a race down each side of her face. "I used to work at The Coliseum and a few other clubs, but ain't a nigga out here who can say they bought this pussy. I promise you that!"

In my head, her words sounded like a desperate plea that her glistening eyes helped to sell. Personally, I didn't care if she was still stripping, and whoever she did or didn't trick with was between her, God, and her gynecologist. She was my people, and even if she had sucked every dick in Detroit, I wasn't with anybody disrespecting her.

Quianna nodded like she read all of that in my gaze. She calmed a bit, used the back of her hand to wipe her wet cheeks.

Seeing her like that stirred protective emotions, which made me feel like a piece of shit for the way I looked at her in the boutique. I got so caught up in the changes the past dozen years had put into her body that I forgot that underneath it all, this was still the girl who had been like a baby sister to me. The shame made me avoid her stare, because those creepy Peterson eyes were too good at seeing straight into my head.

I convinced myself it was just the bit. A decade-plus-two was too damn long to go without a woman. I figured I'd be okay after I fucked someone.

I reached across the console and squeezed her hand just to let her know I had her back, no matter what. Quianna held onto my hand when I tried to pull it back. Laced our fingers and rested our hands on her lap for a while.

Her mood improved after that. We both were still pissed, but she didn't beat up the Hellcat so much, and the conversation was easy.

My guess that Little Goofy was some type of celebrity had been right. He was a local rapper whose real handle was Brody Starrz, and even though I'd never heard of him, he apparently dropped a few mixtapes that got some buzz. Quianna admitted that he had been a regular at The Coliseum when she worked there, even hired her once for a private party.

I committed his name to memory just like I'd done his face. Brody Starrz would pay for embarrassing her with at least one broken bone. I didn't tell Quianna, just quietly made that promise to myself.

It was late in the afternoon by the time we got back to the city. A blood-red sun drifted west and painted the sky a thousand crimson shades. The vibe was so good in the car that we even found a few things to laugh about.

We had left the food court without eating and in the end just hit a Wendy's near the house. I insisted on paying. The girl had dropped a twenty-kit on my gear, so dropping eight dollars for a double with cheese combo felt like the least I could do. My burger was greasy but tolerable.

We had just pulled into the driveway on Monica when Quianna turned to me excited. "We gotta throw a party. Do it big. Make that bitch an event the city gone talk about for a year."

I gave her a look that said, *Hell, fuck naw!*

"I'm gone take care of it. Call some of my people, get a club. Turn up one time to let the streets know you home."

I told her I was straight on that. Her brother Doc was the party type who liked to be the center of attention—I was the one who stood in the corner and watched his back. Plus, the streets were about to find out I was home soon enough.

She was persistent, but I had to shut her down with an emphatic rejection. No party. I told her the bags in the trunk filled with designer brands were enough. In fact, that was already too much.

Quianna pouted and looked a little bit like the twelve-year-old she had been when I went inside. But I also saw a glint of mischief in her eyes that hinted at something sneaky.

Even with the drama, hanging with her had been a fun distraction, but I needed to get back on this mission. I dapped her for the clothes, then sent a quick text to her phone: *Next time save us both the headache and just go with the little nigga.*

Quianna threw a couple of French fries at me. Didn't think it was as funny as I did.

Chapter Eight

No sooner than I ran my bags into the house, I was gone again, back in Punchy's ride and headed to see somebody that I knew didn't want to see me. I took the Jeffries Freeway deeper into the westside until I came up in Brightmoor.

Unlike my hood, Brightmoor was pretty fucked-up before I went in. Time had done it no favors. Today it resembled something from one of those post-apocalyptic sci-fi movies. Burned-out storefronts anchored blocks that only had two or three livable dwellings. Some of the streets were so deserted and unused that bushes had actually started to grow up through the cracks in the pavement. Packs of feral dogs roamed the area looking for sustenance while dope fiends did the same. Driving through as dusk descended made me feel like a kid on one of those haunted hayrides.

The last address I had for her was on a street called West Parkway, just six blocks over from the one she grew up on. She had used so many people to pull herself up from this place—me most of all—so only a serious falloff would force a return.

Proof of it came in the form of a small single-story house six empty plots from the corner. There was no porch, just a collapsed pile of wood under the front entrance. Busy fiends had peeled off half the aluminum siding. Security bars covered the windows and doors, making false promises to the inhabitants.

I parked on the street and chirped the alarm while crossing paths with two heads on the sidewalk. Both looked like zombified extras from *The Walking Dead*. They stared hungrily at the green Chevy, estimating its trade value in crack.

I went to the side door that faced an overgrown field littered with car parts. I knocked hard. The info I had was a few years outdated, and I was gambling. But after thirty seconds, the interior door was pulled in, and I stood face-to-face with her. It took each of us a moment to recognize the other.

Ninety percent of communication is nonverbal. When you pull up on somebody unexpected, that first split-second reaction tells the truth in how they feel. It's instinct, from a part of the brain older than the cerebral cortex. I saw fear, anger, and regret cross her face in quick flashes. I saw the look of a trapped animal unsure whether to fight or flee.

But after that fleeting primal response, the rational part of the brain switched back on, allowing her to weigh options. Her eyes bounced from the locked screen back to me, knowing it wouldn't keep me out any more than it kept out the rats and roaches that bred in her walls.

Escaping me was impossible and trying to fight equally futile, so she rightly chose surrender. She suffered a brief coughing fit, then unlocked the security door. She let me into her modest home.

The side entrance served a stairwell, which led to a small kitchen with rusted antique appliances. A mound of unwashed dishes filled the sink. Empty liquor bottles lined the countertops like little glass soldiers standing at attention. The walls were cracked and covered in chipped paint, while a gaping hole in the ceiling exposed wires and insulation. The stench was a mingling of fish grease and cat piss. Each step had me peeling my Gucci sneakers off the sticky tile floor.

I was invited to sit at a rickety card table like a welcomed guest, although she didn't pretend to be happy to receive me. T'wanda took the mismatched chair across from mine. We hadn't seen each other since the trial. I kept in check the maelstrom of negative emotions her face triggered. I was determined to win this.

She asked, "Who told you where I live?"

I pulled from my pocket the only piece of mail that I brought with me from prison. Every few years, the court's collection agency would send me complaints over back child support, and because it was a legal matter, the plaintiff's name and address were on the documents.

I enjoyed watching her face turn sour at realizing that her own failure had allowed me to track her down. She ran to those white folks and gave up my name looking for a handout. Those same white folks had betrayed her to me, just like she had betrayed me to those white folks. I loved the irony.

She looked from the papers to me and could see that I was assessing her. I remembered paying for hair and manicures every six days, so I tripped to see a headscarf over straight-back braids choked with new growth and chewed-on fingernails. She wore a faded Pistons' T-shirt with juice stains and dirty sweats she probably had on for a week. I didn't try to hide my disgust.

"You ain't gotta stare at me like that, Silence." Insecurity caused her to run a hand over her scalp. "I know I'm lookin' a mess right now."

I saw no reason to disagree.

My first love and the girl once called The Brightmoor Barbie seemed to have declined on pace with her hood. Her once-flawless dark chocolate skin was bloated, sagged, and sprinkled with moles. Puffy black circles ringed tired yellow eyes. The eyes matched teeth stained by years of blunts, Newports, and poor oral hygiene. All the smoking also blackened the pink of her lips.

The body that had earned her the Barbie moniker had lost a protracted battle with carbs and inactivity. That invisible line between thick and fat was well in her rearview. T'wanda was about seventy pounds heavier and appeared to have aged half a year for each pound.

I knew it had to kill her to see me looking my best: eyes white, teeth clean, beard fluffed and oiled with my waves spinning hard enough to make a bitch seasick. I was penitentiary-preserved, and my fifty extra pounds were all muscle. Plus I was fresh from the mall. I slowly shook my head, letting her know she was no longer on my level.

I was still giving her a *What the fuck happened to you?* look when she started coughing again. She was hunched over, forcing spasmic barks into her fist, and I worried if this bitch might have something contagious.

I typed three words into my phone, and when she was done going through it, I held up the screen: *Where is Prime?*

The question creased her forehead with wrinkles. She had assumed I was there about her sins. I still might be.

"Prime?" She acted as if that was a foreign word from a language she'd forgotten how to speak. "Boy, I ain't seen my brother in I-don't-know-how-long. We don't talk no more."

The twirling motion I made with my finger signaled I needed more than that.

"Silence, I don't know. A lot done happened since you been gone. Shit different now."

The Taurus 9 had been tucked under my shirt. I sat it on the tabletop to show her that some shit was still the same.

She glanced at the pistol, then measured me with defiance. "I been afraid of this moment since the day you went in, spent years being afraid. Was so afraid for so long that I had time to get tired of it. So gone and do whatever you gone do!"

I knew T'wanda wasn't easily intimidated. She had never been a scary chick, but her reaction still surprised me.

My reaction surprised her more.

I reached across the table and smacked the shit out of her.

Chapter Nine

I slapped her hard enough to send spit from her mouth in gluey strings. The scarf flew off her head like a strong breeze had taken it. She turned back to me with tears brimming wide eyes, a hand pressed to her cheek.

It's important to note that I'm not a woman-beater. In my personal life, I don't get down like that. During our three-year relationship, I never put hands on T'wanda, no matter what she did. Not when she talked crazy to me, not when she stole my jewelry and pawned it, not even when she committed the ultimate act of disrespect.

I had never hit her as my woman, which was why I had to do it then. I didn't make an angry face or give any warning because I needed her to understand that I was not there as a wounded ex-boyfriend. I'm a goon—I was there in my official capacity.

My palm stung, so I could only imagine the fire she felt in her face. I only hit her with about thirty percent of my actual strength. My bench press maxes out at four hundred and ninety-five pounds, so if I had put my all into that slap, her whole head would've came off with the scarf.

We locked eyes, and it was her turn to make a new assessment of me. The Silence she could manipulate with her smiles, tears, and feminine ways no longer lived behind these eyes. I was a different animal wearing his skin.

She saw this in me, and I saw in her a bit more of that fear that she claimed to be so tired of.

My phone had another three-word question for her: *Is anybody here?*

She shook her head. I chambered a shell into the 9, and a Pulitzer Prize–winner couldn't have articulated a better warning.

I didn't sense anybody, so I didn't do a thorough search. I left her at the kitchen table hacking up a lung. The floorplan allowed me to keep watch on her from the living room. The décor reflected her struggle: cigarette burns scarred a rust-colored velour sofa from the seventies, and a loveseat just as old belonged to a different set. The front windows were covered by cheap-ass rayon curtains.

To the left of the front door, a short hall opened on two bedrooms. In the master, a full-sized mattress and box spring sat on milk crates. From the doorway I peeped that her closet held meager choices—the girl I had once kept laced in Dolce and Prada had a wardrobe not worthy of the donation box at the Salvation Army.

The boy's room opposed hers at the other end of the hall. I just glanced in there. Clothes and trash covered the floor ankle-deep. He at least had a frame for his twin bed.

I returned to the kitchen table with another three words on my screen: *Ja'Quezz live here?*

She was still rubbing her jaw, but that widened her eyes more than the slap. "Stay away from MY son!"

I taunted her with the child support papers.

"He ain't yours." Anger twisted her face. "I just used yo' name to get food stamps."

By my math, the boy should've been thirteen. I'd heard she

had two more kids by a different dude that she lost custody of, but I wasn't interested in them, only the oldest. There was a picture of him in the living room at about six years old. I had hoped for a more recent one to see if he favored me or the dead man.

"I almost miscarried. Stress from the trial. From you. He was born six weeks premature. Only four pounds."

She could kill that weak-ass play for sympathy. I drummed my fingers on the table, made a face to show how few fucks I gave.

"I ain't have no choice. The prosecutor said she could charge me, too." T'wanda's eyes lingered on the gun. "I still get nightmares about the blood."

I figured I had traumatized her as much as what she did had traumatized me. I had thought I could handle seeing her, but all the anger and embarrassment inside me struggled to have a voice. The words were trapped in my head like a legion of screaming demons, too many to pass through my phone, and T'wanda had never learned American Sign Language.

Her expression softened a bit. "Silence, I never meant to hurt you—being young and stupid wasn't no excuse. You were good to me, and I really did love you even though I didn't always act like it."

An apology. I thought I had prepared myself for every place this conversation could possibly go. The T'wanda I knew never apologized for shit. Even when she was dead wrong, she still found a way to make it my fault.

"You did so much for me, Sy. You took care of me, and I fucked over you every chance I got. I'm so sorry." I was totally stuck because, in reading her reactions, this seemed sincere.

The tears she shed were of a different quality. "But what you did messed me up forever. My therapist said it's like I got PTSD, that shit people get in the war. I ain't been able to keep no job— I'm on disability because of that shit, Sy. I still can't believe you could do something so . . . so heartless."

I thrust my phone in her face: *Right back at you!!*

T'wanda started to speak but then got caught up in another coughing spell. I felt something was off. I read her eyes and picked up on what she had been doing even before my nose picked up the scent.

Only it was too late. I turned in time to see a metal pipe coming at my head.

Chapter Ten

What I thought was a steel pipe was actually an aluminum base-ball bat.

What I thought was coughing was actually T'wanda shouting instructions to somebody else hiding in the house. The slick-ass bitch wasn't covering her mouth to be sanitary but to keep me from reading her lips.

The problem was that she had always underestimated me, thought deaf meant dumb. While I couldn't hear the enemy trying to creep me from behind, in a quiet world, so many other things drew attention.

Like the vibrations produced by approaching footsteps through the old and loose floorboards. Like the subtle scent of a body at least two days without a shower along with his nervous breaths that came to me in short, quick puffs reeking of tuna fish. However, the biggest warning of the threat at my back had come from T'wanda's own eyes when she glanced up and they widened with fear and anticipation.

I turned just as he was bringing the bat down on my head like a sledgehammer. I barely got my hand up in time to protect my skull from what could've been a death blow.

Pain danced the electric slide from my forearm to fingertips. The spasm unlocked my grip, and Punchy's Taurus 9 seemed to jump out my hand, a cur pet taking after his master.

My knuckles cushioned the impact, but the blow still dazed me. Colorful lights exploded in my eyes like fireworks. I tried to stand, but my legs were rubber bands. I stumbled over to the sink, knocked liquor bottles to the floor. My world spun as if I had emptied a few of them. The attacker was a faceless blur, one person that fazed into three the next second.

He came again, swinging for my head. I faded left, my movements sluggish, got hit on the shoulder. I ignored the pain and responded with a haymaker that would have destroyed anything I made contact with but only caught air.

I got whacked on the side of the knee and almost went down. I grit my teeth, willed my legs to firm up. I was acting like a wounded animal. I centered myself and remembered my Muay Thai. Bishop Owabala had been my instructor, an ex-Army ranger my father ordered to start kicking my ass at just five years old.

I caught the bat on the next swing, snatched it from my weaker opponent. My elbow clipped his jaw, then followed with a body shot to the kidneys that lifted him off his feet. When he folded around the pain, I took his right arm, twisted, ready to snap it at the elbow.

I was still fuzzy, seeing T'wanda with three faces and all of them screaming. She went for the gun. It was closer to me, but I couldn't pick it up without releasing my opponent. I kicked it down the basement steps, where it banked off the side door and skidded across the landing.

I had dude's bony arm and was about to make sure he couldn't wipe his ass with it for at least eight weeks when his face shifted into focus. A face too young. A face too familiar.

His height had concealed his age. I let his arm go, probably more grateful than he that I didn't break it. He tried to look hard. I backed away to show that I was done fighting.

T'wanda was hollering at both of us. Ja'Quezz because she had told him to stay hidden until I was gone, and me because she wanted that to be now. The boy being there changed the whole dynamic for me, so I was ready to be out before this escalated.

When I reached to grab my iPhone off the table, Ja'Quezz took a protective stance in front of his mother. I appreciated that he had heart.

I typed in quickly: *Where Prime?*

Ja'Quezz was bent over, breathing hard, clutching at his side. That kidney shot would probably make his piss blood tonight. I thanked the ancestors my haymaker didn't connect. I hated that I had put hands on little fella, but when he glanced at the 9-millimeter down on the landing, my eyes warned him not to do it.

T'wanda asked, "Why you want Prime? He wouldn't have nothin' to do with Doc getting killed. The nigga dead and you still running behind him doing his dirty work."

I didn't have time for this. I put on my most fearsome face. I looked from T'wanda to her thirteen-year-old son, threatened to do unspeakable things without speaking.

"You ain't shit, Silence. You ain't nothing but a killer, and that's all you gone ever be."

I couldn't make it all out, but I know she called me a deaf bastard, said she never loved me, said she wished they had given me the gas chamber even though Michigan isn't a death-penalty state. My ex told me all the hurtful and hateful things she had been holding back for twelve years.

Then she told me where to find her brother.

Chapter Eleven

I grabbed the pistol on my way out the side door. Jumped in the Caprice, smoked the tires in front of her crib, then smashed out. I knew it was childish, but that's how I was feeling.

I had convinced myself that going to see T'wanda was only about finding Prime—a lie I used to justify a foolish act based on emotions. Being real, I had just wanted to see her, needed some type of closure. All the years I spent in prison studying the disciplines of Sun Tzu, Machiavelli, and Robert Greene were a waste. The bitch had threw me off my game with that fake-ass apology, could still fuck with my head.

From birth I had been raised to be a soldier, trained in rifles and small arms, multiple hand-to-hand and close-combat fighting techniques, knives and other edged weapons, survival skills like bow hunting and tracking prey, wet and dry demolition. I had been trained to face all manner of threats except the most dangerous: a manipulative woman.

I had met T'wanda at seventeen, fresh out the mountains, a virgin who'd never had a girlfriend. I left the church where the sisters didn't do lace fronts, makeup, or tight clothes, so coming to the hood was a shock to my system. I was good in a fight but awkward around girls. T'wanda put that tight pussy on me, and I was gone.

I drove out of Brightmoor under the glow of its few working streetlights. On I-96, I was driving mad like Quianna leaving the mall. I went around a slow-moving Audi whose license plate shared the first three digits of my inmate number. It felt like an omen.

The boy had only tried to defend his mother. A stranger in our kitchen with a gun on Mrs. P would've made me do the same, and worse.

T'wanda said I wasn't nothing but a killer, a fact I couldn't deny. I was fourteen when I took my first life. He was a boy from my tribe, two years younger than me, a good kid that just couldn't adapt to the mentality needed for our religion. I snapped his neck with my bare hands.

I wish I could tell you that my conscience tortures me with nightmares or that I sometimes imagine my victims standing behind me when I look in the mirror. The truth is, killing just doesn't bother me that much—and I know how fucked-up that sounds. I only regret murder when there's no principle behind it such as Survival, Profit, or Revenge. Or if it was done on some sucker shit, like what sent me to the joint.

I drove but no longer saw the traffic. My sadistic side was again inflicting me with the most embarrassing days of my life.

I can still remember the wood-grain pattern to the doors of our apartment in Southfield. The one in the bedroom stands with a two-inch gap. Clothes on the floor, sweat and sex in the air. On the bed we share, my dark-skinned dime is on her back with her pretty painted toes pointed to the ceiling. Her stomach is five months swollen. The dude from the first floor is on top of her stroking hard like he's trying to kill the fetus. T'wanda is throwing it like she's trying to help.

Thirteen months later, she sits in the witness box conservatively dressed in a Chanel pantsuit, Oakley reading glasses, hair in a ponytail. Through tears she describes the thunderous echo of my .44 Bulldog, the dead weight of her headless lover on top of her and still inside her, the trauma of having to wash his skull and brain fragments from her face and hair in the shower.

T'wanda doesn't look at me, just gives all the details of their affair: how they first noticed each other around the complex in passing, how the innocent flirting led to something less innocent, how he was at my door no sooner than my Denali pulled off and fucking my woman in the apartment that I was paying twelve hundred a month to keep her in. Doc, Punchy, Prime, Louie Boy, Mrs. P, and a then twelve-year-old Quianna: everybody I love sitting in the courtroom listening as the bitch explains how she made a fool out of me for seven months. The lady prosecutor is careful to paint T'wanda as a victim and not a hoe.

The only thing that saves my ass is my lawyer using my disability as a defense. I came home and found a strange man on top of my girl and thinks she's being raped—after all, I can't hear what the fuck's going on. The judge and the prosecutor both know it's bullshit, but lucky for me the jury box is filled with common people who also think deaf means dumb. Out went Second Degree Murder and the mandatory Life sentence I was facing; however, the charge was only dropped to Manslaughter One, and the vindictive judge was happy to sentence me on the high end.

I thought I was over that shit, but seeing T'wanda brought it all back. Whenever exes saw each other, there was always a clear winner and loser. T'wanda no longer possessed anything that once marked her as a bad bitch, but for some reason, I didn't feel like I'd won.

I would've killed her back then, but the baby was the only thing that had spared her, just like he had spared her this night. I rubbed my head to see if Ja'Quezz had given me a lump.

I got a text from the only person who had my number asking me where the fuck I was at, and hearing from Quianna helped to get me back on task. A person's life is punctuated by their death. A ninety-five-year-old woman who goes peacefully in her sleep gets a period. A suicide bomber gets an exclamation point. My best friend Doc's life had ended with a question mark, and I was determined to edit the sentence.

I was getting better with the phone. I shot Quianna a quick one-handed text telling her where I was headed. I took I-96 and connected to I-94, then used that to take me deep east.

It was well into the evening by the time I reached the other side of town. I needed help from my headlights to navigate the surface streets. This was a hood that I'd only been in once back in the day. I didn't know what gang ran things over there. I didn't know what I was headed into.

The area around Mack and Springle was basically Brightmoor East. Mostly abandoned properties and grass fields. I cruised the block slow, searching for an address on houses without numbers. Young thugs stood curbside, watching me cautiously with ready trigger fingers. When you come through a hood like this, an off-brand creeping in an unfamiliar ride had better be delivering for Uber Eats. I was a second away from getting the Caprice shot up.

The spot I wanted was on the corner, a ranch-style house surrounded by a chain-link fence. Interior lights spilled from the open door between two dudes on the porch sipping from red plastic cups. I tried to formulate a strategy to approach these grimy muthafuckas.

I parked on the side street behind an old slant-back Seville propped on cement blocks. Before I stepped out the Chevy, the two from the porch were already hawking me and rose from their seats as I hit the sidewalk. One wore a University of Michigan hoodie, big M on his chest like a superhero. His boy was in a sleeveless T, showing off arms that suggested he'd just done a bit too and had hit the weight pit while he was inside. Both were packing; I could tell by the way they stood.

I let myself in the front gate while trying to put on a friendly face that was no doubt hidden by the dark and distance. Times like this made my six-foot-five, two-seventy a liability in that it intimidated those who knew a very small bullet could reduce it all to dead weight.

I came up the walk that separated a patchy lawn that only saw water when it rained and assumed they were asking me something like who was I or who was I there for. The problem was that they were twin silhouettes backlit by the light from inside, shadows without lips I could read. I stepped onto the porch hands up, doing everything a mute could to tell them I didn't want trouble.

The dumb muthafuckas did the one thing I was praying they wouldn't. They pulled straps on me.

Chapter Twelve

Of course things would be less complicated if I could just walk up and say, "Ay man, I'm looking for Prime." Trying to use sign language might make them think I was throwing up a rival set. I wasn't accustomed to moving in these streets without having Doc at my side. My voice.

Having no way to announce my intent made the drinking partners leery. They raised matching pistols, SR9s most likely bought as a set. I was staring down their twin barrels with thirty-six shots waiting to punctuate my sentence.

I stood on the porch, hands up, trying to do this in a way where nobody got hurt, but Muscles in the sleeveless shirt was doing too much. He barked shit I couldn't make out. Pistol inches from my face. His trembling hand betrayed the hard expression. This clown kept getting more and more agitated. My quiet stare seemed to make him nervous, and his fear fueled mine.

He pressed the muzzle into the side of my head. Mistake. This put him way too close to me, and the size always made people underestimate my speed.

I spun away from his pistol like an inside linebacker shedding a block. I threw myself into his body back-first, pinned him against the house, and took control of his gun hand. I sent a quick elbow back into his ribs, then bent his wrist at an angle that broke his grip on the weapon.

After I snatched the Ruger, I immediately placed it on the ground before his boy spilled my noodles. I went down to one knee, moving slow, palms up. I gave dude in the hoodie an apologetic look that said, *I don't want no smoke but yo' mans was trippin'*.

U of M stood over me talking shit when six more rushed outside. Three of them had pistols; one had an AR-15. One goofy muthafucka actually brought a hammer.

I had my own SR40 with plenty of opportunity to use it. Fake-ass Thor yanked it off my hip. I was on my knees, surrounded with half a dozen guns pointed at my head. Two chicks watched from the doorway; one flicked on the porch light. It was either to give everybody a better view of the crazy guy who ran up on their spot or to give herself a better view of my execution.

I scanned their crew until my eyes fell upon the tall, skinny one with dreads, looking like a broke-ass 2 Chainz. They were all saturated in skunk weed, so it took his red, tight eyes a few seconds before they recognized me under all this new muscle and facial hair.

"My nigga, what the fuck?" The porch light allowed me to see faces, read lips.

He tucked his burner and made the others give me space. His boys began to stand down.

I had to check that clown with the hammer who tried to slip off with my pistol. On that eastside shit. Told him with a look, *Don't get fucked-up!* He passed it back with a sly smile.

Prime embraced me; the only one in the crew who I had to look up to at six-foot-seven. Dude could've hooped at a Division One school and possibly went pro if he wasn't in the streets.

He asked when I got out, and I pointed to my wrist. *This time. Right now. Today.*

He understood. "I know it's looking fucked-up out here, but the city 'bout to come back."

Somebody running for city council president had plastered billboards all over Detroit making the same promise. But the face I made to Prime said, *Shit, I can't tell.*

Prime invited me inside another modest home, cleaner than his sister's but running neck-and-neck in terms of the struggle factor. The two females sat on the couch sharing the blunt with an old man. School looked to be pushing ninety, and hooked to an oxygen tank, but didn't let his lung problems stop him from taking a strong pull off the loud.

The coffee-colored cutie in red was grown but rocked her hair in twin ponytails. Huge lips like tomato wedges shined with a thousand coats of gloss—the type of lips that might have gotten her teased in middle school, back when the boys were too young to know better. Our eyes met, and she gave me a sex look. She was fine but too skinny, not enough meat to feed my beast.

Next to her was the short-haired stallion in pink leggings who had flipped on the porch light. My stare was like, *What up doe?* but her rolling eyes said, *Not a damn thing!*

I followed Prime into the dining room, where a half gallon of Remy Martin 1738 and Dixie cups sat on the table. He poured me the equivalent of a triple-shot, then started with the obligatory guilt trip that people be on when a homie touch down: the I'm-sorry-I-didn't-write shit—the same thing Punchy had done after we untied his girl. I wasn't pressed, because a real one like Doc had held me down until he died; he didn't write or visit either, but those pay receipts came faithfully. I just sipped and looked over Prime while he got it all out of his system.

It was clear he fell off. Before I went in, Prime was getting money, and Punchy used to wash his Lexus. I wanted to know what had flipped out here to where our crash-test dummy was iced out and pushing a 760 while Prime rocked dingy Levi's and curled-up Air Force Ones.

We reminisced over Remy about how I first got down with the crew. At seventeen, I came to Detroit looking for my mother, only to find myself homeless and alone. Doc, Prime, Louie Boy, and

Punchy were already tight, slanging dime rocks next door to the abandoned house I was squatting in. I kept myself unseen, watching from the windows. I didn't know what they were doing. I just knew the four of them were close to my age and I was used to being part of a tribe.

One day two fiends kicked in their door while they were gone; I caught the would-be thieves and sat on them until the boys got back. It still took a while for them to warm up to the big weird dude who couldn't talk. Their respect came when they saw me throw these hands. I didn't know the first thing about dope, but they paid me to be the muscle. Eventually we got cool to the point where Doc invited me to move in with his people.

"Ay Sy, what was that nigga name—the fat one with the burgundy Marauder who had the spot on Stoepel? He was spinning Doc on that bread he owed."

I recalled the incident. I typed the name into my phone and let him read it.

"You dog-walked that nigga down the street in front of everybody, dragged him by the collar, kicking him in his ass. I'll never forget that shit."

We shared a laugh.

"Niggas knew not to get stupid once the Silent Assassin joined the crew."

At my request, we turned off memory lane to cruise more recently paved avenues. Punchy was the first to splinter off, so Prime picked up from there, adding how he eventually broke away from Louie Boy and Doc.

According to him, it was four years into my bit when he found a solid plug out of North Carolina sending up good-quality bricks. The three of them hustled together for about a year and a half, slowly moved up to copping forty at a time on a three-way split: 15-15-10, with Louie Boy taking the smaller cut. Then came the inevitable part of the story where somebody fucked up a good thing. Prime said a youngster working under him got popped down in Cleveland with twenty ounces and put his name in the mix.

"I skated on the indictment, but niggas avoided me like I had that virus. Wouldn't even return my calls. Here it is, we go back to cartoon draws and yo' boys just left me hanging."

He seemed to be fishing for sympathy, but Prime should've known better. When the feds start looking at you, even family members are going to step back.

"By the time the heat was off me, I was down bad and couldn't cover my share. But Doc and Louie just kept on chewing off *my* N.C. connect."

I didn't need to hear the word to know he stressed *my*, even thumped his chest. I also felt the heat coming off of him. Just retelling the story was raising his blood pressure.

"Then I hear Doc and Louie got plugged in with the heroin. While I'm on my knuckles, scraping to get up on four and a half ounces, these niggas on Instagram showing off duffel bags and pouring champagne on top of Lambos."

I read his face as much as his lips. Shoulder-length dreadlocks framed the portrait of a man who was resentful, feeling like he'd been cheated out of something.

I needed to know which did Prime feel most cheated by: friends or fate. Was it just the ordinary saltiness of seeing dudes he was once down with go on to bubble without him? Or was it the type of jealousy that made men murder?

Chapter Thirteen

Doc had known whoever killed him. His Bentley truck had been found in an industrial area where somebody had put two in his head from the back seat. This was the extent of what I had gotten from Mrs. P.

I didn't come to catch up over brown liquor. I came for information—the same reason I had gone to Punchy's house. But just because I didn't kick in a door and tie up anybody didn't mean I wasn't on the same shit. Prime never suspected that I was looking over his crew and the layout of his house just in case I needed to kill him and shoot my way out that bitch.

The two from the porch came in to pour themselves a refill. Dude in the Michigan hoodie was still teasing his boy about the way I disarmed him. "Big Man, that was some ol' Jason Bourne shit you hit my baby with. You gotta teach me some of that."

Muscle Shirt's twisted mug indicated that his pride was still hurt and his boy was rubbing salt into the wound. He flashed me a hostile glare that I didn't feed into.

After I followed him back out the door with my eyes, I texted to ask Prime about the last time he'd seen Doc. I carefully watched his reactions. His face strained with the effort of reaching back into his weed-hazed memory. It seemed genuine.

"Been 'bout six years since we spoke, but every now and then I would see him in traffic—couldn't miss the yellow nigga cause he was always in something exotic. Used to be a lot of Doc sightings in the area of Charles Street and Conant. I think he had a bitch over there somewhere." I knew the area but barely, another eastside hood I had no ties to.

"Word was Doc and Louie fell out over some money right before he died." Prime threw that out there as if it were hardly relevant.

I didn't need my phone. That I wanted Louie Boy's location could be seen in my face.

"I told you nigga's too rich to fuck with me." He let out a dry snort. "I hear dude been buying up houses all over the west—gotta crib and a baby momma on damn near every block." He paused, then added, "Used to have a booty club on Six Mile called Sweet Lou's that got shut down. Too many niggas gettin' shot in that bitch."

After a sip of Remy, his face became serious. "I tried to get T'wanda not to testify, man."

Apologizing wasn't necessary. I should've listened to him from the start. Back in the day, plenty of people had tried to warn me off her slimy ass, none more than her own brother.

"I figure she the one who gave you my info. You done already been to see her then?" Prime twisted the tail end of a long lock, a nervous habit.

I knew what he was trying to ask. I informed Prime that his sister was still alive. For now.

He asked, "You see Ja'Quezz?"

We had the rest of that conversation without words. Then we sat sipping, each making a secret of his thoughts. I was still on my first cup while Prime had just refilled his third.

Babygirl with the lips interrupted our musings. She came in to offer Prime the last quarter of the blunt. After one final hit, she let smoke roll like lazy fog from her mouth to her nostrils, checking me out the whole time. Extending from those red shorts were the long, toned legs of a supermodel. The girly ponytails were a contrast to the mature features of a woman about twenty-seven, five years younger than me. She stared at me in a way that made me shift in my seat.

Doc used to hold court when speaking to a group of fellas, and with the ladies he was a magician. It's a lot harder to have game as a deaf-mute. I sat there trying to think of something I could type into my phone, something clever like my boy Doc might say. I was frozen.

Ponytails broke the ice by complimenting the size of my hands and asked to see one. She placed our palms together to compare how my callused bear's paw dwarfed hers.

"Hope you big like this all over." I couldn't believe when she took my middle finger into her mouth, started to suck it deep and slow.

The newcomers in prison had also warned me about how aggressive the women had gotten, another thing I wasn't ready for. She ran my "fuck you" finger in and out of those wonderful lips with increasing speed, eyes smiling at the *Oh shit!* expression on my face.

The sneak preview lasted thirty seconds; then she made a *gimme* motion for my phone. Her thumbs danced across the screen like she programmed for Apple, tossed it back. She moistened her lips and strutted into the kitchen like the world was her runway. In my contacts, I found a number with a 313-area code under the name Givenya Moorehead. Clever.

Prime was smiling when I turned back to him. "Kierra wanna suck the soul out yo' body. But ain't she too light in the ass for you?" All my fellas knew about my fetish, but Ponytails was so sexy that I was willing to suspend my usual weight requirement. We shared a laugh when he read that.

"Talking 'bout ass, you seen Q-Bands? Got damn!" He used

his open hand to trace a crescent shape in the air. "Li'l Quay-Quay ain't all that little no more."

I frowned to let him know we wasn't doing that. Alive or dead, Doc was still my mans; twelve or twenty-four, that was still his sister.

Prime waved me off. "I ain't on nothing like that with her, either. Quianna was like the only person from that side who checked in on me when I was hurting. She a down-ass chick."

I didn't go there to socialize but got sucked into chilling for another two hours. Most of it was him bragging about the moves he was making. He swore he had bounced back and was getting decent money fucking with the pills. I think seeing me in Gucci my first day out made Prime have to justify why he looked dusty. We had been cool once, so even with all the cap, it was still good to see him again.

I had also been warned about how much stronger the weed had gotten. My tolerance was so low that I tried to take it easy, but just a few puffs had me circling the moon.

Most of his crew was gone by the time we wrapped up. The old man was slumped on the couch with his eyes wide, mouth open. I thought he was dead, but Prime didn't seem worried.

He directed me to the bathroom, where I took a piss, then waited for him on the porch. U of M Hoodie had already left, but Muscle Shirt was still there drinking alone. I stood over him a full minute, giving a *What's up?* look. I wanted dude to know that if he had something on his chest, other than a few prison tats, this was the time to get it off.

I was still feeling some type of way about what happened at the mall. Part of me was hoping to take that frustration out on him. He looked big enough to give me a decent fight.

Muscle Shirt glanced up at me for a few seconds—probably just long enough to not feel like a coward—then retreated from my glare. Ninety percent of communication is nonverbal. His overall body language said he didn't want it, so I left him alone. I'm a goon, not a bully.

Prime came outside and walked me to the Caprice, where he marveled at the green candy and rims. He laughed at learning I borrowed it from Punchy, because we both knew that basically meant it was mine now. He jumped into the passenger seat to check out the pristine leather and wood. I got behind the wheel then made the engine growl for him.

"Even weak-ass Punchy out here shittin' on me." Prime had that sick look on his face again. I didn't pile on by telling him about Punchy's BMW or the house in Sherwood Forest.

He sat next to me with his door open, bathing us in the interior light. For a while he zoned out and just stared through the windshield. It was clear that he had more on his mind. I tapped the gas a few times to show my impatience.

Prime made a face like this was really difficult to say. "Silence, you the type of person where your loyalty will always be your biggest strength and greatest weakness. But loyalty done killed a bunch of muthafuckas when it ain't standing on something real."

That twisted my mug. I needed him to clean that shit up.

He could see I was defensive. "All I'm sayin' is be careful out here. It's a shortage on real niggas and I'd hate to see another fall. Send up the bat signal if you need me."

I wanted more of an explanation, but Prime slid out the car and slammed the door on my curiosity. He patted the hood, then tossed the deuce on his way back to the house.

It was hard enough for me to understand people as it is, so I really hated when they talked in riddles. Prime knew that. I started to go after him but said fuck it.

I took the corner hard while Ponytails waved at me from the porch. I had already forgotten about the cutie with the million-dollar lips. What Prime said had evicted all other thoughts.

Chapter Fourteen

Prime's comments only gnawed at me for half a block. By the time I turned back on the next major street, I chalked up his not-so-subtle shot to envy. Him hinting that Doc wasn't worth my loyalty only proved how tightly the green-eyed monster had him in the headlock. But I reserved the right to revoke that pass I just gave him if I found out it was anything more than simple jealousy.

The needle on the gas gauge drifted dangerously close to EMPTY. The tradeoff for a powerful motor was the cost to feed its insatiable thirst. Before I hit the freeway, I pulled into a 76 gas station that sat right off the service drive.

I parked and cautiously eyed the four dudes posted up near the locked doors to the food mart. I placed them in their early twenties, only prematurely aged by drugs, alcohol, and sleepless nights engaged in dumb shit. All four were on me before I could shut the car door.

I waved off the first in a Georgetown Hoyas windbreaker who claimed to have boy and girl (cocaine and heroin). The second wore a blue plaid fleece and tried to push on me some basic strand he had the nerve to call Five Alarm Kush. After him came another in a Levi's jacket over a white hoodie trying to sell something called a Roku stick that was supposed to have every movie ever made.

The fourth looked the youngest—a nappy afro bulging from under a wool cap—and was the only one peddling something useful. He pulled a stolen gas card from his Carhartt jacket and offered to double me up in exchange for the cash. I gave him dap to lock that in.

Dude pumped my petrol while I went to the window. I had barely hit the weed, but the munchies had me. It took a lot of finger-pointing and hand-gesturing at the attendant to get a pack of Black & Milds, two packs of Tropical Fruit Starbursts, and a Calypso Ocean Blue lemonade.

The dudes who couldn't sell me their products watched the whole exchange with quizzical stares. It took them longer than the cashier to realize that I wasn't going through all this just to be difficult. All three of their lightbulbs flashed on at about the same time.

I must've been buzzing more than I knew, because I fucked up by thoughtlessly pulling out my cash in public. I saw all six eyes start to shine—a broke nigga's hunger and desperation. My measly thirty-two hundred must've looked like a lot more in small bills. I sensed a sudden shift in the energy.

I was in this clean-ass Chevy with a pocket full of money, an off-brand in an unfamiliar hood. I was starting to look like a lick.

And whatever intimidation my size might have brought just got erased when they peeped my handicap. Remember, most people think deaf means dumb.

I walked back to the Caprice, felt their eyes on my back the entire way. I dropped my Blacks and snacks on the seat, then casually leaned against the fender sipping my juice. Thirty dollars bought me sixty in premium unleaded. I slid the kid a twenty and a ten.

The blow man and the movie man stood over by the entrance.

They tried to play it off, how people will talk about you making sure not to look directly at you. They were thirty feet away, and I was able to make out something about my bankroll, the chrome rims I'm rolling that he called Forgiatos, and even my Gucci kicks. Each of them claimed to have a gun.

To my surprise, the weed man wasn't with helping them get me. The blow man explained that three-on-one made for better odds, but young dog didn't fold to the peer pressure. He held on even after the movie man called him a lame and a coward.

The other two were trying to talk themselves into doing something stupid. It was well-lit underneath the gas station canopy, and their lips were easy to read.

The movie man stuck a Newport in his mouth, but I didn't let him and the blow man take three steps toward me before I froze them mid-stride. I calmly lifted my shirt to reveal the .40-caliber riding my waist. I met them both with a grim look, gave the subtlest headshake that said, *Don't even think!*

Trick no good. They were going to hit me with the old, "Hey brother, can I get a light?" routine. And while I distracted myself searching my pockets for a lighter, they would pull guns and strip me butt naked.

The sight of my burner quickly made them abort mission. The wannabe jack boys smartly chose to remain petty hustlers. Returned to their post at the entrance of the food mart, trying to conceal defeat and embarrassment.

I waved over the youngster in the blue fleece and bought two hundred dollars' worth of Five Alarm Kush. I still didn't want the homegrown trash that smelled like grass clippings, just rewarded him with my business for not feeding into the bullshit.

Dude next to me with the gas card had no clue of what nearly went down. He gave me a nod like, *Almost done* when the meter topped fifty dollars.

I turned up the Calypso, downed it like a wino, and continued to watch Blow and Roku. Just because I spooked them off the move didn't mean I was gonna let these little muthafuckas rock me to sleep.

My attention was so focused on them congregated by the food mart that I didn't notice as quickly as I should've the silver sedan pulling into the gas station. Way too fast.

I, along with young dog pumping my gas, barely had enough time to jump out the way when that car smacked head-on into the Caprice.

Chapter Fifteen

They were three deep in some kind of late-model Nissan that looked like every other mid-sized, mid-priced sedan on the streets. A man jumped out each front door followed by a female who rode in the back seat.

I didn't know if the driver was drunk or just happened to let the wheel get away from him. The Nissan didn't skid; no tire tracks stained the cement to show he had tried to brake. This muthafucka just plowed into the front of my shit like he didn't see me.

Lucky for all of us, he didn't have the speed for a serious collision, only came in doing about twenty miles per hour. No one who'd been inside the car appeared hurt, but me and the youngster pumping my gas could've got fucked-up if we didn't jump out the way.

I assessed the damage. Our rides looked like a couple meeting for a kiss. The older, steel-framed Chevy only suffered a slightly punched-in bumper. The little plastic-ass Nissan's entire front end was sagging on one side, the grill shattered.

The driver was staring at his car like, *What the fuck?* He was a sloppy-built six-foot-two, about two hundred and fifty, wearing a

Cleveland Indians windbreaker. He was dark-skinned and had a low sloping forehead with the heavy brow of a caveman.

The passenger matched my brown skin tone and had a similar build, bulky in the upper body but was probably thirty pounds lighter. He was also close to my height at six-foot-four but was nowhere near my swag, rocking a nameless black tracksuit with old dusty work boots.

The girl was in all black, too: leggings and a knitted sweater. She was brown-skinned, still fuckable despite being skinny with a nose like a shark's fin. Her short hair hardly reached back into a nub of a ponytail.

I was pissed, not as pissed as I would've been if this had been my car. So you could imagine how confused I was when the driver approached me with the attitude. I was expecting him to offer me a couple of dollars, would have even been straight with a simple "My bad." But when this muthafucka walked up on me trying to spazz, I thought he might be drunk for real.

He looked at me, speaking slowly: "Ay man, we gotta swap info. I hope you got good insurance."

The frown I returned said we wasn't swapping shit. I ain't never had a driver's license, so we wasn't getting insurance involved, and damn sure not the police.

Besides, he's the one who ran into me. I figured his goofy ass didn't need my help to raise his premium.

The meter hit sixty dollars, and I threw a head nod to the gas man as he put the nozzle back in the cradle. I was about to be out. When dude in the Indians jacket tried to block me, I shook my head to let him know he didn't want this problem.

"Hell naw, nigga. Don't think you just 'bout to leave. Look at my ride. We gotta figure this shit out."

To me, it wasn't shit to figure out. Punchy's whip would only need a bump out, while his would need a whole new front end.

But as the driver was still in my face talking crazy—like I'm the one who ran into him—I peeped the passenger lining me up.

He was preparing to sucker punch me.

Chapter Sixteen

My peripheral vision is the most important tool in my box. I can't brag that mine works any better than yours, only that I lean on it more since I can't hear someone trying to sneak up on me. So even when I got something going on right in front of me, I'm giving as much attention to everything going on around me.

Like how the three youngsters over by the food mart entrance had eased several feet closer to the pumps, either to be nosy or to scope an opening to jack me. How the female was lingering a few feet behind the driver, and I could tell she was going to be a problem by her energy and the bulge under her sweater. But more pressing was how the stocky dude riding shotgun had inched to within arm's length of me, and from the way he angled his body, set his feet, I knew he was about to put everything he had into a big swing from his right hand.

Looking over his arms and shoulders, I judged he had quite a bit of power but not speed. When you were taught to fight young and trained rigorously, your ability to size up an opponent flowed from instinct rather than intellect. This was why I felt his punch coming as if I had thrown it myself—a looping overhand right with terrible form.

I dodged that so easily, it could've been in slow motion, then counted with a quick but effective combination: a rabbit punch to the solar plexus stole his wind, and I followed with a hook to the kidney. My uppercut caught him under the jawbone and made him bite his tongue. He stumbled back dazed, wheezing with bloodied lips, hit three times before realizing he'd been hit once.

The sloppy-built caveman came in at the perfect angle to catch a spinning back fist. I switched my fighting style from boxing to Muay Thai, put together a four-piece using my elbows and forearms.

I landed a quick hammer-punch to the throat with the side of my fist. A gut-shot folded him, and I took advantage of the momentum that already had him bowing to me. I grabbed the back of his head and bounced it off my rising knee. That threw the driver backwards to where his skull bounced a second time off my car door and a third off the ground.

From the corner of my eye, the four gas station hustlers laughed and cheered like spectators at Monday Night Raw.

The big-nosed chick went for that gun. She unholstered the pistol, but there wasn't much distance between us. Her eyes went buck at seeing how fast I closed the gap, and that I already held her wrist. Twisted until I felt her bone snap. I watched her face contort with a scream as the gun dropped from her limp, dangling hand.

I was still manhandling the woman when the passenger finally shook off that three-piece I put on him. He caught me from the blindside with a glancing blow that skidded off my temple but still stung.

Unarmed, she was less of a threat, and I needed my hands free. I used those years of weight training to sling Big Nose like I was an Olympian going for gold in the hammer throw. Her bony ass flew clear over the hood of the Nissan, where she disappeared on the other side.

The bitch was still in the air when dude tried to sneak me

again—seemed to be the only way he knew how to fight. He put everything into another big haymaker, but I dodged his fist and used his energy against him this time. I grabbed the collars of his tracksuit, guided him right along with his momentum to put his head through the Nissan's rear passenger window. He shattered it with his face, then landed flat on his back in a pile of broken glass.

Only his hand fell right next to the pistol I stripped from ol' girl. A closer inspection revealed it to be a Glock 19. He glanced from it up to me standing over him, squinting from the cuts on his forehead leaking blood into his eyes. There wasn't even time to throw him a warning glare not to do it.

We reached in the same instant. His fingers curled around the grip but had to bring the pistol up to take aim. Once I freed the SR40 from my waistband, the gun was already pointed downward. My shorter, therefore quicker, path allowed me to get off first. I popped twice before he squeezed off a round. Both shots hit him center mass.

His head sagged back against the pavement, and his gun arm fell at a right angle to his body, pointing as if he died giving somebody directions.

Shit just got too real for the spectators, so they were ready to break out. I gave Weed and Gas a pass but caught Blow and Roku before they bolted. I ran over, arm extended, giving them a closeup view of the pistol I flashed earlier. They had seen enough to know they'd almost fucked with the wrong one, so they didn't try to reach or run. In a bit of irony, I made those two check in the same guns they were going to use to rob me along with whatever else they had in their pockets. Then I let them catch up with their boys, who had sprinted off into the night in the direction of Harper Street.

The blow man had a nice little H&K P8M7 while the movie man was packing some old-ass German Luger that probably hadn't been fired since World War II. I dropped the Heckler on my passenger seat and the Luger in the trash.

I stepped over Big Nose, who was still between the Nissan and the gas pumps writhing on the ground, hissing in pain, and gripping at her broken wrist. In stretch pants, she had no pockets I could run for cash and didn't feel like searching the car for her purse.

That knee to the face still had the caveman on his back looking dazed, but he was lucid enough to immediately throw his hands up when I turned the barrel on him. I didn't think he was armed but still gave him a quick pat-down just in case. Transferred the contents of his pockets straight into mine.

Shots had been fired, and even though I didn't see the clerk in the window, I didn't doubt he was ducked down somewhere inside calling the police. I hurried to scoop up Big Nose's Glock, kicked the driver one more time just to be petty, then hopped in the Caprice.

I made my own exit out the gas station. I backed away from the Nissan, swerved around the body, and drove over the grassy embankment at the edge of the property, over the curb. I fishtailed on the service drive, then punched it through a yellow light and down the on-ramp for I-94.

I was surprised by how out of practice I was for the gangsta shit. I had just caught a body in front of six witnesses. I hadn't been worried in the moment, but during the drive, I found my leg bouncing with nervous energy. My heart was beating too fast. One hand held the wheel, the other the .40-caliber on my lap; both trembled enough to bother me. Plus I was driving like somebody fleeing a crime scene.

I took a few deep breaths to calm myself. I needed to reduce my heart rate and speed. I tore open a pack of the Starbursts and stuffed five into my mouth like a greedy kid. After a few minutes, the sugar helped to soothe my adrenaline. My hands stopped shaking; my heart rate stabilized. I merged into the far-left lane and stopped racing the other drivers.

But the second half of the Starbursts didn't help to ease my paranoia. My eyes shifted from the windshield to the rearview mirror every three seconds, searching for the swift approach of flashing police beacons or any civilian headlights that might be following me.

It was a total coincidence that almost got me robbed by the youngsters. I just happened to pull up at that 76, and they just happened to see my cash. They were simply being opportunistic.

But the dude in the Nissan running into me wasn't a random act. That shit was a setup.

Chapter Seventeen

I fired up a Black & Mild, let tobacco help the relaxation therapy the sugar started. After a few minutes and miles passed without flashing lights, I calmed down but stayed in my rearview all the way to the westside. I crept through the alley and stashed the Caprice in Mrs. P's garage.

Quianna's Charger was gone, but there was still a bunch of muthafuckas at the house. I didn't like that shit, thought about evicting people. Had to remember it had been the same way when we were younger; this had always been a chill spot for everybody in the hood.

Doc's son Trayvion had about five of his boys on the back porch caked up with four chicks age-appropriate for them. I thought it was too damn late for the little kids to still be running around on ten. Inside, a pair of ladies closer to my age were at the kitchen table partnered up against two unknown dudes in a game of spades. I had to squeeze past another girl leaning against the stove just to get through.

In the living room, a deep valley of mahogany cleavage snagged my attention. Long pencil-thin braids framed a cute, round face. She wore a linen sundress with a plunging neckline. She easily tipped the scale at two-twenty, but her heavy-duty bra supported forty of the pounds.

I looked in on Mrs. P, who was lying across her bed asleep in front of the news. I stood in her doorway long enough to catch the final fifteen minutes. Some of my tension lifted when WDIV never broke or recapped a story about a gas station shooting. I pulled the door closed, even though Mrs. P slept unbothered by all the ruckus.

I went into the basement to find it unchanged other than a new front-load washer-and-dryer set. Against the rear wall sat the same fold-out sofa bed Doc had let me crash on when I was seventeen. It was covered by trash bags filled with miscellaneous junk.

I cleaned off the sofa, then flopped down hard, exhausted from a day of constant motion. Prison makes you too used to sitting still. Institutionalized. It was half past eleven, and I had been up since four a.m., ready to sprint out the gate like a horse at the Belmont Stakes.

I nearly dozed off thinking about the crazy shit at the 76 when I remembered to check my pockets. I didn't expect too much but was still hopeful for a surprise.

The blow man did have boy and girl, just not much of either. I only took cash off the movie man and the driver of the Nissan. I tallied up the bills to learn that I had gotten them for under sixteen hundred, bringing my grand total to forty-six after deducting the two I spent on the Five Alarm Kush.

I hid the dope and the bullshit weed under the sofa cushion. I ain't never been a D-Boy, so in the past, whenever I hit a lick for drugs or jewelry, Doc had always sold it for me. He would've been way too major for these crumbs but having those sacks reminded me of my loss. My best friend wasn't with me. My voice. My guide.

I lay across the musty sofa and followed my thoughts down a rabbit hole constructed of memories and imagination until sometime later. I came up from the basement to find that the house had finally settled down. Doors were closed and lights were dimmed. Practically everyone was gone except for half a dozen kids who slept all over the living room floor.

The microwave clock read 1:24, and through the front window, I saw the Charger was back in the driveway looking like a crouched panther. I sent a text asking Quianna if I could come up to talk but the request went unanswered.

While I was away, Quianna took over the second-floor flat that had once belonged to Doc. I slipped into the hall and crept lightly up the stairs that joined the units. I tried to move quietly by chance she was asleep, but I'm big, heavy, and never quite sure how much noise I'm making.

The door to her flat wasn't locked and opened up on the kitchen. Black and white linoleum tiles, stainless steel appliances all shined even in the dark. Cedar cabinetry matched the breakfast table. It was a recent remodel; I could detect the scents of fresh paint and new wood.

The floorplans for the up and downstairs units were identical. Mrs. P's flat was stuck in the eighties, but everything up here was new and modern. Fresh carpet, a huge glass and wrought-iron dinette set, brushed-suede living room furniture. A huge liquid-crystal TV dominated the wall.

Shifting light drew me to the end of the hall. The door to Quianna's bedroom was open; had it been closed, I would've turned back and simply got with her in the morning.

The flickering light came from a lavender candle on the nightstand. The scent mingled with good weed and sweaty bodies.

After the candle the first thing I saw was a big, black ass. A slender waist tapered those round cheeks to a narrow back draped by silky blue weave. She was facedown, waist in the air, positioned like she was waiting for somebody to thrash her from behind. I was faced with a fat, moist pussy with a swollen clit, and from between the plump lips, the pink called to me. The mystery girl had the body of a chocolate goddess, but her face was buried in more pussy.

Quianna was on her back, knees pushed up to her chest. Body oil and perspiration caused her skin to shine like pine under many coats of varnish. Her perky A-cups were crowned with nipples that looked sharp enough to cut glass. She tugged at the sheets, chewed her bottom lip, eyes closed. Her head rolled from left to right. The lovemaking was so intimate and beautiful that my presence felt like an intrusion.

I eased back down the hall, through the kitchen and down the stairs. In the basement, I fired up another Black and puffed like I wanted lung cancer by morning.

I sat on the couch, then pulled out my money to count it again. It wasn't that I expected the amount to change, just hoped to take my mind off what I saw upstairs.

My beast was beating against his cage, trying to get me to do something stupid. He was convincing me to drive the hot-ass Caprice back to the side of town where I just committed murder, to risk it all for Kierra's lips. I flashed back on the way she sucked my finger. I stared long and hard at the contact she left in my phone: *Givenya Moorehead.* I needed some of that.

But I had to move smart until I figured out who was following me and for what.

They made every attempt to make it seem like that was some random altercation. The drama at the gas station was a poorly-orchestrated hit. It was the driver, the caveman in the Indians jacket, who exposed their hand.

When he first spoke to me, it was really slow with emphasis on each syllable. This is how people not used to talking to lip-readers think they are supposed to speak. He knew I was deaf, which meant they knew who I was.

But they had no way to know I'd be in an unfamiliar hood at a gas station I never used unless they'd been following me. They had to be on me at least since I left Prime's house, probably since T'wanda's. Maybe even before then.

I thought over the short list of people who knew I was home. Could Punchy have hired these clowns for the way I came through his spot earlier? Did T'wanda call Prime and have her brother put somebody on my head for the shit with her and Ja'Quezz?

Punchy and Prime knew me well enough to send real hitters who would shoot first and not be stupid enough to trade hands with me. That shit was amateur hour.

I thought on that for a while, then hit the side door, needed fresh air. I walked to the liquor store two blocks over, making sure to check my six for anybody who might be following. I slid through right before it closed. I wasn't a real drinker, so I just bought the first vodka I saw and a pack of Backwoods. Back home, I rolled up some of the grass clippings I bought off young-ster.

Niggas in prison always daydream about how they would cele-brate their first night out. It usually involved champagne, strip-pers, and twenty friends treating them like King for a Day. A watered down, affordable imitation of the lifestyle portrayed in the rap videos he had to live vicariously through during his sen-tence.

I passed on Quianna's Do-It-Big party in exchange for this sad celebration involving dirt weed, cheap liquor, and no pussy. I got fucked-up by myself down in a dank, moldy basement.

Worst was that I ran around all day, even caught a body, but didn't learn anything. I wasn't a single step closer to finding out who killed Doc.

Chapter Eighteen

I felt somebody touching me and jumped straight to my feet into my fight stance. I regained my senses to take in the dim light falling through the tiny casement windows, the water-stained cinderblock walls, the stench of mildew competing with fabric softener.

And the little girl kneeling on my fold-out bed in Wonder Woman pajamas. She was one of the kids from upstairs, about five years old in afro puffs. It had been her tiny hand tapping my shoulder to wake me up out of a vodka-induced coma.

In prison, a Slumber Party is a sneak attack where a blanket gets tossed over your head followed by a shank being pushed into your neck. This programs a convict to sleep light and to wake at the slightest provocation prepared to fight for life. I was thankful I didn't hurt the girl.

The darling had a message for me: "She said get up and come eat 'fore she come down here and beat yo' ass!" The words were slow and mechanical, obviously rehearsed several times. An adult had given her permission to curse, and that just tickled her to death. She covered a gap-toothed smile to giggle in her hands.

I rubbed the crumbs from my eyes, found an expression that I hoped looked friendly. I tipped her ten dollars just in case I scared her by jumping up like that. She looked at the bill then back to me in disbelief before scrambling back up the stairs.

I followed her after a minute. I went to use the bathroom, then stepped into the kitchen wondering why I didn't smell food. I was still wearing sleepface when Mrs. P noticed me.

I didn't know the short sweeping bob she wore the day before was a wig until I saw her without it. Wispy patches of thinning silver strands sprang from underneath a stocking cap.

"You in the wrong place lookin' for something to eat," she informed with an unlit cigarette perched between her lips. "Better take yo' ass upstairs. I ain't feeding no grown-ass nigga in the morning unless they done spent the whole night feeding me dick!"

I waved my hands to stop the old lady, didn't want the visual. I often wondered what my father would think if he knew my surrogate mother was a tiny white woman who smoked Newports, only dated brothas. and said the N-word more than the grimiest rappers.

The scent of fried meat welcomed me before I reached the second floor. Quianna's door was ajar, and her lover stood over a stove that belonged in a professional chef's kitchen: dual ovens, a broiler, eight gas burners and most of them going. The cook only wore a gray T-shirt and black thong.

She was Hershey-bar dark, five-foot-nine and crazy-thick. She balanced all that body on shapely calves, small feet with polished toes. For a minute I just took it all in from the doorway.

I knocked to announce myself, and she turned to me with the large expressive eyes of a Disney princess. She had full lips and a slightly upturned nose that fit her face. I saw no flaw other than that to me, the neon-blue weave didn't work well with her skin complexion.

She looked me up and down, just like I did her, only with pursed lips. Those pretty brown eyes rolled in their sockets. Her invite came through a dismissive wave toward the kitchen table.

As I settled into a chair, she tugged down the hem of her shirt to cover her ass, then tossed me a *Fuck you!* glare. I guess the view wasn't meant for me.

It only took a minute to guess what her problem might be. Quianna was the one with the angle to see me, and must've told her girl that I was spying on them like some pervert. The two seconds I stood there was too long to see something not meant for my eyes.

Maybe I got called up here to get checked. This started to feel awkward.

I was ready to slip back downstairs when Quianna stepped in. She wasn't dressed yet either, despite the clock showing a quarter to eleven. A silk Versace bonnet on her head and she wore nothing else but an oversized wife-beater and cotton panties.

I frowned to say, *Go put on some clothes* and got hit with my second *Fuck you!* glare.

I didn't even know she had a pet until the cutest little puppy followed her into the kitchen on the heels of her bare feet. The pit bull was about six weeks old, smoke-gray coat with a bluish tint, pink eyes, and a red nose. He sniffed around my ankles, then chased his mistress into a well-stocked pantry that she kept secured with a padlock. Inside, Quianna emptied a small can of Cesar gourmet dog food into his bowl while another seventy-five-pound bag of Pedigree leaned against the shelves. He attacked his meal, busy little tail wagging nonstop.

I was still trying to get a read on Quianna's energy as well as scripting my explanation for being in her hall last night when she handed me a pre-rolled blunt and a lighter. The first couple of puffs choked me. This strand was so potent that it was disrespectful to even call that bullshit I bought real weed. I was still coughing when Quianna made introductions.

The chef's name was Lexy, and I was surprised when she offered her fist to me. I gave some dap then passed her the blunt. She accepted with a smile that I easily saw through.

As Quianna moved around the kitchen, I didn't know what to

do with my eyes. She was braless under the wife-beater, flashed me every time she leaned over. The tattoo drew me to her upper thighs and the print she was so proud of.

Her girl served us Belgian waffles, scrambled eggs, turkey sausage, hash browns with onions and peppers. "The shit ain't about to get up and walk away." I didn't realize I was eating fast with my head down like I was still in the chow hall until Quianna spoke on it.

"Why the fuck you sleeping in the basement?" The question blindsided me.

I texted that I wasn't too good for it back in the day, and I wasn't too good for it then.

"I got an extra room I ain't doin' nothing with." I did notice that all the kids and company remained on the first floor. Quianna clearly wasn't having that in her second-story penthouse.

Still I refused her hospitality. When I really started knocking heads off, I planned to find another place to stay anyway.

"Nigga, it's damp down there, it stank, and you probably gone catch something. It's a full-sized bed back there and a dresser for your clothes." She said that like it had already been decided and I wondered if moving me in was what had her girl so salty.

Quianna tried to pass the weed back to me, but I declined. Last night's hangover still had me, and the things I needed to do that day required me to be clear-headed. She offered the blunt to Lexy, who made sure to give me a funny look behind Quianna's back.

I seemed to skate on getting caught, so that brought me back to the original reason I climbed those steps last night. Through my phone I asked Quianna if she heard anything about a falling out between Louie Boy and Doc right before he died.

According to her, Doc hadn't been around much the last couple of years. He occasionally pulled up in something shiny and foreign. She said, "I heard he was leasing a condo down on the waterfront but lost that when he moved in with Darnia. He bought her a house over on Radom."

Quianna read my raised eyebrows. "Yeah, fucked me up too when I heard about it. They say it's nice as hell: four bedrooms, den, attached garage, big backyard."

"I heard" and "they say" indicated she'd never seen the house or the condo. I remembered the Petersons as a close unit. Did Doc cut ties with the family? I didn't want to believe it, but the evidence stared me in the face when I walked in the day before. Doc cashed out on a new house for some random bitch while Mrs. P was sitting on the same furniture.

I asked Quianna what's up with that and watched anger tighten her eyes. "Fuck what Prime and whoever else told you. Bro was deep in these streets. He ain't stop fucking with us—the hustle kept him busy. If me or Momma needed anything, he would move Heaven and Earth."

Sounded to me like she was trying to justify some shit, but it didn't surprise me. Quianna had always looked up to her big brother and would fight to protect his name.

But I couldn't imagine the same person who had supported me my entire bit leaving his people on stuck unless they fell out over something major. This wasn't adding up.

Then I'm looking at Quianna's flat full of new furniture and appliances. A new Hellcat outside on Ruccis. Even the shopping spree she treated me to. It was obvious that she had recently come into some money.

My friend was dead, and everybody kept telling me how there's no loyalty out here. It came off like an accusation, but I point-blank asked Quianna where all this cash came from.

I let her see in my face that I wasn't going for that "don't worry about it" shit she hit me with last time.

Chapter Nineteen

This was my best friend's little sister and had been as close as a sister to me. After all she'd done, I felt like shit for asking but had to. My father was a paranoid conspiracy nut, and I had inherited the defective gene.

Quianna stared at me for a long moment, her champagne-colored eyes searched mine—I couldn't guess for what—then she called over Lexy. Quianna spun her girl around and snatched up the back of her shirt.

The ink hardly stood out against Lexy's dark skin, which was why the first time I missed the elaborate tattoo on her right cheek: B.S. drawn into a shield over crossed swords; BANDS Society encircled the crest in gothic lettering. Quianna brought my attention to a smaller version of the same logo on her wrist hidden within all the Asian art that sleeved her.

"B.A.N.D.S. Society! Bitches Are Now Dominating Shit. Beyond Average Niggas and Dusty Sluts. Broke-Ass Niggas Don't Sex."

Lexy chimed in, "Breaking A Nigga Down Swiftly. Bring A 'Nother Dollar Stupid." I got the hint. They had a bunch of acronyms for it.

"That's my crew," Quianna announced with pride. "It's the takeover."

She explained that being in the clubs forced her to deal with all the pettiness and jealousy between the girls until she met a chick named Tuesday who changed her life. Instead of competing for tips, this mentor convinced Quianna to form a small group of dancers who worked together and split their profits. That simple idea blossomed into something more, causing Quianna to spend the next four years recruiting the baddest strippers in Detroit. They danced, they hosted parties, worked as escorts, even pulled scams with Quianna running it all and collecting a percentage. She was basically a madam.

She reached across the table to put a hand on my forearm. "Don't look at me like that. I just plan and organize. I meant what I said in the car."

She was doing it again, wrongly assuming I was judging her. I had no moral aversion to how she got her money. I just needed to quiet the nagging little voice in the back of my mind trying to connect her to something slimy.

Quianna pulled up their official Facebook page and showed me some of the members—the type of dimes who made eights feel like fives when they entered the room. In the pics, they weren't just at the local clubs and events. They hit up Black Bike Week in Myrtle Beach and the NBA All-Star weekend. "The Society is eighteen deep and growing."

She joined Lexy at the stove to receive the last quarter of the blunt, and studying them side by side, I could see why they were leaders in some bad bitch association.

Quianna blew smoke through her nostrils while she spoke: "My girl Tuesday helped me understand the importance of having a team. She was a boss bitch who bought her own club and had a crew hitting licks on the side. She told me that pussy was the ultimate drug. Dope boys, jack boys, weed heads, and crack fiends, all of 'em are addicted to it, but you got these dumb bitches out here fucking for free. Imagine a dealer just giving away his product."

While it hurt my heart to hear Li'l Quay-Quay talking like that, I couldn't argue with her philosophy. Prostitution was the world's oldest hustle for a reason. Pussy was so powerful that, even though I knew Lexy couldn't stand me, I still found myself staring with hunger.

Her booty was big enough to get a disability check and each step broadcast its softness. She didn't snatch her shirt back down, left the view open as she walked back to the stove. I followed with my eyes, and when I turned back to Quianna, her eyes had followed mine.

She used the phone to quietly ask if I wanted to sample that. I tried to downplay how embarrassed I was that she caught me stalking her girl. I hurried to delete the text and Quianna laughed at me.

I got serious again, asked her about the club on Six Mile that Louie Boy used to own, and of course she was up on it. She confirmed that Sweet Lou's had gotten shut down but reopened under a different name. Louie still ran it, and a few of her girls danced there. Quianna didn't seem happy when I asked for the address.

"Prime. Louie Boy. What's next, you gone go try to find Punchy's weak ass, too?" I had already found Punchy's weak ass but let her make her point.

"Why is you in a rush to chase behind these niggas who ain't did shit for you your entire bit?"

Through my phone, I tried to run game that tracking down my old crew was just a friendly reunion, but Quianna was too good at reading me. She saw through the lies on my fingers and gleaned the truth in my eyes.

"You think one of them had something to do with Doc." The blunt had been smoked down to little more than a tail. She tapped that out in a crystal ashtray stationed between our plates.

"And now yo' ass about to run around playing Sherlock Home-boy and get to the bottom of it."

I stuffed two entire sausages into my mouth. Let her see in my eyes that I was going to do more than just get to the bottom of it. I was going to kill any and everybody who played a part.

I expected her to try to talk me out of it. Thought she was going to hit me with the whole *You-just-got-home* shit, and the *Ain't-nothing-gone-bring-Doc-back* shit. I expected her to try to put this dog on a leash.

Quianna surprised me.

"Before you go see Louie, pull up on Darnia first—the one Doc was living with. That bitch know something."

Chapter Twenty

Quianna was smart enough to figure out that I must've got into some shit when I told her I needed to park the Caprice for a while. Once she and Lexy finally put on some damn clothes, she ran me up to a used car lot on 8 Mile Road. I cashed out on a '93 Lincoln Mark VIII that performed decent on the test drive despite having over two hundred thousand miles. Burgundy over tan, few dents, and minor rust. It wasn't as pretty as the green-apple Chevy, which was exactly why I chose it. Being followed last night convinced me that I needed to be more low-key.

My revenge fund had stood at forty-six hundred, but the car, tags, and insurance drained me of all but eight. I had needed Quianna to put the paperwork in her name because, thanks to my pops, I didn't know my social security number or the actual name on my birth certificate.

Paper tags in the back window, I parted with Quianna and Lexy at the lot. She headed west in the Charger to handle BANDS business, and I headed east to handle my own.

On the way to the lot, I had asked Quianna about the police investigation into Doc's murder. She explained that the fam had received the news from two detectives out of the Tenth Precinct.

A stocky white dude with a buzz cut and a white woman. The female had done most of the talking, and had talked a lot. A tall lesbian by Quianna's description. Quianna admitted that she didn't hear much else after learning that her brother was dead, only that it was being treated as a drug deal gone wrong. They had no witnesses or suspects.

A few weeks later, the female detective had come back with a different partner: some four-eyed black dude who looked like an accountant. Quianna claimed they had a bunch of follow-up questions about Doc's lifestyle, friends, and enemies, which she knew nothing of due to him keeping so distant. As far as the family knew, no more had come from the investigation, because that was two months prior, and the police hadn't been back since.

It took a while to find the address Quianna had sent me. This Darnia chick stayed on a block called Radom that was tucked into a confusing neighborhood with too many one-way streets and dead ends. I cruised past a nice brick Colonial with an attached garage. It was well-kept just like every other home in the area, manicured hedges with fresh lawnmower tracks.

Along with the house, Quianna said that Doc bought this bitch a new Escalade ESV. The gray long-sleeve was in the driveway next to a raggedy-ass '79 Monte Carlo on flats.

Quianna made it clear that she didn't trust Doc's girl but gave no reason for the suspicion. As little as that was, it was the first time I felt I had something real to go on. If Darnia did know something, I was prepared to make her tell it. I parked the Mark VIII at the corner. I stuffed the SR40 in my waistband.

I found three pieces of mail in the box. I knocked hard, but it took a full two minutes before somebody answered, some dude in a Lions jersey way too frail even to be a kicker.

He snatched the door wide with an attitude. He clearly had been asking "Who is it?" from the other side and was pissed I didn't respond. His mug was tore up, but that changed when my size registered with him.

I held up an energy bill addressed to Darnia Stallworth. He

looked from it to me. I didn't have the patience for this slow muthafucka to figure things out, so I just forced my way inside.

He tried to grab my arm to stop me, a natural response, just not the smart one. I elbowed him hard in the throat. While he coughed and gagged, I patted his pockets and the waistband of his jeans. I closed the door behind us once I was sure he didn't have a pistol.

The interior didn't disappoint. To the right was a living room designed to be a showcase: burgundy leather furniture over white carpet. Going left, a more-utilized dining area led into a large kitchen with a prep island and farm sink.

Dude was still hunched over coughing. I showed him the envelope again, and that shot to the throat seemed to improve his thinking. He held his neck, shook his head.

I learned my lesson from what happened at T'wanda's. I grabbed his skinny ass by the collar and took him through the house room by room. It was a split-level where the living room looked down on a sunken family room with a TV so massive that I couldn't imagine how they got it inside. A den was on that level, along with a half bathroom. Below that was a cellar I didn't feel the need to explore. But I did check the three bedrooms upstairs and a master bathroom with a jack-and-jill vanity. All were empty.

Back in the dining room, I noticed one of those corny-ass wooden carvings of the word *Love* with a couple's photo in the heart-shaped O. I recognized Darnia from the Instagram page Quianna pulled up for me. In the picture, this clown was draped all over her.

For some reason I had assumed dude was a brother or family member. This slut was shacked up with another man in the spot my friend paid for. That heated me up, brought up some of my own issues. I gave the bony muthafucka a kidney-punch just because.

He folded over, stumbled back into the table. I snatched him by the neck again and made him read the message on my phone: *Where that bitch?*

"Work. I gotta go pick her up right now."

And his weak ass ain't even riding. I had already guessed that broke-down Monte leaving oil stains in the driveway was his. He drops her off so he can slide around in the Escalade, something else my boy paid for. This earned him a bitch-slap that nearly made him fall.

After regaining his balance, he cupped his cheek and snarled at me. Being punched was one thing, but slapping a man always fucked with his pride. A butcher's box of large kitchen knives sat on the prep island about five feet away. His eyes flashed on it.

I dared him to go for one. I even took a step back to give him a clear path. I wanted a reason to tear this whole fucking house up, to drag his scrawny ass all through this bitch breaking everything like cheap Christmas toys. A little smirk parted the black hair of my heavy beard. I begged him with my eyes to please do something stupid.

Darnia's man proved to have more common sense than body mass. He dropped all that hostile energy.

A few seconds later, he reached for his phone, and I made him show it to me before he answered. She had texted a strongly-worded reminder that he needed to be on his way. Apparently he had a problem with being late to pick her up.

I made him text Darnia back that he was headed there now. She didn't need to know that company was coming along for the ride.

Chapter Twenty-one

We waited in the Escalade outside of some nameless telecommunications company headquartered in a squat building of mirrored glass, way out near 13 Mile Road and Dequindre. I let dude drive but confiscated his phone to make sure he didn't pocket-dial the police. I rode shotgun, keeping the silent threat of the pistol on my lap, but climbed into the back seat once we reached Darnia's job.

We were about fifteen minutes late, which was purposely my doing. I had us bullshit at the house, then stop at a Dairy Queen, where dude was nice enough to treat me to a cookie-dough Blizzard.

I scooped spoonfuls while watching a slow stream of employees spill from the lobby, mostly whites who looked like low-level office types, before a pretty brown woman in her late twenties burst out the entrance. Her face was etched with frustration and fatigue.

Darnia yanked the passenger door open, ready to spazz on her man for his tardiness, until she spied the big fella in the back seat holding the pistol. A surprise concealed by the limo tint on the rear windows.

An instant after our eyes met, her face went blank. She spat the word *Fuck!* but didn't cry out or make a scene. It was hardly the reaction I expected. Darnia calmly got in, shrugged her purse, then ordered dude to pull off.

We drove about a quarter mile before she turned in her seat. "What do you want with me?" She made sure I could see her face and spoke slowly, which told me she already knew who I was.

What I wanted was for us to talk in private. I made dude stop the truck, then strip off some of his clothes. I put his skinny ass out right there on the side of the road. We were miles outside Detroit city limits, actually closer to Warren, and them white folks damn sure wouldn't be too quick to pick up a black stranger walking without his shirt and shoes.

I also warned that if by chance an officer stumbled on him and he repeated what happened here, that wouldn't be too good for his woman. I jumped in the passenger seat, gave Darnia the wheel, made her skirt off and leave the clown walking barefoot on the gravel berm. I threw my half-eaten sundae at him and laughed when ice cream splashed his bird chest.

As her man shrank to nothing in our mirrors, I used my phone to let Darnia know I was seriously considering taking the Escalade and burning down her house.

She twisted her mug. "Boy, Doc been dead for months."

I frowned to let her know how I felt about that timeline. Three months was kind of soon for a grieving woman to get some dick, but way too soon to already have a new man moved in. She was clearly fucking the skinny dude while Doc was still alive. I used my phone to share my observation.

She glared back defiant. "And? You know how many hoes Doc was fuckin'?"

I imagined it was a lot, but I let her see in my eyes how little that mattered.

I typed: *Doc told you who I am?*

She confirmed what I already knew with a nod.

Next I asked: *Did he tell you what I do?* Darnia flashed me a look to show that she wasn't scared.

We didn't communicate much on the way back to the city other than me telling her which turns to take. I directed her to the westside, an old warehouse district not far from our hood. We pulled onto an out-of-the-way service street. It was a long dead end spaced with empty lots and large dilapidated factories. Behind buckled and rusted fences stood the fossilized remains of these dinosaurs of the Industrial Age, rendered extinct by Amazon, Google, and outsourcing. Without eighteen-wheelers coming back and forth to pick up or drop off inventory to the long-dead manufacturers, the service street had no purpose and saw practically no traffic.

I made her park in the loading dock of one of those factories. This widened her eyes. It was the first time she showed any real shock. Darnia already knew this was the perfect place for me to kill her and leave the body.

We both knew. This was exactly where it happened to Doc.

Chapter Twenty-two

The shadow of the now-defunct Nature's Way Juice Company spilled over the Escalade. The naked branches of a leafless bush scratched at the windshield like the Reaper's skeletal fingers.

"Look, I don't know nothing about what Doc was doing or who he was doing it with." Darnia said that as if it would be her final words on the matter.

I reached over and put my large hand on the back of her slender neck, needed her to see how easy it would be for me to snap her shit. I wanted to know what Doc was doing here that night. Who was he here to meet and why?

"Doc didn't tell me shit."

Quianna was sure this chick had information for me, and I knew she wouldn't send me on a dry run. I squeezed Darnia's neck to the same degree that I doubted her words.

She grit her teeth. "You think we was the type of couple where the man come home every night at five-thirty and we discuss all the details of his day? This wasn't that. Yo' boy only dropped through when he wanted some head, and we didn't talk about what, or who, he was doing."

Quianna mentioned Doc having a condo somewhere on the riverfront. I asked Darnia what happened to that.

"He lost it about two months before he—" she avoided the word as if it might jinx her. "He put all his stuff in storage and was staying at the house with me."

I asked about the storage unit, thinking there might be something useful in there.

Her eyes shifted to the floor. "It's already gone. Wasn't nothing but a bunch of his clothes and some furniture."

The bitch was basically saying that she already pawned off all his shit.

Doc living with her definitely made it harder for the skinny dude to slide through, and Doc being out of the way left her free to do her thing, with a house and truck already paid for.

Darnia felt me staring at her, finally looked to meet my eyes. I didn't need the phone. She read the accusation there.

"Doc treated me like shit, but that didn't mean I wanted him dead."

She already knew what my next question was going to be and answered before my fingers could tap it out. "Because he was a fine nigga with good dick and a lot of money." She sneered at me. "What? You think I'm a gold-digging piece of shit?"

Of course I did. But lucky for her, I didn't think she was a murdering, gold-digging piece of shit. Under Doc, she had been a kept woman who only had to sit on a dick every couple of days. That piece of mail I pulled from her box told me more than just her government name. The shut-off notice stamped on the front of her energy bill told me that Darnia Stallworth was now struggling to keep a house she couldn't afford, all the while supporting a lame nigga with no hustle on about seventeen dollars an hour from her new telecom job. Darnia struck me as the type of woman who was too smart to butcher her cash cow.

But I still could tell she was holding something back. My next message asked: *What the issue Doc had with Louie Boy?*

She knew what I was talking about. She shook her head for a denial, but I saw her spine stiffen and concern flicker in her eyes.

These were called micro-reactions, and I was good at reading them. I didn't learn this in the church; in prison I studied a few books on body language. A widened eye, a flared nostril, a finger twitch or a subtle bodily adjustment—these subconscious responses happened in split seconds and told on a person.

I only had to apply a little more pressure before she folded. "Around the same time he moved in, Doc told me that Louie robbed him. They was working together on something, then Louie Boy did some slimeball shit."

I wanted to know more about this slimeball shit.

"He never gave no details. Just said that Louie got him for some bread. He didn't say how much, but I could guess it was a lot. He was mad about it up until he—"

I didn't remember the Louie Boy I used to run with being that type of guy. He was a flashy cat who loved to trick but had always played the game by the rules.

But then again, the years had changed a lot of other things. Punchy was up, Prime was down, and Li'l Quay-Quay was a pimp. Louie Boy might have switched up, too, considering that I was also hearing shit about Doc that was outside of his character.

I pressed, but Darnia swore she didn't have any more than the scraps she already fed me. "I only know that Doc had took a helluva loss—so much he couldn't afford to keep his condo no more. Between that and all he spent on getting this damn building, his money was fucked-up for a while. At least that's what he told me every time I asked for some."

I stopped her, made her back the fuck up. I asked if she meant that Doc had bought this building. The one we were parked behind, the same one he had been parked behind the night he got murdered. I felt that was information important enough to be shared up front. I typed the question into my phone and frowned to let her know to stop playing with me.

"My bad nigga, I thought you knew already. He bought this old fucked-up piece of property—a juice factory that's been closed for like thirty years. Kept going on about how it was gone get him all these millions."

Seemed like Doc had plans to go legit. I asked what type of business it was going to be.

Darnia waved me off. "He was full of shit about this just like everything else. He spent all that money and this raggedy mutha-fucka just sat here."

I asked her if she knew how much Doc had spent on this building he never used.

"Too damn much!" She punctuated that with a neck roll. She clearly felt the money would've been better spent on her. "And I don't think he never even stepped inside of it."

I threw open my car door, because that's exactly what I was about to do.

Both of us. I looked over to her like, *Bitch, come on.*

Chapter Twenty-three

The building was vast and stretched for about an eighth of a mile, surrounded by broken beer bottles, trash, and untamed weeds. Most of the white paint had peeled away from the exterior to expose scarred cinderblocks the local gangs had decorated with graffiti. Across the top was a row of large plate windows in rusted frames; the few that weren't boarded over had served as target practice for little bad-ass kids with rocks or bigger kids with guns.

We had to make a quick run to a hardware store for a large set of bolt cutters. On the dock in the rear was a trio of loading doors, and I snipped the padlock on the middle one.

It was mid-afternoon, but the interior was too dark to navigate, even for my sharp eyes. Darnia used the flashlight on her phone. I was still new to this tech shit, so I gave her mine to turn on for me.

She had begged to stay in the truck, but I wasn't about to leave her outside so she could pull off on me. She entered the factory a few feet behind me, hoping that whatever attacked would feast on me first and give her time to run.

We both used our shirts to protect our mouths and noses from the stale air. Darnia claimed she saw the paperwork to prove that Doc had spent nearly five hundred thousand dollars on what was basically just a ninety-five thousand square-foot breeding ground for rats and mold. All the processing and bottling machinery that had once belonged to the Nature's Way Juice Company had most likely been sold off years ago to satisfy creditors. Without the equipment, the main floor was a large empty space that ran the length of two football fields and was nearly one wide. Huge I-shaped beams were spaced every fifteen by thirty feet—I used my steps to mark them.

Hanging from the ceiling fifty feet above was a system of old rusted steel-mesh catwalks that had allowed foremen to look down on the production area. A switch-back staircase that looked like an old fire escape led to those catwalks. Darnia followed me up, a nervous hand clinging to the tail of my shirt. We got to the top and looked down, but I damn sure wasn't about to trust that old rusty catwalk with my precious two-seventy.

There were smaller rooms in the foremost part of the building, and in some of these it was nearly pitch. We did have a scary moment when a raccoon scurried by our feet to scare the shit out of us. Other than that, all we found were empty offices, breakrooms, and restrooms the crack fiends had left as gutted shells—all the toilets and salvageable furniture plucked a piece at a time during their numerous raids. Copper was the real buried treasure in these old buildings; nearly every wall and ceiling had been hacked open in search of piping or wiring.

I tried to see this place through Doc's eyes, wondering what his vision had been. Why would he blow half a mil for an old factory? Darnia reiterated that he had been bragging that this place was going to pay huge dividends, but neither of us could guess how. The building had plenty of usable space, but the renovations would cost millions. Darnia agreed with me that, while Doc had a golden hustle hand, he didn't have the type of money to pull that off. It seemed that just getting the property had stretched him thin, and whatever happened with Louie Boy had put him on his knuckles. We eventually tired of the smell along with trying to ask and answer our own questions, so I concluded the tour.

Back outside, we caught three mangy malnourished dogs hanging around the Escalade. To them, the shiny Cadillac SUV must've appeared to be trespassing in their territory and deserved a cautious investigation. They sniffed around the tires briefly before the emaciated trio continued on their quest for food.

I let Darnia take the driver's seat when we climbed back in. I could tell by her expression she was trying to decide if that was a good or a bad sign.

I asked with my phone what else did Doc tell her about me.

"He said you were his right hand. Said it wasn't a nigga in these streets that could do nothing with you when it came to throwing hands or pistol play. Doc was the type who didn't trust a muthafucka, but it sounded to me like he trusted you."

That gave me slight case of the warm fuzzies. He was about the only person in the world that I trusted without fail, which was why Louie Boy was going to have to answer some hard questions when I pulled up on him.

"But Doc wasn't looking forward to you coming home though."

Darnia damn near knocked me sideways out the passenger door with that. I needed her to repeat it to make sure I didn't misread her lips.

"Doc knew you was getting out soon. He was worried about it."

She tried to just breeze past that like it was nothing, but I needed her to be specific. Worried like how? What had he told her?

Darnia rolled her eyes, wishing she hadn't touched that subject. She tried to downplay it when I pressed for an explanation. I pulled the .40, cupped her face, and forced her to look into the eyes of a killer losing patience.

She stared into the barrel with wide eyes. "He didn't say nothing. I could just tell."

I twirled my finger to indicate that I needed more than her intuition.

Panic caused her to speak fast, making it hard for me to follow along. "If my best friend coming home after twelve years and I'm out here getting to a big bag, I'm excited. I can't wait to put her up on all the new stuff: fashion, food, clubs, cars. I'm looking forward to spoiling her. We about to act a fool—I'm talking a nonstop party for a least the first two months." She used hand gestures for emphasis, and I nodded once I eventually caught her meaning.

"When Doc spoke about you, it wasn't with that same energy. I'm not saying he wanted you to stay locked up. But—" Darnia took a second to more carefully script herself. "Seeing you again wasn't a cause for celebration. It was a cause for concern. Wasn't nothing he came out and said. I just saw it in his demeanor."

As much it hurt to hear, I was apt to trust her judgment. I know better than most that ninety percent of communication is nonverbal.

That sent me into my thoughts. I stared down the service street for three-quarters of a mile to where the road terminated in a dense grouping of untamed trees and a tilted sign that read NO OUTLET. I don't know how long my eyes were focused there, seeing none of it.

Chapter Twenty-four

Darnia was disloyal and kind of slimy, but she had done nothing that should cost her life. I had her drop me off at my car, which was on the corner of her block. I didn't want her to think she was totally off the hook, so I left her with my customary warning. Told her what the penalty would be if I was forced to come back because she had lied to me about anything.

Then I immediately went back west. Deep west.

My next stop was to an interfaith cemetery out past Telegraph Road where Plymouth turned into 5 Mile Road. The family had put him away somewhere nice. The grounds were maintained, no litter, the headstones weren't vandalized. Mostly white people buried out here, so it was the type of place they locked at night and patrolled with rent-a-cops.

I followed the little service road about half a mile in, parked the Mark VIII, and jumped out with the brown bag in my hand. The three-o'clock sun hovered over a cloudless sky, but the temperature was about ten degrees cooler than the previous day. I was in a navy Balmain outfit with short sleeves, and a steady breeze assaulted my clothes.

I honestly hadn't planned to make this visit until after I dealt with his killers, wanted to face him with my gun still smoking, their blood dripping from my hands. But that conversation with Darnia had me feeling like this was something I couldn't put off.

The Jordan 9s had come fresh out the box that morning, but a careless step in the factory had already left a rust scar on the right toe. Right then I stepped over the damp grass expecting more stains. He was another few hundred yards from the service road, up over a crest that took my car out of view. I found his marker next to a lady with a long Russian name who had lived ninety-eight years. Darius Peterson had only seen thirty-four, and I felt like my nigga got cheated.

Doc had always seemed older than his age. He only had me by one year, but it felt like ten. At seventeen I came to the city I'd left as an infant, knowing nothing about its people or culture. It was Doc who took me under his wing and taught me the streets. Even at eighteen, he was like a wise OG telling me how to move, what to look for, what to avoid.

Back then, I had been lost without the church, without my mom. I was one of those people who needed a cause and didn't know if it was my nature or the old man's programming. I'd killed for the church then for my crew, but without either, I wasn't sure where my direction should be. Doc didn't just give me a voice; he gave me a purpose. Without him, I sort of felt like a Ronin—a samurai with no master.

I sent him a couple of letters from inside, but it became clear in the first few months that he wasn't about to write back. He was too heavy in the streets, too busy. I wasn't mad at that. The money was appreciated, but it still would've been good to hear from my friend.

I got ambushed by a montage of memories laughing, chilling, even disagreeing with Doc. I felt emotion swell inside my chest, eyes tried to squeeze back tears.

Everybody was making it seem like my best friend had changed into somebody I wouldn't recognize. All I remembered was a smooth yellow cat in an Al Wissam leather who could talk a dude out his cash and a girl out her ass within ten minutes of meeting them. The same cat who put me on my feet, took me from broke and homeless to crispy white Ones and a Yukon Denali on chrome within months. This new person who pushed Lamborghinis and Maseratis but wouldn't take care of his mother was a stranger to me. I couldn't even picture him.

I pulled a pint of Hennessy from the bag and filled a plastic cup. After he got his dollars up, I figured he graduated to the top-shelf cognacs or champagne, but back in the day he used to sip straight Henny. I sat his drink at the base of his headstone and offered the rest to the dirt.

Prison was a world I could easily navigate on my own. I'm big, strong, can fight with my bare hands, and I'm used to structure. In no way am I saying that I liked being locked up. It's just that I'm an apex predator, so being in a pond with guppies ain't shit to a gator.

But now I have to navigate these streets on my own. The thought of that scared me.

I don't know how long I stood there having a quiet conversation with my friend, asking questions, making promises. I headed back to my car after a few parting words.

Coming down a ridge crested with stone markers, I caught sight of the Mark VIII. But there was a new Camaro ZL1 parked on my rear bumper, gray with powder-blue racing stripes.

A driver and passenger jumped out to meet me as I approached. The black guy was only five-foot-seven, short afro, wire-framed glasses with thick lenses. The driver was a tall white woman rocking short blond hair and men's clothes.

The two detectives who came to the house were just as Quianna described them.

Chapter Twenty-five

I left Doc's grave to find detectives waiting by my ride. I couldn't imagine how they found me, but they had every reason to be looking. I'd been on bullshit from the moment I stepped out the joint.

Darnia might've called them after I left, or maybe the parole officer I never bothered to meet might have reported me as Absconded. In either case, they might be there to arrest me.

My first impulse was to not even find out, just blow both of them down. I scanned my periphery and didn't see any backup. The cemetery was empty besides us. Both had their service weapons in view, but neither were poised to draw. They were too close to me, and my quickness was always underestimated. I could be on both of their asses before they unholstered those Glocks. It would be a short trip to their final resting place.

And I definitely would've done that had the energy coming from them been aggressive. The lanky white chick came towards me the way you approach something you know to be dangerous, walking slowly with her palms up.

"We just want to talk and took this to be the safest place." She was also clearly aware of my handicap. She did that whole thing of speaking slow and overemphasizing each syllable. "We figured you'd come here eventually."

Ninety percent of communication is nonverbal, but for me zero percent of that communication is with the police. I breezed right by them like their presence hardly registered.

They followed. The black dude put himself between me and my car door. With a look I told him that I wasn't above moving him.

The woman lightly touched my arm, turned my attention to her. "Nobody's here to play Starsky and Hutch. I just need five minutes, and you need these five minutes more than me."

I looked her over, six-foot-two, dressed in a man's dark-gray suit minus the tie. A lavender shirt under the jacket added some color, and on the front of it, her golden shield hung from a thin chain. The pale blue eyes seemed to be assessing me, too.

"I'm Sergeant Gamble, and this is Detective Bates." The four-eyed brotha nodded when she introduced him. I had already guessed by her demeanor that she was the superior.

She mouthed, "The Silent Assassin. I've only been working the Tenth Precinct for eight years, but I've read enough open cases with your name attached to become a fan."

Normally I wouldn't entertain this bullshit, but these were the cops working Doc's case. They had information I wanted. That was enough to make me stop and listen for a minute. But I flashed my impatience as a warning to tread carefully.

"We know you just got out of prison yesterday, and we pretty much know what you've got planned." I frowned to tell the white girl she didn't know shit.

"We know you've been dropping in on the old crew. You've already been to see Eric Sims aka 'Punchy' and T'Ellis Caldwell aka 'Prime'. We can easily guess your old friend Louis 'Louie Boy' Pollard is next on the list." That came from the brotha and caught me off guard.

Bates got jumpy when I reached for my pocket, put his hand on his pistol. I stared at him like, *Nigga please.* I moved slowly to pull up my iPhone.

Fake-ass Norbit was clearly a clown and not worth my addressing. So I typed something in my phone but faced it towards fake-ass Ellen instead.

I asked about the investigation, wanted to know who had been suspected and questioned.

Gamble squinted hard to read my screen against the glare of afternoon sun, then flashed those blue eyes back to me. "That's the whole point of this meet-and-greet. You have questions; we have questions. Maybe we can find the answers together."

I crossed my arms, made an attentive face just to play along. I would see what I could get from her but wasn't giving up nothing.

"Look we're not gonna pretend Darius was a saint. We already know the type of stuff he was involved in, but that still doesn't mean he deserved—"

Bates interrupted to quip, "A real pillar of the community. I wonder if we'll get a paid day off when he gets his own holiday."

He didn't know how close that sarcastic smile was to getting his glasses slapped off.

Gamble seemed to notice. She checked him with a reproachful glare that drained the humor from his face before turning back to me. She repeated, "It doesn't mean Darius deserved what happened to him. And it damn sure doesn't mean somebody deserves to get away with it."

Believe me, bitch, they ain't. But I offered her the slightest nod to cosign her point.

"Darius was ambitious, maybe too much for his own good. He came up a long way since he had you beating up delinquents for running off with thousand-dollar sacks." She added, "Other than drugs, did you find out what else he was involved in right before he died?"

Only that he had been killed on his own property. I answered with a headshake.

She asked, "Would you even tell me if you did?"

Could only respond to that with a guilty smirk, and she returned a nod.

She said to Bates, "Do me a favor and make sure a bird doesn't shit on my hood."

For a second, he looked at her confused, until she shooed him away. He went to stand by the fender of her Camaro and stared up at the sky like a dummy.

She led me away from our vehicles. "Sorry about him. New partner. Gotta housebreak some of them like puppies."

Normally it would bother me to see a white person treat a brotha like that, but he was one of those Uncle Toms, so fuck him five times over. We only walked twenty feet or so, I imagined just far enough for Bates to be out of earshot.

"Back when I was fifteen, I went full-on Goth: black clothes, jet-black hair, nose and lip piercings. Because I still hadn't accepted certain things about myself, I didn't think friends would, either. So I was that sheltered girl who spent all of her time up in her room watching movies. Tarantino, Spike Lee, John Woo—to me, the nineties was the golden age of film. I even considered going to school to learn direction and cinematography."

Quianna wasn't lying when she said this bitch liked to talk. I flashed that impatience again, made a twirling motion with my finger that implored her to get to the fucking point.

"Silence, you are what the biz would call an Avenging Angel. An anti-hero who's ready to go on what the studios would advertise as a bloody revenge spree to find your friend's killer."

She brought out her own phone and pulled up something that turned my stomach sour.

I was looking at a shot of Doc's crime scene photo. The picture was taken from outside the Bentley Bentayga of him slumped forward in his seat. Blood and brain matter splashed his face and the dashboard console. The gruesome crater in his forehead was where the slug exited his skull. His face rested against the wheel, turned to the window. The hazel eyes he shared with his mother and sister were half-open, staring into the beyond.

I had seen worse, because I had done worse, but still had to turn away from her phone. Rage tightened my face. I suddenly felt like I had electricity running through me.

I finally looked back at Gamble and read the subdued satisfaction. I'd given her exactly the response she had wanted. I hated myself for that.

"Now as for my role. This is typically the scene in the movie where the asshole cop, preferably a young Jodie Foster, would show up to tell you to stay out the investigation. She would nag about this being a police matter and threaten to lock you up if you tried to interfere."

I wasn't a movie buff, but I had seen this flick too and a thousand just like it.

"Well don't worry, because this isn't that type of movie," she explained with a smile. "In fact, I want you to get involved. I want you to crack some heads, to do what you do and get to the bottom of this. I just need you to report to me whenever you find out something significant."

Me work with the police? I looked at this bitch like she was crazy.

Gamble didn't seem surprised by the rejection. "I never made it to film school, but I do dabble in my spare time. I recently directed a small independent project that I'm really proud of. Tell me what you think. And be honest, because the criticism will only strengthen me." She pulled up something else on her phone, a video this time. It took me a second to realize what I was looking at, but the sight made me sicker than seeing Doc's dead body.

If I had a voice, I would've cursed loud enough to wake half the people in that cemetery.

Chapter Twenty-six

The video on her phone was recorded with harsh light and at a weird angle. It had to run for a few seconds before I realized that I was looking at a bird's-eye view of myself putting the ones and twos on the caveman in the Indians jacket, then tossing the female over the Nissan. The footage had clearly come from an overhead camera mounted under the canopy at the 76.

Gamble explained, "They were supposed to do this without guns. But I guess you were enough to spook even three trained officers."

She enjoyed the look on my face at learning they were cops, because we both knew what came next. There was me breaking the window with the stocky dude's head. Then I witnessed myself the way God must do as I put two in his chest.

"We hardly ever get video this sharp from surveillance cameras with no obstructed views," she said through a smile that was genuinely excited. "And thanks to the excellent lighting, we see every feature of our hero's face, so there's no mistaking you for a stunt double."

On the screen, I watched myself empty the driver's pockets, give him a kick, then back the Caprice out the frame.

"Three counts of Assault and Great Bodily Harm, four Armed Robberies, and one Felony Murder of a city police officer." The sergeant used her fingers to enumerate my crimes.

She raised her hand to stop me as if I were really about to interrupt. "This whole thing was supposed to be sort of an audition for you. After hearing so many stories, I just wanted to see if you lived up to the hype—which you totally do, by the way.

"But Officer Clements was stupid for drawing her weapon, and Evans was more stupid for reaching for it. I'll take the blame for that. He was actually a late addition to the cast after I had a short-notice cancellation. My original was supposed to really test you."

I had known the shit at the gas station was a setup, never would've guessed the motive.

But you don't spend twelve years in prison and not learn few things about the Law. Running the entire tape would prove they initiated the fight, were the first to draw a weapon and never once announced themselves as police.

Gamble must've saw that I was calculating and liking my chances. "I suppose a good lawyer might be able to argue self-defense supposing anyone sees the whole unedited version of this video, which I promise they'll never find. Then you still have to justify taking their money.

"Including myself, three decorated officers will testify that you knowing and willingly murdered our colleague. Any jury—who'll most likely have more people with my skin tone than yours—is going to take one look at all that big, black muscle and come back with a guilty verdict. Especially when they learn you haven't been out of prison one day for killing somebody else.

"You got off lucky the first time. Do you really want to roll the dice again?"

I don't get squeezed; I usually do the squeezing. She had come here with only one other cop. A mistake. I judged the distance between me and Bates, confident that I could quick-draw, kill her, and squeeze off another kill shot on her four-eyed partner before he returned fire.

The lean lady with the masculine swag seemed to be psychic. "Oh big fella, you could bury me and my phone in the deepest hole in Hell. That video would still have you on a level-five yard doing pushups for the rest of your natural life. Hardly a noble end for a proud warrior from the tribe of Shango."

That stunned me, and she peeped it in my response. "I told you I'm a fan. I know about your father's . . . uh, let's just call it his religion."

My eyes warned she needed to leave that alone. She was already playing with fire fucking with me. Digging into the church was like playing with something radioactive.

She either didn't get it or didn't care. "I need you to find out what happened to Darius. You got three days."

I texted to ask how did she expect me to do in three days what she couldn't do in three months.

"By going places I can't get into and using means I can't legally."

I had already planned to have Doc's killer folded up in an oil drum by then, but this shit felt shady. A cop making a goon find a killer. Why was she giving me such a short window? Why just three days? I presented the last question on my iPhone.

"Because the video is evidence in an active investigation into the murder of a police officer. We have a thing in the department called Chain of Custody. I can only keep this for seventy-two hours before I have to pass it along to my superiors. And once it's out of my hands—"

She left the threat dangling. If I didn't turn over Doc's killer before she turned over the video, I was cooked.

With that, we were done. I turned my back on her, headed back for the cars, brushed past Bates, who was still standing there looking like a kid on timeout.

I jumped into my old-ass Lincoln, hit REVERSE, and purposely slammed into her Camaro hard enough to crack the bumper. I skirted off mugging Gamble with my middle finger up.

I came home only thinking about the enemies I'd have to deal with: street thugs, conniving hoodrats, but mostly whoever was in the back seat of Doc's Bentley.

I pulled out of the cemetery with no idea of how to deal with the dirty cop who was blackmailing me.

Chapter Twenty-seven

I had kept my composure in the moment but left the cemetery driving like a road rage incident waiting to happen. Learning that the police had been following me this entire time wasn't what had me so pissed off. It's that I should've been paying closer attention.

My whole life, the old man had been warning me that white folks had a thousand ways to put the black man in a trick bag. Gamble had been looking into my past, even knew about the UOTA. I wasn't sure if my father knew where I was or simply didn't care. Either way, I wasn't just playing tough when I warned her about that. If she looked too deep into it, the white bitch might get us both killed.

You might have already guessed that the church I grew up in isn't like the one you probably attend on Sundays where a slick-talking preacher in a ten-thousand-dollar suit lectures on piety and humility, then after eleven different collections, smashes off in a brand-new Rolls-Royce. The Universal Orthodox Temple of Alkebulan is a black nationalist organization started by my father and a few of his cronies.

After spending time in the Nation of Islam and the Moorish Science Temple, he found them not radical enough, then drafted his own manifesto. The old man had done time, too, back in the eighties. He came home fucked-up on that angry militant shit. The LA riots sparked by the Rodney King beating convinced him that a race war was inevitable, and that blacks weren't just out-numbered, but pitifully unprepared. One of his favorite sayings was, "We're teaching our kids to shoot hoops while they're teach-ing theirs to shoot us!" He rounded up enough people who felt the same way then convinced them to sell everything they owned to buy nineteen rural acres in Washington state near the Cascade Mountains. They built a compound. He even used his knowledge of the Uniform Commercial Codes to get the land declared as a sovereign nation.

I blame my father for a lot of shit: running off my mother, rob-bing me of a normal childhood by raising me in a black militia, even for losing my hearing to a treatable disease because he re-fused to trust the white man's medicine.

I used to blame him for making me a killer. The UOTA raises their children like Spartans; to be a warrior in the tribe of Shango, the training is as lethal as the skills taught. One of their favorite exercises was to snatch up a group of kids in the middle of the night, take us deep into the woods or up into the mountains, then leave us butt-naked to fend for ourselves until the adults came for us, which could be as long as six weeks. Fear, meekness, senti-mentality: we were mercilessly grilled by instructors to never suc-cumb to these. So when a younger boy in my group started to freak out in the middle of wilderness training, I stepped up as the elder chief's son. I snapped his neck. This was the only time the old man showed any measure of pride in me.

Not long after that, my mother left. Maybe she couldn't stand to see what my father was doing to me or maybe she just couldn't get down with his new views on polygamy. She had called it a cult back before I knew what that word meant. She ran away from the church, and I did the same two years later when I came to Detroit to find her.

I was too deep in my memories, snapped back when the car in

front of me stopped for a yellow light. I had to brake hard before I plowed into the rear of a Chrysler 200. Raised a hand to say, *My bad* when the driver threw back a sour look. Her bumper sticker urged me to vote for Corliss Henley: the mechanic we need to tune up the Motor City.

With my thoughts back in the present, I refocused on current problems.

Gamble had already known I was looking for Doc's killer. It made no sense why she would go through the trouble to black-mail me into doing some shit I was doing anyway. She clearly needed me to handle things my way, and fast. The upside was that the sergeant obviously was going to keep the police off my ass while I worked. But still, I was in my mirrors watching more cautiously for anyone tailing me as I drove to the club on 6 Mile Road.

It was a freestanding building with a navy and sky-blue color scheme. The Pastry Shop could've been one of those places that sold erotic desserts—the dick-shaped cakes women ordered for bachelorette parties. The sign featured a sexy cartoon fox in lingerie and a chef's hat.

I paid cover at the door and got frisked by a bouncer who stood six-foot-seven. He had me by a few inches but was intimidated by my physique. He advised me that I'd better not be a problem. My eyes advised him to be ready, because I might.

Inside I was surprised by the décor and the amount of square footage. Hardwood floors, walls of exposed brick, recessed lighting. Tables, chairs, and a curved bar matched the blue in its exterior and were trimmed with neon lights. A second-story VIP terrace overlooked the stage. They played on the theme by hanging framed pictures of souffles, crepes and other whipped-cream-covered sweets alongside promotional photos for dancers who had names like Angel Cakes and Honey Buns.

After being shut down, Louie Boy had obviously spent some bank trying to revamp the club to attract a more upscale clientele. What he attracted right then were the type of thirsty dudes you'd expect to be at a strip club in the middle of a weekday afternoon. Sitting in parties of one, they looked so pathetic the strippers should've thrown dollars to them. I was there on business but was still a little embarrassed to be even mistaken for one.

I felt the vibrations for a deep throbbing bass line while the girl on stage rolled her hips to it in slow circles. She wouldn't make the cut for Quianna's BANDS Society. I only expected to see the benchwarmers on this shift while the baddest bitches took the nights and weekends when the money showed up.

I claimed a stool at the bar and was greeted by a bartender who looked better than the dancer. She rocked short hair permed into thick shiny waves. Friendly brown eyes invited conversation, while enhanced double Ds in a push-up bra invited tips.

I used my pen to scribble something on a fifty, then slid it to her. She took the bill, and when she returned with two double-shots of Patron, I had another twenty waiting with a one-word question: *Louie?*

She leaned over the bar and tried to whisper to me. I motioned to let babygirl know my ears were only for decoration. Made her just speak the words, since the loud music clearly didn't affect me.

According to her, Louie Boy usually didn't come in until later, if at all, but luck had been with me that day. He had an office in back. I offered her another twenty if she sent a message that an old friend was there to see him.

Business was slow, so she could briefly leave her station. She stepped from behind the bar wearing sheer leggings with cutouts. My eyes followed her ass across the room until she disappeared through a door reserved for employees.

I downed my first shot thinking that somebody was going to get robbed soon. Buying the Mark VIII had dealt a serious blow to my revenge fund.

I felt the song switch to one with a faster, more aggressive bass line. Girl on stage was twerking hard enough to throw her spine out, but the customers were stingy. I supported her hustle with a light sprinkling of singles, more out of pity than anything else.

Watching her clap those modest cheeks reminded me of how mandatory it was that I fed my beast soon. Givenya Moorehead hadn't just been a clever pun, but a promise. I texted Kierra to make sure she kept it. My corny ass even did a little fist pump when she sent back confirmation that we were locked in for later. It was deeper than me just being horny; the shit at the cemetery had me feeling like I needed some type of win.

The bartender was gone under two minutes, and even before she spoke, I saw *No* on her face. Apparently Louie Boy was busy and couldn't be bothered, even by old friends.

He clearly didn't know who was out here, because he knew better than to play me like that. Shorty with the waves refused to try again, even for another twenty. Her energy told me that the boss must've cursed her out the first time.

My thanks came through a smile, let her keep the other twenty anyway.

I was about to act a damn fool and didn't want the lady to think it had anything to do with her.

Chapter Twenty-eight

After I swallowed my second double-shot of Patron, the bartender looked at me crazy when I climbed on top of the bar. I tracked Jordan prints across the top of her clean workstation and dared somebody to come do something about me. I spotted the mounted cameras that every boss has to spy on their employees, threw out my hands like *What's up?*

I jumped down from the bar and headed to kick in Louie Boy's office, but dude who searched me, along with a second I hadn't seen, blocked me at the employee door. Both wore navy-blue T-shirts with The Pastry Shop's logo. The first was close to my height, but his extra twenty pounds were soft in the middle. His partner was a little shorter than me and closer to my build; his two thirty-five looked solid.

I didn't have my pistol but wouldn't need it. Bouncers were typically just big muthafuckas the club hired because they looked intimidating. They could manhandle and toss out the average dude. Few of them had any real fight training. Nose, throat, solar plexus, kidneys: those sensitive targets always lit up on my opponents like icons on a computer screen.

We stood in a three-way staredown. Even two-on-one, they didn't have shit coming. In the few seconds we faced off, I'd already played out our fight six different times in six different ways. None offered them a win.

I waited for either of them to start our two-step when Louie Boy came from the back. His belt was unfastened, and part of his shirt was caught in his zipper. The reason followed him through the door: petite and favoring a young LisaRaye in *The Players Club*.

Louie Boy stepped between us to put his dogs on a leash. "Y-y'all niggas back the fuck up before somebody get hurt." The bouncers fell back, wearing smug faces as if that "somebody" referred to me, but their boss and I knew better.

He gave me a smile, and I gave him a look that told him how close he came to having his club shut down again.

We embraced the way real niggas do: tight but quick, with pats on the back. Louie Boy had put on the few extra pounds you'd expect when somebody's getting money. I saw where the weed and Remy had aged him; his brown skin looked leathery, and that wavy-ass Indian hair that used to make us question who his father was had thinned. But all in all, he shined. He was still fresh-to-death, draped in the Louis Vuitton that was part of his name and swag.

"God d-d-damn man. You built like a muthafuckin' action figure. Wanna b-bounce for me?" And he still had that stutter that fucked with my lip reading.

I typed something quick into my phone and let him read it.

"I couldn't afford you. A-Ain't that a bitch." He laughed. "This how you t-talking now?"

Louie Boy didn't bother with the I'm-sorry-I-didn't-write formalities, just took me around the club to show me his pride and joy. Then he grabbed an entire bottle of 1800 from the bar when we retired to the rear. The employee door led to a long, narrow hallway that ran lengthwise across the back of the building and terminated in a fire exit. Louie Boy's office was a small window-less space near the end that was probably meant to be a storage room.

The air still carried the scent of fuck-sweat. A tray with two undone lines of white powder sat on the desk, and Louie Boy hurried to put that out of sight, knowing I don't fuck around.

"Goddamn, Sy! Twelve y-years over that nothing-ass slut T-T'wanda. C'mon man! All this m-m-muthafuckin' pussy out here." He eyed me from across the desk with a pitiable head-shake, and I couldn't shoot back. Truth can't be argued with.

Sucker-stroking over a bum bitch had lost me over a decade of my freedom. I just didn't see why Louie Boy felt the need to rub that in. Like I didn't spend the past 4,667 days torturing myself with the same damn thought every time they locked me down for count, every time a skinny white CO spoke to me reckless as if I couldn't twist off his head like a bottle cap, every time I dreamed a bad chick like Quianna's friend Lexy was on top of me going buck only to wake up alone and with my dick harder than the iron bars that caged me.

"An-and I saw yo' girl, too. The b-bitch hit now anyway. All f-fat and dusty-looking."

As I sat there getting a sermon from the Book of Louie, he reintroduced me to a core part of his personality. Even when we were younger, he had always been a trick; owning a strip club meant having a dollhouse full of disposable pleasures. Louie Boy was a man whose dick measured his bottom line. The fact that I'd let one piece of pussy take me away from all the pussy in the world to him wasn't just bad math, but a cardinal sin. He only wanted to save my soul.

After he preached to me on the evils of tender-dickery, he told me about all his accomplishments, but in a way that didn't seem like bragging. I was just a passenger while he drove the conversation. Louie Boy knew where I wanted to go but took the scenic route.

Then finally, our destination: "Y-yeah man, when I h-h-heard

Doc was dead, I couldn't believe it. Th-that was some f-f-fucked-up shit, man."

I dove in a little too eager. I shot rapid-fire texts, typing misspelled words in long run-on sentences until my fingers cramped. I caught him up on everything I got from Punchy and Prime but left out the stuff from my conversation with Darnia. I wasn't going to expose all my cards.

He offered me another drink, but I declined. My tolerance was still low, and I was starting to feel the shots I'd done at the bar. Plus, it seemed to me like he was stalling.

He downed a glass and poured another. "F-first off, I gotta c-correct you on some of the bullshit they done fed you. St-starting with Punchy."

I sat back in my chair, got comfortable for what I figured to be a long explanation.

"Punch always been a clown—nigga, you know that. I c-c-can't believe you bought that whole started-from-the-bottom bullshit about him t-taking over Fenkell. Nigga st-stop it! Punchy couldn't take over a playground at a middle school for sp-special kids."

I had only listened to Punchy's story, never said I believed it.

"Meeting th-that chick Tyeisha was the best thing to happen to Punchy. She the one who-who got the bread. Her people own office buildings and shit, heavy in commercial real estate. They was already fucking with the vending machines and threw him a bone. Every now and then he'll try to shake a little bag. But mostly he just works as a property manager for ol' girl's family. Dude was a flunky back when he was with us, and j-just a better-paid flunky now."

That seemed about right to me. Punchy never had the discipline or disposition to be an effective hustler. The girl's rich family would explain the house in Sherwood Forest, the cars and jewelry, but also why I found so little cash and no drugs other than some paraphernalia.

Louie Boy dissected Prime next. "And that s-s-sob story my baby ran on you? After the indictment, we b-backed off for a minute—of course, nigga you hot! Honestly, D-Doc did cut him loose, but I was still rocking with dude when the heat cooled off.

"Some people fall down and get right b-back up; Prime fell down and j-just kept bitching about it. I was still eating pretty good off his Carolina plug s-s-so every time I came through shining, I could see it hurt his heart. I tr-tried to throw him a few lifelines, but I just got tired of watching that nigga feel sorry for himself."

I had caught a glimpse of that, remembered that sick look on Prime's face when we sat in the Caprice. It's sad when your friends can't wish you well because they're too busy comparing your situations. It wouldn't have been long before I got tired of that shit, too.

Punchy and Prime were just the undercard. It was time for the main event.

Louie Boy tossed back more tequila. He was stalling again.

"I knew Doc longer than you, Punchy, or Prime. We went all the way back to matching B-big Wheels and shit. He was a smooth, shit-talking nigga, a people person who made you like him. Even when he pissed you off, it was hard to stay mad for too long."

He took another shot. I realized then he was looking for courage in the liquor.

"Sy, I loved Doc, but you w-w-worshipped him. Everybody in the crew saw it from Day One. You don't talk but you d-damn sure don't hide how you feel either. And y-you made it clear to all of us that Doc was your favorite.

"I'm just giving you a heads-up b-before I say anything else. I know you think that nigga walked on water but . . ."

Louie Boy was basically asking me not to fuck him up if he said something that offended me. I sat across the desk from him, arms folded, making no promises.

Chapter Twenty-nine

"Don't get it twisted. I ain't knocking the nigga or disrespecting his memory. I got rich fucking with Doc. I'm j-just being one hundred, so check your temperature."

The look on my face seemed to scare Louie Boy. I fought to keep it neutral.

"We ate good off North Carolina for years, but it dried up and things was slow. Then one day Doc just p-p-pop up with forty ounces of raw. Won't tell me nothing about the plug, just w-w-wanted my half on a ticket that was so lovely I thought it had to be a joke."

I didn't know much about heroin, because my crew was mostly dealing in cocaine before I went away.

"That dog changed our lives, Sy. Every one we get we pressing that into three and the bag still going s-so hard, so fast that—" Louie couldn't seem to find the words, just motioned with his hands to indicate it was mind-blowing. "The product ain't consistent, but the pipeline was steady, and the prices so low you can't help but turn a fat profit."

I could tell it was an exciting time for Louie Boy by the shine of his eyes. "I scooped up every HUD house I could and dropped cash on a primary out in Grosse Pointe. Doc did the riverfront, was pushing every whip in the Dupont Registry. Was even bragging he about to b-be the real Sebastian Caine." We shared a laugh at that.

Sebastian Caine was supposed to be this mysterious drug lord out of Detroit who ran the entire Midwest; rumored to be Big Meech, Michael Corleone, and Satan all rolled into one. Despite his name ringing hard in the streets for almost twenty years, you won't find a single person who's actually met him or seen his face, earning him the moniker: The Invisible Man. His MO is that he never does business in person. Most dope boys who are actually heavy in the game don't believe dude even exists. An urban legend.

Gamble had just put me on the clock, so I pressed fast-forward. I held up a message on my phone for Louie Boy: *Skip to the part where y'all fell out.*

Surprise altered his features. I wasn't supposed to know about that.

Louie Boy claimed it started when Doc came with the deal of a lifetime. Their mystery supplier offered them a whole twenty pounds at Black Friday prices.

"Sy, that's o-o-over nine kilos of raw!" Louie said that like I couldn't do math. "We always used the Holiday Inn out in Southfield for our stash spot. When the work was gone, we spent thirty-six hours up on pills counting up. T-time we done, it's over three million and eight hundred thousand stacked up on the bed."

Goddamn. I tried to imagine the feeling. Sitting in a hotel room with close to four million in trap money. Figured it had to be some combination of pride and paranoia.

"I get an emergency call from Baby Momma Number Six saying my second-youngest girl in the ICU. I leave Doc with the stash while I run all over the city, hospital to hospital, before I realize it's b-bullshit. So I haul ass back out to Southfield.

"Doc gone, but it's five niggas in sk-ski masks bagging up the money. They came ready: big straps, duct tape, zip ties. Strip me naked and l-laid me facedown in the tub. Dude with the twelve-gauge sat on me with the barrel to the back of my head." Louie

Boy ran a shaky hand through his slick hair. "I always thought in a situation like that, I'd be calm, say some slick shit like in the movies. In real life, I cried and begged for my life. I even shitted on myself."

People sometimes felt safe telling a mute things they would never share with a talker—I was used to that. I didn't know how to respond to his confession, though. I was usually the one on the other end of the gun making people shit themselves.

I didn't fault Louie for grabbing the coke tray to vacuum up a line. It even made me reach for the 1800 again.

"Our childhood friend got me for one-point-nine. Th-That's your boy."

I'd heard a different version of this in the Escalade: Louie had pulled the slimeball shit, and Doc took the loss. Darnia had been convincing, too, but I couldn't deny the truth I saw in Louie's eyes. He didn't just retell the story; he relived it.

Louie Boy read my text and frowned like it was a stupid question. I felt my boy deserved the benefit of the doubt.

"We the o-only two who knew about the count-up. Plus, Doc had some youngsters off Joy Road working for him at the time. They the ones he had do it."

Louie Boy had just admitted to having nearly two million reasons for wanting Doc dead. He read the accusation on my furrowed brow.

"Look Sy, I was heated at th-the start—even thought about putting some money on that nigga head." The way I leaned forward in my seat made him put his hands up. "Just thought about it. But I-I let that shit go."

I made sure he saw my doubt.

He glanced away from me to the surveillance monitor on the corner of his desk. The screen held six simultaneous views being fed by the cameras around his club. Mid-afternoon business was slow. I watched the cute bartender lean against the bar to play with her phone.

"I was in that bathtub, duct-taped and sm-smelling like shit, for eleven hours before housekeeping found me. That's a long enough time to have a conversation with God."

I hit him with my *Nigga please!* look. I know he wasn't going to run some bullshit about finding Jesus when he was just in this bitch sniffing cocaine off of stripper titties.

"I ain't saying I got saved. I just left the game alone. D-done seen enough money—I wanna see my babies grow up. I started focusing on my l-legitimate businesses."

I had trouble believing he took a loss like that on the chin and kept it moving.

"L-look Sy, if your plan is to holler at every person in the c-c-city who had a problem with Doc, you gone be a b-busy muthafucka. He done stuck niggas, done sold fake dope, done bought real dope but paid with fake money. And I g-got it on good word that he even helped put a few niggas in the fed."

That put me on Louie Boy's ass before he could react. I yanked him across the desk by his shirt collars, spilling the shot glasses and coke plate. I choke-slammed that muthafucka to the floor then pinned him there with my hand on his throat.

To say my boy stole was one thing, but calling him a rat was over the line.

Louie Boy pried at my fingers. His strained face made his lips harder to read. "These d-dudes cr-credible. I wouldn't put a snitch label on a stranger without proof, let alone a friend."

I dared him to say it again. My fist hovered over his face.

"I'm-I'm just telling you what the streets saying."

The two bouncers appeared in the doorway of his office, followed by the young stripper. I could only guess they were drawn by the sound of the commotion. His security saw I had their boss on the floor underneath me and charged in to help. These clowns wouldn't have been a problem if I wasn't down on one knee.

Being low did put me at the perfect height to give the fat one a straight shot to the nuts. I hit him so hard that the rest of his children would probably be born fucked-up. He stopped in his tracks and grabbed at his pain. He staggered back into the wall to support himself.

The muscular dude actually had those hands. Before I could get to my feet, he caught me clean with a big right. I was suddenly on my back looking up at the ceiling lights, trying to figure out why they were swirling.

He stood over me to rain a couple of punches, and I deflected what I could. Louie Boy was up, tugging at dude's shirt to hold him back, but his employee was too eager to earn his pay.

He fucked up when he tried to stomp on me. He got in one good shot before I caught his foot. I twisted the ankle in a direction God never intended. I saw his face brighten with pain. He stumbled away from me as I scrambled to my feet.

Louie Boy jumped in front of me with his palms up. "C-c'mon Sy, j-just come with me."

I was still dazed and embarrassed that I let myself get dropped. Once I unleashed The Hulk, I couldn't turn back into Bruce Banner until I whipped a proper amount of ass.

"Sy, take this ride with me please!" Louie begged. "I think I know who k-killed Doc."

Chapter Thirty

Louie Boy kept his ride locked in a gated breezeway that separated his club from the neighboring building, an abandoned credit union. His silver-and-black Wraith was easily the prettiest car I'd ever seen up close but looked out of place in the hood. I left the Mark VIII in the customer lot, agreed to take that ride with him, but grabbed my pistol first.

The Rolls-Royce had me feeling like a passenger on a spaceship. The interior was immaculate: wood grain over rich bespoke leather with temperature-controlled seats. We were pulled along by a powerful V-12 motor, and the suspension made Detroit's rough potholed streets suddenly feel like goose-filled cushion.

You couldn't drive five blocks on any major street without running into a campaign sign to re-elect Councilman Corliss Henley. I learned from Louie Boy that dude was a lock to reclaim his position as president of the city council, as well as his bid for the mayor's office in another two years. Louie turned to me beaming with enthusiasm. "You know the city's coming back?"

So I'd heard, but all my own problems had me not giving a fuck about civic pride right then. Still, though, I was surprised that Louie Boy followed politics so closely.

The whole thing about knowing who killed Doc started to seem like a ploy just to get me out of his club. For a while I thought we were just wandering aimlessly until we ended up in an area where the two major arteries of Grand River and Joy Road intersected.

We crept down a residential street named Cascade that saw the same amount of blight as the rest of the city. However, wedged between the burnouts and trashy fields, a large Venetian-style house stood out: fresh paint and siding, new roof, a shiny new eight-foot fence surrounding it and the neighboring lot, which had been paved over to create a full-sized basketball court. A Benz G63 Wagon, two SRT-8 Challengers, a new Corvette, along with an assortment of old-schools were parked within the fence, all on big chrome and shiny red paint.

Half a dozen youngsters sat on the porch, wearing more than enough of the same color. They watched the Wraith cruise by, mugging us, like they were the only ones allowed to be riding good. One even felt the need to lift his shirt to show us he was in-sulated—holding heat.

Louie Boy turned off their block and brought us back to Grand River. "Th-those the li'l niggas Doc was fucking with right there. They flipped and turned on him."

I needed more proof and let him see it in my expression. If this was the same crew Doc supposedly had used to rob him, I thought Louie Boy might be using me to get back for him.

"I t-told you I ain't tripping on that, Sy. That loss hurt, but I-I'm still up. I still had a decent run before that, still got the club and a rib joint doing a profit, st-still got thirty-two tenants paying me rent every month on the first.

"Whatever Doc did to me don't change the fact that we was once boys. I didn't have warm feelings for the nigga but d-didn't want him dead, either. Two to the back of the head is a fucked-up way for anybody to go out. Somebody need to pay for that."

I flashed back to that picture in Gamble's phone. Somebody

was going to pay for that. I just needed to know these were the right people.

"My BM from this way and a few of her g-girls fuck them niggas. Y-you already know these young muthafuckas can't keep they mouths closed about nothing nowadays."

Louie Boy sent a text, and a few streets over, he parked in front of an unimpressive brick house. A woman already waiting on the porch came down to lean into his window. She was brown-skinned, top-tier fine, early twenties, and short. He actually introduced her as "Baby Momma Number Six," and she didn't seem the least bit offended.

"Baby this m-m-my guy Silence. He can't talk, so don't think he acting funny when he don't say Hi." We acknowledged each other with perfunctory head nods.

Louie Boy gave her his phone. "Show me th-that shit you showed me before. What them li'l niggas posted around the time Doc died."

Baby Momma Number Six pulled up the Instagram page for somebody tagged as JoyBoyDirtyRed. In the short video, a chubby light-skinned dude was wearing a heavy thirty-two-inch Figueroa link chain with a huge copy of the Detroit Tigers' signature Old English D encrusted in diamonds. He flossed and danced around in the chain like it was a fresh acquisition.

Louie Boy paused the video, then enlarged the image. "That's D-Doc's chain!"

He then went to his own Facebook account to show me a photo taken five months before, back when he and Doc were still on good terms. They appeared to be at a club, holding up bottles; each had a hoodrat twerking against his crotch. Doc was wearing a short, hooded mink jacket with the same chain hanging around his neck.

I leaned against the passenger door, didn't want to look at any pictures of my boy. Seeing him in Life made me imagine him in Death. He drank and partied that night, not knowing in two months his body would be a feast for worms.

I asked Louie Boy if Doc had been a member of Blood Nation.

"D-Doc wasn't affiliated but fucked with s-some of everybody. Stones, GDs, Pirus. Only c-colors that mattered to Doc was pink and green." I got it: pussy and money.

For a while, Louie Boy pensively stared at the photos of Doc, eyes cloudy with emotion. Each of us was deep in our memory of that mutual friend when his girl interrupted the vibe.

"This all you wanted?" She stood outside the car, arms folded, looking on us agitated. "Cause if that's all you came over here for, you can leave."

Her obvious play for his attention worked, because when she tried to storm off, Louie Boy jumped out to stop her just like she wanted. Number Six didn't fight when he snatched her by the arm, pulled her body into his.

She had the height of an adolescent child, but the orange sweatpants covered the form of a full-grown woman. At four-foot-nine, she even made Louie look like a giant. He had to stoop over to meet her lips, and I watched his hands caress her soft parts. They leaned against the Wraith's fender, the public make-out session escalating in intensity.

I knew it was coming before Louie Boy hit me with the *one-minute* finger. She dragged him towards the house, and I dragged a hand across my face. This was why I used to hate riding with his trick ass back in the day. Left me sitting in one of the grimiest areas in a four-hundred-thousand-dollar car with the motor running. I put the SR40 on my lap and my head on a swivel.

Louie Boy was in the house for twenty-three nerve-racking minutes before he and Number Six appeared in the doorway. He was adjusting his Louis V. outfit while she was in the same shirt, minus the sweatpants. He pulled a thick cash roll and peeled her off several bills.

He bounced down the porch steps and strolled back to the car with the relaxed posture of somebody who'd just busted a good nut. I expected to have that same swag in a few hours—right then, I was moving as stiff as a robot.

He jumped into the driver's seat, did a K-turn, then led us back to Grand River. He was looking off into traffic before realizing I had him under a quizzical glare.

What about that emergency phone call he got at the hotel? I asked what's up with that.

"That's how I-I know for a fact it was Doc who got me. Had to choke her little ass up, but she told it all." Louie shrugged nonchalantly. "Y-you know how it is. She a young b-bitch still impressed by shiny shit. She never had a chance a-against a smooth-talking pretty boy like Doc, yoking a Lambo with all that ice on. He caught her out at the club and took her down.

"Had been fucking her about a month before the lick. She claimed not to know what the whole plan was; he just told her to make the call. D-dumb bitch said he only gave her a stack."

If Doc had used his girl to set him up, then Louie Boy was being awfully cool about it. He clearly forgave the BM for her role. Still, that didn't mean he forgave Doc.

"C-c'mon man, don't act like I'm the only one who done got snaked by the homie. The good doctor was known for making house calls on someone's lady." He gave me a curious look.

I turned to stare out the window, slipped back into my head as a few tortured city blocks rolled by my vacant eyes.

After a mile, he nudged me with an elbow to reclaim my attention. "So w-w-what you wanna do, Sy?" He ran a hand through that good wavy hair again, waiting for my response.

I sat there pretending like I hadn't already made up my mind. Louie Boy knew as much as I did that I was about to take a look at these Joy Road niggas.

Chapter Thirty-one

Since Louie Boy had all the money, we agreed he would finance the cost of the mission. I needed assault rifles. The Joy Road Boys had a fort with God-knows how many men and weapons inside. I couldn't just run up on an army with my few pistols and hope for the best.

I was stuck in a holding pattern until Louie Boy plugged me in with some big guns. I got back to Mrs. P's around six, left the driveway empty for when the alpha female returned.

For the first time, there wasn't two dozen people on the porch, just Trayvion and a single friend. They scanned the block sharing the restless quiet of teenagers who were bored and broke.

The more I looked at the boy, the more I saw a slightly darker version of Doc at nineteen, minus the bleached afro.

I could tell that Trayvion still wasn't comfortable around me, so I decided to break the ice. I still had the weed I bought at the gas station. I warned them it was trash, but enough of it might get our heads right. I let Trayvion roll a few heavy blunts with the Backwoods I bought the night before.

The youngsters must've been used to smoking bullshit, because they had a higher opinion of the trees. We passed the blunts as they talked about different stuff that mattered to them—which young dudes were starting to become hustlers, which young girls were starting to become sluts. I asked a few questions through my phone to stay in the conversation. I didn't push but skillfully turned the discussion from the streets to the family, and from the family to Doc.

Trayvion shared a few memories from his childhood, back when he worshipped Doc as much as Louie Boy said I did. He recalled his father dropping him off new outfits, picking him up in some new convertible, wearing more jewelry than the rappers he saw on TV. "He was kind of like a star to me back then. But that was before my mom died and I came to stay with Mrs. P."

According to Trayvion, Doc had acted more like a rich uncle who occasionally popped up with cash and gifts. He claimed that he didn't feel neglected, just not prioritized.

"Like I knew my ol' dude was ballin'. We wasn't tight like that, 'cause he was always handling his business. I ain't tripping."

It seemed to me he was making excuses for Doc—like Quianna with less skill. I sensed pain there, even when he tried to hide it behind a bunch of generic maxims like "It is what it is."

Trayvion told me that he had briefly tried to get Doc to invest in his music aspirations. He was another wannabe rapper like so many young dudes I met in prison. I asked him to spit for me, more out of courtesy than genuine interest. No sooner than he read the request on my phone, he sprinted into the house and came back with a battered, dog-eared orange composition book. I waited while he thumbed through pages and pages of sloppily scribbled rhymes.

I'd had people rap for me before, and I am able to pick up much of what they say. Only without emphasis or the inflections in tone, it just seems like they're talking shit in a manner slightly faster than conversational.

But I could still judge bars, and Trayvion's were mediocre. He recited a young hustler's fantasy of being rich and fucking beautiful women. I liked when he gave a shout-out to his auntie Q-Bands, calling her the realest chick in the D, but other than that, he said nothing that surprised me. I still bobbed my head in time to theirs and smiled like I was impressed.

I didn't ask for an encore but was treated to a second song called "I Got the Juice." It was more original than the first: a testimony about overcoming adversity, his own doubts, and his haters. I could see in his emotion that this song was more personal and had come from the heart.

I dapped up Trayvion and his mans, gave them the rest of the weed since they liked it so much. I also threw him three of the few hundred dollars I had left.

The problem with drug dealers was that the job didn't come with a pension, and they seldom had the foresight to buy life insurance despite the high mortality rate. Doc had hustled for years and had touched millions, but his son would only be left with pictures and memories.

He took the cash excited, saying, "Good lookin' Unc." And that made me feel good to be a part of a family again.

In the house I ran into the same little girl who woke me up that morning, still running around waving the ten-dollar bill like a flag. Mrs. P passed along the key to the upstairs flat Quianna had left for me.

My new room was small but was an upgrade from the smelly basement. The full-sized bed had new sheets, and when I checked the closet, I discovered all the clothes she bought for me already hung up there. It didn't even occur to me that I needed socks, T-shirts, and underwear until I saw packs of all three on the dresser.

I took a shower, my first as a free man, and I washed like I was trying to scrub the penitentiary off of me. It had been so long since I could control the temperature and water pressure. I spent a half hour reveling in that until I considered Quianna's utility bill.

With the crib to myself, I walked around in my boxers and had forgotten all about her puppy until he startled me. His name was Chino. We played tug-of-war with one of my used socks.

Back in my room, I put my phone on the dresser and stretched across the bed. It was probably a cheap mattress, but years spent lying on a thin plastic mat made it feel decadent, the Bentley of beds.

I felt myself being watched. I snapped back into consciousness violently. I suffered a time skip. The windows were black, night pressed against the glass, and again I had to scan around to get my bearings.

The eyes I felt on me belonged to three women staring in my doorway. I mugged them with a grim sleepface, didn't understand what the fuck they were looking at until I glanced down.

Not only had I fallen asleep on top of the covers wearing nothing but boxers, my beast had woke up before me. He had worked his way out the front of my shorts and was showing off for company. I was standing tall and stone-stiff like the Washington Monument.

The ladies erupted in laughter as I quickly tucked myself in. These were obviously friends of Quianna. All three were young and too damn fine to be anything other than members of her BANDS Society. I didn't catch what was said through their giggles, but the smiles proved they were clearly impressed by what I was working with.

Quianna appeared behind them. She gave the girls a look that cleared them out of the doorway, then came in holding my phone. "Givenya Moorehead—that's what you doing?"

Kierra! I jumped up, still trying to figure out how long I'd slept. I snatched a pair of jeans off the hanger, quickly stepped into them, and demanded my phone.

Six missed texts from Kierra but none from Louie Boy. It was after one-thirty, and her last message came an hour ago. I was about to hit her back when Quianna snatched the phone.

"You ain't chasing that bitch. By now she done already lined up another dick to suck."

It was probably what bricked me up in my sleep: my beast psychically picked up on Kierra's juicy lips. I cursed myself, still couldn't believe I let her slip my mind. And that I'd slept over six hours.

Quianna saw the frustration in my face. "You missed out on some wack pussy—boo hoo. It ain't too late for you to make this bread though."

That raised my eyebrows. My money was definitely funny.

"BANDS got an event tonight—bachelor party. These niggas the type who get drunk and might start disrespecting. I just need you to come and make sure shit don't get too rowdy."

I stroked my wavy Caesar, face not hiding the fact that I wasn't feeling this. The idea of running security for some strippers was beneath my goon talents. You don't ask a five-star chef to microwave a Hot Pocket.

But Quianna had already done too much for me to refuse her in good conscience. Plus, nothing had changed since earlier; I was still stuck waiting on Louie Boy. I surrendered more than accepted, and Quianna's bright hazel eyes beamed with gratitude.

She shrugged a white Gucci bag off her shoulder, pulled out some cash, and counted out two grand in hundred-dollar bills onto my bed. "That's upfront. You'll get another five percent of what we pull down after the count up."

I slipped on the black Huaraches she bought for me. I swore to Quianna on the souls of the ancestors that no harm would come to her girls. And I resigned to take only one percent.

Chapter Thirty-two

We left in three cars: me, Quianna, Lexy, and nine other women, all in sheer catsuits or sexy dresses with thigh-high slits. I trailed the Hellcat and a late-model Toyota through post-midnight freeway traffic. Two of the ladies drew the short straw and had to ride with me in the old Lincoln. We arrived at the Hilton hotel out in the suburbs of Novi a little after two a.m.

The clients were waiting on the sixth floor. They rented an executive suite with a large conference room attached. Middle-management types typically negotiated business deals at the twelve-foot table, but this night, it was stacked with bottles of champagne and hard liquor. Two basic chicks already danced naked on top of it.

I counted twenty-one men who all stared like predators when the BANDS Society came through the door. While they sized up the girls, I sized them up. I made mental notes of which ones were packing, which ones were aggressive.

I also checked the heat coming off the other two strippers. They looked salty, the way hating bitches do when superior stock enters their ranks.

What had been a pitiable sprinkle for them exploded into a

category-five storm when our ladies turned up. They stripped down to pasties and thongs. Ass was everywhere: bouncing, clapping, getting smacked. The dollars fell like confetti.

Quianna kept her clothes on, despite the endless requests. She was friendly but firm, made it clear that she was not a part of the entertainment. All business. Didn't smoke or drink. She just walked around the way a boss is supposed to, keeping eyes on everything, especially the money.

I copied her example, let my vibe reflect that I was a professional. I found a spot that gave me a view of the entire suite, then posted up against the wall, letting everybody see the .40 on my hip. I didn't have a drink despite the fact I could've used one. And I didn't get too caught up in watching the show.

At least not until Lexy did her thing.

The other dancers were just the opening act for Lexy, who was presented as the headliner. She came out the bathroom in a royal costume with plastic crown and scepter. Another girl attended her like a faithful servant and removed the red velvet cape to expose all of Lexy's chocolatey goodness. I marveled at those insane curves which were wrapped in nothing but a fishnet body stocking and a sash that read: BOOTY QUEEN.

The man of the hour was seated in a chair while everybody formed a circle around him. All eyes and phones were on Lexy's seductive movements as she did handstands, splits, and contortions that should have been impossible for a body that thick. Through it all, her humongous ass wobbled almost effortlessly, as if it were its own living thing. She grinded on top of the bachelor, who looked ready to explode in his pants. A monsoon of cash was rained upon her.

The party really cranked up when the show went from NC-17 to X-rated. Thongs came off, and the toys came out. There was a pussy-eating contest that had four girls lined up on the conference table while the guys placed bets to see who would cum first. Another pair of girls were on the floor going cheek-to-cheek on a two-sided dildo.

That's when the real money started to get made. After brief negotiations, fellas were led into the bedroom, the bathroom, even closets for more discreet services. Some didn't even opt for privacy as one dude got sucked off on the couch not three feet away from me.

Quianna had said, "Pussy is the ultimate drug," and I watched her make a killing pushing their product. After every transaction, the girl would report back to turn in any fees and tips. Quianna walked around carrying a large Fendi diaper bag stuffed with cash, and the heavier it got, the more alert I became. I made sure she and it never left my sight.

I noticed Lexy only gave lap dances but refused multiple offers for sex. Disappointed tricks who couldn't ride the pretty black stallion sought out secondary choices among the others. One super-thirsty dude had bid Lexy up to seventy-five hundred, then got on his knees and literally begged. She clearly wasn't for sale at any price. I wondered if her and Quianna's relationship had something to do with that.

I played it cool on the outside but was bubbling like lava on the inside. All these gorgeous women walking around in flawless flesh had my beast aching for his turn to play.

I momentarily got caught up watching the action happening on the couch next to me. She was one of the girls who had rode with me in the Mark VIII, brown-skinned with almond-shaped eyes. She had the face of an R&B singer but the technique of a porn star. Her mother could've been a carnival sword-swallower who had passed along the trade secrets. She made love to his dick like they had history, like she had five of his kids and wanted a sixth, like it gave her more pleasure than him. Dude's head was tilted back with his eyes closed and lips trembling. I wanted to be wherever he was in that moment.

It was such a beautiful performance that when she was done, I tipped her a twenty just for the pleasure of watching. She introduced herself as Chun Li and tried to earn her way deeper into my pocket. I shook my head, made a crucifix of my fingers. Her wicked grin said, *You better be scared!* She strutted off wearing only earrings and the BANDS tattoo on her lower back.

Two dudes got into it over something minor, a brief shoving match that fizzled out quickly. It had nothing to do with the girls, so it had nothing to do with me.

It was close to five a.m., and the party had started to wind down. The numbers had dwindled as tricks stumbled toward the exit two and three at a time, buzzed off cognac and satiated by rented pleasures. Most of the girls were already dressed as we waited for the last two customers to trade their cash for semen. Lexy was helping Quianna scour the floor for loose singles that might have drifted under the furniture.

Up until then, no situation had occurred to pull me away from my wall, and I was content with imitating a statue. The gig was starting to feel like easy money.

But Fate was a bitch on her period. I had jinxed myself by even having the thought that I would get through this drama-free.

I was just about to sit down, treat myself to some of the left-over Hennessy, when there was a commotion in the back. Quianna and a few of the girls ran towards the bedroom, causing me to follow.

Chapter Thirty-three

We sprinted to the bedroom to find this shirtless muthafucka holding one of ours by a fistful of weave. Chun Li's eyes were wide with terror. The prettiest gun I'd ever seen—a chromed-out, pearl-handled .45 Magnum—was pressed to her temple.

After what she showed me on the couch, I doubted the trick was complaining about the head, but dude was clearly pissed about something. Too many people stood between us for me to read his lips. Quianna, a bunch of her girls, and some off-brand dude were all trying to speak to him at once, but their efforts only made him more frustrated. He made threatening gestures with the gun. He was accusing Chun Li of something that he obviously felt should cost her life.

I stealthily eased through the crowd, got closer without drawing attention to myself.

"The bitch sold my box . . . stole my socks." His speech was too slurred for me to understand.

I was eventually able to piece together that this was the best man, the one who had arranged the entire event. At some point during the party, he had lost track of a platinum Daytona-series

Rolex with a black face that he claimed to be worth sixty thousand. He was of the opinion that Chun Li had taken it.

The off-brand standing next to me was a friend trying to talk his boy off the ledge. He offered that Chun Li was naked and could not have his watch. He reminded the best man of his own complaints about the watch being oversized—the band had needed a link removed—and that it could have slipped off his wrist. Also that a lot of the fellas at the party were just casual acquaintances, and one of them might have scooped it. He offered to help him search the entire suite for his property or at least discover who had taken it, if he let the girl go.

Quianna vouched for the integrity of the BANDS Society. "We hustlers, not petty thieves!" She offered to let him strip-search every member of her crew, starting with herself.

The best man had celebrated harder than the bachelor; liquor was affecting their ability to reason with him. He was sure Chun Li had taken his watch, and attempts to convince him otherwise only fueled his anger. He swayed on spongy legs, swore he would blow a bitch's brains out if his Rolex didn't turn up right then, even placed the barrel under her chin. Tears streaked Chun Li's face while she blubbered pleas and promises.

I had made my own promise to Quianna that no harm would come to any of her girls. I raised my pistol to take aim but used a second to assess the situation.

I could easily put a bullet through his left eye, but the logistics were bad. Even if he didn't paint the ceiling with Chun Li's brains on reflex, I still had eleven women who all had to get dressed, descend six floors, pile into three cars, then get out of Dodge before the cops showed. The police response time was fast in the suburbs. If I pulled the trigger, we would all get off the elevator just in time for me to shoot it out in the lobby with Novi's finest.

I took a deep breath, really examined dude: his stance, the gun, the way he held her by the hair, the fury in his eyes as he barked threats. I processed all that data like a computer, then tucked the SR40 back on my waist.

Everyone had given him a wide berth. I made my way through the crowd and just walked up on him. Quianna, Lexy, and all the girls panicked, couldn't figure out what I was doing. His boy even tried to grab my arm. I snatched it away and threw Quianna a look that said, *I got this.*

I circled to the same side of the bed where he held the girl. I approached him calmly. He shrank behind his hostage, threatened to shoot her and me if I didn't back the fuck up. I didn't. I kept coming forward, even dared him with my eyes to do something. Chun Li stared at me wild-eyed like I was trying to kill her.

The inebriated best man started to look more frightened than her as I got within three feet. He took the chrome Magnum away from her head and thrust it into my chest, just like I hoped he would. The move required precision and speed, and I'd only practiced it in a UOTA training room, never in a life-or-death scenario.

I took hold of the barrel with my left hand, then jammed the thumb of my right hand into the trigger guard. He couldn't squeeze with my thumb acting as a backstop to the trigger. Then I bent his wrist at an angle that broke his hold and wrenched the gun away from both of us.

The maneuver happened in under a second. I pulled Chun Li aside as he stood there trying to figure out how he lost the pistol. He stared at his hands, then at me like I'd just performed a magic trick.

He lunged at me, but I bombed his drunk ass with an overhand right that sent him into a Michael Jackson spin. After the pirouette, the best man fell face-first onto the bed and into a premature blackout that the liquor would have eventually caused without my assistance.

Chapter Thirty-four

The way I handled the situation earned me a few cool points with the ladies. I received a few hugs and pats on the back. Lexy still hit me with the usual eye roll and Fuck you! glance.

I expected that, but not the hostile energy I got from Quianna. "The fuck wrong with you trying to play Supernigga?"

She wasn't trying to hear it, but I didn't just walk up like I was bulletproof without cause. My assessment told me dude wasn't a killer. True killers don't carry shiny-ass chrome pistols—only those who wear guns like fashion accessories. Real shooters pack shit they could put a body on and throw away at a moment's notice. I rightly guessed he wouldn't pull that trigger unless he was pressed, and I hoped to be close enough by then. I didn't think Chun Li needed to know the extent to which I gambled with her life.

Back at the house, Quianna dumped the Fendi bag out on the dining room table, and loose bills practically covered it end-to-end. Singles were in the majority, tips they got from twerking, but I saw a lot of fifties and hundreds the girls had earned the hard way. A celebratory blunt was rolled as three of the ladies sat down and started to separate the denominations.

Nobody asked me to leave, but I went back to my room and closed the door while they counted up. I wasn't BANDS, only freelance. I didn't want it to look like I was watching anybody's pockets.

I sat on my bed and played with my phone. It was damn near six in the morning, but I was wide awake. Adrenaline had me gassed, and I was still rested from sleeping through the whole evening. Despite the hour, I left Kierra a text that I know made me look thirsty.

After a while, somebody cracked the door to my room, and I hardly expected it to be Lexy. She extended a hand that was filled with twenty- and fifty-dollar bills. I didn't know the final tally, but it looked like a lot more than the one percent I agreed to. I placed the cash on the dresser, didn't bother to count it.

I blinked my thanks, but Lexy lingered there like we had more business. I stared at her, and she stared at me. I know she wasn't waiting for me to speak. The vibe was weird.

I thought she was finally about to leave, but she pushed my door closed. She undid her skin-tight jeans, fought the denim down to her ankles.

My first expression said, *Damn!* but my second asked, *What's up?*

She responded, "You know what it is." Only she didn't speak the words. She signed them with excellent form.

When I asked how she learned American Sign Language, she gave a curt explanation about being raised by a deaf uncle. It was clear she had been taught young, because she didn't have to mouth the words like most beginners. She could sign better than me, was probably as good as Mrs. P.

She pulled off her shirt, tossed it. Stood before me topless with hands on wide hips. Her upthrust titties were barely a handful but formed into perfect teardrops. The dark nipples resembled Hershey's kisses. "Let's just get this over with."

For a moment, I sat there awed by her the way museum patrons were awed by Monet. I wanted her. Bad.

But I didn't want her like this. Even as I admired her, those large doe eyes scanned me with contempt. I'm built like a mutha-fuckin' tank, eight-pack, big dick, and ain't never been no ugly nigga. "Let's just get this over with." Bitch said that like I'm some unpleasant chore to be done, like scrubbing a toilet. I felt some type of way.

I spoke with my hands. "Go tell Quianna I appreciate the funds, but I'm straight on you."

Her hands responded to mine. "Q said I'm sleeping in here." She climbed into my bed. "Whether we fuck or not don't matter to me either way."

She curled up under the sheets, put her back to me. Told me to cut out the light when I was done like we were some old married couple.

Thinking back on the party made it dawn on me that Quianna had this planned from the jump. Lexy wasn't tricking because she'd already been lined up for me, and little sis was thoughtful enough to not have me fuck right behind a customer.

I could've kicked her out my room. I could've hollered at Quianna myself, refused the gift. A few minutes later, I cut off that light and stripped to my boxers. I slid beneath the sheets, telling myself I'd stay on my own side of the bed. I felt like I was better than this handout.

I put my back to her just like she had done to me, where I could ignore her Princess Jasmine eyes, her full lips, her body with the exaggerated curves of some pagan fertility goddess. But as a man who'd slept alone for so long, I couldn't ignore the heat coming off of her. That or her sweet scent.

I started to brick up and cursed at my beast. Told him we didn't need this. I asked him to be patient, promised that Kierra's plunger lips would be slobbing him down soon. We'd waited twelve years; what's another twelve hours? I reminded him of the clown-ass nigga at the bachelor party, on his knees begging for the pussy; if we caved in, we would be less than him.

My beast retorted by reminding me of Lexy's performance—how flexible she was, how those lap dances showcased her dick-riding skills. He told me to forget her and whatever her problem was, to pound this bitch until all her saltiness turned to sugar.

My pride and dick were having a chess match, only my dick was Magnus Carlsen and checkmate came in nine moves.

I turned over, drawn to her celestial body like gravity.

Chapter Thirty-five

Lexy let my hands explore her, neither blocking nor encouraging me. I rubbed her breasts in slow circles, then flicked the nipples. She only moved to give me access to the places I wanted to touch. She showed no interest in my body, which was a blow considering how hard I'd worked on it. But my ego wasn't too wounded to stop me from losing my boxers. When I tried to ease down her underwear, she impatiently yanked off the thong and tossed it.

I would've loved a more enthusiastic partner, but should a starving man refuse a meal?

I engaged in a little more one-sided foreplay. I caressed her and teased her with my tongue. I barely got a response when I played with the clit, slipped my middle finger inside her.

I mounted her, and it was the first time Lexy touched me. It was a light tap on the shoulder to give me a condom she had been palming the entire time. She apparently knew that men were weak-willed creatures.

Lexy must've thought I was average. I trashed that little-dick Trojan, grabbed one of the Magnum XLs I bought for Kierra. I slid into something made for big boys.

She spread her legs to invite me, but her eyes remained cold. I wasn't feeling this. I had fantasized too long about coming home to my first piece, but it was nothing like this in my mind. I had tricked before, so I could do sex without intimacy, but this felt like a distant cousin to rape.

Enough of dawn's light spilled through the window for us to see each other, and I asked with my hands if she were okay with this. Lexy rolled her eyes, gave me a *Shut the fuck up!* look, then grabbed my dick and pulled it to her.

At that point, I was like fuck her feelings. She wasn't very wet; most of the lubrication came from my condom. I slowly worked until I got the head in, then pushed hard. I slid about eight inches inside her before she was ready. I enjoyed watching her eyes go wide as golf balls.

Within a few strokes, I was giving her the whole ten. She was scrambling back, trying to run from the dick. I grabbed her by the shoulders and pulled her back into me with each thrust.

I was surprised by how quickly she adjusted to me. She turned on the faucet. She wrapped her legs around my waist, bucked back with the same force.

Because I'm not able to appreciate the soft falsetto moans or the breathy whispers of a lover calling my name, I need to see the expressions she makes from the pleasure and agony my beast provides. Lexy was doing all she could to keep a straight face to make me feel like I wasn't doing shit. What we had wasn't sex but a battle of wills. Her goal was to make me nut quick and get me off of her as soon as possible; my goal was to punish her vagina until she begged for mercy or begged for more. This became the game.

I dragged her to the edge of the bed, where I could stand up in that shit. I held her ankles to my shoulders and pounded her like I was drilling to the bottom of Forever. I watched her try to fight the feeling: grit her teeth to bite back the screams. Lexy closed her eyes, and I saw pleasure soften her features for a few seconds. But she quickly shook it off to stare daggers at me again.

She grabbed the back of my thighs and started pulling me into her deep. I fell into a groove, and the sex got good to me. I almost slipped up. I just barely fought off a premature orgasm.

For the next hour and twenty minutes, the bed was our battle-field. Each of us would get the upper hand for a moment: I killed it while she lay on her back and side; Lexy took charge when she rode me. I guess the bed was rocking too hard, because she stopped in the middle of a stroke to stuff our extra pillow between the wall and headboard.

It didn't really seem to be about pleasure for either of us. It was more about the game, and neither of us wanted to lose. She was on her back again, ankles pushed behind her ears, and I was thrashing her to no effect. The blue weave was sweated out, and her dark skin shined like patent leather. But I saw in her eyes the grim focus of a runner determined to finish a marathon.

I realized then that I had been relying solely on my power game, nearly forgot about finesse. I experimented with a few different strokes until I cracked Lexy's code—in and up but slightly to the left. I saw the *Oh no!* look on her face when I hit her G spot. I grinned like, *I got your muthafuckin' ass now!*

Once I started pushing that magic button, her body responded to me against her mind's wishes. She closed her eyes, grabbed me by the back of my neck, and bucked to the new rhythm. My beast took her three levels deep into an orgasm that made her curse God then me before she covered her face with a pillow. She didn't want me to savor my victory.

She panted like she couldn't catch her breath, so I gave her a moment to recover. I thought she was ready to tap out and declare me the winner, but I didn't know she had been biding her time, waiting to use her own secret weapon.

The backshot. That dark-skinned dime looked back at me, throwing pussy that seemed to get wetter and better with each stroke. I made my own *Oh no!* face. Her expressions and all that ass jiggling as I bounced off it was too much for me to take. Lexy kept sending back like she was trying to break my pelvis. I felt my climax cresting and couldn't do a damn thing to stop it.

So instead of trying, I went in hard. I gripped her waist and rammed her like she was responsible for all the wrong that happened in my life. I could've been having a seizure; my spine jerked with each ejaculation. After nine or ten powerful spasms, I fell onto her back. Lexy stretched out on her stomach under me. I noticed then that I was covered in as much sweat as she.

For a while, I lay on top of her, savoring that sweet release and the headrush that came with it. At around the same time, we seemed to realize the moment had passed. We rolled away from each other like boxers returning to their corners.

After catching my breath, I went to take a piss. It was nearly eight a.m.; morning brightened the flat. The company was gone, and Quianna slept behind her closed door.

Back in the room, the smell of our sex was like perfume to me. Lexy had covered herself with a sheet, asleep or pretending to be. Her job was done, and her back was to me again. I eased into bed, trying not to disturb her.

I closed my eyes, thought about Doc, thought about Louie Boy and the Joy Road mission. I thought about the gas station footage, that ticking time bomb Gamble had dangling over my head. I was thinking about a thousand different things when I felt Lexy tap my thigh.

I turned over and found her eyes waiting for mine. It was the first time she didn't look like she despised me.

She signed to ask if I was tired. I told her I wasn't.

She asked me if I had another condom. I told her I did.

Chapter Thirty-six

As much as the first time we fucked was combative, the second time was cooperative. The foreplay wasn't one-sided, the pleasure indulged, reciprocated. She slipped the Magnum on me without using her hands. We touched and teased and offered up orgasms freely. The energy between us had me harder, her hotter and wetter than before. The Booty Queen got murdered by the Silent Assassin well into the morning.

I woke up around noon. Lexy wasn't in the bed next to me, just wrinkled sheets that hung half off the mattress and a wet spot from where I'd been tapping that ass. I figured she made her way back to Quianna's room. My short lease on her body was over.

I got up, stretched, muscles felt loose. I finally got that gorilla off my back. My pockets got heavier, and my balls got lighter—the way the night is supposed to go for real niggas.

The money on the dresser came up to thirty-two hundred. Including the two bands I got up front, fifty-two hundred seemed like a lot just to hold up a wall for three hours and punch a drunk dude in the face. If Quianna still paid me off at five percent, the BANDS Society had pulled down sixty-four grand last night.

That estimate seemed high, but only Quianna and her girls knew the actual amount; again, I wasn't trying to pocket watch.

My phone had several texts from Louie Boy. He would be pulling up on me in two hours. I showered, washed Lexy off of me, and dressed. Quianna's door was still closed, so I decided not to disturb them. I went into the kitchen and made enough breakfast for three.

Chino, the red-nosed pit, watched me cook with hungry eyes. His breakfast would have to wait until Quianna got up to undo the padlock on the dry goods pantry.

I tried my hand at a western omelet: cheese, diced green peppers, and tomato with lean turkey meat. I play with guns, not spatulas, but thought I did pretty decent. The ladies would have to judge for themselves once they got up. I left an omelet for each of them in the oven.

I finished the last quarter of a blunt that the girls had left in the ashtray from the night before. The weed gave me cotton mouth, and since Quianna didn't have a beverage in her refrigerator that wasn't at least eighty proof, I went downstairs to raid Mrs. P's.

I was in that refrigerator, bent over, looking for something cold and sweet, when I felt a hand tugging at the back of my jeans. Touching me while I'm in a vulnerable position is another no-no. This had nothing to do with me being institutionalized. Just as a man, I'm not feeling it.

I jumped and spun around, ready to punch somebody in the throat. In doing so, I damn near knocked over the little girl with the afro puffs.

It was the second time in two days we had a moment like that. If she wasn't already scared of the big weird guy who couldn't talk, I was practically making sure she would be.

I quickly put away my twisted mug, my balled fists. I tried to fake a friendly smile that probably made me look like an animal aggressively baring its teeth.

By far, lip reading is the hardest to do on children: they don't have pronunciation down yet and have a tendency to look every-where but your face while talking to you. So it took a frustratingly long time for me to figure out that the little cutie was asking me if I could take her to the store. Everybody else was too busy or dis-interested, and the ten dollar-bill I gave her the day before was burning a hole in her pocket.

At some point, I learned that her name was Nika, and she was the daughter of that BBW with the supersized titties who was crashing on Mrs. P's couch. I didn't yet know big girl's name or her connection to the family.

Louie Boy was still an hour off, and I was fiending for a pink lemonade, so I took Nika to the store. I had to walk slower than I liked to let her little legs keep up.

Nika reached for my hand when we had to cross the street, and it brought up memories of doing the same with Quianna back when she was nine and I was seventeen. Nika's small soft hand held on to mine even after we made it safely across.

At the store, she went crazy, looking to blow her whole ten on nickel candy, chips, and Skittles. It was her money, but I felt I wouldn't be a responsible adult if I didn't cap her spending at five dollars. I copped a Calypso, and Skittles too, because seeing hers made me want some.

It might have been the sugar that had Nika so talkative on the way back. She was too short and walking at my side, so I didn't catch anything she said. She just chirped along between handfuls of Skittles, happily swinging my arm as if she didn't need me to respond.

For a moment, she had me wondering if this could be my life. Could I do a house in the suburbs? Could I do play dates and pizza parties? Could I do a minivan filled with six-year-olds on their way to soccer practice? Could I really do Daddy?

T'wanda had never given me a chance to find out, and that was probably for the best. My first interaction with Ja'Quezz was me damn near breaking his arm. I could still see his mother's face screaming that I ain't nothing but a killer.

As much as I enjoyed the image of wrestling on the living room floor with a baby girl in barrettes and braids who had my eyes, I knew it was never meant to be. I'm a goon. Period. She would either get hurt by people trying to hurt me, or I would have to train her the same I was, thus robbing her of any semblance of childhood and innocence. Either way, she would become collateral damage of my life choices.

But it was still fun to hold Nika's hand for a while and pretend. I indulged in fantasies of father-daughter dances and Christmas mornings where I spent way too much money on shit she was just going to break in a week's time.

Back at the house, Nika scrambled through Mrs. P's living room with three other kids on her heels begging for some of her candy. I watched her go, thinking what could've been in a different world if I was a different breed.

Chapter Thirty-seven

Upstairs, Quianna was on the living room sofa with Chino, watching Divorce Court on her eighty-six-inch television. She was in yoga pants, a sports bra, and a Gucci satin bonnet. The all-but-finished remains of the omelet I made sat on a plate next to her. She smoked another blunt while Judge Lynn dispensed sage advice to a young married couple circling the drain.

I sat next to her and received no acknowledgment other than a no-look pass on the weed. I puffed conservatively, because me and Louie had business that I had to be sharp for.

I still felt like she overpaid me for the party, so I pulled out the fifty-two hundred and offered back half. Quianna just looked from the cash to me as if we were both trivial sums.

I used my phone to ask if Lexy was still there. Quianna only said, "She gone!" and I detected a level of hostile finality that suggested they might not have parted on the best terms.

It was also clear that some of that hostile energy was directed towards me. She glared quietly at a commercial for Windex, the unattended blunt burning in her fingers.

She finally asked, "Did you use the condom she gave you?"

I didn't mean for it to come off like a brag when I told her that the one Lexy had was too little, but I did have my own protection. I promised Quianna that I hadn't raw-dicked her girl.

It wasn't the reaction I expected, just an eye roll and a snort. I had definitely needed some ass but wouldn't have touched Lexy if I knew it would stress things between me and Quianna.

I made a face that asked, *We cool?*

She studied me for a long time before her features softened. She nodded but muttered something I barely made out about a bitch not following directions.

We switched lanes to get into what happened with Darnia. The previous night, both of us had been preoccupied by the BANDS event, so I caught Quianna up on everything I'd learned.

I started with the one thing that I thought provided the biggest motivation for Doc's murder: the hotel robbery. I recapped both versions I got from Louie Boy and Darnia so Quianna could compare notes. Either Doc or Louie Boy had shot a move to walk away with the whole three-point-eight million in cash. They were basically pointing fingers at each other.

Even his adoring baby sister didn't think that Doc was above such a shady move for the amount of money involved, and when we factored in Baby Momma Number Six's admission that Doc had paid her to place the call, me and Quianna were in agreement that Louie Boy was more credible.

But I also shared my belief that Louie Boy wasn't telling the whole truth. He was being a little too forgiving for my taste, but I was going to play the game of keeping my enemies close.

I put her up on the Joy Road Boys and that video they posted. Quianna watched the link with a grim face, those thick Peterson brows hovered low over her focused eyes. She confirmed that it was Doc's chain that this Dirty Red character had on.

"So it's looking like Doc crossed Louie Boy, then these niggas crossed him."

It was the only thing that made sense. I relayed all the fly whips I saw parked inside the fence of that house on Cascade: Benz truck, Corvette, Challengers, and old-schools. Wouldn't be too hard to stunt like that if you just came up on four million tax-free. I told Quianna they were on my list as soon as Louie Boy lined me up with some hardware.

Then, as an afterthought, I asked Quianna if she knew what Doc had planned with the old juice factory. Learning that her brother had owned the abandoned building he was killed behind was news to her. She could offer no insight on Doc's intentions.

Something about this still didn't add up to me. Darnia had sworn that buying the building had crippled Doc financially, so much so that he lost his apartment down on the riverfront and had to move in with her.

Quianna finished the thought with words that I had started through text: "After the robbery and up until he died, it looked like Doc was down bad." She suggested, "But playing broke might have just been his way of throwing Louie off his trail."

Trying to figure this whole thing out by myself had been leaving me drained. It felt good to have another head on it.

I slipped off into my own mind for a moment, still bothered by that shit Darnia said about Doc being nervous to see me come home. I started to text Quianna something about that when she leaned over and kissed me. It was on the cheek but close enough to my mouth for me to taste the omelet on her lips.

I leaned back like, *What the fuck!* Not angry, just caught off guard.

Those light eyes beamed something at me that felt like gratitude, even though I hadn't done anything yet. "You was always so good to Big Bro."

I didn't know if brothas as dark as me could blush, but my cheeks suddenly felt warm. I started to feel other stuff too that made it hard to look at her.

Something about the expression I wore made her laugh out loud. "Boy, you been knowing me forever. Why I make you so uncomfortable?"

She made me so uncomfortable because I'd been knowing her forever.

Her playful mood turned serious on a dime the way only a woman's mood could. "I ain't trying to see your ass locked back up. If it was on me, I'd tell you to just leave this shit alone. But I know your pedigree. Know you can't stop until you handle this."

I nodded, confirming what we both already knew.

Quianna leaned in so close that I thought she was about to put another kiss on me. She only told me to let her know if I needed her help.

Chapter Thirty-eight

Louie Boy was pulling up by the time I took a shit. Because of the move we had to shoot, he said he would be riding low-key; apparently low-key for him was a triple-white Range Rover with the Overfinch package, rolling on twenty-eights. His sounds slapped hard enough for me to feel the tremors running through the house. Louie Boy parked in the driveway behind Quianna's Charger, where the Range gleamed like a diamond in the afternoon sun.

I stepped outside to catch one of Trayvion's little female friends on the porch trying to get chose. Burgundy weave framed the face of a sixteen-year-old, although her body was much more mature and I figured with a bunch of hard miles on it already. The homemade cutoffs exposed a lot, and she made sure to strut around to advertise.

I jumped in the passenger seat and warned Louie with a shake of the head. He pulled off smiling, trying to downplay it, but I knew his trick ass was about to scoop up that jailbait.

We rode to the eastside, and in the last day and a half, I'd spent more time on this side of town than I ever had. This was the hood near Gratiot and 8 Mile Road. I knew them Eighty-deuce boys were thick over here, because I met enough of them in the joint.

According to Louie Boy, guns had been harder to come by ever since Face died, who had been the biggest arms dealer in the city. The man had been found crushed to death in a car compressor in his own junkyard, and even I thought that was a fucked-up way to send somebody out. Louie said he tracked down the recipient of Face's stolen surplus, who was some fat muthafucka named DelRay. Louie Boy explained all this to me on the way, and it felt like he was trying to earn points by showing me he had went through a lot.

We parked on a side street of a block called State Fair and waited while he placed a call. It was clear that Louie had never done business with these people. His nervousness put me on high alert.

After the call, we left the Range and walked towards a house two away from the corner. This was a clean, well-kept piece of property with gardenias and plastic flamingoes decorating the front yard. A garden gnome stood next to a replica antique lamppost hanging a sign that introduced the occupants as the Martins.

A shiny black '96 Chevy Impala SS owned the driveway, looking clean enough to have rolled off the assembly line this year. I admired that as we passed it on our way to the side door, where a youngster with nappy dreads waited.

The flowers and garden gnomes made the outside look like your grandmother's house, but only after stepping inside did I appreciate the genius of that. The renovations done to the interior were extensive and proved we were in a place of business. Serious business.

The moment we were let through the side door, we found ourselves inside a small pen. The landing to the basement, on which we stood, had been caged. It was weird to see an actual chain-link fence built inside a personal residence, but a gate with a heavy chain and padlock stood atop the three steps to the left and prevented us from ascending into the kitchen, while a second gate directly in front of us blocked the way to the basement. Dude with the dreads closed the door behind us—a wooden door that had been reinforced with a solid iron plate—then locked it with four bolt-action cross bars. That shit at the gas station had me searching for cameras everywhere I went; I spotted three tiny ones inside the cage covering us from different angles.

An old head who looked like a fiend appeared on the other side of the kitchen gate holding a Sig Sauer 556 SWAT pistol. He didn't point it at us, just let us know we were to comply while Nappy Dreads gave us a pat-down. He got the .40 off me and a big .454 Casull from Louie.

Upon surrendering our heat, the old head unlocked the gate and led us through an empty kitchen, where I assumed nothing other than dope got cooked, beyond it into a dining area, where two more dudes sat a table cutting the pungent buds from a bushel of marijuana plants. They stood as we approached.

DelRay was one of the few people who could actually call me Little Fella. At six-foot-nine and pushing four hundred pounds, he looked like a grizzly bear standing on its hind legs. His heavy cheeks accentuated a face that looked friendly but not soft. Louie Boy said he used to be a bouncer, and I believed it; he eclipsed the ones who worked for him at The Pastry Shop.

We sized each other up the way two big men do when first meeting. Despite his size, I thought I'd still fuck him up, and he was probably thinking the same.

None of us knew or trusted one another, so everybody was on edge, but the tension really shot up once Louie Boy introduced me. Hearing my name caused curiosity to spread across DelRay's huge rubbery face, and it suddenly didn't seem so friendly.

"Silence? I know that handle. You did some time up at Bellamy Creek?"

This newfound popularity was starting to piss me off. Everybody I met lately already seemed to know who I was: from Darnia, to Gamble, and now this dude. I don't fuck around on the eastside, so this man had no reason for knowing me.

"I gotta nephew who came home eighteen months ago, little Seven Mile Blood named Ricochet. Skinny-ass nigga, always rappin' and talking shit.

"That was until neph came home with his mouth wired shut—jaw broke in three places. Word was he had a problem with this cocky-ass deaf nigga with a reputation for hurting people."

I never broke eye contact with the big man. I didn't confirm or deny anything he said. My slow nod only indicated that I understood.

DelRay sneered at me. "Nephew said you was in that bitch trying to play Debo. Hating on a young nigga for getting money and visits."

The funny thing about Detroit is that it's big geographically but somehow too small at the same time. Everyone is connected to everyone else in loose degrees of association, and it has the weirdest way of popping up to bite you in the ass. Even with the sharp decline in population we saw in recent years, there's still almost seven hundred thousand in the inner city. Only a mathematician could calculate the odds that a little punk who I had to put hands on up in Ionia, Michigan, almost two years prior would be related to the gun plug. The one person who I needed most right then. The one person who at the moment had me trapped in his spot with no weapon.

It felt like the temperature in the room shot up by ten degrees. Louie Boy had an *Oh shit!* look on his face. All of DelRay's people tensed up.

The junkie with the Sig Sauer semi-automatic had the business end trained on me, laser sighting painting a red dot on my chest. He looked to his boss, waiting for the word to air me out.

Chapter Thirty-nine

There was about eight feet between me and the head covering me with the Sig Sauer. I was nowhere near fast enough to span that distance before those 5.56 rifle rounds cut me in half.

The quiet one sitting next to DelRay also had a strap tucked. He hadn't pulled it yet, but that pistol would come out to play the moment I made my move.

DelRay continued to stare me down. "Rico said y'all was bunkies and you stole from him. Y'all rocked out and tore up the whole cell. Said when it was done, y'all both had to spend a month in the hospital."

That actually made me chuckle. Ricochet would only be a buck-o-five wearing twenty-pound boots, and he fought me to a draw? In what world? It didn't surprise me that he would try to change the story, but his version could've been co-written by Kevin Hart.

First off, the whole jealousy angle was bullshit—Doc kept money on my books, and the only reason I didn't get visits was because I didn't want them. I wouldn't have put the ones and twos on little dude, but Ricochet broke one of the ten commandments of the joint: THOU SHALL NOT JACK OFF IN THE

CELL. I woke up at three in the morning, bed shaking like we having an earthquake. I caught the little freak on the top bunk beating his dick right above me, so I snatched his ass down.

Even though he deserved more, all I did was give him a few bitch slaps, then kicked him out. The incident that got his jaw wired popped off a week after, when Ricochet and two of his Seven Mile boys rolled up on me with a couple of razors. Two of THOSE niggas spent a month in the hospital while I spent ten days in the hole.

I could've used my phone to explain all this to DelRay but didn't want to. I just stood over the table asking him with my eyes if this was going to be a problem.

He didn't retreat from my glare. "My nephew spent six months drinking his meals through a straw. I told myself if I ever met the man who did that, I owed him something special."

He mugged me for another five seconds before his lips stretched into an easy smile. He extended his fist. "Let me buy you a drink!"

Everyone hid their anxiety behind a phony laugh as I dapped him up.

"Good lookin' my dude," DelRay mouthed. "You gave me a six-month vacation from having to hear that little nigga mouth, running all day and spitting them wack-ass raps."

We didn't drink, but DelRay's right hand rolled a blunt from the buds they were stripping off the plants, and I honestly didn't see any harm in smoking with them. They already had our guns, already had us locked in. If they still wanted to do something dirty to me and Louie Boy, they didn't have to rock us to sleep first by getting us high.

These dudes didn't just have a trap; they had a fortress. Another gate separated the dining area from the living room. Every window was fitted with wire-mesh screens mounted from the inside. All the walls that faced the street had been reinforced floor-to-ceiling with sheets of the same thick bulletproof glass you see in banks or liquor stores. The front door was also steel-plated, had more bolts than the side, with the additional support of a huge pole braced between it and the floor. And on the off chance the jack boys or SWAT team somehow managed to get through, they would find themselves trapped in another fenced pen. I admired their layout, thinking one day how I might do something similar to my own place.

After the preliminary bullshit, we got to the business. The big man led us to the cellar, unlocking and relocking barriers as we went. The basement had also been renovated: all non-load-bearing walls were knocked down to create an open space, and the windows were bricked over. It was a large vault.

DelRay switched on an overhead light to reveal the subterranean space was dominated by five long picnic tables, each one covered with munitions. Every pistol, shotgun, and assault rifle I had ever heard of—and a few I hadn't—was either lined up on the tables, stacked against the wall, or just lying in careless piles. Everything looked military-grade and fresh out the box.

We looked over his inventory, but I didn't touch anything until DelRay granted his permission. I saw a Smith & Wesson .500 Magnum that I really liked, played with it even though I didn't need another handgun.

I needed big shit, and fat boy had it. AKs galore, SKSs, semi-autos converted to fully, even those 20-millimeter cannons that could punch holes in a tank.

Louie Boy and I shopped around like a couple of housewives browsing at Walmart before I selected a FN P90 Herstal fully automatic and a Benelli M4 rapid-fire tactical shotgun. I inquired about C-4 and grenades, but DelRay chose not to deal in explosives. Luckily I knew how to make shit that blows up, so in the end, I settled on those two weapons with extra ammo for each— 5.7 rounds for the Herstal and 12-gauge solid slugs for the Benelli.

DelRay was cool, knocked a couple hundred off the ticket for me. "You know li'l Ricochet still talk with a slur to this day."

I tapped my chest like, *My bad.* Offered that as a half-ass apology I didn't really mean.

DelRay told me I was welcome to come shop with him any time, and I was already scouting items for my return trip. I saw too much shit down there I just had to have. I was like a sneaker head at the Nike outlet.

Louie Boy paid the tab while dude with the nappy dreads wrapped our order in a garbage bag. Business handled, we were escorted through the pen at the side door. The pistols we came with were returned at the same place they were taken.

We walked back to the Range Rover, and I had just climbed into the passenger seat when Louie asked, "So wh-when we gone do this?"

He said *we*, speaking French, like he was about to go on this mission with me. Louie Boy was a notorious player and a decent hustler, but he damn sure wasn't a shooter. I was willing to bet that big-ass .454 revolver he carried didn't even get popped at the sky on New Year's Eve.

I told him through my phone that I planned to watch the Joy Road Boys first. I was taught always to do a little recon on the target before engaging them.

Louie Boy asked me to keep him informed.

Chapter Forty

Louie Boy dropped me back at the house, where I swaddled the Herstal and the Benelli in an old baby blanket and stashed them in the basement.

Then I jumped in the Mark VIII, headed back over by Joy Road, down the block from the house on Cascade. I parked on a side street called Kay that gave me a clear view of the whole block through an empty lot.

Even without the shiny vehicles out front, the big gated Venetian saw enough activity to confirm it was a dope spot. The majority of the traffic was handled by three dealers: one stood on each corner with another in the field directly across from the house. Two minutes wouldn't pass before another car pulled up, sometimes two at a time when the second customer would be waved to the dealer down the street.

They also saw plenty of walk-up business. Quick hand-to-hand transactions were conducted with dusty muthafuckas who habitually scratched themselves. These were the low-end junkies buying in small amounts.

Occasionally a car pulled up to the house. I imagined only their top-tier customers were privileged to enter their gated premises:

the working-class fiends who could afford to spend heavily or other dealers looking to buy weight. The money hit Cascade in an endless stream.

None of the Joy Boys I saw looked older than twenty. Just like youngsters to get away with four million clean and still be out here selling dope. I remembered what Louie Boy said about the heroin Doc came up on and wondered if killing him was also about getting his mysterious connect.

I was only there a few minutes and didn't plan to stay much longer. Somebody just sitting on the street watching the business would get suspected of being the police, or worse, a snitch.

Just as I had that thought, the actual police turned onto the block. An unmarked black Ford Explorer with crash bars had a CB antenna that announced itself even without DPD decals and beacons. It rolled at an infant's crawl, but the block didn't seem to notice or care. The customers were unfazed, and the corner boys continued to slang like they had a vendor's license. The two silhouettes inside the car weren't interested in jumping out to make arrests.

I started to break out right then, but curiosity kept me posted a little longer. Something about the way these cops were creeping had me vexed. If I needed to strike off quickly, I could; the Mark was already in Drive with my foot on the brake.

The Explorer cruised to a stop right in front of the Venetian, and seconds later, that muthafucka came out the front door. Dirty Red. I recognized him from the Gram, the light-skinned, chubby muthafucka with skinny braids. He bounced down the porch steps, belly fat jiggling all the way. He was flamed up in a red Adidas jumpsuit with orange stripes, rocked it with the throwback Adidas Crazy 8s in the same color scheme—the original Kobes that dropped before the Black Mamba signed on with Nike.

I saw a different type of red at seeing the iced-out D hanging from his neck. Sunshine struck the stones and made the charm dance on his chest. Wearing my boy's chain in broad daylight like he ain't got a care in the world. I wanted to jump out and fuck him up right then.

Dirty Red came through the gate and climbed into the back seat of the squad car just long enough for a one-minute conversation. He got out with a large paper bag that he ran to the house.

The unmarked pulled off, driving faster as it approached me from the opposite end of Cascade. I slumped low in my seat but made sure I got a good look at the two occupants as they drove past me at the corner. Black driver and white passenger.

They continued north, and I watched them go, so fucked-up by what I just saw on the block that I hadn't been paying attention to the side street. It wasn't until I looked up and turned to my driver's side window to meet somebody staring me right in the face.

The red Challenger I'd seen parked inside the fence the day before had crept right up next to me. Anybody else would've heard the growl of that SRT-8, and I hadn't been checking my mirrors. I straight got caught slipping.

They were two deep, the passenger closest to me. Dude was another young dread head with a face full of tattoos. He was barking at me but talking too fast for me to catch on. I could guess he wanted to know what the fuck was I doing spying on his set. And I'd just seen some shit I wasn't supposed to see.

I had no response for him. That seemed to make him angry and impatient. I knew what was coming next.

I smashed the gas before he could get his pistol up and out the window.

Chapter Forty-one

I hit the gas so hard that the Mark VIII fishtailed, and I could've gotten shot waiting for my bald tires to find traction. I stabbed down that side street, then took a left on the next major one called Broadstreet. I hit that corner sharp enough to lose a hubcap. I sped north.

Broadstreet is residential, where a kid might dart out in front of you at any moment. I blew down that bitch doing seventy with the Joy Boys right on my bumper.

I didn't even realize they were shooting at me until the holes appeared in my rear window. I got my big-ass head down low and drove old-lady style hunched over the wheel.

Tactical driving was another skill taught in the Universal Orthodox Temple of Alkebulan. My father and the other tribe leaders figured that during the great race war, one of us might need to escape the police. A course was built right on the compound with fake streets and storefronts. Twelve-year-old boys and girls were put in practice cars and taught defensive driving techniques: how to detect the spike strip and how to avoid the PITT maneuver. As a chief's son being groomed for leadership, I was expected to excel at everything, so my training started early. I'd been driving since I could barely see over the dashboard.

Even with training, the Mark wasn't about to do shit against a brand-new Challenger coming off the assembly line running six-hundred horses, especially when my engine was thirty years old with miles galore. I wished I had Quianna's Hellcat. I'd give these niggas a run for their money—Dodge versus Dodge, Hemi versus Hemi.

I had two things in my favor: first, they were riding twenty-eight-inch chrome, not racing wheels; second, I gave no fucks if I tore up this piece of shit, so I was free to be more reckless.

Coming up on the next intersection, I had a choice to make. Left would take me west, back towards my hood. So naturally I bent a right and made them follow me east.

I flew down Davidson, weaving through traffic. I had to slip into the bike lane to avoid a slow-moving Fiat, then quickly back out to avoid a pick-up truck illegally parked there. I clipped it and lost my passenger sideview mirror. Too many years inside had my wheel skills rusty.

To his credit, dude driving the Challenger matched my every move. Lucky for me, his partner wasn't too eager to bust the gun on this busy main street.

I blew through a red light on Dexter Avenue and damn near got T-boned by a garbage truck. My pursuer took the light with me, not giving a fuck. He swerved around the garbage truck and stayed right on my tail. Clearly the Challenger was insured, or maybe he was just getting so much money on Cascade, he could easily buy another.

I was rapidly approaching the Linwood Avenue intersection. I used the emergency brake to drift into a wide left turn from the wrong lane. I cut off east and westbound traffic on Davidson, forcing cars to screech to a halt. I hit the cross street with my tires smoking.

I didn't expect them to catch that turn, but the Challenger slid onto Linwood Ave at an awkward angle that told me the driver had overcorrected the wheel. He sideswiped a Camry headed in the opposite direction and scarred that shiny Dodge red with Toyota blue.

I had the Mark VIII up to ninety, blowing through all stops and reds. Boarded-up industrial buildings, vacant residentials, and unused parks with waist-high grass all raced past me in a blur. I led them by half a block, but through my rearview, I watched the SRT-8 quickly make up that ground.

Then my back window completely exploded. The dread head was shooting again. He hung halfway out the passenger window with an FNX-45, letting loose like the clip was bottomless.

Some of those rounds made it into the car. Stuffing erupted out the front passenger seat as a slug punched through my glove box. Anybody riding shotgun with me would've just been killed. I was expecting his next shot to catch me in the back.

I had the .40 but couldn't aim backwards while keeping an eye on the road. So I pointed the gun over my shoulder and squeezed off three times—a deaf nigga shooting blind.

That made them back off a little bit. The driver only retreated a car length.

The city was broke, and Linwood had needed to be repaved even before I went upstate. Potholes had the Mark shaking like an airplane in heavy turbulence. The asphalt had craters larger than its manhole covers. I chose this route because riding in Punchy's donk showed me how rough streets could be treacherous to the thin meat on those low-profile tires. I was hoping the Challenger suffered a blowout or bent a rim.

But dude was apparently used to riding chrome on the fucked-up city streets. He navigated the potholes like a pro and still stayed on my ass.

To make matters worse, the Mark was starting to lose acceleration. The oil light glowed. I felt strange vibrations, and for all I knew, this old muthafucka was probably about to throw a rod.

There was a slight incline at the railroad tracks just before the next major cross street. I hit the gas and went over them fast enough to get about two feet of air. I came down hard, damn near lost control, and bounced through the intersection still fighting the wheel. I was lucky Linwood traffic had the green light.

Through my rearview, I watched the SRT-8 fly over the tracks, pull off a more graceful landing, and blow through the light on yellow. Dude could drive, but it was nut-check time.

After the John C. Lodge overpass, I crossed the center line and put myself right in the path of the oncoming traffic. I was in a dangerous game of Chicken with everybody traveling south. I gripped the wheel, my body tensed and ready to take a head-on collision.

As I suspected, most people seemed to place more value on their lives. Cars, SUVs, and minivans all swerved to get out of my way—probably with blaring horns and more than a few curses. Some even jumped the curb and hit the sidewalk.

I looked back and saw that the Challenger was stuck behind the carnage left in my wake. A Buick LaCrosse had spun out in the middle of the street and stalled. I might've gave the old white lady driving it a mild heart attack, but she couldn't have done a better job if we planned it together. Her sedan was turned sideways, blocking the road for me.

I got my ass back to the right side of the street by the time I reached the intersection at Puritan Ave. I headed back to my way with smoke coming from under my hood.

I was thinking how much more complicated my mission had just become. Not only did I lose the element of surprise, but I was sure the Joy Road Boys were selling drugs for the police.

And if that wasn't enough to fuck with my head, I recognized the black female driving the Explorer. That same bitch had pulled a Glock on me at the gas station.

Chapter Forty-two

I made it back to my way leaving a trail of black smoke and leaky fluids for my enemies to potentially follow. I didn't know what was wrong with the engine. I'm a goon, not a shade-tree mechanic—Smith & Wesson makes the tools I work with, not Craftsman.

And since I wasn't about to cash out on a new motor and back window, the Mark was done. I torched that bitch in an alley about half a mile away from Mrs. P's.

I stomped down the street cursing myself for how I let the Joy Boys creep me on that side street. A true Shango warrior is always aware of his surroundings. Dreads in the Challenger could've blew me with that FNX and I never would've seen it coming. Ja'Quezz had crept on me, too, and it was starting to make me seriously doubt my skills.

I turned on the block to see Quianna's car was gone. We put the Mark VIII in her name, and she would need to report that stolen just to cover her ass.

The downstairs flat was jumping as usual, with a dozen kids running around. Trayvion and some of his boys were having a cipher at the dining room table, spitting rhymes written on napkins and crinkled sheets of scrap paper. My godson had his trusty orange notebook.

The door to Mrs. P's room was cracked, so I peeked inside to make sure she was decent. Decent for her was a long purple nightgown, its function expanded to day and evening wear. She was lying across her queen-sized bed on her stomach with a folded pillow stuffed under her chin. I shook my head when I saw she was watching *Love & Hip Hop*.

It was an old lady's room with old lady smells—didn't stink, just carried a staleness like she hadn't opened a window in months. The mahogany dresser and vanity that dominated the entire wall had school-age pictures of Doc and Quianna tucked into the edges of the mirror; some older, cracked and faded photos of Shaft-looking brothas from the seventies with parted afros and porkchop sideburns; a few throwback flicks of Mrs. P during her twenties that showcased the hazel-eyed dime she had been once—Quianna without the African features; some other pictures of white folks that might have been siblings from a family that Mrs. P never spoke about.

I always assumed her tastes for menthols and black dick caused her to split from her people way back in the day. Doc and Quianna didn't ask about their white side of the family, so I never felt I had the right to.

The room was dim despite being three in the afternoon. She kept the curtains pulled tight, as if she didn't want to see the changes brought to the world outside her window.

Mrs. P was so immersed in the females squabbling over nonexistent music careers that she didn't acknowledge me until I dropped my weight on her bed.

I signed to ask if she was hungry, let her know I was contemplating a Coney run. She used her hands to inform me that Coney Island didn't get along with her arthritis medication. The army of pill bottles on the dresser suggested she had a medication for everything.

For a few minutes, I sat watching with her, hardly interested in the drink-throwing and table-flipping. I had something I wanted to ask her but was afraid to approach the subject. At a shriveled ninety-five pounds, she was still the most intimidating woman I knew.

She must've sensed that. During the next commercial break, she flat out asked me: "Nigga, I know you ain't spend all that time in there waiting to sit up under my stankin' ass."

I had learned all I could from the streets and had less than forty-eight hours before Gamble turned over that tape. Since coming home, I saw the sadness in Mrs. P but also that she was reaching a place of healing. I felt like shit for having to peel the scab from her wound.

I asked what the relationship was like between her and Doc before he died. My question took her by surprise. Those thick Peterson eyebrows came together like mating caterpillars.

I shared what Quianna told me about Doc not coming around often. I also had to be honest and comment on the state of the house. Everybody I talked to had agreed that Doc was getting to a big bag. I didn't see proof that he had been taking care of his mother.

She perched on the edge of the bed with me. "All I ever wanted for my kids was y'all to be unapologetic in who you was. Quianna is unapologetically Quianna, and Darius was the same. I ain't never felt entitled to nothing but that."

I reminded her that when I lived there, me and Doc used to help her out. We always dropped something on the rent, even bought that living-room set out front.

"YOU always dropped something on the rent," she corrected. "And y'all ain't buy shit. I knew from Day One you thieving muthafuckas stole that furniture off the back of a truck."

I could only offer a guilty smile.

I told her I was hearing a lot of negative things about Doc out here in these streets.

Mrs. P looked to me without surprise. "I know who my son was and who he wasn't."

On screen, two ladies charged each other and had to be restrained by security. "I'm able to enjoy this so much cause I know it's fake. Them gals really don't wanna fight each other, gone be laughing and high-fiving soon as the cameras turn off. The problem with a lot of y'all coming out of prison is that you be done made your own reality show and don't even know it."

I didn't understand her meaning. She saw that in my quizzical glare.

"For starters, y'all be stuck in the time and place where y'all first went it. Using those memories of home and what's familiar help keep y'all sane, but the mind is a muthafucka. Over time, it's got a way of editing the past: erasing certain things and rewriting other stuff. So enough years go by, and you'll be working off a script that's far from reality. Then those of y'all lucky enough to make it back end up coming home fucked-up. 'Cause not only has everything changed, but the shit you thought you knew wasn't real in the first damn place."

I asked Mrs. P if I was seeing the world through a fiction I created in there.

The old lady said, "I think you see damn good. But only at what you want to look at."

And with that advice, I took a more critical look at her and everything around her room. The nightgown in the middle of the day, the stocking cap covering thin patches of silvered hair, the closed curtains despite the sunny day, and the line of pill bottles on the dresser.

I made praying hands, then pointed to her. I tapped my forehead with the middle finger on my right hand at the same time I tapped my stomach with the middle finger on my left. I put it in the form of a question, but the certainty of my expression presented it more as a statement.

"You're sick?"

Chapter Forty-three

Osteosarcoma—she had needed to finger-spell that. A fancy-ass word for some type of bone cancer.

The diagnosis came fourteen months prior, and she'd been hospitalized six times since. The disease was aggressive. The prognosis was grim. We were in mid-April, and she didn't anticipate seeing Labor Day.

"That cemetery plot Darius in was already paid for. My baby boy was supposed to put me in it, not the other way around."

I bit down on my lip, tried to squeeze back the tears that threatened my eyes.

The old woman waved me off like I was being overly dramatic. "Don't do it. You ain't that handsome to start with, so you don't need to be making no ugly cry faces."

I didn't realize I was working my hands in and out of fists until she said, "Boy, quit that, too! It's cancer—bad genes as much as bad habits. Ain't nobody do this to me. Ain't nobody for you to beat up."

That was probably what made it sting so badly. There was no enemy to face. I couldn't avenge this.

She rubbed my back as a tear escaped to streak my face. "Nigga, I'm the one who sick. The fuck you crying for?"

I sat on the edge of the bed, shaking with rage, forcing the dying woman to console me.

Mrs. P told me she'd had a fantastic life and enjoyed her time—of course there were regrets, but none that disturbed her sleep. She'd loved and been loved. She'd taught her kids to thrive, despite that they might have been rejected by both cultures. She listed the things that she was most proud of and counted me as one of them.

I had been indoctrinated to be a radical black nationalist, been taught since I was a toddler to hate white people for no other reason than being white. But after my very black mother abandoned me, I came to one of the blackest cities in America to find a white woman who took me in, taught me how to sign, and loved me like a son. This was proof for your ass that, not only is God real, but that He's got a sense of humor.

We didn't communicate for a while, just watched TV. The petty squabbles that unfolded on *Love & Hip Hop Atlanta* took her on an emotional rollercoaster: she smiled, laughed out loud, got mad, and cursed at the screen. She offered to switch on the closed-captioning for me, but I told her that wasn't necessary. Watching her enjoy it was enough for me.

I pecked her cheek and stood, ready to bounce, when she spoke again: "You always saw the best in Darius, and in a lot of ways, you brought out the best in him. But ain't nothing you about to do out there gone bring back the boy he was or the man he became."

She squeezed my hand, surprising strength in her bony arthritic counterpart. "Lutalo, you got a second chance, which is more than a lot of folks get. You ain't daddy's toy soldier no more. You can do more than just hurt people. Figure out what you enjoy doing and make a hustle for it. Find you a good woman to put some babies in—shit, find three of 'em!"

I gave her another kiss. Instead of Coney Island, I offered to bring her some of that fried perch I knew she liked from the fish place two blocks over.

I couldn't bring myself to tell her that hurting people was what I enjoyed doing. I was unapologetically Silence.

Mrs. P stopped me as I turned to leave. I assumed it was to impart one final piece of wisdom, to drop one last jewel.

"Nigga, don't be kissing me on my face like that," she said through a frown. "Nowadays y'all young muthafuckas be out here eatin' ass."

Chapter Forty-four

I then understood why Mrs. P liked having so many young people running through the house. The dying preferred to be surrounded by life.

I could've went upstairs to Quianna's, but the basement still felt like my domain. I worked out my anger with some shadowboxing. I would've preferred an opponent who could hit back.

Mrs. P's bombshell threw me for such a loop that it temporarily made me forget the reason I'd initially gone into her room. I had been looking for advice on this Doc situation.

Punchy lying about his come-up; Prime crying about his falloff; Louie Boy accusing Doc of a setup; an off-brand out here wearing Doc's chain. And as if shit wasn't confusing enough, let's throw a few crooked cops in the mix. My mind was like a blender trying to break down all these rough ingredients into something smooth and digestible.

I'm built for forward momentum and punching on shit, always had Doc to help me with anything more complicated than that. Solving a murder wasn't as easy as the cops made it look on *The First 48*—but then I didn't have some snitch muthafucka to serve up all the information.

And with that thought, a plan started to take shape in my mind. I knew what I had to do next. The problem was that I still had about five hours of daylight to kill.

I got tired of punching air, so I dropped down to do some pushups. I was on the floor, muscling through my fifteenth set of fifty, when I spotted feet in my peripheral.

Quianna stood over me looking fresh from the salon. Her head was still shaved on the sides and back with the fretwork cut into it, only the top was styled in big bouncy curls. Her face was made up with bronze eyeshadow, false lashes and liner, lipstick in firetruck red.

"I need you real quick. The girls got this event downtown."

I only had about thirty-six hours before Gamble turned over that video of me killing a cop. I avoided the details but tried to tell Quianna that I didn't have time to play bodyguard.

She hit me with a stern look. "I'm typically not the type of bitch who put strings on shit." She didn't need to finish the statement. We both knew I owed her. "Boy, bring your ass."

In the room she was loaning to me, a nylon garment bag waited on the bed. Twenty minutes after a shower, we were walking toward the door in his-and-her red bottoms. I was bossed up in a dark-blue Ralph Lauren suit, crispy white button-up with cufflinks, and a platinum Rolex. Quianna was stuffed into a strapless bronze mermaid dress made of a saffron material that shined like polished metal.

I was far from a man with a normal build, so she had done an excellent job to guess my measurements. The pushups had my chest and arms swollen, but other than being a little snug around the pits, the suit hung on me like it was tailored.

Quianna's dress was so tight that it looked as if a deep breath would split the seams. I joked that if she passed out, I wouldn't be doing CPR to save her.

I figured BANDS was having some sort of black-tie trick party for its VIP customers. I told Quianna she could get me for a few hours, but I had to be out as soon as the evening came.

She tossed me a key fob. I had thought Louie Boy's silver-and-black Wraith was the prettiest car I'd ever seen, but that was before stepping out on the porch.

The Aston Martin DBS Superleggera parked in our driveway was finished in an intense metallic blue over gray leather—so cold that it made our house look worse by comparison. All the kids from downstairs had it surrounded, staring like it was a spaceship. Every neighbor on the block hung out their doorways: the nosy aunties, the thirsty rats, especially the hungry jack boys.

I had forgotten that scams was the other side of how the BANDS Society ate. Thanks to the credit card numbers of a Mr. Justin Wilson, the Aston was hers to play in for two days. When Quianna asked if I could drive a stick, I gave her a look that said, *Girl, stop it.*

We didn't immediately go to the event. Quianna directed me to Black Rock Steakhouse and introduced me to stuffed mushroom caps. I tore into a twenty-four-ounce porterhouse plated with truffle parmesan fries and grilled asparagus. I tried not to eat like a convict.

We conversed between bites. Our phones were out, and my iPhone delivered the responses too complex for facial expressions and hand gestures. Quianna would smile, give me these looks while playing with the straw in her drink. She told me that we would meet the girls later at the MGM Grand, and I wanted to know how much later because I had shit to do.

While she sat next to me looking like an IG model, I still remembered a skinny tomboy, a straight-A student who had wanted to be a veterinarian. For some reason, Quianna hated to be reminded of that girl. I risked pissing her off but had to know what had diverted her path from there to the strip club. Again, I tried to ask this in a way that didn't come off like I was judging.

"Life happened!" It was an emphatic statement delivered with attitude. She almost made it seem like it was somehow my fault.

I left that alone, told her about the car chase and shootout. I suggested she put a theft report on the Mark VIII, but she thought it would be less suspicious if we waited a few days.

We hit the MGM Grand and got the Aston Martin valet-parked. I wasn't one for dressing up, so I didn't quite understand what a man in a suit did to some women. We walked in the hotel, and the eyes were on me like I was candy.

Quianna said we had time to hit the casino first, and it was so many people in that bitch that it triggered my inbred paranoia. I wasn't a gambler, but Quianna apparently liked to fuck with the dice. I watched five thousand in chips slowly get siphoned by the crap table. The whole time, she siphoned the complimentary drinks, like that was an even trade.

She gave me a couple of stacks to play with, and I tossed the rocks a few times just so I wouldn't seem lame. I could see that Quianna wanted this to be fun for me, so I made an effort. The casino was jumping, wall-to-wall women in that muthafucka too, so I got the appeal for other men. But I'm not into large crowds or wasting money.

Everybody around me laughed, gambled, drank, and had a good time. I just felt out of place. I was ready to get back to what was fun for me.

Chapter Forty-five

Casinos were designed for gamblers to lose track of time. Even with my frequent glances at the Rolex, I couldn't believe how fast five hours got away from us. It took that long before bad luck and reckless betting allowed the blackjack table to drain the last of our chips.

Quianna wobbled in her heels as we left the casino floor. All the complimentary drinks had taken their toll. She had to lean on me as we rode the elevator up to the twelfth floor.

The accommodations made those used for the bachelor party look like some bullshit. A luxury corner suite with a thousand square feet, including a comfortable seating area, a room with a king-sized bed, full bath with walk-in shower and jacuzzi, floor-to-ceiling windows offering skyline views of the Ambassador Bridge spanning the Detroit River to Windsor. The décor was Art Deco.

I looked around, taking in all the amenities, but what was missing stood out the most. No customers. No girls. There wasn't a party happening up here, and a while back, I began to suspect there wouldn't be. We were alone.

Quianna stepped out her Louboutins the instant I closed the

door. She was already saucy but padded barefoot straight toward a cart waiting in the center of the room, where a bottle of rosé chilled on ice. She filled a champagne flute until suds spilled on the carpet.

Through the windows, the sky had slid from the deep blues of pre-evening to night violet. The city lights shone like artificial stars. It was creeping up on eleven-thirty, and I had expected to be out of there two hours before.

I used my phone to ask where everybody was, but Quianna ignored me. She sucked down her champagne like a lush and poured a refill.

"It's something I been wanting to ask you for ah minute." The liquor had her speech slurred. "What did you do in there when you got horny? Make some white boy touch his toes?"

Anybody else would've got checked. I knew she was using comedy to ask a serious question. TV and movies have given the public some fucked-up notions about prison on this subject. People, especially women, assume that men are so sex-consumed that if he's done any real time, then he's indulged in homosexual activity. They don't understand that there is no such thing as Situational Sexuality, where a straight man becomes gay just because he's locked up. The men who fuck men in there would fuck men in the streets. You are either gay, straight, or bi-sexual; nothing about location or circumstance puts something in you that wasn't already there.

Again, if this was somebody else, I would've spazzed. Instead I simply texted Quianna one question: *If there was no more weed, would you start shooting heroin?*

She sneered at me as if offended. "Do I look like a dope fiend to you?"

And with that, I just waited for her to realize that she made my point for me.

I asked her again when exactly was this event supposed to start. Quianna gave me a playful look. "Pour up, nigga. You been actin' stiff all night."

She tried to get me to sit next to her on the couch as she put together a sloppily rolled blunt. Quianna was clearly drunk, and this wouldn't be easy for a smooth talker on a sober chick.

Through a series of texts, I explained to her as gently as I could that this wasn't about to happen. She was my boy's baby sister—and the fact that I actually lived with the family for a year made it less cool. While I acknowledged that she had grown into a beautiful woman, in my eyes, she would always be Li'l Quay-Quay. I explained my feelings probably to the point of over-explaining.

Quianna read everything I texted her slowly, as if needing time for it to penetrate the alcohol. She stared at her phone for so long that I was tempted to send another text to ask if she were okay.

Quianna was only five-foot-five, and I was pretty sure I could take her in a fight, but when she stood and looked up at me, those sharp hazel eyes scared me into taking a step back.

"You actually think I brought you here to fuck?" All the slur gone from her speech.

Us getting all dressed up, the restaurant, the casino, and finally a hotel; the shit kind of felt like a date to me. And what about the event BANDS was supposed to have planned? To me, that seemed like a play just to get me here alone.

"Stupid muthafucka, the event was for YOU!!" She stabbed me in the chest with a finger. "A couple of girls on the way now. They was already supposed to be here." She showed me texts in her Galaxy from Chun Li apologizing for getting held up. She claimed to be thirty minutes away with three other girls from their crew.

Quianna still swayed on drunk legs. "You said you didn't want a party, so we was gone do something low-key. Just you and a few dancers—Chun was down because you pulled her out that situation." I remembered that sneaky look she had in the driveway after the mall. "Just because you didn't want a big party. I still wanted you to do it big. That's why I rented the car, got you suited. I figured after all the time you did, you deserved a night like this."

A smart man would've left it alone right there, but for better or worse, I just had to go down swinging. I asked her about the clothes, the extra money, the kiss. What about all the walking around half-naked? I even brought up the tattoo on her thigh: the finger over the lips.

Quianna looked at me like I was biggest idiot in the world, and by the time she was done talking, I felt like it.

"First, I dress how the fuck I wanna dress around my house, because I'm a grown-ass woman. Second, I copped you a couple of 'fits because you my people, and I knew you wasn't coming home to shit. I even let you fuck my bitch because you was around here lookin' thirsty."

I scratched my beard, knowing I should've quit while I was ahead.

She continued unloading on me. "And what I got tatted on me ain't none of your damn business. It was just something slick I wanted because I don't like bitches with loose lips. For real, nigga? You saw that shit and thought I branded myself . . . for you of all people?"

I could've shrank down from six-five to three inches right before her piercing glare. I typed: *I'm sorry*, but those two words didn't offer enough compensation for a fuckup this major.

She barked, "Just because a bitch try to look out for you don't mean she wanna give you some pussy! She might just feel sorry for your weird ass!"

She looked at me with a slow headshake. "Keep the room, it's paid up for the night."

Quianna emptied the rest of the glass in one swallow, then went to collect her purse and heels. She no longer listened to me through the phone, so I had to chase her down. I stopped her at the door and tried to express how bad I felt for spoiling a night that she had obviously put a lot of thought into. I also suggested that she should stay, and I'd leave. Quianna had a lot more to drink than me. Plus

I felt too much like an asshole to sleep in the luxury suite that she paid for.

I offered another silent apology with my eyes, but her mouth responded with *Just get the fuck out!* She shoved me towards the door, a hand in my back.

Once we reached the threshold, Quianna spun on me with the same fury she had at the mall with Brody Starrz. "And this whole honor thing you're trying to stand on is funny as hell to me, where you think being with your best friend's little sister is some type of violation."

She smirked at the confusion that clouded my features. "You so gullible, you still ain't figured out the truth. You wasn't never Doc's friend. You was just his muthafuckin' flunky!"

With that, she shut the door on my face. Probably would have made a bigger impact if I could've heard the slam, but it still provided the adequate punctuation.

Chapter Forty-six

I left the hotel by cab. A regular cab. I still wasn't with this Uber shit, where you just jumped in any random person's car. I was more concerned about the wrong driver catching me than me catching the wrong driver.

Luckily a cab stand was posted just outside the casino, ready to ferry home the dejected gamblers who left their mortgage payments on the tables. I felt like one of them.

I slipped the female cabbie a twenty along with our address scribbled on a note. Her friendly smile told me she was ready to talk. The frown I returned told her I wasn't. She left me undisturbed in the back seat.

I was going back through my mind, replaying every exchange I had with Quianna since coming home. My stupid ass misread her and embarrassed both of us. Was my self-esteem so low that I could take simple generosity—or pity, as she called it—and twist it into attraction?

My relationship with T'wanda and the one with my real mother proved that I didn't relate well to women—one had betrayed me and the other abandoned me, which is just a more passive form of the same. Quianna was the only person who had been any real help to me since I touched down. Now I'd fucked up that relationship. Unlike the others, this one was on me.

By the time we'd exited I-96 at Livernois, I hopped off the couch, stopped trying to be my own therapist. I had to get on with the business. I had moves to make this night, potentially murder moves, and needed to be focused.

My last thought on the Quianna subject was that part of me was glad this cat-and-mouse game was over—the is-she-or-isn't-she-flirting-with-me shit. I was tired of the endless merry-go-round of lust and guilt. While she had been my biggest source of support, she had also been my biggest distraction. Now I could do exactly what I came home to do.

The driver dropped me at Mrs. P's, where I did a quick change of clothes. Stripped out the suit and traded the Louboutins for my black boots. It was nice to get bossed up for a minute, but what I had to do next required sweats and a dark hoodie. I was back on my grimy shit. I left the Ralph Lauren on the bed in Quianna's spare room that I never intended to use again.

I walked to the liquor store, not the closest one to our house, but still in our hood. I didn't need a drink, though. I scanned the parking lot but saw nothing that fit my plans. I hung out at the rear of the lot, away from the lights, where darkness could conceal me. I waited until an old Buick Electra 225 pulled in. Late seventies or early eighties—couldn't place the exact year. The yellow behemoth was dented and pocked with tiny rust spots like bad acne.

I checked my wrist, cursed myself for forgetting to take off the Rolex, but read that it was after twelve. The two who jumped out the Buick looked like they were just old heads trying to get in that last bottle of Johnnie Walker. I pitied them, because their night was about to go bad—how bad was totally up to them.

I watched the two enter the store; then I moved along the back of the lot to wait closer to their vehicle.

After three minutes, they stepped out. They were lit by signs advertising liquor and lottery, and I could see that they both looked about sixty. The driver wore a dirty trucker hat while his boy was bald. Not Johnnie Walker: the passenger carried a brown paper bag with what looked like the neck of a gin bottle coming out the top. I slipped in step right behind him.

He was at the passenger door and never felt my presence when I grabbed his head and bounced it hard off the roof of the car. He went down with his liquor, the bottle shattered against the asphalt.

I looked at the driver from the other side of the car, but School must've been somebody in a former life. He was quick on the draw. Before the gin could soak through that bag, he had already brought up an old revolver. I was moving too fast to see if it was a .38 or .357.

I got low before he could squeeze off. I used his big, long Electra for cover, scrambled along the side. Poor lighting or eyesight might have made him misjudge my route. He thought I slipped around the rear and was aiming that way with a shaky hand when I popped up behind him. He turned in time to see my pistol up and ready.

I had the drop on him. I motioned for him to throw down that ancient-ass revolver before I put him up on this new shit.

But School was hesitant, like he was thinking about trying me. I couldn't see his eyes under the visor of his cap, but I warned him with mine not to do it. I know his pride was probably telling him to defend what's his, that he still had some of the gangster left in him from his youth. But he couldn't win here. I begged him not to make me blast him for this raggedy-ass deuce and a quarter.

I was relieved when he raised his hands in surrender and extended the gun as if ready to drop it. But like they say, Ain't no fool worse than an old fool. He faked the motion, then tried to swing the revolver towards me and got his dumbass shot. The impact spun him around and sent the gun flying from his grasp.

When I went to check him, he was on his back, eyes wide and watery. The bullet I put in his arm had went straight through. He should've thanked me. I knew that at his age, if a .40-caliber slug had hit him anywhere in the torso, he would have been done.

His lips were moving, but I was in too much of a rush to make out his words. I ran his pockets for his keys and wallet. I didn't take his couple of dollars, just the driver's license.

I learned my lesson from the gas station, kept my hood up and my back to the camera covering the parking lot. The Buick was still going to be hot in an hour or two, so I didn't waste time. After a quick stop at the house for my bolt cutters, I drove straight over to Joy Road.

I didn't turn down Cascade but the block just past it. I left the Electra parked under a dead streetlight.

I hit their block on foot and saw that, even at midnight, business was still slapping. Like before, three dealers were out handling the walk-up traffic: one on each corner, with a third standing in the field at the center.

I had already targeted the dealer working the corner farthest from the house, but his face became familiar as I approached him. It was dude with the dreads and face tats who had shot at me earlier from the passenger side of the Challenger. The one who got a good look at my face.

He was posted on the same corner they had crept me on, and that probably should have been enough for me to abort the mission right then. About ten feet separated us, and another customer kept him distracted. After their quick hand-to-hand, it was my turn to buy.

My casual stroll didn't reflect my nerves. Hood up, eyes down. A folded twenty palmed in my fist. This was another one of those times when my size did me no favors, made me too easy to remember. Once I was three feet from him, I thought for sure he would pull his gun, because I was ready to go for mine.

But the young dude stared right through me as if I were just a window to a far more beautiful world. He was high as fuck. The closer I got, I could smell weed and a mixture of white and brown liquors coming from his pores. I also peeped that shine in the eyes of somebody who had sniffed something strong. He was out here serving on autopilot. That made me walk up boldly, certain this clown wouldn't recognize me.

I was on a hot streak when it came to being wrong.

The moment I pressed the cash into his palm, he looked up at me and seemed to sober up immediately. Like a thrown switch, he just somehow turned off all the liquor and drugs in his system. I saw recognition flash in his suddenly-clear eyes.

His hand went to his waist, but like so many before him, he'd already fucked up by letting me get too close. I twisted that arm. I watched his lips part, but I slipped around his back at the same time my arm slipped around his neck.

Hopefully I choked off that scream before he got it out.

Chapter Forty-seven

I only chose the old Buick because it had a massive trunk, just hated that the old man made me pop him for it. The corner boy was sharing space with a bumper jack, a four-way lug wrench, and some oily rags. I didn't think anybody saw me dragging his slack body off the block. I lost one of his shoes on the way to the car and didn't risk going back for it.

A good choke hold can strangle a person in about four minutes, but applying the right pressure can render them unconscious in under sixty seconds. The length of time they stayed out varied with the individual. He had slept through my post-midnight shopping trip, and as we reached our destination, I still felt no movement coming from the rear. I took his phone, but for all I knew, during the past three miles, he could've been back there screaming "Police!"

The city's financial crisis had hit its peak in 2008, forcing a rash of closings that touched nearly half the Detroit public schools. A few were renovated and reopened years later under a marginally improved economic climate. The wrecking ball claimed some to make way for the big box stores like Circuit City and Dollar General. Most of these vacated school buildings were still spread out across the D as huge eyesores, crumbling memorials to the children they failed.

I chose the elementary school that Doc and Louie Boy had attended as kids. The rusted chains on the fences had been cut long ago, allowing me to creep around the back with my lights killed.

Odd that my first time in a public school would be at one a.m. in one that had been closed fifteen years. I grabbed one of the LED lanterns I bought at Target and did some exploring.

The fiends and scrappers came through just like they did Doc's juice factory, claiming everything salvageable and searching for the precious copper. They had hacked into every wall and ceiling. Debris chunks of crumbled plaster and acoustic tile littered the dust-covered mastic floors along with a heavy sprinkling of rat droppings.

I borrowed a huge room in the center of the first floor without windows that looked out onto the street. All that remained was a series of long waist-high counters that housed wash sinks with rusted gooseneck faucets. It might have been used for a science lab. I popped the trunk to find the Joy Boy still napping, and I didn't wake him until class was in session.

His red eyes snapped wide, trying to figure out if he were still dreaming. Two LED lanterns sat on the counters and were the only thing pressing back the darkness. Duct tape kept him strapped to his seat and unable to scream. I stood before him as a hooded silhouette, looking like the Angel of Death.

The straight-back chair kept him propped up with his wrists secured to the armrests. He shimmied and struggled against the tape, and this part always amused me. At the start, people always thought they were just going to muscle their way out the restraints—I blame all the damn superhero movies. I let him get it out his system.

It was interrogation time, but this wasn't *The First 48*. I had Louie forward that club photo to me. I pointed to Doc, then gave dude a kidney shot just so he understood the rules.

After that explosion of pain made them go buck, his eyes

tracked back to me, and I brought them back to my phone. I wagged my finger before I pulled the tape away from his lips.

"The fuck you on, blood. I be—"

I hooked his ass to the kidney again. He grit his teeth, leaned the other way as if trying to scoot away from the pain.

I held up my phone again. Doc's picture and my two-word question shared the screen.

"I don't remember nobody. Eat a dick. Blood Gang. Joy Road for li—" The straight right to the solar plexus interrupted his tirade by stealing his wind. For a while, I watched him gasp like a fish out of water. When he finally drew breath, it came with a string of violent coughs.

Over the next twenty minutes, I asked him about Doc and the D chain his boy was rocking. I asked him about security on Cascade: how many men and guns were in that house. I even asked him what was their connection to the police.

His responses varied from "I don't know shit," to "Fuck you, old nigga!" and said that like I looked a lot older than my thirty-two years. He made some slick comments about my mother. During that time, I worked over his midsection to the point where I knew I'd fractured at least three ribs and put him on the donor's list for a new liver and kidneys.

He kept up the tough guy act, even after I went to the head. His left eye was swollen shut. He was down one front tooth, but his leaking mouth still called me all kinds of bitches and hoes.

As I stood there beating on him like a drum, it might be hard to comprehend that there was some part of me that was actually proud of this little nigga. He wasn't giving up nothing. I appreciated his loyalty and resolve. No matter how much I punched on him, young dog held firm, represented his flag, refused to betray his friends.

But my own impatience had me ready to turn up the pressure. The little fella had heart. I hoped he had brains enough to realize that sometimes in life, you have to compromise.

I had the heavy bolt cutters that I used to break into Doc's building. I hadn't just brought them in case the school was chained and locked. I held them up for him to see.

He mugged me through his one good eye. "I'm supposed to be scared, nigga?"

Hell yeah, he was. The words *Bloody Savage* were tattooed over his left eyebrow. He was about to learn that I was the real savage here.

One of his shoes was already lost when I dragged him off the block. I got down on one knee and snatched the sock off that foot. He tried to squirm and dance away from me. Li'l dog had stood ten toes but after tonight wouldn't be able to say that literally. Blood spurted from his foot like a water gun when I snipped off the pinky and the one next to it.

I couldn't imagine the pitch to his screams but watched his other reactions to the pain. He drummed his heels against the floor, and his body mimicked the spasmatic convulsions of someone being tased. He shook his head as if to tell himself that didn't really just happen.

Next I put the stained bolt cutter around his index finger. Ninety percent of communication is nonverbal. It was a silent promise that he understood. I was about to make it real hard for him to ever throw up his set.

His heart must've been in his toes, because as soon as he lost them, he lost all that tough-guy shit.

After Bloody Savage got all the screaming out, he told me everything I wanted to know. He even told me a few things I didn't.

Chapter Forty-eight

Bloody Savage was still strapped to the chair when he looked up at me with a face lumped-up and bloodied, the question of what happens now in his one good eye.

The answer came when I palmed the SR40 and slipped behind him. I squeezed off a single shot. He spat the slug from his mouth along with a few more teeth and some pink tissue that might've been gum or inner lip. His final movement was to slump forward in his seat.

You could respect an enemy, but that didn't change what he was. And it damn sure didn't change what you had to do.

He deserved better than to just be left there for the rats to gnaw on. I used one of the lanterns to find my way down the hall to the boys' gym shower, carried his body there, and stuffed him in a locker like a fifth-grade bully. A metal coffin was the best I could provide.

He had just dropped a lot of info on me, and I was still trying to sift through it. Coming out of the locker room, I was so busy thinking about my next conversation with Louie Boy that I barely spotted the moving shadow out the corner of my eye—much too big to be a rat. This came right before I was blinded by flashlights and a brief series of lesser flashes.

The dust that sprayed my face came from a bullet striking the wall less than an inch away. My cheek burned, and I knew that one had been close enough to graze me. I raised my gun to fire back, still blinded.

I slipped back into the locker room. It wasn't a deep space but constructed like a small maze of six-foot lockers with benches centering the aisles. The showers were at the rear.

I tossed my LED lantern, dropped my retreat into nearly pitch blackness. I could barely see but figured I couldn't be seen. Moving quickly through those narrow passages, I banged my shin on a bench and was grateful that the string of curses in my head couldn't be vocalized.

I didn't know how many shooters there were or how they found me. I could only guess the Joy Boys had big guns. The muzzle flashes suggested something fully automatic.

I ran my thumb over the side of my clip. Five rounds. My spare pistols were under the seat of the Buick, and the M-90 was still in Mrs. P's basement. I wasn't expecting a shootout.

My dark-adapted eyes found an opening at the rear of the shower room that led to a short hall. This was lined with a few gated pens that I imagined had once been used to store gym equipment. I sprinted down that hall, through a hanging curtain of cobwebs, to the door at the end. This was secured with a thick chain and padlock—and of course I'd left the damn bolt cutters in the other room. The gated pens on either side of the hall weren't locked but didn't offer a place to hide.

I went back to the doorway that led to the showers and concealed myself there. The shower room was a twelve-foot cube with ceramic tile walls of a pale color; although dulled by years of grime, they offered just enough ambient light.

The only advantage I had was surprise. I let them come to me. This was a weak-ass ambush, but the best I could do in an unfamiliar setting with no time to prepare. I peeked from the other side of the threshold, waiting for one of them to step inside my killbox.

After a few seconds, multiple silhouettes slowly crept against the backdrop of the shower walls. They had cut their flashlights. Three were coming my way, all carrying big choppers. I got the spike of adrenaline that told me it was time to do work.

The first one passed me at the doorway as a shadow holding an assault rifle. I put my free hand on his gun and my gun to his head. I splattered his brains, then quickly turned the .40 on his partners. In the same motion, I stripped the weapon from the first one before his body could drop.

Seeing their boy lose his brains caused the other two to freeze up. My pistol caused them to scramble backwards. I thought I hit one but couldn't be sure. The SR40 was empty.

But I had traded up. Had to get the new weapon in my hands to realize it was a Chinese SKS with a folding stock. I got the interception. I came out the short hall ready to play offense.

The locker room was much darker and offered too many places to hide. The narrow aisles created by the lockers could be a trap. Rather than pin myself in, I edged along the back wall.

Someone darted by about ten feet ahead of me. He was a phantom swimming through ink, gone by the time I took aim.

Keeping my head low and moving quickly, I followed that rear wall until it met a corner, then followed that to a dead end.

Pain in my right shoulder caused me to spin and bring my gun up. A shadowy figure stood blocking the way I'd just come. Muzzle flashes from his rifle created a stroboscopic effect.

I got low, fired back from the SKS. His jerky dance was the only indication that my shots struck home. He stumbled back into the wall, then slowly sagged to the floor.

I couldn't be worried about stealth any longer, since the bullet exchange had already given up my position. I clamored over that six-foot wall of lockers and landed in another aisle. I came down on the bench and banged the same damn shin from earlier.

It hurt, but I couldn't stand there bitching about it. I kept limping forward.

Right then my leg hurt more than the slug I had caught in my right shoulder. I expected that to change. That throb would become a much sharper and distinct pain before long. The SKS started to feel heavier. I wouldn't be able to hold the rifle in my dominant hand much longer, didn't like my chances to get out of this shooting lefty.

But I had killed two. Would help to know how many were left.

I gingerly made my way to the end of that aisle but stopped short of the corner. I didn't step into the cross aisle, didn't need to poke my head out to know there was a shooter waiting. He was trying to pull off an ambush just like I'd done in the back hall.

I might've returned the favor if my nose didn't help to make up for the deficit of my ears. Over the acrid scent of ignited gunpowder, I could detect skunky weed on his skin, and the subtler scent of his short nervous breaths, probably from a burger with heavy onions.

I counted to three, then dove out into the cross aisle, firing as I fell. I caught dude by surprise and riddled him with a short burst. He fumbled his assault rifle as he went down.

But I was caught by surprise when I realized there were two shooters. Another stood a foot behind his friend. My nose had confused their combined scents for one individual.

And there was no split second of shock at seeing his boy die like I got from the ones in the shower room. He returned fire as soon as I hit the floor.

I was down. Helpless.

Chapter Forty-nine

Darkness probably aided me more so than his poor aim. In a well-lit room, I have no doubt the second shooter would have hit me from a distance of seven feet.

But his return fire struck the floor less than a foot away from my legs. I had to half-crawl, half-scramble to get to my feet, doing my own awkward dance. I struck off down the parallel aisle while a spray of bullets peppered the metal lockers above my head, throwing off sparks.

He must've called to his boys, because I looked back and counted at least four of them pursuing me. They were using their flashlights again, beams slicing through the darkness. I got myself as low as possible. I hit corners quickly and in no particular pattern.

That momentary spike of adrenaline had numbed my leg, but the running was bringing back the shin pain. Plus the slug in my shoulder started to burn.

I didn't plan to go back to the shower room, was pressed that way. I couldn't get out the locker room with the exit cut off to me. I again stepped into the short hall and over the body I left there.

Limped back to the door at the rear as if expecting it to no longer be chained.

I was trapped and out of options. I couldn't expect for them to fall for the same trick twice. Those gated pens were on each side of the hall, still offering no place to hide.

But maybe an escape.

I missed it before, concealed by the years of dirt coating the glass. High in the wall of the second pen on the right was a tiny casement window.

I hurried to it. The window was the type typically found in any residential basement: a rectangle that was maybe eighteen inches tall by two feet wide, operated by a hand crank that rolled it out-ward. This was going to be a tight fit on the off chance I could get it open.

The rusted crank fought me for every inch, and I only got it a quarter of the way before it froze. Another time when my size worked against me—a crackhead could've squeezed through. I tried to muscle it wider, but my shoulder made reaching up with my arms complete agony. I unfolded the stock of the SKS, then used the butt to shatter and clear out the glass.

I threw a nervous glance to my back, expecting those boys to appear in the hall behind me. My escape hatch was only about eight feet high, but my sore leg wouldn't let me make what should've been an easy jump. I saw an empty waste can in the cor-ner. I turned that over and dragged it back to the wall.

One of them sprinted by the pen, spraying wildly, causing me to fall back on my ass. I returned fire, but wasn't even close with my bad arm. The SKS had started to feel like a hundred-pound dumbbell.

A second shooter briefly poked his head around the corner, then disappeared without firing. They were playing me cautious, respecting my skills, and that was the only thing saving my life. I was outnumbered and wounded. If the four of them just strapped on their nuts and ran up all at once, I'd be done.

The one dude tried another walk-by, only going back the opposite way. He sprinted past the pen spraying again, but I was ready.

I swept low at the same time, around knee-height, and let him run right into my firing line. He did a front flip when I cut his legs out from under him, then landed on his back. I switched the SKS to my stronger left hand once he was down and pumped a few into his side.

My clip was low, could tell by the weight of my gun. I had to get the fuck out of there.

I got up to the window using the waste can as a step stool but hated this next part. I had to toss the rifle through first, leaving myself butt naked.

I scrambled up the wall like a cat, then got my head out, but that tiny rectangle was snug on my shoulders. My beard got snagged on something. The rusted window jamb scraped me hard across the back, right over the wound, and made me tear up.

I had only passed my arms up to my biceps when I got stuck. Halfway in, halfway out. I was caught in that most-vulnerable position and couldn't shake the embarrassing thought of dying from a slug shot right up my ass crack. It took a lot of squirming and wormlike undulations to finally work my way through.

I fell headfirst, landed in gravel, came down weird on the back of my neck and the bad shoulder. I told myself to get up but was paralyzed by the pain. If one of the Joy Boys poked their head out the window right then, they'd had found me flat on my back. A perfect target.

I rolled onto my stomach and needed every ounce of my strength in reserve to push up to my feet. I couldn't call what I did running but some clumsy imitation of it.

Gravel kicked up at my feet. One of them was shooting at me from the window.

Chapter Fifty

My tires sprayed gravel as I peeled out the school parking lot. The bodies left inside would eventually get noticed, but I didn't have time to worry over that.

I had more questions for Louie Boy. This time the wrong answers would get his stuttering ass more than snatched up and choke-slammed.

I smashed to Seven Mile in the big Electra 225, taking corners hard and blowing through yellow lights. When I pulled in at two in the morning, The Pastry Shop had a parking lot at capacity. The triple-white Range Rover was locked in the gated pen that separated the buildings.

I left the SKS but snatched the Heckler from under the seat.

Two different bouncers covered the front door from the ones I fought last time. The expression on my face should've warned them that a pat-down wasn't happening. I went to bowl right through them until one tried to reach for me. A mistake.

The kidney shot dropped him to one knee like he was proposing to me and put him at the perfect height to eat my knee. The second one ran into my spinning elbow, caught that to the nose, then got KOed by a three-piece finished by the left.

I handled that easily, but the movements made me see white spots as every nerve in my right shoulder screamed in rebellion. I was practically tearing up when I snatched open the doors.

The club was slapping, unlike my first visit. Customers claimed every table, barstool, and the VIP terrace, waving bottles and raining singles. And these dancers definitely weren't the B-team—bad bitches worked the stage and walked the floor with nothing but pasties over nipples and strings flossing asses.

I didn't ask a bartender to announce me this time. I went straight through the employee door, down that service hall that led to Louie's office.

Another female had him too distracted to check the cameras. I saw the shock on his face when I appeared in his doorway. I was just as shocked at seeing Lexy. They weren't fucking. It was more like I interrupted a conversation.

I used ASL to ask what she was doing there. She responded with two fists, palms down, the right wrist tapping the left hand two quick times in imitation of a hammer striking an anvil. *Working.* I detected more of that hostility I thought we had gotten over with our second fuck.

She was definitely dressed for some type of work: a cheerleader with an S&M fetish. She stood over the desk in a black leather bra top, matching stiletto heels, and a pleated skirt hemmed so high that it left the bottom quarter of her ass in view.

I slid into the small storage room that was Louie's office, rubbed against the door jamb, and didn't realize I smeared it with blood until Louie Boy jumped to his feet. He turned me to inspect the hole in the back of my shoulder and the wet stain spreading across my hoodie.

"Damn Sy, m-man you shot!"

As if I didn't know.

He claimed to keep a first aid kit behind the bar and sent Lexy to get it. She made sure to hit me with another eye roll.

I dropped myself into the chair that fronted Louie's desk, didn't realize how weak my legs were until I got off of them. He tried to pass me a shot of Casamigos that I rejected.

I didn't waste time with warmup questions. I flat-out asked Louie if he knew that he and Doc had been selling dope for the police.

Before Louie Boy answered, I could tell he had at least suspected something was shady about their mystery supplier. "I never met them. Doc said he the only one who get a f-face-to-face. Five-o though?"

I told Louie that there was this big stud sergeant at the Tenth Precinct who had a crew of dirty cops doing for Doc the same thing I used to do for him back in the day: shutting down competitors and taking their product. I didn't know if they stole it all directly from the dealers or took it once it hit their evidence room. Either way, this explained why the heroin was never the same cut or quality but always priced so cheap.

Doc had been using the Joy Boys to move his share of the dope. It took two toes to get the truth, but Bloody Savage swore that days after Doc died, Gamble showed up saying Doc owed a big debt they were responsible for. From that point on, Doc's former workers had become hers.

Lexy returned with the first aid kit. She didn't seem too enthused about playing nurse but still signed for me to pull off my hoodie. The weight and wetness of the fabric indicated how much blood I'd lost. I couldn't see the wound, but the glances that passed between Lexy and Louie Boy told me that I really needed to get my ass to a hospital. My glance told them that wasn't happening. I just needed her to slow the bleeding. Wasn't shit I could do about the slug right then.

I leaned forward in my seat while she cleaned and dressed the wound. Lexy made no effort to be gentle.

Louie Boy seemed confused, and I read the moment he puzzled out why Doc would owe a debt. All this time, Louie had thought they were buying the heroin outright, but Doc was pocketing Louie's fare, getting the drugs on consignment, then paying the cops on the back end. Whatever Doc did with the cash from the hotel, Gamble and her crew didn't get their cut. That was probably why Doc had tried to blame Louie for the robbery.

Louie Boy just smirked at me, shaking his head. "Still th-think that nigga was Jesus's light-skinned cousin?"

My twisted mug told Louie I wasn't in the mood for any of that shit. There was still too much about this that didn't make sense. Each answer I pulled out of Bloody Savage only brought up two more questions.

Lexy passed me my hoodie to let me know she was finished. I dove into it, but the pain was so intense that I needed her help to guide my right arm through the sleeve.

"Tell yo' girl Q I'm just making a couple of extra dollars doing bottle service." Lexy's comment caught me off guard but did explain the outfit. It wasn't street-appropriate but more than what the strippers had on.

I signed to asked why she couldn't relay that message herself. I already knew they were beefing.

"I failed to secure something the queen wanted." I'm so arrogant that I thought they fell out about me, because Lexy had let me get more than one free ride.

For a small consolation, I let her know Quianna was pissed at me, too, but didn't go into the reason. I still felt stupid about overplaying my hand at the MGM Grand.

Louie Boy broke in on us by waving for my attention. He directed me to the monitor on his desk offering different views of the club.

A panoramic scene of the parking lot was in the upper right corner. Four red vehicles had parked in front of the entrance, not bothering to slot themselves among the customer parking or cut their headlights. A '68 Chevy Chevelle, a '78 four-door Malibu; both were donked out on big chrome rims, club lights dancing off their candy paint jobs. The G63 Benz Wagon was the current-year model and met the Chevelle nose to nose. I was familiar with the Challenger.

I was also familiar with the stocky light-skinned nigga who jumped out the driver's door of the Benz with the D-chain swinging. The alpha dog had joined this hunt.

From the small office, our six eyes watched the screen as the four vehicles disgorged ten men. Each one of them had an assault rifle.

Louie Boy looked at me with panic and desperation on his face. His club was definitely about to get shut down again.

Chapter Fifty-one

Lexy signed to me: "Did he have a phone?"

I was lost, didn't know what or who she was talking about. The view on screen of ten shooters coming into the club made my previous thoughts beyond recall or relevance.

The monitor offered six simultaneous views of the property. We watched the Joy Road Boys pass through the scene that framed the entrance to appear in the frame that covered the club's interior. Mostly in red attire, they carried Israeli Tavor X95s, Belgian FN SCARs, and German HK416s in open view. Streetwise patrons and strippers hit the floor, while the more brazen gambled for the exit.

The Joy Boys sprayed like trigger-happy youths more enamored with the destructive power of their weapons than shooters selecting targets. Holes got punched in the promo posters of dessert-themed dancers, the lighting fixtures over the stage, the liquor bottles behind the bar. Holes got punched in a few people if they just happened to be in the way.

The lower left corner of the screen winked to static as the camera providing that footage was cut down. A few of those slugs burrowed through the plaster and wood behind the bar, crossed the hall, and entered the open door to Louie's office.

I pulled Lexy to the floor, landed on my belly, but the impact still ignited my shoulder. Those white spots exploded upon my field of vision, did a short frenzied dance, then melted away. The pain tightened my jaw.

We couldn't stay pinned down. Once they got tired of wasting their ammo in the business area, a search of the entire building would start.

Louie Boy was lying behind his desk wearing an expression that told me he was more concerned about property damage and insurance premiums versus the people who might be dying out front. I flagged his attention, but he couldn't make any sense of my hand gestures.

My phone was on top of the desk and out of reach unless I was willing to raise my head from the floor. I wasn't.

Lexy was down on her side next to me. I tapped her shoulder and signed my instructions.

I drew my Heckler and made Louie give me his Casull—we both knew he wasn't about to do shit. I army-crawled on my elbows and knees, swallowing the pain of that movement.

In the hallway, I got to my feet, but remained in a low crouch. I duck-walked to the end of that service hall, toward the fire door, P7M8 in my left and .454 in my right.

I sensed a presence behind me. I spun quickly on my heels, ready to shoot.

A girl dressed only in purple bikini bottoms was crawling on her hands and knees. She stared at me over the two guns, then fell back on her haunches to raise trembling hands. One fake eyelash was stuck to her cheek; mascara tears streaked her face. Her bottom lip quivered.

I didn't know if she was trying to speak, but I put a finger to my lips in imitation of Quianna's tattoo.

I trained my eyes and guns back to the opposite end of the corridor, where the service door led back into the club. I expected more panicked civilians or enemies with guns. I waited long enough for the second hand to make one smooth circuit around the face of the Rolex.

I motioned for the dancer to come, and she followed me on all fours like a stray dog. I reached the end of the hall and booted the fire exit. The sign was joined to a LED light that flashed in bright pulses. I imagined this was accompanied by the high-pitched scream of an alarm, and for once I was grateful for my disability.

I waved her out the door, then watched from the hall as she struck outside. She ran barefoot down an alley scattered with broken glass and brown puddles. She bent a corner at the neighboring block, then disappeared into the freedom of the night.

I wasn't being as helpful as one might think. The Joy Boys could've had a few shooters covering the rear. If she had gotten cut down, then I would've known.

After I peeked out to double-check that the way was clear, I hurried back to the office. Lexy got up and hustled outside without me having to call, was even mindful enough to grab my iPhone off the desk. I had to make the *C'mon* motion to Louie three times to get him moving.

A red Givenchy shirt appeared at the far end of the hall. I fired three times before I was even sure he was one of the ops. His skull snapped backwards when his forehead caught the slug. The man in red juggled the FN that hung from a shoulder strap (a weapon I only saw after my bullet turned his body). He fell flat on his back.

I knew that if the alarm hadn't already, the gunshots would surely summon his boys. I backpedaled with the burners stretched out before me, covering our retreat.

I met Lexy and Louie Boy where they had waited for me in the alley by the gated pen that housed his white Range Rover under a chain and padlock. A brief flicker of its head- and taillights signaled that he killed the alarm.

I kept the rear exit covered. Bust twice when two figures appeared in the doorway. They fell back briefly, then responded with the short spray of an X95. The shots were wide and high.

We were outmanned, outgunned, and out in the open. I turned back to Louie Boy, wondering what the fuck was taking him so long to pull the truck out. He patted himself frantically, then gave me this panicked look that explained his fuckup without words. He couldn't unlock the gate. He had his car keys, but this dumb muthafucka had left the key to the padlock back in his office.

Another volley of slugs shattered the rear tailgate window on the Range and flattened a tire. I saw Dirty Red along with a second darker-skinned dude taking shots at us. They used the door jamb for cover but were preparing to come out in force.

I switched the heavy Casull to my stronger left hand and let that bitch go twice. The .454 had almost twice the power of a .44 Magnum, and the sound alone was enough to back them up.

But I knew not for long. I turned to tell Lexy and Louie Boy to run.

It fucked me up to see that my homeboy was already halfway down the alley. Doing his Usain Bolt impersonation. Not even glancing back for us.

Chapter Fifty-two

"Did he have a phone?" Lexy signed this question to me. It felt like déjà vu.

I was curled over the wheel, more focused on my mirrors than a response.

"I g-gotta chick who live right 'round here on Asbury Park. Y-You can just dr-drop me over there." After reaching up to tap my shoulder from the back seat, I used the rearview to read this off Louie's lips. "Y-you ain't gotta worry b-bout getting me all the w-way to the crib." This weak attempt to make it seem like he was doing me a favor almost got him slapped.

From the passenger seat, Lexy shot me a side glance and an irritated eye roll that wasn't directed at me for once. "He probably need to change his draws." I assumed she mouthed this without volume.

We were both still pissed at him for running on us. He had followed the same path the half-naked dancer took: down the alley and hung a left on the next side street that took him north. It took us a block and a half to catch up with him—the whole time Lexy running in four-inch stilettos. Then it took a couple of minutes just to calm Louie Boy down, because he wouldn't stop bitching about his truck and club.

I had to calm him down again after I put down a play to get us a vehicle. We were still walking up a residential block in the direction of 8 Mile when I peeped someone pulling an early-nineties Chrysler New Yorker into a driveway. I crept up in the dark and caught him dragging his trash bin to the curb, jammed the .454 in his face. He was only nineteen but already had more sense than Old School with the yellow Buick. Young Dog ran those keys without a fuss. He was also smart enough to understand the implied threat of me taking his driver's license.

Louie Boy hadn't even wanted to get in, and the whole thing about being dropped at his girl's house was just him trying to get the fuck away from the drama as fast as he could.

"She stay on A-Asbury and Outer Drive," he repeated. "B-but you can just leave me at the c-c-corner, and I'll walk to the—"

I ignored that clown in the back seat and turned to Lexy, who was signaling me. I caught her halfway through what she was saying, some shit about a phone again. My shoulder throbbed, my head pounded, and those white spots were back in my eyes. My hands asked her to repeat it.

"Did he have a phone?" She mouthed this with an exasperated glare. My quizzical reply only frustrated her more. "The nigga you took!" She smacked a palm against the dashboard. "Did he have a phone?"

I nodded that he did, because I took it off Bloody Savage when he was choked out. Didn't want him to wake up and call the police from the trunk. In fact, I still had it.

When I fished his phone from my pocket, Lexy snatched it the way you'd take scissors from a child.

She frowned at me. "How in the fuck you think they keep finding you?" I shrugged, and Lexy shook her head like I was helpless. "You been locked up so long, you don't know shit. They tracking his phone, dumbass!"

I was still new to this technology shit. This whole time I had been leading the Joy Boys right to me. Would eventually have to toss Louie Boy a "My bad" for bringing them to his club, but right then he was acting too much like a bitch to get an apology.

Lexy was about to drop Savage's phone out the window, but I stopped her. It might still be useful. For now I just needed her to disconnect however they were tracking it. If she could get into it, because the phone was password-protected.

Lexy reminded me that she was a female, so of course she could break into any man's phone. Her quick tapdancing thumbs glided over the screen, and she navigated his security features in the time it took for us to travel two traffic lights on 8 Mile.

I believed the New Yorker had to have belonged to Young Dog's grandmother. Burgundy over burgundy, and had cloth interior saturated with the scent of menthols and softer old woman smells like those in Mrs. P's room.

I caught Louie Boy trying for my attention again, waving his hand in the mirror. I was so tired of his shit that I just pulled over and put his ass out right there.

Louie Boy pretended to be salty. He hopped out the car wearing a thin veneer of indignation but underneath showed the relief of an inmate who'd just been pardoned.

The hurt feelings only became real when he asked me to return his .454 Casull. A weak-ass nigga had no business with a gun this powerful. I pulled off and left him standing in front of a closed Home Depot.

According to the dashboard clock, we were only minutes away from three a.m. Traffic was nonexistent, which made patrol cars easier to spot.

Lexy lived all the way on the south side of town, and at that point, my head felt like a helium balloon ready to drift off my shoulders. She obviously saw in my weighted eyes that I'd plow us into a stop sign before she ever got home. She made me pull over to give her the wheel.

In the passenger seat, I angled myself against the door in a way that allowed me to recline comfortably without resting on my tender shoulder. I don't remember nodding off, even though it had felt inevitable. We were traveling eastbound on 8 Mile Road, the boundary line for the north end of the city; then after a time skip, I felt myself being nudged awake to find we were already parked in the area of Tireman, the boundary line for the south side of the city.

I could've woke up nineteen hours later in Texas and still not felt rested enough. I told myself what I felt was ordinary fatigue, but the smarter part of me knew better.

I turned to Lexy. Her eyes were filled with unvoiced concern. I worked the kinks out my neck, offered a nod that said I was okay. She looked no more convinced than I was.

She snatched the keys out the ignition and pushed open the driver's door. I guessed I was expected to follow. I dragged myself out the car and was surprised by the effort it took to stand.

Lexy had sense enough to park the stolen New Yorker half a block down and across the street from her house. She lived in a small single-story unit that fronted Tireman Street. The exterior was wrapped in beige siding trimmed in white, and an aluminum awning that covered the porch. It was a nice house but probably still wouldn't sell for fifty thousand because of the area.

It did stand out in contrast to the rest of the block, which resembled a bottom row of bad teeth. Each empty field was a missing tooth, each burned ruin a rotten one riddled with cavities.

Lexy glared at me, clearly reading my silent judgment of her hood. "You know the city 'bout to come back, right?" I just gave a nod but swore to myself that I would choke the shit out of the next person who said that.

Trailing Lexy down the street, even with one foot in the grave, I couldn't help but be drawn to her form. That skirt left the bottom of her ass hanging out, and it was just so fat that it had no choice but to shift and jiggle as she walked.

As I watched her climb the porch steps, my mind actually wasn't in a sexual place. It was obviously a bonus in their profession, but I wondered if she and Quianna found having curves like that to be more gift or curse. I flashed back to the incident at the mall with the little rapper Brody Starrz. Lexy must've had to deal with that type of bullshit every day.

At the door, she spun on me suddenly to catch my eyes lingering. Lexy of course had that sixth sense all women develop at puberty, that almost-psychic feeling that warned them when their bodies received unwanted attention.

The raw umber dimepiece scanned me through cold, narrowed eyes. "I'm only letting your ass in to take a quick nap. A few minutes to recharge, then you out."

I nodded as she twisted the key in the lock. Gave a silent but solemn promise to be on my best behavior.

"I ain't playing, Silence." She mouthed the next words with extreme emphasis so I could see them clearly on her lips: "DON'T EVEN THINK PUSSY!!"

Chapter Fifty-three

Lexy gave me another long hawkish glare while we stood on her porch, a warning for me not to be on bullshit. I assured her that I only wanted a half hour to rest my eyes. Visually admiring her was worlds away from trying to fuck. The bullet in my shoulder had ignited every nerve in my back. Liquid fire. Even if I could take my mind off the pain long enough to wake my beast, I knew my stroke wouldn't be shit.

The invitation finally came by way of her pushing in the front door. Before stepping inside, I saw enough to be impressed.

The interior had the look of a museum. The living room set was composed of contemporary black leather furniture that resembled pieces of modern art. The coffee table was granite and stained glass, matching the dinette table in the anterior room. It was a small space but thoughtfully adorned. Everything was new and immaculate, particularly the huge television that centered the wall opposite the sofa, twin to the one in Quianna's living room, and most likely purchased with the same card numbers.

The hardwood floor was polished to a wet shine that reflected a glowing circlet of orbs from the overhead lights. When she stripped off her shoes at the door, my boots followed.

My time in the church drew me to the African art. A set of tribal masks bracketed the entrance to the dining room. On the coffee table stood an eighteen-inch wooden figurine of Aset (Isis to the Greek plagiarists), solar disk balanced upon her head and stomach swollen with Heru, seed of Ausar.

But I was totally held captive by the six-foot-wide mural above the sofa. This was a hyperrealistic portrait depicting Queen Ana de Sousa Nzinga of the Mbande, sitting on the back of one of her kneeling soldiers during talks with Portuguese colonizers. When the hosts refused to offer the Queen a chair, a faithful servant folded himself into a seat for his general and Majesty.

I turned to Lexy, and in a split second, an entire conversation was exchanged between us without lips or ASL. She, like her home, offered a rich interior not expected from its outside appearance. I apologized for thinking she was no more than a pretty face and big booty.

My two-seventy felt like twice that, and I was ready to drop myself into a seat when Lexy stopped me. She disappeared, then returned a few minutes later carrying a folded cotton blanket. Lexy draped the blanket over her fine leather sofa, boasted that it was a Tacchini, as if the brand were known and respected. She demanded my black hoodie and again had to help me get it over my head, along with the shirt underneath. Both were drenched in blood, so she went to the kitchen and offered them to the trash.

She came back with a pot of warm water and a few rags, turned me to inspect my shoulder. I figured the gauze she applied at The Pastry Shop still held, because after a brief peek at the wound, she carefully replaced it, then wiped down the rest of my back with the damp rags. This felt soothing but was hardly enough to quiet the pain.

After drying my back, she tossed me a clean shirt. A Hanes tee in a 3XL that still fit snug once we both wrestled me into in. Only then was I allowed to sit. I eased myself slowly against the backrest until my shoulder told me it was okay.

During those few minutes Lexy was in back, she had also

changed into something probably intended to take my eyes and mind off her body. The billowing pink top looked like a tent-sized T-shirt, so long that it hemmed around her knees.

Lexy ran the rags and water pot to the kitchen while I adjusted myself on her sleek but uncomfortable sofa. I found myself staring at the framed photos on a tall metal stand with a series of shelves that stood in the corner. Most of the pictures starred a four-year-old girl who could've been Lexy's clone.

Lexy tracked my eyes as she padded barefoot back into the living room. "She ain't here—yo' ass wouldn't be if she was." I took no offense. Most people didn't want me around their children any more than I wanted to be around them.

In one photo, the girl was sandwiched in a two-armed embrace between Lexy and a brown-skinned dude rocking a pair of Cartier glasses studded with thirty-pointers.

At reading my inquisitive glance, she immediately ran her hand across her neck, throat-slit motion. She made it clear that her and dude were just co-parents, nothing more. "I already made a bad dick decision that left me connected to one asshole for eighteen years." I could tell this bit of information wasn't just for me, but something I was expected to relay to a third party.

I reminded her that I wasn't the one to get her off of Quianna's shit list. My own name was probably at the top.

She changed the subject, asking instead about the drama at the club. "Are those the guys who killed Q's brother?"

I contemplated that for a few seconds before confessing that I didn't know. I closed my eyes before she could ask something else. I was physically exhausted and mentally drained from trying to figure out this Doc shit.

On top of everything else, I only had about twenty-four hours left to deliver Doc's killer. I was even less sure of who that was.

Chapter Fifty-four

I checked the borrowed Rolex: it was a quarter to four. Lexy only then noticed the watch, glanced to my wrist and back wearing a half-smirk and something less friendly. I was too tired to go into the meaning of that look. I promised me and the New Yorker would be gone by six.

The pain that started in my back behind my right shoulder had claimed that entire arm and crept up my neck. I turned to Lexy, laying one hand faceup. With the middle finger of my other hand, I drew a small pill-sized circle in the center of my palm. In ASL most of the signs were logical once given some thought. Particularly this one for *medicine.*

Lexy claimed to have nothing in the house stronger than Children's Tylenol. When she returned with a glass of water and a pill bottle, I tossed back a handful like M&M's.

I sat back and closed my eyes but couldn't get comfortable on the sleek Tacchini sofa. Every move caused me to wince. Lexy watched me with unblinking brown eyes, behind which I detected some degree of calculation.

She urged me down to the sofa's edge, where I could lean against the armrest. She slid over an ottoman that matched the couch so I could prop up my feet. This helped. Then I learned that Lexy planned to make me a LOT more comfortable.

With me seated at the far left end of the sofa, this allowed Lexy stretch across it lengthwise on her stomach. Her head hovered at my lap. Before I could shoot her a look to ask her what's up, she let me know. With one yank, she snatched my sweatpants and boxers halfway down my thighs.

I tapped her, signed a joking reminder of that warning she gave me on the front porch. She had told me, "Don't even think pussy!"—and to be honest, I hadn't.

Lexy responded that only *I* wasn't allowed to think about it. She claimed to owe me a treat for saving her life at the club. I was to blame for bringing the Joy Boys there in the first place, but didn't let the facts get in the way of a good story.

The problem was my dick hung like a wet rope, so after two minutes, her constantly tugging on it only annoyed and embarrassed me. I expressed my appreciation for the thought but didn't think there was any way I could brick up with the amount of pain I was in. Lexy treated that as a challenge, not a concession. She used her tongue to duel me, but my sword was soft and unresponsive.

Next she started running her fingernails up and down the inside of my thighs. This was a slow gentle raking, not hard enough to leave scratches. According to her, it was supposed to stimulate blood flow to the groin area.

And this worked, because it only took about thirty seconds of this to send a single weak spasm through my limp, bendy dick. More followed, and I started to grow slowly. When I asked where did she learn a trick like this, *None of yo' damn business!* was written in her rolling eyes.

Lexy kept up the raking while sprinkling me with thin kisses. That faint flicker of life became a steady pulse. Then she scooped me into her mouth like a predator. After three smooth inhalations, I was hard enough to stop flopping. By the fifth, my sleeping beast was fully awake.

Lexy continued to take me into her mouth but used her hands to help. Twisting and sucking in a technique made famous back in the day by Karrine "Superhead" Steffans. She loaded her mouth with so much spit that it dribbled over her hands and leaked down my balls.

After four minutes of her neck pumping like a piston driving an engine, Lexy stopped and stood. She straddled me, then sat facing away. No panties were under that long shirt. Her first three motions only accepted five of my inches. After that, she was taking all of me.

Lexy rode me like an exercise bike. Her repeatedly dropping her weight on me wouldn't have been a problem under normal circumstances, only the impact was fucking with my shoulder. It was slow and seductive, but pleasure and pain in equal doses.

Lexy then hiked up her long shirt, giving me a view of that masterpiece she covered every day in designer denim. The ass was round and perfect. It was only marked by the BANDS crest over crossed swords. I didn't realize she could twerk it while riding the dick. The Booty Queen made it shake in six different ways.

But just as she had me to the point of hypnosis, she suddenly stopped. She tugged her shirt back down. Just dropped the curtain and killed the show.

Even though she never stopped riding me, I wanted more entertainment. But when I pulled at her shirt, Lexy smacked my hand like I was some naughty child.

Our first encounter was like a sparring match, but this was a game. Apparently, no touching was one of the rules.

Peek-a-Booty. Lexy would hike up her shirt tail, twerk that ass for a while, then cover up again. She might shake it for a full minute; it might be quick as a flash. Or she would fake me out by easing up the hem part of the way, then snatching it back down.

And she did this while switching up the rhythm and pitch of her ride. She would go from a forceful bounce to a circular motion. She might take me to the balls and grind back and forth. The anticipation of the next time she would flash and twerk left me excited, amplified by the fact that she got wetter as the game progressed.

Eventually the temptation became too much, and since I ain't never been one known for following rules, I had to smack that ass.

Can't let it be said that I'm a selfish lover who only thinks about his own pleasure. I slipped my left hand around her waist and into the warmth between her legs. I felt her shudder.

The thumb on my right hand ringed her asshole for a few turns before plunging inside to the knuckle. I used both hands to tease her ass and clit with a rhythm that synced up. It would've been better if my right arm wasn't numb from the bullet moving through me, possibly causing permanent nerve damage.

Lexy loved this once she caught on to the rhythm. The little game was forgotten; teasing me became irrelevant as she approached her climax. Her bouncing became fast and violent. The couch thumped against the wall so hard that I feared the Nzinga mural might fall on my head.

Lexy looked back at me with a face that asked, *Nigga, what are you doing to me?* She cursed me, cursed my beast for feeling so good. She even cursed Quianna for some reason.

Lexy came with closed eyes, a half-open mouth, and a quivering bottom lip. She filled my palm with so much wetness that my first thought was that the bitch pissed on me.

I permitted her a brief intermission to savor that moment of satisfaction while I stealthily cleaned my hand on that tarp of a shirt. She opened her eyes, stared at me with some mixture of anger and affection. Lexy seemed to be battling something when it came to me—there was a part of her that just wanted to hate me.

That might have been the part that took over when she started riding me again. She grabbed my knees, lowered her back, and bounced on my beast like she was mad at him.

It felt good but not ecstatic. I closed my eyes and brought up images that I thought would bring me home: Lexy in her leather skirt, Lexy in her crown and sash at the bachelor party.

And then, totally unwanted or called for, I got ambushed by a fat pussy print bursting out of some yellow shorts. My balls tightened; my dick started to throb like a heart muscle.

Lexy stopped bucking the moment she felt me blow. It was like the last of my energy left me with that nut. My head fell back, my eyes closed. I drifted off wondering if Louie Boy and Doc had used to count up at the same Holiday Inn back when they were still fucking with Prime.

I suffered another time skip. I didn't realize I'd dozed off or for how long until I felt Lexy tapping my thigh. I could've been out for fifteen minutes or thirty, but not hours—I could tell from the way night still dressed the scenery outside her windows. Hours were what my body begged for. That and Motrin in eight-hundred-milligram capsules.

When Lexy woke me up, I was no longer in her. She sat next to me, and my sweats were pulled back up. I was busy shooting her a furious glare, too tired and irritated to focus on her hands.

Her eyes were wide; silent alarm bells rang in them. Bloody Savage's phone rested on her lap. Lexy signed to me that I needed to get my ass home right then.

Chapter Fifty-five

I raced back to the house, blowing through red lights and stop signs like I had sirens.

The haste was triggered by what Lexy found digging through Savage's phone. I still believed he had answered my questions truthfully while grunting and puffing through the pain of his lost toes; however, I just learned that he didn't give me the whole truth.

During those precious few minutes I was allowed to sleep, Lexy had found a Facebook account with the same handle: Bloody Savage. He had made several posts that day, most of them just of him being a young wild nigga doing what young wild niggas do: smoking wax, clowning one of his mans, playing with a gun nearly as big as him. The relevant posts had been uploaded thirteen hours before.

From the vantage of his phone camera, I could see the interior of a car: the glove box, dashboard. Coming into the frame was a disconnected arm thrusting a FNX Tactical 45 out the open window. The pistol jerked forward several times, spitting fire and ejecting tumbling shells high from its head. The camera panned upward, giving a view out through the windshield: of the car's red hood, the road ahead, and the rear end of an old Lincoln struggling to keep pace a few feet ahead. Two bullets pinged off the trunk; one cracked a taillight. A third shot completely shattered the back window of the fleeing car.

This stupid muthafucka actually posted our car chase, of himself shooting at me.

After about fifteen seconds, that video ended, and Lexy showed me another, the one that knotted my stomach, woke me all the way up, and had me out her door without a goodbye hug or dap for the ass she just gave me. This posting had only come minutes behind the first, obviously after I lost them near John C. Lodge behind a traffic jam I created by going kamikaze.

The phone was pointed down at the scarred and cratered asphalt street as legs that terminated in throwback Pippens walked over tiny pellets of sparkling glass. A slip of paper was attached to a huge chunk of back window that had shattered but not broken apart. The paper shivered in a slight breeze until a brown hand picked it up. The camera zoomed in on a temporary plate registered in the name of Quianna Peterson.

I got back to the hood in record time and hit the corner at Monica damn near on two wheels. I was still a block down from ours when I saw the ambulance.

My first thought was Mrs. P. I sped down to the house cursing myself.

Enough people were out on the block to include every neighbor from this street and the next two. They stood on the curb opposite our house, gawking.

Along with the ambulance, there were two Detroit Police squad cars. The uniformed officers on scene weren't even bothering to question the onlookers. They knew better. This was the type of hood were everybody saw everything, but nobody witnessed shit.

The congestion on the block kept the New Yorker from getting any closer than three houses past the corner. I stomped the brakes and jumped out so fast that I forgot to shift into park. I had to catch it from rolling into the car in front of me.

I immediately noticed our house. The bank of four windows that looked in on the lower living room were completely shot out, making the front of our home look like a grinning face with missing teeth. Bullets had knocked chunks out of the brick façade. The spray pattern indicated that at least three shooters had stood out front with fully automatic assault rifles.

This made me rush towards the ambulance. I needed to know who was in back.

I was making my way towards the rear doors when I spotted Mrs. P coming down the porch steps leaning heavily on Trayvion for support. I finally took a breath—didn't know how long I'd been holding it, but my lungs seemed to burn from the want of air.

I scanned the crowd and saw a few of Trayvion's boys were huddled in conversation over by the rusted fire hydrant at the curb next door. I spotted most of the kids.

But the ambulance with its swirling beacons painted their strained faces in colors that alternated between the pale violet of the mercury streetlamp and that ominous red, refusing me the delusion that everyone had escaped unharmed. My gut told me who it was. Even more than I wanted it to be nobody, I wanted it to be somebody else.

But I was a child blowing out candles or tossing pennies into fountains. My eyes confirmed what my stomach already knew when the BBW was escorted from the lower flat. Her face was wet with tears, and she was going crazy. The uniformed officer struggled to restrain her.

Two EMTs followed them out on either side of a gurney. Little Nika with the afro puffs lay stretched out, eyes closed. A clear plastic mask was over her face, and one of the paramedics forced oxygen to her by squeezing a rubber bag that was connected to it.

A dark crimson stain had blossomed across the shirt of her Wonder Woman pajamas.

The tears never stopped, but Big Girl calmed enough to make the ride with her daughter. She seemed to realize in the moment that what Nika needed was a steady anchor to tether her to this world and not the screaming hysterics of a mother already grieving for her.

Big Girl allowed herself to get helped into the rear of the ambulance. They zipped away no sooner than the doors were closed, taking one of the squad cars to provide an escort.

I went to Mrs. P, and the second our eyes met, she knew this was on me. I had allowed my bullshit to blow back on the crib. Only this wasn't the time or place to go into it.

I pointed to the burgundy Chrysler, told her to take the kids to my car. When she tried to sign back a question to me, I dismissed it by waving my hands and aggressively responded with the gestures for "Just do it!" I'd never bossed up on the old lady like that before. I saw the anger and confusion flash across her face, but this was superimposed by a quiet acquiescence. Mrs. P knew I wouldn't come at her like that without a good reason.

Mrs. P wrangled the kids and hustled them to the car while I sent Trayvion back inside to grab her a few changes of clothes. She was going to be away from home for a while.

I followed him into the house but hit the basement steps. The M-90 and the M4 I got from DelRay were still where I hid them.

I was running that out to the New Yorker and nearly dropped the shit when I saw the gray Camaro out front. Gamble, Bates, and a third white detective stood in the street getting briefed by the pair of uniformed officers who remained on the scene.

And they had just happened to be parked on the rear bumper of the vehicle I just carjacked. While I just happened to be carrying an armful of illegal, unregistered weapons.

Chapter Fifty-six

The three detectives spotted me at the same time I spotted them. My guns were still wrapped in a blanket. I hurried to the car, and Bates moved to intercept, flagging for my attention. I played the deaf card while we had a foot race to the New Yorker. I popped the trunk, dropped the load in, and slammed the trunk closed a second before he pressed up on me.

He asked me what did I just put in there. I typed to ask how badly did he really want to know, because the cost of finding out was one broken bone.

Gamble and the white dude joined us when Bates looked to his superior. "He threatened me. You saw him." Bates yanked the handcuffs from his belt.

Gamble tried to warn him: "You might not want to do that."

This dumb muthafucka actually tried to arrest me. The instant he put a hand on my left arm, I grabbed and twisted his wrist, then sent an elbow into his throat. I spun him like a dance partner while he was still coughing and spitting, then snatched his cuffs. A second later, he was the one facedown against the New Yorker with his hands behind his back. Through the magnifying lenses of his thick glasses, Bates had the confused look of somebody who needed what just happened explained to him.

I was still quick enough, but the pain of the movements made me tear up.

Gamble laughed so hard that her cheeks flushed hot pink, but the male detective was unmoved. He studied me without expression, and I could tell he was sizing me up. I remembered him riding shotgun when Big Nose made the drop-off on Cascade. He was six-foot-four in a black T-shirt and khakis. His muscular build and buzz cut screamed ex-military.

The two uniformed officers unholstered their Glocks and sprinted over to intervene until Gamble held them back with a raised head. She stood at my right hand, again dressed in a men's button-down shirt and slacks. The gold shield around her neck twinkled in the reflection of the Camaro's headlights.

"You are aware that you just assaulted a detective-ranked member of the Detroit Police Department in full view of four other officers?" I kept Bates's head smashed against the trunk like I was the cop and he was the perp, let Gamble read the few fucks I gave in my return stare.

Everybody in the car must've heard and felt the thump. I looked up and saw Mrs. P, Trayvion, and all the kids twisted in their seats watching out the back window.

Gamble peeped when my eyes flashed to them then back. Her smile took on a more sadistic quality. "It's so much easier when your actions only affect you." She gestured at the two officers slowly inching towards me with their pistols leveled at my head. "I'm sure that your family doesn't want to see you lying next to Darius."

She must've seen something dangerous flash through my eyes at the mention of Doc. From her reaction, it was something she feared but admired.

Her energy softened. She asked almost humbly: "Would you please release my partner?"

I let him go. Bates's square ass sprang up looking angry and embarrassed. He still fought to clear his throat, all the while muttering some incoherent threats I couldn't make out.

Gamble told him to go wait in the car; only she and the other dude with the buzz cut left him wearing his own cuffs. So it was comical as hell watching him struggle to open the car door with his wrists locked behind him. Gamble waited for him to go through all the trouble of maneuvering himself into the passenger seat, and the moment he got settled, she yelled: "Back seat!" It was nearly three more full minutes of humiliation watching him fight to get himself out, raise the seat, and climb into the Camaro's cramped rear space with no hands or help.

Even though Bates was a sellout by all accounts, seeing his white coworkers clown him still pissed me off. It stirred up the black nationalist bred in me.

The sergeant dismissed the two uniformed officers. Reluctant glares passed from them to me. They clearly wanted to see your boy on the ground while they got in some baton practice, but retreated back to their car looking like kids sent to bed without dessert.

The street was pretty much cleared at that point, anyway. Most of the onlookers had left with the ambulance except for the nosiest aunties.

The shooting at The Pastry Shop had made the news. Gamble guessed I was involved and called herself checking me. "Four dead, seventeen injured. The case is being handled by another precinct, but lucky for you, I have friends there. I had to call in some big favors to protect you."

More like protecting herself. She needed me on the streets, and she was making too much money on Cascade to have the police looking into her crew. I didn't bullshit with it, flat-out told her that I knew those gangbangers moved heroin for her, just like Doc used to.

For the first time, she let her game face slip. "This is waaay bigger than Nino Brown."

I typed: *Why didn't you look at the Joy Boys for Doc's murder?*

"Because I know for a fact Dirty Red and his boys aren't responsible for Darius. He was their plug. They had more to lose than gain by killing him."

I rebutted that three million and eight hundred thousand is a lot for anybody to gain. That text widened her eyes. I just fucked her up again. I wasn't supposed to know about the money.

She hid her shock behind a smirk. "What else did Louis tell you?"

Enough to know that for her, this was never about finding Doc's killer. But I kept that to myself. Plus I just learned something from the incident with Bates that I was still processing.

Gamble waved her hand, prompting me to look around our block, where the early dawn showed crumbling multi-family flats outnumbered three-to-one either by burned shells missing roofs or empty plots. Some of the abandoned cars parked out on the street should've been towed back in the day when I was still a virgin.

"I always found the words *black community* to be an oxymoron, since you don't actually have your own community. You pay rent to white landlords and can't buy a cheeseburger, pack of cigarettes, or a gallon of gas without going to the Arabs. Most of the streets you have so proudly tattooed on your chests are named after English lords or American slave owners, and yet you are more ready to die for them than the real owners who actually profit off the land." The sincerity in her blue eyes disturbed me. I would've felt better if she were mocking our people, but to her, we were a sad and pitiable race. "And in six years, none of you will even be able to afford to live here."

Gamble saw how that screwed my face up. "Something really big is coming down the pipeline in the next few weeks, and Darius had a share in it before he got greedy. If you're smarter than him, that share can be yours."

That really screwed my face up. Doc might have been cool

working with the police, but not me. Even this relationship had my toes closer to the line than I was comfortable with.

"You've got less than a day to figure this out, or I can promise you'll be brought up on multiple murder charges." She saw the sour face I made at the word *multiple*. "I'll connect you to the strip club. Plus, we have a few open homicides we need to get off the books."

Gamble talked like she didn't get that I had no plans on going back to prison. If it came down to that, court was being held in the street, pistols and assault rifles my only representation.

Ninety percent of communication is nonverbal. I let her see that in my face.

"Like I said before, it's easier to not care when it's just you." She glanced to the car, where the family waited on me, wearing their nervousness like Halloween masks. "Collateral damage is a bitch. You're already the reason why a little six-year-old girl is on the way to Detroit Receiving with a fifty-fifty shot at pulling through.

"Dirty Red didn't kill Darius, so squash this shit so each of you can focus on your respective tasks." She turned and headed back to her Camaro like she was giving me an order and there was nothing else to discuss.

The Joy Road Boys had just racked up a whole new bill for what happened here tonight.

During my entire exchange with Gamble, the dude rocking the buzz cut had just stood there like a portrait of fake intimidation. When he finally turned to follow her, he gave me a pat on the shoulder that wasn't meant to be friendly.

It was a hard clap right on my wound. I knew it wasn't coincidence. Those white spots exploded upon my field of vision, and the pain almost buckled my knees.

Chapter Fifty-seven

I could tell Mrs. P was pissed at me for having to leave home, even more so for the reason and the consequence. I expected to get cursed out about all of this soon. She probably just didn't want to do it in front of the kids.

I took the Davidson Freeway back east. When I parked on that short residential block in front of the brick split-level, Mrs. P signed to ask where were we. I silently cursed Doc, then hit her with the *one-minute* finger.

It was a quarter to six when I knocked on the door. The motion sensor activated the porch light, but every window was a slate of darkened glass. I assumed I pounded hard enough to rouse the sleepers. My last barrage went on for a full minute, hammering with the bottom of my fist.

I was just about to unlock that door with my boot when lights in the dining room began to glow. I peeped two shadows under the doorway that represented feet. They were too nervous to open the door, which told me they knew who was on the other side. I was probably spied through a window or a doorbell camera. I pounded again and punctuated that with a sharp kick.

Darnia's man finally answered. The door parted about two

inches, then was checked by a security chain. He stared at me through the gap. I glared at the chain, then him, gave him a *Bitch please!* look.

The skinny loser nodded, then fully opened the door. He was shirtless and barefoot, only in a pair of faded gray sweatpants.

I saw the small .32-caliber he had tucked by his leg. I gave him another *Bitch please!* look. He handed that over with the solemn face of a kid caught playing with daddy's lighter.

We both turned to Darnia, who stood about twelve feet away in the dining room wearing a long gray top that matched his sweats. I guess she expected her man to handle my intrusion. She called him a hoe-ass nigga, then asked me what the fuck I wanted.

When I told her, she didn't seem to get the point right away. I hadn't misspelled a single word on my iPhone. and nothing in my face suggested I was joking.

"The fuck you mean I gotta go?!" I could tell by Darnia's expression she screamed this. "This my shit! I pay bills in this muthafucka!" Barely. My dude bought the house, and she only started paying the bills after he died. And was struggling to do that.

I didn't bother explaining that Doc's mother needed a place to kick back, and it was going to be there. I just made it clear that she had to find somebody to stay with for a while.

That didn't go over well. I didn't expect it to. Darnia basically acted an ass.

I tried to channel Doc and called myself running game the way my voice would've done.

I explained to Darnia that for her own safety, she needed to relocate, just for a short time. I made it seem like some of the drama surrounding Doc was about to blow back on her—which wasn't totally a lie. I emphasized that I was looking out for her.

But I couldn't do with texts what Doc could do with slick talk and hazel eyes. Darnia was hesitant and too damn inquisitive. She wanted to know so many whats and whys that she burned through my teaspoon's worth of patience. I was mentally and physically drained, had more aches than I could count, and let's not forget was also shot and still bleeding. I wasn't in the mood or condition to be smooth about this. I resorted back to doing shit my own way.

A box of knock-off brand heavy-duty garbage bags stood on the kitchen counter. I snatched two off the roll, dropped them at their feet, then told Darnia her options: a) she and her man could walk out the front door carrying a few outfits in them, or b) get dragged out the back door stuffed in those bags.

I watched from the bedroom doorway while they dressed and packed. The whole time, the couple kept throwing glances at me, as if waiting for me to reveal this was a prank. I told Darnia she only needed a few days' worth of clothes, insisted it was temporary.

I walked them out to the Escalade thinking how lucky the bitch was that I let her keep the truck. I gave my customary warning of what would happen if the police came knocking.

As soon as they bent the corner, I waved in Mrs. P, Trayvion, and the kids from the car.

The old head in the Buick wasn't the first person I'd carjacked. There had been several times when I'd gotten jammed up and needed wheels in a hurry. For me, the gun was a lot quicker than breaking into the steering column.

But tonight was a first for me. I'd never house-jacked anybody before.

Chapter Fifty-eight

Between the refrigerator and cabinets, there was more than enough food. Between the four bedrooms and the den, there was more than enough places for everybody to sleep.

The kids were still shaken up and apprehensive in the new environment. I thanked the ancestors for Trayvion, who helped the vibe by pretending that this was a game: being awakened by the sound of gunshots, sirens, and screams; the car ride in the early morning; coming to this strange new house was all a part of the adventure. He pulled them into the fantasy, cheered them up when one of their moods began to darken and it was clear they were worried about Nika. He guaranteed she would be okay, and his blinding optimism fed their faith. And mine.

The little ones adjusted quickly the way kids do. Once Trayvion cut on the PlayStation connected to that giant TV in the family room, everybody under ten was happily distracted.

Mrs. P wasn't so easily placated. She had what felt like a thousand questions. I told her this was Doc's house, told her she and the kids would be straight there for the time being. I told her that during the day, I would swing by Monica and grab whatever else she needed from home.

Upstairs and out of sight of everyone, we had a heated and animated conversation with our hands, but still not the one she probably wanted to have. I'd been stupid and reckless. Back in the day when me and her natural son were neck-deep in beef, we had never allowed drama to blow back on the house. As big a slimeball as Doc eventually became, Mrs. P had still been insulated from his choices. The old lady just wanted to die peacefully in her own home surrounded by laughter and life; I hadn't been back three days and already fucked that up for her. She didn't say any of this with her mouth or hands, but I saw it in her disappointed eyes and knew the words waited just behind her closed lips.

Mrs. P looked the type of tired that ran deep down to the spirit. The old woman had puffy dark bags rimming her eyes; her sagging skin seemed ready to slough off her bones. A stocking cap covered the few patches of silvery hair that hadn't been eradicated by chemo. Even while shriveled by cancer, she had the nerve to tell me that I looked like shit.

I imagined I did after the day I'd had. I felt dead on my feet and light in my head, but I still had business. Mrs. P could tell by my manner I was in a rush to be out.

I tried to put her up in Darnia's room, but she wasn't with sleeping on a strange bed, even after I offered to flip the mattress and change the sheets. She agreed to be settled on the living room couch. I fetched her a pillow and a clean blanket.

I used the mirror in the master bathroom to confirm that I looked as bad as she said. The bullet that grazed me outside the locker room left a horizontal scar going across my cheek that parted my beard. That needed a trim; I also needed a cut and lineup. My eyes were sporting dark circles and were yellowed from the weed as much as the lack of sleep. I already looked five years older than the crispy version who had tried to stunt on T'wanda.

My legs weakened and threatened to become unhinged. I

swayed a bit and had to lean against the sink. I blinked out the white spots that zigzagged across my vision like fireflies.

I peeled off the T-shirt and dressing Lexy provided, both sticky wet with blood and sweat. I twisted to inspect the bullet hole in my shoulder. Centering the field of bruised, purple skin was an ugly puckered ringlet crusted in dark crimson paste that ran down my back and stained my boxers. The slug was still in me, and I had no way to know how close it was to something vital or if it might travel.

By virtue of practice, Detroit Receiving Hospital has one of the best trauma centers in America when it comes to treating gunshot victims—it was in these very capable hands that little Nika's life then resided. The problem for me was that anyone coming in with a gunshot wound would be held for police interrogation.

Darnia didn't have anything close to a first aid kit, but a search of her bathroom turned up some useful personal items. I covered the wound with a sanitary napkin designed for heavy flows, then secured it to my shoulder with packing tape.

I exited the bathroom, headed down the hall toward a short flight of five stairs that led to the kitchen, when those white spots started fucking with me again. They swarmed my field of vision. I couldn't blink them away this time. The fireflies multiplied until white was all I saw.

I never remembered making it to the bottom of the stairs. Was told later that I did reach the kitchen, but flat on my face.

Chapter Fifty-nine

Consciousness came back to me slowly, in stages. I vaguely remembered a blackness that could have been the daughter to actual Death. This wasn't a cold void, something to inspire thoughts of vast emptiness. What I felt was warm and velveteen—as hard to break away from as a side-piece begging you to stay the whole night out from Wifey.

I was facedown, head hanging halfway off of someone's full-sized bed. I realized I was connected to an IV; the line coiled my arm and crossed my body. The stand was next to my bed, something I'd only seen in hospitals. The thin metal crossbar hung two plastic bags of clear fluid. The fluid came to me in the slow monotonous drip of leaky faucet, and I'd already drained one whole bag and was a quarter of the way through a second.

Right then, I had to piss so bad that I couldn't be bothered with the obvious questions. I staggered into the hall, dragging behind me the IV stand that I had forgotten about that quickly.

My memory was also feeding me on a slow drip. Darnia's house: I had brought Mrs. P and the kids there. I was standing in the upstairs hallway in my dingy black sweats, no shirt.

In the bathroom, I pissed for so long that I had time to stare out the window at an afternoon sky and wonder how long I'd been out. My legs became tired, had to press a hand against the wall to steady myself. By the time I was done, I could've refilled Lake Michigan.

I flushed, turned, and saw Quianna watching me through the open doorway. She was dressed in a tan and black Fendi top that covered her torso in a print of forward and backwards Fs. Underneath the sweater, she wore black denim.

Her face was unreadable. The last time I'd seen her at the hotel, she had been furious with me. She had more of a reason to be then.

"I would've brought you something to pee in. You shouldn't be up yet." Her eyes scanned me, unblinking. "Heard you dropped like a tree—wish I would've been here to see that shit. It was a bitch getting your heavy ass back up the stairs."

I turned my shoulder to the mirror and saw fresh dressing, not the packing tape and maxi-pad. These were real medical supplies. Better than what Lexy used and not so sloppily done.

"Lucky I had my girl with me when Momma called. Damn near lost her job for you."

Part of me was still in that black place, so I barely recognized the Afro-Asian who stood behind Quianna in burgundy hospital scrubs. Chun Li. Still fine as fuck in a ponytail with no makeup. An ID badge clipped to her shirt read: LATRISHA SOMMERS, LPN.

The ladies helped me back to the spare bedroom that had been my recovery ward, as well as the OR where my triage had been performed. Apparently while I was out, Chun Li stole surgical supplies from Sinai Grace, dug the bullet out of my shoulder, and gave me a transfusion after running a test to determine my blood type—something I'd never known. Once I was refueled with four pints of AB negative, she had started me on a solution that was pure saline mixed with electrolytes to replenish my fluids. The fourth of these one-thousand-cc bags was being dripped into my arm, which explained why my bladder already felt full again.

I consulted the Rolex to learn that I had burned up eleven of the twenty-four hours I had left. I stood to get dressed and asked Chun Li to remove the IV, but she refused. Quianna showed me how weak I was with one small push. I flopped down hard on the bed.

I wasn't in so much pain, because Chun Li had also stolen me something from the hospital pharmacy: a bottle of thirty-milligram Percocet. I offered my thanks for everything with a hug, but she claimed this only made us even.

Thinking back on the bachelor party, I texted to ask if I could call her the Head Nurse. I thought that was funny, but she and Quianna just rolled their eyes like I was corny as hell.

Chun Li left; then Mrs. P, Trayvion, and a few of the kids all stopped by to check on me after word spread that I was awake. There was relief for me, but I also detected a different energy that was subtle and sad. The family had conspired not to tell me, but I was able to guess before they broke down to confirm it.

It was bad news concerning Nika. The large-caliber bullet that punched through the wall at Mrs. P's had punched through her tiny body, destroying a portion of her large intestine. Surgeons had labored for six intense hours to repair the damage, but during post-op, Nika had slipped into a coma. Her doctors weren't optimistic.

Little Nika with the afro puffs, who one day before had happily swung from the end of my arm making me fantasize about alternate possibilities. And I couldn't avenge this, because I was too much of a coward to kill the person responsible.

I couldn't put the pistol to my own head.

Chapter Sixty

I was ready to swim forever in those warm endless oceans of that Other Place, but my strange lover wouldn't commit to me, wasn't ready to introduce me to her father.

As much as I hoped I wouldn't, I woke up to shadows claiming the borrowed room. Through the windows, deep violet skies hovered over the darkened silhouette of the neighbor's pitched roof.

My final saline bag hung deflated on the stand, so I disconnected myself from the IV. In the bathroom, I took another one of those long pisses that made you contemplate the capacity of the human bladder. I felt better than I had in a while.

At least physically.

I hadn't faced the fam since learning about Nika. In the past seventy-two hours, I had stared down more guns and dodged more bullets than most people will in a lifetime. It still took more courage to walk down that short flight of five stairs to the main floor.

Mrs. P was in the kitchen pouring spaghetti noodles into a large pot producing a violent boil and column of steam. The kids were still in that sunken den perched cross-legged in front of that wall-sized television arguing over the video game.

I had hoped to slip out unseen, but Mrs. P spotted me creeping to the front door. She beckoned me from the stove.

"This Darnia bitch don't know how to keep no kitchen. I can't find shit in this disorganized muthafucka." She ordered me to check the cabinets for garlic salt. I located garlic powder, not salt, on a shelf above the sink. It must have been close enough, because Mrs. P added a generous dusting to five pounds of ground beef that fried in a blackened pan.

I figured it was finally time for us to have that conversation. The old woman looked in my eyes and saw everything I wished I had the words for, then sent me into the refrigerator for a bell pepper. After cursing me out for not dicing the pieces small enough, she made me stir a simmering pot of sauce to keep it from sticking.

"Kids ain't ate nothing all day. Gone be hungry as Iranian hostages when they finally tear they asses away from that game."

I couldn't say if her yelling at me wouldn't have been worse than the guilt I felt from her not bothering to. I only knew that in that moment I loved her more than I had ever loved anybody.

I was so deep in my own thoughts that I don't remember when I stopped playing prep cook and drifted into a seat at the dining room table.

With so much happening so fast, I nearly forgot about what I had stashed in my pocket. I pulled the wallet, opened it on Detective Bates's badge and ID. He hadn't notice that I picked his pocket when I had him facedown on the car.

For a nigga with big hands, mine had a light touch. That had allowed my fingers to run across something else Bates carried. Another ingredient just got tossed into this weird gumbo. I was still trying to figure out a way to capitalize on this new information when Mrs. P joined me at the table.

"Boy, you need to quit pumping quarters into that ass-kicking machine." She assumed from my expression that I was sitting there still beating myself up over Nika. Part of me was.

I didn't feel like revisiting that right then. I asked about Quianna and Trayvion's absence only to change the subject.

"You know that girl dropped everything the second she heard you was hurt. Brought her nurse friend over here and sat with your ass the whole time. Even now, her and Tray done ran back to the house to get you some clothes."

I signed to let Mrs. P know how much I appreciated Quianna, but also my surprise that she was going so far out of her way for me.

"Boy, if you had a bigger head, you'd be a bigger damn fool."

I knew what she was hinting at and shook my big head. I'd already made that mistake. Told her about how I embarrassed myself at the MGM Grand.

"The fuck you expect?" The old woman looked at me like I was clueless. "Rejection hurts. When you wound a woman's pride, she gone do what she can to save face. You really think she meant that shit she said, drunk and in her feelings?"

It had been enough to convince me, and I'm basically a human lie detector.

Mrs. P pursed her thin lips. "Do you think she'd be doing all this shit if you was just another one of Darius's friends? Think if Louie Boy had went away when she was twelve, she would've cried herself to sleep every night for six months? Think she would've went out and got a job at sixteen just to help keep some money on Prime's books?"

I was speechless, figuratively as much as literally.

Mrs. P confirmed it with a slow nod. "During that first year or so Darius sent you money, probably felt he owed you that much. When I saw his interest in you start to drop off, I covered you for a few years by sending what I could, only it got tight after I stopped working and ain't have shit but my disability check.

"For the past eight years, every penny you got in there came from that girl. Still thinking it was just cause she felt sorry for you?"

Whenever I got those JPay deposit receipts under the name of D. Peterson, I had assumed it was Darius, as in Doc. I never put this together, because the old lady was known as "Mrs. P" even to her friends close to the same age. Being so seldom used, it was easy to forget her government name was Dolores.

The comment at the steakhouse about life happening suddenly made sense. Quianna had started dancing to support me, and I really didn't know how to feel about that.

"That girl been in love with you since before she was old enough to understand what love is—hell, I knew it before she did. When Darius first started bringing you around, I still remember how her face used to light up. Shit, she turned cartwheels all through the house when she found out you was coming to live with us. I thought it was just puppy love.

"Why you think she ain't got a bunch of babies or a thousand niggas pulling up to the house? Cause she been waiting on you, dummy!"

Honesty has a way of being contagious. I admitted to the conflict I felt about Quianna.

"I don't see no conflict. Eight years is a case when it's between nine and seventeen or twelve and twenty. Eight years don't mean shit at twenty-four and thirty-two. Y'all both legal."

I explained that it was more than just the age difference. The Petersons had welcomed me into their home, accepted me into their family. I signed to Mrs. P that it felt like a betrayal.

"Betrayal?" The old woman threw her head back for a deep laugh that made her shoulders jump. "You only betraying yourself. You should've been whooping that bitch the first night you got home. It ain't just hazel eyes that run in the family—good pussy, too."

I cringed. Mrs. P loved to fuck with me by making shit weird.

She shifted in her seat, as well as in her demeanor, to reflect a more serious tone. "You my son as much as Darius, and Quianna is my daughter. But don't it twisted, this ain't no *Game of Thrones* shit—y'all muthafuckas ain't brother and sister. Lutalo from the tribe of Shango, don't fuck around and miss what you looking for just cause it's too close to your face."

She shuffled back to the stove on stockinged feet, swallowed by and dragging her oversized nightgown across the floor like some wizard. Wise and powerful.

I needed a moment. I was already a soaked sponge trying to absorb more water.

Soon the smell of ground beef, onions, and tomato sauce became too much to ignore. My stomach was running on about twenty hours empty, and she let me know the spaghetti was done.

I used my hands to ask: "Isn't Quianna going to be upset with you for telling me all of this? Both of us. Either she didn't want me to know or wanted me to figure it out on my own."

Mrs. P waved me off. "Shit, nigga, I'm dying—she cain't be mad at me for too long. You, that's another story."

Chapter Sixty-one

It was no knock on Mrs. P's cooking to say that the spaghetti made no impression on me. I sucked down saucy noodles and ground beef without really tasting it. I didn't eat, just refueled. Shoveled myself with forkfuls like a worker feeding coal to a steam engine. I scraped a full plate and a second helping in under ten minutes.

I sensed before seeing the car pulling up out front. When multiple doors opened on an unfamiliar minivan, paranoia had me reaching for my gun.

My hand went from Louie's Casull back to my fork when I saw one of Trayvion's friends slamming the driver's door. He came up the walk with the other two youngsters I'd seen in the rap cipher at Mrs. P's dining room table.

I didn't mind the half dozen kids who were already there, but we were supposed to be low-key. Trayvion had obviously invited his friends to pull up. I was thinking me and my godson was going to have to talk whenever he and Quianna got back.

The minivan's rear sliding door opened to reveal someone I had hoped to avoid. It hadn't felt right to just keep calling her Big

Girl after what happened, so while bringing Mrs. P and the kids east, I had learned that she was known as Pooh.

Pooh came up the driveway being aided by a girlfriend on whom she leaned heavily. She was dressed in the same clothes worn when she climbed in the back of the ambulance. The friend had needed to guide Pooh to the house because she kept a hand shielding her eyes the entire way, as if refusing to gaze upon a world cruel enough to threaten her baby.

The spaghetti suddenly received no more of my interest. I dropped my fork onto the plate and readied myself.

Still aided by her friend, Pooh came through the door looking broken and disheveled. Half of her head was in a short afro; I imagined that while Nika had surgery, Pooh had nervously started undoing the pencil-thin braids during the torturous wait. Her pendulous breasts swung free under a T-shirt stained with her daughter's blood.

She removed the hand from her face to reveal eyes like wounds: beet-red and circled by puffy dark flesh. Her plump cheeks were still marked with the dried streaks of salty tears.

When Pooh looked upon me, her face contorted from shock to something that looked like disgust and finally to rage. I stood so she could get a good look at all six-foot-five of me. I met her eyes, but there was no challenge in mine. Just a quiet acceptance of what I knew was coming next.

I wasn't the only one who knew. Trayvion's friend had read Pooh's reaction to me and tried to block her path. But he was maybe one hundred and sixty-five pounds in the way of two-twenty charging with a full head of steam. He got knocked aside like a rodeo clown.

She came into me with enough force to send me two steps backwards. Pooh started swinging on me, windmill style. I offered no offense or defense. I was hit three times in the chest and once in the face before somebody grabbed her arms. I deserved that and more. None of it hurt as much as both of us wished it could. It took a group effort to pull her off of me.

I made a silent promise that I was going to make this right somehow, even though I had no power to heal wounds or possibly raise the dead. Pooh clearly didn't care about my apology, because she came at me again but was held in check.

She spat when she couldn't get to me. I jumped back as a sticky wad landed on my shirt.

I normally don't play getting spit on by nobody but gave her a rare pass. I just got myself out of there before me and that bitch fought for real.

I had left the stolen New Yorker parked on the street. I popped the trunk to look in on my children. The Benelli and the Herstal were still swaddled in the baby blanket.

Back inside the house, I took the stairs in two strides and searched the master bedroom. I was hoping Darnia had at least held onto some of Doc's old paperwork. It didn't take five minutes to find what I was looking for. A Nike shoebox high on the closet shelf was stuffed with important-looking documents in the name of Darius Peterson. I took the box.

I jumped in the New Yorker, bent a corner, then another. I didn't know where I was going to lay my head that night but knew I had to put some distance between me and the family. Everywhere I went, Death seemed to be walking right on my heels, a shadow cast by a low-hanging sun. Since the fam was on the eastside, I made my way deep west. Telegraph Road was the boundary line for that end of the city.

It was early evening when I cruised the strip lined with used car lots, fast food joints, and a shitload of cheap motels. I had to visit four before I found one that met my requirements: accepted cash, no ID, and parking that couldn't be seen from the street.

My second-floor room was surprisingly clean, a fifteen-by-twelve-foot space dominated by a king bed not laced with bedbugs and cum stains. I had a television, a chest of drawers, and an old recliner from the seventies. A small half-bath was attached where I could shower.

I brought the guns in from the car and stashed them where

some nosy-ass motel manager wouldn't stumble across them. In low-budget spots like this, the rooms typically got robbed by the same person you paid for the keys.

I didn't need to hide the guns well, because they were about to get put to use very soon. I checked the cylinder in the .454, only had three rounds, and these would probably get put to use even sooner.

I was ready to settle this shit with Gamble and the Joy Road Boys, but I had to pull back up on somebody else first. It was an itch I just had to scratch.

Chapter Sixty-two

It only required a short drive down southbound Telegraph Road followed by a left on Fenkell Avenue to bring me back to Brightmoor. I knew this hood was grimy after dark but felt that anything out on the prowl in those desolate streets needed to be more afraid of me.

I still kept alert as I sat two empty fields away from T'wanda's house in the darkened New Yorker. I needed about ten minutes to properly arrange my thoughts and to script our conversation. Some of what I was about to propose seemed crazy, even to me.

When T'wanda answered the side door, I saw more fear on her face than the last time. The same scarf I smacked off her head covered the same braids sprouting an overgrowth of new hair.

She stared at me though the bars of her security door while I waited to be invited inside. This had nothing to do with her brother Prime; she seemed to know that. She also had known this visit was coming sooner or later.

T'wanda told me that Ja'Quezz wasn't home. She had been my woman once, so she was able to tell by my expression this was something I already knew. I don't believe in repeating previous mistakes. This time I'd sat in the car and watched the movements at her windows long enough to be certain she was alone.

T'wanda unlocked the security bars with a quiet resignation. She led me inside and again seated me at the wobbly card table in the kitchen.

I didn't think it necessary to waste either of our time. I loaded my phone and went in headfirst: *You and Doc fuckin the whole time we together?*

She looked from the screen back to my eyes without blinking. An ashtray on the table between us was filled with a different kind of roach that scrambled across her cracked and greasy walls. She fingered through it until she found a thin blunt in a tan leaf that had about half an inch remaining. She perched it between blackened lips, then added fire.

"Before. During. After." She finally said in response to my question. "While you was staying with them on Monica. When we had the apartment in Southfield. A little more after you went away." There was nothing in her eyes to suggest she was trying to rub this in to be hurtful. She seemed emotionless. It was honesty, brutal by nature but delivered without spite.

I leaned back in my chair, remembered the coaching I gave myself in the car. I refused to get in my feelings like last time. I took slow breaths to keep myself composed while I asked what type of slut bag would fuck on two homeboys at the same time.

She admitted without any trace of apology that she had been sleeping with Doc since she was thirteen, and had only started sleeping with me because he paid her to. T'wanda exhaled sharply after saying this, as if it had weighed on her for a long time.

"He knew you liked me. Both of us did. I saw the way your eyes used to follow me whenever I came around." She sucked another puff off the micro-blunt. "You was big and most of the girls thought you was—" Scary. Dumb. Weird. My mind supplied those adjectives when she faltered.

I was shy and awkward and had nursed a crush on Prime's

fine-ass sister just like half the men on Detroit's westside. Then one day, out the clear blue, she approached me. I had never thought she knew even I existed before then.

T'wanda swore that she only got paid the first couple of times. She claimed that real feelings for me had developed, and she stopped taking Doc's money.

But not his dick! She rolled her eyes after reading that on my phone.

I was back on sucker shit. I wanted to know every detail of how the only woman I ever loved and my best friend had humiliated me. I even asked the questions that I knew I shouldn't have, rush and rage causing me to misspell: *How mny times you let me eat you rght after y'all fucked? How many kisses did I get with Doc's dick on yo' breath?*

But T'wanda wouldn't feed into it. "You only wanna know so you can make this easier." She gazed at me with the professional detachment of a therapist. "You need to believe that we took pleasure in hurting you. That we was slapping high fives and laughing behind your back."

She took the final two puffs, butted a tail so short that it melted her fingernails. "I'm not giving you the gas for your little revenge fantasy. Plus not knowing is going to hurt worse. It'll never be as bad as you make it in your head."

At some point while listening to her, I totally forgot about my breathing. My hands curled into fists without my permission.

"I was a bigger slut than you'll probably ever know. But still not a killer like you."

I proved her wrong with my very next message: *That second year. The miscarriage?*

That shot the bitch down off her high horse. Her eyes shied away from mine when her lips formed the word *Abortion.*

I figured that had been Doc's, just like Ja'Quezz. This was the real reason she had wanted the boy to stay hidden during my first visit. I had thought Ja'Quezz might belong to the dude I killed, but while he hadn't inherited the hazel eyes, I recognized other

Peterson features, namely those thick eyebrows. He wore his father around the nose and eyes, just like Trayvion did.

T'wanda claimed that both pregnancies had been a coin flip between me and Doc, and she had gotten rid of the first because she didn't want to take the chance.

"Doc wanted me to get rid of this one, too—even gave me the money. But." She claimed she couldn't bring herself to terminate another child. She'd had her first one yanked at thirteen, and Ja'Quezz would've made three. T'wanda said she'd known girls who'd had multiple abortions, and it affected their ability to carry to term when they were finally ready.

"He was scared, Sy. We both was." Her eyes found mine again. It was the first time I saw genuine emotion. "We didn't know what you would do if my baby came out looking like him."

I typed something quick, then held up my phone again. T'wanda shook her head. "Doc didn't know 'bout me and Jayson." Might sound cold but I'd totally forgotten dude's name from the first floor, even though I blew his brains out and did twelve years for it.

On that day, I was halfway back to the city when I got the message from Doc telling me to shoot back to the apartment for the digital scale.

It took of a lot of typing to explain my theory to T'wanda. She took it all off my screen with a skeptical frown, then tried to poke holes in it. "How could Doc know when me and Jayson was doing something? He wasn't psychic."

I rebutted that it made perfect sense if Doc put dude on her the same way he put T'wanda on me. To me it wasn't that far-fetched. Doc pays this Jayson to start fucking my girl, then sets it up for me to catch them. I tried to make her understand that Doc knew that I was a naïve, tender-dick with an unnatural talent for violence. His intent most likely had been that I'd kill T'wanda and her side-dude in a jealous rage, totally solving Doc's problem for him: no T'wanda, no Jayson, no baby. And me upstate doing triple-Life.

T'wanda couldn't accept this, because it would mean she had been played by both of her lovers. I made no effort to convince her. Believing me or not didn't change how this was going to play out.

When I asked her what happened at the time of my trial, I saw something flash across her face. I peeped some slight weakening of her resolve that made my accusations at least plausible.

"I wasn't lying when I said the prosecutor was pressing me to testify against you." T'wanda's tired, yellow eyes shifted from me, and I followed them to some hole in her wall.

She finally confessed, "I went to Doc and asked him what I should do."

And if I had a voice, I would've broke in to finish for her. He told her to testify. Probably even paid the bitch again.

Chapter Sixty-three

I moved the car up the block to the corner, in front the vine-covered ruins of what had been a pet store back in the day. Ten minutes after ten glowed dimly on the digital dash clock, and I sat draped in darkness again, avoiding the head or interior lights. I waited for the telltale signs that it was okay to pull off, pondering the difference between Possibility and Plausibility.

By the time I was seven years old (before I lost what remained of my hearing), my father had me, along with everyone else on the compound, thoroughly convinced that the UOTA's need to raise its own cattle and crops was not primarily due to our self-sufficiency as a sovereign nation, or any of the economic benefits. Our elder chief preached with absolute certainty that fast-food restaurants in the ghetto poisoned our people with additives designed to keep black folks overdeveloped physically while mentally stunted. He claimed that the White Man required speedsters and high fly-ers to support its multi-billion-dollar sports complexes; however, required the niggas too stupid to ever use their millions to orga-nize and buck the system. According to dad this also explained why our fifteen-year-old girls already had bigger titties than their mothers, had dropped out in the seventh grade with their second bun in the oven. Once I left the church, I realized that his theory about fast food was at least possible, but not plausible enough to keep me from fucking over a Whopper with cheese.

The rest of my conversation with T'wanda was her insisting that I was prone to the same wild conspiracy theories as my old dude. She agreed it was possible that Doc had set it up so that I would catch her cheating, even conceded the possibility that Doc had hired her lover. But to T'wanda, the whole thing was implausible. Jayson was just a guy in the same building who talked her out the pussy. The phone call that sent me back to the apartment, pure coincidence.

As far as my suspicions that Doc's plan was for her to die along with her lover, she wouldn't even entertain the possibility.

She swore that Doc never paid her to take the stand against me. In T'wanda's words, he had simply advised that she look out for her own best interest and that of the unborn Ja'Quezz.

T'wanda confessed that her last conversation with Doc had happened six weeks before he died. He had bragged about having friends in high places and gassed her with promises that she and their son would soon be set for life. According to her, Doc spoke like somebody who knew he had the winning numbers to the lottery's Mega Millions jackpot. But like everybody else, she was a dry well when I tried to pump her for details.

It was clear from her responses that T'wanda still loved him, and it was more than she had ever loved me. Doc hadn't been fucking my woman—I had been fucking his. She had just been on loan to me the same way Quianna had lent me Lexy.

It eventually became time for us to reach that unspoken but mutually understood conclusion. I offered T'wanda the courtesy of doing this somewhere else. The last thing I wanted was for Ja'Quezz to come home and be traumatized by an unpleasant scene.

T'wanda countered that if she just disappeared, he would be more traumatized by the possibility that his mother had abandoned him. I couldn't argue with that.

T'wanda showcased more courage and grace in her final moments than I thought her capable of. No crying, no begging, didn't even curse at me. She only asked not to suffer long, and I obliged. She also asked me to stay away from her son, which I also promised. The only comment she made even close to condemnation was her saying that even before the incident at our apartment, she always knew that I would kill her one day.

It was the last thing she said. I rose from my seat and stood behind hers. She didn't fight or claw at my arms as they slid around her neck. I snapped it quick and clean. True to my word.

I could've done it for cheating on me and having another man's baby. I could've done it for helping to send me away. Like she was prone to remind me, I am a killer. T'wanda knew the penalty for breaking a killer's heart.

I had lain her body gently across the sofa in the living room, then went back to the New Yorker for the gas can I filled up before I arrived.

That was seven minutes earlier. I remained parked on the corner, turned in my seat and staring through the car's rear window at her stripped-down home.

It took longer than I expected before waving arms of orange-yellow light grabbed hold of those flammable rayon curtains. Heat imploded the glass, feeding oxygen to multiply the creature's size and appetite as it scrambled up the exterior to the roof. Only then did I drive away, thinking that the charred ruins of another house would hardly be noticed in Brightmoor.

Chapter Sixty-four

I had spent twelve years fantasizing about that moment. I didn't know why I thought it would be as gratifying as it had been those hundreds of times in my head. Nothing ever is. Killing T'wanda felt no different from any other life I'd taken in the name of self-preservation, profit, or honor.

It was only once I was back at the room with no welcomed distractions that I began to fully absorb the implications. It was looking like a person I had killed for, would have honestly died for, had conspired to get me out the way. What Darnia said in the Escalade made sense. Of course Doc hadn't been looking forward to me coming home. Not with T'wanda's thirteen-year-old boy walking around with his face and eyebrows.

I always knew Doc was capable of fucking over other people. But never me. Not possible or plausible.

Soon my fifteen-by-twelve-foot room with king bed and fake walnut furniture felt too cramped for me and my growing rage. The need for fresh air drew me outside into the crisp night, but a spinning sign glowing in the distance beckoned me further. A convenience store two hundred yards away promised liquor, cigarettes, and snacks. I was craving two of the three to take my mind off the bullshit.

I walked across six lanes of street traffic separated by a grassy center island sprouting dandelions. At the liquor store, I chose a fifth of cranberry Ciroc, Twinkies, and Skittles in honor of little Nika.

I returned to the room, lined my stomach with sponge cakes before I started in on the vodka. I wasn't trying to get fucked up, since I still had business on Cascade, just needed to be a little out of my right mind. I was a third deep into the bottle when somebody beat on my door.

Of course I can't hear when someone's knocking, but in certain situations I can feel it. Vibrations. Subtle ones that go undetected by those of you who have spent a lifetime spoiled by your ears. In a small space when I'm standing close to the door, I can feel sound crawl over my skin like ants, and use my own unique form of sonar to trace the source back to the entrance. From there my eyes were able to detect the slight rattle of my door in the jamb, the jingle of the chain lock. These visual cues were enough to inform me that somebody was outside my room, banging on my shit hard and aggressive.

Like the police.

All I could think was that somebody saw me torch the house and then reported me. It had to be that. Nobody knew I was here.

I still had three shells left in the .454 since I hadn't needed to spend one on T'wanda. I crept to the door on my toes. The big revolver raised and ready.

Chapter Sixty-five

My uninvited guest knocked with a fury that signaled losing patience. I gently lifted the chain lock out of the groove, then turned the switch to retract the bolt so slowly that I hoped the click wasn't heard.

Again, surprise was my only advantage. I yanked the door open, brought my gun through in the same motion. Ready to blast at the first glimpse of a police badge or red shirt.

Staring down the wide bore of a .454 definitely surprised Quianna. Her eyes snapped into circles showing white all around her hazel irises.

I must've been wearing an identical mask of shock. I don't know how long we stood there like that before she had to push the gun out of her face and bully her way inside when I failed to extend the invitation.

By the time I closed the door and turned around, Quianna was already well into cursing me out. I came in late and wasn't really paying attention. I did get: "The fuck is you doin' way out here?" and "How you gone leave before I got back?" She had a complaint about my cheap-ass room.

I took another long swig of Ciroc. She finally stopped bitching and registered concern when she picked up on something deeper than just my general disinterest.

She mouthed, "I heard about you and Pooh. Don't trip. You know she just fucked-up right now about Nika." It was one of the few times Quianna misread me. Normally she would be able to gauge by my dark eyes and equally dark mood I was dealing with some shit that made the little altercation seem like a firecracker to a grenade.

I typed: *How you know where I'm at?* then felt stupid when I realized that I was literally holding the answer to my own question. I glanced at my phone then back to her with a sour look. Quianna wore the guilty smirk a woman puts on when she knows she's busted and has no comeback. I tossed the phone onto the bed next to where she dropped off her Birkin bag.

I glanced out the window and saw the metallic blue Aston Martin parked two slots away from the burgundy Chrysler. I just folded my arms, asked with my eyes why would she come here driving that hot-ass rental.

She asked me the same question but used her lips. She was saying I should've stayed at the house to protect Mrs. P and the kids.

Protecting the family was the reason I was clear on the other side of town. And the reason she needed to go. I nodded towards the door.

She crossed her arms, mirrored my stance.

"The fuck you doin' at Lexy's house four in the morning, nigga? Y'all crept and fucked behind my back. Bitch got your nose open just like triflin' ass T'wanda used to."

That skinned my lips back from my teeth. It was the wrong time to hit me with that one.

I was through being played for stupid in these streets, by Doc, by Gamble, and especially by Quianna. She didn't think I would be slick enough to figure out that her sneaky ass only bought me

SILENCE • 267

the iPhone to keep tabs on me and probably had the GPS installed right there in the store. Just like I wasn't supposed to know that the platinum Rolex she let me wear was the same one me and Chun Li almost got shot over at the bachelor party when she stole it.

I already had the truth and was done with her head games. I was still wearing the embarrassment from the MGM Grand when I had been right the entire time.

I closed the distance with a step and a half. While she was still in the middle of asking me some shit about Lexy, I just cupped her face and kissed her on the mouth to shut her up.

The surprise caused Quianna to stiffen for a beat; then she invited in my tongue. It was a sloppy kiss, longer and harder than it probably should've been. I palmed her body with huge eager hands. I broke our kiss just long enough to snatch Quianna's shirt over her head. Her small perky A-cups were in the satin confines of a lacy turquoise bra. I gave the left a quick tease with my right hand, just until I felt her nipple sharpened against my palm.

A black and gold Hermès belt matching her bag snaked the loops of skin-tight denim, and with two quick flicks I unfastened the belt and top button of the jeans. Quianna looked at me curious when I roughly snatched them down over the wide spread of her hips.

Under the pants was a thong that matched the bra. For a moment, I just took it all in. Quianna had a small waistline that made her curves seem that much more extreme. Large spiral curls draped one side of her face. A golden goddess with cat eyes. While my preference ran towards darker skin, Quianna was so gorgeous that sometimes I hated her for it. Part of me had wanted her to strip as bad as those fellas at the BANDS event.

When I snatched down the panties, Quianna covered her crotch with her hands. I gestured for her to move them. She had been trying to show me this shit since that day at the mall. I gave her a look that asked why in the fuck was she being shy now.

She obeyed but not before giving me a nervous eye roll like she was embarrassed. Her pussy was so fat, a pretty shaved peach. It had the tight youthful look of a vagina with low miles that hadn't spit its first child.

I grabbed her by a fistful of hair. I spun her around and bent her over the edge of the bed. I pushed my sweats down to my knees and freed my beast.

Chapter Sixty-six

I stood behind Quianna, enjoying that view of her bent over the bed with her hands pressed down into the mattress. The problem came trying to get up in her. Quianna was dry and super-tight, tight to the point I thought she was sealed. The inner gates were closed. Locked.

Quianna stared back at me with contradiction filling her eyes. There was a part of her that wanted this, but her body didn't respond to me because it was controlled by another part. This was the part that caused her to look at me like I was a stranger, some-one totally unfamiliar.

I rubbed my dick head all around her inner lips but she wouldn't lubricate for me. Impatience made the few minutes I spent trying feel like much longer. Eventually my beast started to soften and bend.

I gave up frustrated, just left her standing there while I flopped down in the chair. I didn't even bother to pull up my sweats when I turned up the Ciroc bottle.

Quianna sat on the bed for a moment facing the other way. Then she stood, back to me, yanked up the jeans and thong gath-ered around her ankles, then dove back into her shirt.

When she snatched her keys and bag off the bed, I glimpsed her profile. There were tears on her cheeks. I hiked up my sweats and blocked the door before she opened it.

I embraced her, wouldn't let her go when she tried to pull away. She drummed my chest with her fists then used them to cover her eyes. Her body shuddered from hard sobs.

I would've taken three more bullets to the back over the pain I felt in that moment. I leaned back on the door, banged my head against it a few times, feeling like a total piece of shit.

I didn't realize how drunk I had gotten or how hurt I was by Doc and T'wanda. But I couldn't blame it on alcohol or anger. There was no excuse for this.

I wanted, no needed, Quianna to see the apology in my eyes. She continued to weep into her hands and wouldn't let me pull them away from her face.

Right or wrong, I wasn't letting her leave like this. I scooped her up like a honeymooner, carried her back to the bed, eased her down. Quianna rolled away from me on her side and continued to cry. I climbed in bed with her. She still wouldn't face me but let me spoon with her. I rubbed the shaved side of her head, planted soft kisses on the stubble that said, *I'm sorry.*

This girl had spent half her life waiting on me, had hustled to hold me down when even my closest friends didn't send me a dollar. I repaid her patience and generosity by trying to slut her in a cheap motel because another chick had me in my feelings.

I felt my own tears burning in my eyes and no amount of effort kept them from falling.

Soon I was crying as hard as Quianna, and the reasons bled one into another. I cried because my mother didn't love me enough to stay in the church or enough to take me with her; I cried because my father didn't love me enough to save my hearing or come after me when I ran; I cried because Pooh was across town crying over love; I cried because even with all the slimy shit he'd done, I still loved Doc; I cried because even with all he slimy shit she'd done, I still loved T'wanda, and killing her had hurt more than I dared to admit; I cried because Ja'Quezz wasn't mine and I had just guaranteed he would never love me. Most of all, I cried because I would always be difficult to love.

I was so inundated by my own tears, I hadn't realized that Quianna's had stopped, and she was facing me. I buried my face while she made efforts to console me. Our roles reversed.

I eventually purged a lifetime of liquid pain, and we were finally able to look at each other at the same time. Lamplight reflected constellations in her moist bloodshot eyes, and I figured mine had to be the same deep shade of orange-red. Quianna was in tune with me again, so our eyes were the only vehicles necessary for conversation.

She explained how much it had hurt for me to treat her like that. Because of the stigma she'd labored under, because of niggas like Brody Starrz and what he'd done to her at the mall. I promised on all the names of God ever uttered that I would never disrespect her like that again.

I explained to her that I'd been fucked over by everybody I'd ever loved and could only respond by fucking over somebody who loved me. I opened those soul windows, let her read in me everything Mrs. P had told me at Darnia's kitchen table. Her secret was written there.

She tried to shy away again, embarrassed, but I turned her face back to mine.

It was time for my own confessions: that I'd wanted her from the moment I surprised her in Mrs. P kitchen, that all the Li'l Quay-Quay shit was just me trying to fight the feeling, that she was the only good thing in my life.

We shared our first real kiss—not my rough sucking on her tongue where I mistook rage for passion. The first two were short, sweet exchanges of sentiment, but the third consumed us. It was a long escalating engagement, and at some point, either I had rolled on top of her or she had somehow slid under me.

Quianna snatched me out my shirt the same way I did her before. She made a point to rub every muscle in my chest, arms, and back, appreciating the hard work I'd put in. I kept my hands above her clothes, explored her dips and swells.

She pulled off her shirt and flung it aside; the motion swept her purse off the bed and spilled its contents to the floor. She unhooked her bra, then fed me her caramel nipples.

When she fought her jeans off like they suddenly hurt to have on, I had to hit the pause button. I understood that our moment was supposed to happen after we partied with Chun Li and the girls in the suite at the MGM Grand. I felt Quianna deserved better than a shitty motel that rented rooms by the hour, especially after the way I just played her.

But even as I silently asked this, I knew we were past the point of turning back. Quianna was running hotter than a car with a bad radiator: her chest rose and fell in quick breaths; her forehead had already broken out in tiny beads of sweat. I could feel the heat rising off of her and its scent was pure sex. She answered my *should we wait?* face by putting a hand on my dick.

That was enough to get me off that chivalry shit. I eased down that turquoise thong, and she lifted her weight to help me.

I was staring at that pretty pussy again. I glanced from it to Quianna with a sly smirk that promised we would get properly introduced shortly, but first I danced my tongue around in her belly button, making her giggle and swoon at the same time. I left a trail of kisses down the rounded curve of her hips and watched those legs part for me with eagerness.

I studied up close the finger over sealed lips. It was cruder than the Asian pattern that sleeved her arm. Probably her very first tattoo, clearly the work of an amateur.

I gave Quianna an upwards glance that said, *Girl, quit playing!* Again she wore that guilty smirk of a woman who's busted. Finally she confessed that she had only been fifteen years old and in love with an older man in prison. She rolled her eyes at me, said this bad decision was my fault. I apologized by tracing the thick sloppy line-work with the tip of my tongue.

I finally came face-to-face with Miss Fat Cat and introduced myself. A clit as thick as my pinky finger was shy at the start but quickly came out to make my acquaintance.

I dined on her, savoring the taste and smell. I didn't waste time licking circles around the inner lips. I listened to her body, and her body told me to just focus on the clit.

From the way she was breathing, clawing at my head, clamping her meaty thighs around my neck tight enough to choke me out, I thought Quianna was enjoying herself. I knew I was. So it threw me when she stopped me after a few short minutes.

She was in such a rush to get my boxers down that she accidentally scratched my thigh with a thumb nail. It occurred to me that Quianna could get ate out by Lexy or any other chick in BANDS who went that way. What she wanted from me was dick.

I could've been off a pill. My beast looked so stiff and swollen that it surprised even me.

The gates that were locked to me just twenty minutes before were open and glistening with anticipation. The tightness still required a few seconds for me to work the tip inside. But I'll swear under oath that once I was in, I didn't push but was sucked deeper into her. Half my beast disappeared without effort.

The first few strokes were enough to let me know I'd just fucked up big time. This was a life-changing mistake.

Chapter Sixty-seven

I'm a goon, ain't never been one of these player-types out here bagging chicks left and right. But even I know that for ninety percent of the women out there, the term "good pussy" is a self-deception that lives in the mind of her lover and is mostly the result of the couple's emotional connection during sex. However, there are a small minority of women who really have Good Pussy (capital G, capital P). It's more than a mind-thing. Good Pussy is physically superior—tighter, wetter, better muscle-control. Many ladies who are just average might think they have Good Pussy because they've been gassed up by the men who are in love with them, while in truth, only about two in every ten women have Good Pussy.

But then I've stood on the side and watched fellas have conversations about an extremely rare breed of demi-goddesses who have GOOD PUSSY (all caps). This is the one in ten thousand. According to them, GOOD PUSSY goes beyond mind and body; the experience is almost mystical. And the wielders of this magical box cannot be discerned by appearance: Rihanna might have it; your three-hundred-pound aunt Mabel Jean might have it. GOOD PUSSY can cause a man to abandon his values and moral codes: make a devout Catholic leave his thirty-year marriage and five kids, make a radical Skinhead tattoo over his swastikas and march with Black Lives Matter.

I used to think these women were a myth and the niggas who swore on them were like the country-ass white boys who swore they saw Bigfoot.

That was up until the moment I slid into Quianna "Q-Bands" Peterson. After my first three strokes, I knew what I'd fell into and knew I was in trouble. You don't just fuck GOOD PUSSY: you sign a contract with it, and your dick is the pen.

She felt like home. Her box grabbed me, held me, sucked and pulled my beast like something hungry. Quianna was so hot, she could've been running a high fever, so wet that after an hour, we'd have to flip the mattress.

Not that I would ever last that long. Just ninety seconds into her, I was fighting off a premature nut. I tried to alter my stroke to stay alive.

Quianna stole the rhythm, hooked her legs around my waist, and put it on me with a deep bucking of her hips. She started chasing her own nut, and I was trying like hell to let her win that race. She was on her back, eyes closed, biting and chewing on her lips. I pinned her arms over her head and pounded hard.

Her orgasm came in the form of a wet, sticky bomb that I felt explode deep inside her. She opened her mouth for a gasp and clutched at the muscles in my back. Tears slipped from the corners of her eyes.

My nut came five pumps after hers, and I was lucky to hold off that long. I blew hard enough to scare me. I shuddered, shook, felt like she was connecting me with God as I offered up pieces of my soul.

When Quianna opened her eyes, I could only give her a look of apology. I felt like I had cheated her. As long as she had waited on the dick, for me to not last three minutes had me looking weak as hell. And I couldn't use that fresh-out-the-joint shit as an excuse because I'd been with Lexy. I shook my head, miming the point that this never happens to me, but I guess all niggas who weak in bed probably use that one.

Quianna smiled at me, even though I saw some disappointment behind it, and pulled me to her for a kiss. I collapsed on top of her while she made Miss Fat Cat chew on me like a toothless mouth, milking those last drops of cum out of me.

I laid there enjoying that, thinking about the moves I still needed to make later that night, and thanks to me being quick on the draw, our episode hadn't killed enough time. Then thinking of time reminded me that I was nearly out of it with Gamble.

Quianna saw the concern in my eyes and misread it. Her insecurity caused her to fear that I might be feeling guilty about what just happened, that I might backtrack and start looking at her like Li'l Quay-Quay again.

With a kiss, I reassured her that we were all good. I was aware of the moment's significance, the fact that we had crossed a line we couldn't come back from.

But surprisingly, that didn't worry me. Maybe because she had already shown me time and time again that she was down for me. Maybe because with all the arguments and drama and her secretly tracking my phone, she had already been acting like my woman.

I was still inside her, half limp and receiving a soft massage from her vagina, when she used her fingers to trace a message on my back. I felt an *I*, a heart, and a *U*. I stared into the hazel eyes of this half-black dime wondering why.

It made some sense when she was younger; I was right-hand to the big brother she adored, so I picked up on some of that affection through transference. But I couldn't understand why after she grew into this bad-ass bossy bitch what made her stay focused on me when she could literally have any man she wanted. It was my own insecurity that made me ask with an inquisitive stare and hand gestures.

Her answer was so cute and clever that it made me smile. "Because other niggas talk too much!"

My phone was still on the edge of the bed, and I was able to grab it without leaving her sanctuary. I used it to tell her that I just learned T'wanda's son wasn't mine. I kept Doc's name to myself. I buried that right along with my belief that her brother had set me up.

Quianna looked furious but not surprised at hearing T'wanda did me dirty. She hissed, "Give me the nod and I'll drag that slimy bitch! I been wanting to."

I pecked her nose to show I appreciated the sentiment. Didn't think it necessary to tell her I'd already handled that, then quietly worried about a relationship built on so many secrets.

This compelled me to confess to the ride that I got from Lexy at her house. I thought if Quianna knew that me picturing her in those yellow shorts was the only thing that helped me finish, it might make her feel better. It didn't. She made her pussy clamp down on my beast so hard that I cringed. Her Kegel game was no joke—she could probably crack a walnut.

I also told her that I had walked up on her and Lexy getting down that first night I was home.

"I saw you," she said, giving me a sneaky, playful look. Then came her own confession that I was supposed to catch them. She had purposely ignored my texts to bring me up to her flat, the same way she had purposely left the door to her room open. "Scary ass just gone stand there and watch. Why you ain't come in?"

The thought of being the meat between a Quianna/Lexy sandwich sent a strong pulse through my semi-sleeping beast. Quianna felt it. She ejected the dick, rolled me on my back and took it into her mouth.

She sucked my dick like she loved it—the way Chun Li sucked dude at the bachelor party. Quianna was throating my shit and I could tell she was receiving as much pleasure from the act as she was giving me. The whole time her smiling eyes watching me go crazy.

I had to return the favor. I pulled her to me, and we sixty-nined. She devoured my dick while I teased her clit with a quick and nimble tongue. The stimulation heightened her technique, and had she kept that up I would've blown again.

She must've sensed that, too. She stopped, then straddled me. Quianna just sat there. I felt the proof that the foreplay had turned her on. I couldn't believe she was actually hotter and wetter than before.

She smiled down on me. "Let's just take it nice and . . . SLOW." She put emphasis on the last word by starting a slow wind as she twisted her fingers through my beard. "And maybe you can last longer than five minutes."

Quianna laughed like I was joking when I held up eight fingers. I was dead-ass serious.

Chapter Sixty-eight

GOOD PUSSY is like a scalding-hot bath: you feel like you can't handle it when you first dip your toe into the water. The trick is easing into it slowly, giving your body time to adapt.

Quianna seemed to understand this, which is why she took it easy those first ten minutes or so. Eventually I adjusted, and she was able to ride a little harder a bit at a time. Before we both knew it, she was bouncing on my beast like an exercise ball, from the front, then reverse cowgirl.

That first time had been intimate, but still over faster than a Pop-Tart came out the toaster. I felt I had to earn some of my respect back. So, that second time, I manhandled her.

I dragged Quianna to the edge of the bed where I could stand up in it and flipped her on the left side. I picked her up to carry her around the room, pinned her against the wall, WWE-slammed her back down on the bed. I pounded her cakes and spanked them hard enough to turn those yellow cheeks hot pink. I was in a groove, laying pipe the way your boy knew he was capable of. We'd been fucking for an hour-twenty, and I had enough stamina for another two.

But Quianna was panting hard, sweat glossed, spiral curls

bouncing with each thrust while looking back at me, eyes begging for my nut. So I gave in to the soft sucking of GOOD PUSSY and blew. Not as hard as the first one but still strong enough to weaken my legs. It sent me into a thirty-minute nap where I ended up lying in the wet spot from Quianna's overflow.

When I woke up, she was sitting next to me, back against the headboard and resting on a stack of pillows. She was still ass naked and downing the last of my cranberry Ciroc.

At her side, she had the Nike shoebox filled with all of Doc's paperwork. Nearly forgot I brought it with me. I had planned to go through it but got distracted. Quianna had started while I slept. Half of the documents were scattered across her side of the bed.

I went to the bathroom, spent four minutes pissing out the last of the saline solution, then rejoined her. I nodded like *What's up?*

"Mostly lease agreements from European Motors." There were plenty of those. Doc's flossy ass had wanted to play in a different exotic car every four to five months.

Quianna beamed when she thrust the deed to 11879 Radom in my face. It was in the name of Darius Peterson. This just made Darnia's eviction legal and permanent.

That seemed to be the treasure Quianna was looking for, but I kept digging. I wanted bank statements, info on savings accounts or safety deposit boxes. Anything to disprove my theory.

I searched everything left in the shoebox and doubled back over the paperwork she'd already picked over. Brochures for studio equipment: thirty-two-channel digital mixers and drum machines; property tax receipts for the house; a glossy six-page pamphlet for something called the Urban Renewal Project. I found records showing that Doc had purchased the Nature's Way building for four hundred and thirty-nine thousand through a limited liability company he had formed. I scanned articles of organization and an operating agreement in the name of Deep Pockets Productions, LLC. I also found receipts for a bunch of business checks that went back to the previous year, but these were fewer than ten grand each and had been paid to Doc. I was sure I wouldn't find any financial trail that might relay where he had stashed the four million.

Quianna claimed to know nothing about Doc's company, the checks, or how these might tie in to the old juice factory. Gamble herself had confirmed that Doc was on the verge of a huge payoff. It was like solving a jigsaw puzzle without the picture to guide me. I knew I had all the pieces in this box, just couldn't figure out how they fit together.

It was after one, and Quianna was intuitive enough to know I had someplace else to be. She had a sour look waiting on me when I came out the shower. She crossed her arms over the brown aureoles of those perky A-cups, looking like *So it's like that?*

I dropped on the edge of the bed, went in for a kiss that she backed away from. My look said, *Come on girl, you know this ain't no toot-it-and-boot-it. I just got business.*

Those thick Peterson eyebrows drifted high on her forehead to ask, *What business?*

We could do simple conversations with facial expressions, but I needed my phone to explain that I was about to take a look at the Joy Road Boys. While she read the text, I slid into my boxers and sweats, stuffed my feet back into the boots.

She watched me pull the heat from the bathroom linen closet. I sat the blanket on the floor and unwrapped the M-90 Herstal and the Benelli M4. Quianna looked over the guns, then me. "So you sure these the niggas who killed him?"

I admitted that I wasn't sure of shit at that point. This really wasn't about Doc anymore.

"Then why is you still doing this?" She tilted her head the way women do when they're getting impatient. "What, cause they shot you?"

No, because they shot Nika. Because it was time to get Gamble off my ass, too.

But the most important reason probably couldn't be explained so easily. Because this is who I am and what I do. Because, at the end of the day, I just like fucking shit up.

I underestimated Quianna, because she read that in my eyes. Her frown indicated that she wasn't happy but clearly understood at least a portion of it.

She made one last-ditch effort to tempt me into staying. Crossed the bed on her knees and stood chest-to-chest with me. She put my hands on her ass, then reminded me that she still had a hole that I hadn't been in yet. I immediately bricked up again.

Nice try but trick no good. She smirked, knowing she almost had me.

Quianna was going to sleep at the motel, then head back to the house in the morning. I didn't like her being there alone, especially with the Aston Martin parked out front. I gave her the .32 pistol I took off of Darnia's man, advised her to be careful. I received the same advisory to not get my dumb ass killed.

I shared with her an epiphany I had while laying inside her. I believe that I had been moving so reckless before, not because I was out of practice, but because some part of me honestly didn't care if I lived or died. But I would move smarter now that I had so much to live for. From that day on, getting safely back home to her would be my motivation.

Quianna read my phone, sucked her teeth, and called me corny. But I knew it was just her trying not to get choked up. My baby was a street chick. A street chick will fight to stay hard even in the softest moments.

But ninety percent of communication is nonverbal. Her goodbye kiss told me how she really felt.

Chapter Sixty-nine

Prime had told me if I needed him to shine the bat signal. It was time to find out if he was ready to put his cape on—even though he would be playing Robin to my Dark Knight.

His house was one of those spots where the party never stopped, just alternated in size and intensity. A light burned in every window, front door wide open, five dudes on the porch holding red plastic cups and two blunts in rotation.

I must've made an impression on my first visit, because I didn't have any trouble walking up to the door this time. Once I laid out my proposal, I didn't have any trouble convincing Prime to help me, either. It was actually harder to convince him to do it my way.

Forty-five minutes later, me, Prime, and eight of his boys were headed back to the westside—not the clown with the hammer who tried to steal my gun. One rode with me in the New Yorker. Prime followed, driving three others in a Hummer H2 with scarred paint that was probably the last token from his former life when he was still getting real money. Three more trailed him in a beat-down '83 Buick Regal that had needed a jump to get started.

First we made a quick stop at a Super K for a few items. With the fam over on Radom, we were able to use Mrs. P's spot to finalize the details, and for me to do a little chemistry.

Next we headed over to Cascade to the Joy Boys' trap. I pulled Punchy's Caprice out of hibernation and drove in it alone. Prime and his boys hung back near the corner and waited for my signal.

I raced up the well-lit block, saw that two dealers were out and appeared to be doing decent numbers even at three a.m. The eight-foot fence that surrounded their house and the neighboring property was their security barrier, and my turn into the short driveway stole much of the speed I needed to ram open the gate. I only managed to punch through half of the Chevy's front end before the chain-links trapped the car like the webbing of a baseball glove.

I figured that would bring the dealer working the field directly across the street. He ran towards me on instinct, a Glock in his swinging arm that should've been up and firing.

I rolled out the driver's door with the Herstal raised and sent a short burst of four rounds into his chest. He was a dead man running those last three steps, carried forward only by momentum. Then his body crumbled like a puppet with cut strings.

The second street vendor working the far corner clearly had a transmission system installed by Mercedes-Benz. He had also been coming to me full sprint, but at seeing his man go down, somehow stopped on a dime and shifted into reverse faster than I would've thought possible. He jogged backwards as easily as Ali danced around the ring, all the while shooting at me with some pistol too far away for me to identify.

I got low on the side of the Caprice and returned fire. It took my third burst to change his graceful backpedal. He stumbled onto his back to contemplate the heavens.

I had been totally deaf since seven, but even before that age, I'd had plenty of experience with guns. Still, it had been so long that I sometimes forgot the jarring effect the sound of a fully automatic could make. Roosting birds lifted off from their trees, dark wings beat against a darker sky. The walk-up fiends quickly beat their feet off the block to go spend their money elsewhere.

Six vehicles were parked inside the fence on the basketball court. The Benz SUV, the Corvette, the Challenger, and the old-school Malibu I recognized from the surveillance cameras in front of Louie Boy's club. Resting alongside these were two more cars I'd never seen: a shiny Cadillac XT6 and a basic-ass Hyundai sedan that seemed out of place amongst the company. The number of cars couldn't account for how many people might be inside the house.

I snatched the Benelli off the seat, used the shoulder strap to drape it over my back where it would be out of my way.

The front door opened, but I made the ops think twice with a wild looping arc of bullets I sent at the porch. I wanted them to come outside and play, just needed a bit more time to put some space between us.

I eased back across the street toward the grassy field, still peppering the face of their house with 5.7 rounds. A few of the Joy Boys had leaked out onto the porch to shelter themselves behind the brick railing. Some cleared out the glass to return fire from the windows.

I was falling back, trying to lure the ones on the porch into coming forward. All the working streetlights gave them a good view of me. I stood in the middle of the field, making a target of myself, basically waving a flag that said, *Come get me!*

But to their credit, these youngsters weren't that stupid. I counted on them being aggressive because of their superior numbers, but they didn't come out in force. Maybe they sensed a trap, or maybe our previous run-ins had warned them that I was something special. Either way, the Joy Road Boys rightly stayed on the porch, firing at me from cover.

We traded bullets from across the street, and if any of those little niggas had aim, I'd already be dead. But a stray bullet can kill, too. And with so many shooters firing wildly, some were coming dangerously close just on dumb luck. This made me retreat deeper into the thicket of chest-high cordgrass. I took my own cover behind the skeletal frame of an old torched car whose make and model was unrecognizable. Rust flakes and tiny bits of char rained on me as their slugs pinged the ruined metal.

I emptied my first clip and ducked to reload. That reprieve and my pinned position must've been what finally emboldened my enemies. Those in the house filtered onto the porch. Those on the porch filtered into the yard, where they fired at me from their side of the fence.

I could've took aim and dropped two or three of them, but I purposely misfired. I just needed a few more to feel brave enough to slip down the porch steps, to get closer.

What felt like ten more minutes of me trading fire might have only been sixty seconds. I was sure Prime's boys were getting anxious, and I couldn't waste all my ammo on this part of the plan. It was time.

I took a few more errant shots, then ducked out of sight. I pulled out my spare phone and momentarily turned night into day.

Chapter Seventy

Bringing forth light from the darkness for me was not an act of God, rather an act of Science. Sugar, liquid oxygen, and ammonia in proper amounts created a rising fireball that for a few seconds resembled a giant and blindingly fluorescent jellyfish swimming upwards from a murky depth of ocean. The flash briefly eclipsed the streetlights with the intensity of a lightning strike. Then the bright jellyfish morphed into a column of dense smoke with a mushroom top.

It would've been so much easier if DelRay had C-4, but for me that wasn't a problem, because you've probably already guessed that the UOTA also had demolition classes that taught us kids how to make several different types of explosives.

I used the Caprice to deliver my package. I left my surprise in the trunk connected to a remote detonator that I rigged from a cheap corner-store minute phone.

As I gazed over the rusted roof of the car I'd been using for cover, I saw everybody was down across the street. There were a few fatalities, but most people were writhing in agony.

That had been the cue. The Regal and the Hummer immediately skidded to a stop in front of the house, doors opened. Prime and his boys sprang out in ski masks.

I had made them promise to spare anybody who surrendered, and this had resulted in much of the debate back at Prime's. These grimy-ass eastsiders had wanted to kill everything on Cascade. This wasn't me going soft, especially after what they did to Nika. I had a long-range plan that might make these youngsters useful. So Prime's crew just took the guns away from those who were down and hurt. Though it was understood that any Joy Boy still armed who wanted to die for his set was fair game.

It couldn't be helped that two dudes had been standing too close to the Caprice. One body had been thrown up on the eight-foot fence, folded over the top as if he'd fallen asleep halfway through trying to climb over. All I glimpsed were pieces of the other; the biggest was a smoking Jordan 4 with part of an ankle and sheared piece of shin bone sticking from the top.

Punchy's donk had been reduced to a smoldering hunk of twisted metal. The trunk and roof of the cab reminded me of the bodies in those *Alien* movies where the creature bursts out the chest cavity. That part of the fence was blackened and warped into a strange geometry.

My bomb had only been roughly the equivalent of five sticks of dynamite. If it had been my intention to take out all of them, I would've given it a much bigger kick and packed it with steel ball bearings to maximize the kill radius.

I had mostly wanted everybody outside too stunned to put up a fight. They were down from the concussive effects of the blast, looking dazed, probably with a high-pitched ringing in their ears, momentarily sharing my handicap. Prime and his boys had already started rounding them up, emptying their pockets. I left them to that while I jogged up the porch steps.

The interior was what you'd expect from young niggas with too much money and too little supervision. The wooden floor was covered with cigar tobacco they emptied to make their blunts. A busted old sofa and folding chairs were the only things to sit on, but they had a huge new Samsung on the wall with a game of Ghost Recon still paused on the screen.

Upstairs, there was a brief firefight with one of the Joy Boys who had wanted to go out in a blaze of glory; Prime's boy in the muscle shirt obliged him with a short burst of the Drecco. The three others we came across decided that laying down their guns was preferable to laying down their lives.

I knew we didn't have long before the sound of that explosion brought police cars, fire trucks, and probably the National Guard. We went through the big Venetian room-by-room.

I eventually found a secret one in the basement hidden behind what was supposed to be a plain linen closet. If they had used a better carpenter, and not some dope-fiend uncle, I wouldn't have noticed that the back wall of the linen closet was fake. It was actually a door that only took me three kicks to unlock.

The nine-by-twelve-foot panic room gave me flashbacks of a prison cell, cement block walls and a single bulb hanging from the ceiling. Inside was a sizable stash of money and a refrigerator holding the unsold heroin. Prime's crew began to bag everything up.

I took the dude who had been in there hiding with it. This was the stocky, light-skinned guy who was supposed to be The Man over here. Dirty Red.

He held a Sig Sauer P365 XL, but we both knew if he hadn't used it by then, he wasn't going to. I held out my hand, and Dirty Red came off that without having to be told.

I tucked the pistol on my waist, then held out my hand again. And without having to be told, he slipped off Doc's chain.

Chapter Seventy-one

Dirty Red was actually younger than I previously thought, just prematurely aged by the streets and stress. I didn't take him to an abandoned school for us to have our discussion, because hopefully this wasn't going to be that type of talk. I brought him back to Mrs. P's house and saw no reason not to, since he'd already been there when they shot the bitch up.

He wasn't tied to anything but made no attempts to run. He sat on the porch looking eerily detached and subdued, a prisoner of the mind, as I stood in the driveway concluding my business with Prime.

The plan had gone as well as I could've hoped: no casualties on our side. I only asked for an equal split on the cash, Dirty Red's truck, and Doc's chain. All the dope and guns along with the rest of the cars and jewelry was for Prime's hungry pack to carve up any way they liked. It was a deal that worked heavily in favor of the eastside homies which was why it had took so little convincing.

I didn't know how much dope they hit for, but the celebratory mood suggested they were more than satisfied. Most of them had already skirted off in new Challengers, a Corvette, and a few shiny old-schools headed for the chop shops.

I stood with Prime in front of his H2, brightened by the glow of headlights, casting thin elongated shadows that stretched the length of Mrs. P's driveway. An unseasonably chilled breeze pulled at our shirts, made the bushes thrash like stationary monsters.

Prime wanted to say "thank you," wanted to tell me how badly he had needed this, but knowing it would shatter the illusion that he wasn't down as bad as we both knew he was. His face expressed the gratitude that pride kept off his lips. Ninety percent of communication is nonverbal. On the oil-stained pavement, our dark elastic doppelgangers embraced the way real niggas do: tight but quick with pats on the back.

This had also been about repaying some of my debts. He would find out about T'wanda soon enough, and whether estranged or not, they were still brother and sister. I didn't think the couple of dollars from this lick made that right, just thought he deserved a painkiller.

After the Hummer backed out my driveway and I watched it and the raggedy Regal disappear down Monica, I returned to the porch. I sat with Dirty Red in front of the windows he and his boys had shot out. We'd left without bothering to hang up plastic, so the house appeared to breathe through its toothless grin, animating the living room curtains like spirits.

He stared at me with eyes that weren't fearful or angry. I'd seen too many times the resigned look of someone who figured he was about to die and just wanted to do so with dignity. Some of the fellas with Prime had mistaken his surrender as cowardice, but I detected no fear in him when he handed me the gun, just like I detected none then. This wasn't a hoe nigga begging for the mercy of his enemy; I detected in him a cool tactician with the vision to see that the game was lost and had simply tipped his King. Others, myself included, might have decided to shoot it out in the small stash room hoping to take a few of the ops with him, but a perceptive eye using a strong lens could even glean the cowardice in that form of suicide.

I pulled my phone and put him up on how I communicated. My first question was a two-for-one. Did he know this was Doc's mother's house, and did he know they'd shot a civilian here, about the only kid I actually liked.

He shook his head, and I assumed it was in response to both questions. I let him read off my screen facts that should've been obvious even to somebody with no GED: First, I could've had him and all his boys killed on the spot. Second, he was only here because he had information that I needed. I was down to have a gentleman's discussion but warned that any attempts at bullshit would force me to grab the bolt cutters and get it like I did from Bloody Savage.

To all this, he responded without a nod or headshake, just stared back at me unblinking. For a minute he had me thinking he was a mute, too.

But Dirty Red eventually had to use his words to tell me everything he knew about Doc's relationship with Gamble. Red started a year back, when Doc first put his team on with the heroin, then worked forward past the time of the hotel robbery and Doc's murder. A lot of it was ground that Bloody Savage had already covered, but there were some points of correction for tidbits Savage unknowingly got wrong.

Dirty Red swore that the chain had not been stolen but a gift from Doc himself two weeks before he died. Other posts he showed me from his Instagram page JoyBoyDirtyRed proved a close relationship with Doc, their roles like teacher and protégé.

But regardless of that, hurting little Nika had put him in my debt, and for shit like this, repayment would usually mean his life. I let him know the loss he took tonight was connected to that and exactly what the cost would be going forward. Fucking with me would save his life, his reputation, and take Gamble's foot off his neck.

We sat on the porch breaking it down through texts and lip reading from four a.m. until the eastern horizon paled with dawn's approach. Too much blood had been spilled between us to ever come away as friends. However, we did reach a mutually favorable agreement that, by the time we were done, had us dapping each other. I even gave him back the D-chain.

But I couldn't let Dirty Red get off that easy. For what he'd done to Nika, the additional cost was two broken bones. And I thought that was cheap.

Dirty Red looked at me like I was joking when I told him to give me his hand. The alternative was that I could just shoot him in the face right then with his own pistol.

He made the smart decision to offer up his left. I bent the middle and ring fingers into a position that God never intended until I felt them snap. His face brightened with pain, but he bit back the screams.

And if for whatever reason little Nika didn't wake up from that coma, the cost would be expensive. His life, plus the life of one person he loves for the interest payment.

I didn't let Dirty Red know this, just quietly made that promise to myself.

Chapter Seventy-two

I made it back to the Radom house around eight-thirty to find half the house still sleeping. Mrs. P was up, and if true to schedule, had been since five a.m. Quianna made it there before me and appeared fresh from having slept at the motel. The few kids up on their feet shuffled like zombies, yet to have the sugary cereal that would kick-start their morning of hyperactivity.

I pulled up to Quianna's rented Aston Martin in the driveway audaciously parked backwards, as if sending a message to the neighbors that we were more than just temporary guests. I was still surprised to see how completely settled in the family had gotten. Trayvion had claimed the upstairs room where I made my recovery. It couldn't have been easy for Pooh and her friend to be crashing in the one next to it with pink walls that was clearly for a little girl, even though for a childless Darnia, it had remained no more than a guest bedroom. Trayvion's boy was knocked out in the lower-level den with his shirt and socks off like he was at home. That was the room I would've preferred for Mrs. P, but she still seemed content on the living room sofa. The same as on Monica, the kids just dropped in whatever random spot they finally ran out of gas.

Quianna took the master bedroom, and I peeked in there to see the bed fitted with new sheets, the television she brought from home waiting to be mounted, and her pit Chino napping in the corner with his head on his paws. His big seventy-five-pound bag of Pedigree was in the closet along with the rest of Darnia's clothes, already knotted in garbage bags.

It had finally been time to ditch the New Yorker. Quianna peeked out the front windows in the dining room to see what I had parked at the curb. She started to ask a thousand questions, but I dismissed what would be a long and unnecessary explanation with a quick shake of the head.

I was still trying to keep my distance from the family. I had overshot Gamble's deadline and didn't know what form her retaliation might take for what I did on Cascade. My plan was to only be at the house long enough to make the drop-off. But Quianna told me to sit down and eat something, said this like it wasn't up for debate.

The preteens had a choice between Lucky Charms and Apple Jacks, but for the adults, Quianna was preparing a breakfast hash whose smell reminded me of last night's weak-ass dinner of Twinkies and Ciroc. She was at the stove whipping scrambled eggs, loose ground beef, potato cubes, and diced onions all in the same skillet.

Even when I wasn't looking at her, I could feel Quianna watching me. I sensed a growing irritation, and of all the mysteries I'd had to solve since coming home, this was by far the easiest.

Quianna wanted to know how was I going to play our new situation in public. Were we keeping things low-key? Did being around the family make it too weird, and was I going to just pretend the motel never happened? This was written on her face for me each time I glanced in her direction, with increasing imperative and narrowing eyes. These weren't just unvoiced questions about our status; they were challenges.

Whether question or challenge, I answered both when I stood to meet her at the stove. I pulled her into me and kissed her long and deep right there in front of Mrs. P and the kids, then looked to the fam like *This is what it is!* The kids made comical faces, disgusted by any form of adult affection. Mrs. P's wrinkled mouth curled up in the corners as she offered her approval with a slow nod.

I turned back to Quianna with a look that said, *Now shut the fuck up!*

Two minutes later, I was at the table with Mrs. P, devouring my hash. The old woman looked at me with a sly smile. She made a circle with one hand, and with the other used her index finger to run in and out of it. This wasn't American Sign Language, just her juvenile way of telling me she knew what me and her daughter had done.

I had scraped my plate clean by the time Pooh finally came downstairs. She wobbled into the kitchen wearing a fresh change of clothes, unpermed hair still wild as a lion's mane. I imagined her and her friend were headed back to the hospital to spend the day at her daughter's bedside.

When we locked eyes, even the kids became tense. She scanned me then Mrs. P with tight yellow eyes that asked what was I doing there. Quianna moved to put herself in between us.

With a look, I told everybody it was cool. I approached Pooh slowly in a manner that showed I didn't want trouble. She looked ready to spit on me again. I had a small brown paper bag—about the size you would get when buying a combo meal—half-filled and stuffed in the cargo pockets of my sweatpants. I pulled that out and had to make several head motions for Pooh to take it. She gave me another long, hard glare, then snatched the bag from my hand. I expected those tired yellow eyes to open fully when she peeped what was inside.

I didn't care how much dope we got, but back at Mrs. P's I kept a close eye as Prime and his boys counted out the cash. One hundred and thirty-eight thousand was the final tally: sixty-nine of that was my cut, and what I had just handed Pooh.

Next, I passed off the key and directed her to the window. The Mercedes-Benz AMG G63 SUV retailed for about one hundred and sixty thousand, even though she would never get that much on a trade-in. I used my phone to explain that the title would be transferred later that day. That was only a part of the understanding I had come to with Dirty Red on the porch.

The kids forgot their cereal, ran outside, jumping up and down like the family of someone who just won the car on a game show. Quianna had a hand over her mouth, wearing a face like she wanted to cry.

Pooh stared at her new Benz long enough for a tear to race her round cheek, but she wiped it, then turned back to me with a grim frown to indicate that this didn't change shit between us.

The frown I shot back let her know that it wasn't supposed to. Fuck her. I did what I did for Nika.

Chapter Seventy-three

Quianna really appreciated the way I looked out for Pooh. My baby stared at me like she was ready to do something to me right there in front of the kids. So after breakfast, when she told me to come upstairs real quick, I knew what was up. I knew I should've headed back to the motel, but GOOD PUSSY was mind-bending, so I let my beast overrule the objection raised by my better judgment.

Quianna showed me enough gratitude for Pooh and three other women. She got on her knees, capped me off sweetly and serenely as if she could do this forever.

She stood up, wrapped her thighs around my hips so I could push into her. I pinned her against the wall, held onto her neck and a fistful of good weave. She only needed a seven-minute choke-n-stroke to take her to a Level 5 orgasm. A few minutes after her, I erupted in a way that turned my legs to jelly.

I flopped down on the bed that formerly belonged to Darnia. Just like the smell of food reminded me of my empty stomach, the softness of the mattress reminded me that I'd pulled an all-nighter. I was suddenly and urgently exhausted. I stretched out on top of the sheets with the oscillating fan blowing cool over my naked skin.

I asked Quianna to wake me in a half hour. There was something in her eyes that I didn't trust, so I held up three fingers and shook them to emphasize thirty minutes. I kept stressing thirty minutes until she rolled her eyes and snapped that she wasn't stupid.

So of course it was four hours later when she finally woke me with her mouth. I raised my heavy head off the pillow and stared through grainy eyes at the alarm clock, not believing my time skip. Then I looked down at her.

She stopped long enough to answer the question on my face. "Nigga, shut up. Yo' tired ass needed that." Then went right back to sucking me.

I couldn't disagree, because I did feel recharged in my body and mind, but I also knew the extra rest hadn't only been about me. Quianna was acting like a girlfriend now, not a just a homie and far from a little sister. Letting me oversleep, kept my black ass around the house and out the streets a few more hours.

I frowned at her and said with a look, *Bitch, you ain't slick.*

Either Quianna was a nympho or just felt we had to make up for lost time, because that head led to another short but vigorous session that only lasted twenty minutes and remained in one position. It was ladies' choice, and the freak didn't hesitate to prop herself on knees and elbows, facedown/ass up. Even though we just got it in a few hours before, she felt just as hot and hungry. Chino spied on us for a while, then must've decided my technique wasn't shit because the puppy found more entertainment playing with the laces of my boot.

Afterward, I dressed in the Polo 'fit that she brought from the other house while she watched me from the bed chewing on her thumb. She told me I was ugly and my dick was weak. I responded that I didn't fuck with yellow girls no way, and she punched me hard because she knew it had some truth to it. As I left the room, she gave me the finger then rolled over for her own nap.

Fucking with Quianna had killed my morning, but I could still salvage my afternoon. It was minutes after one and I wondered if I had time to put everything in motion before that night. I needed to get back west. I finally caught up with the times, called myself an Uber.

Mrs. P was back on the sofa curled up under a blanket, facing the wall. Passing through the living room made me frown, because the old lady must've farted in her sleep. I stepped outside to wait on the front porch, grateful for the fresh air.

Trayvion and his boy were rehearsing their music. His man supplied a beat with his mouth accompanied by an ink pen he tapped against the metal leg of his patio chair. Trayvion quoted from the trusty orange notepad resting on his lap. He stopped rapping when I sat down.

It might have been pride or something else that had Pooh not drive her new gift to the hospital; Trayvion glanced skeptically at the Benz truck, then back to me, knowing I hadn't paid for it. I hadn't sensed that type of nervousness in him since I first came home. I was kind of disappointed we still weren't past that.

I sat with them for eleven minutes until a blue Scion pulled up to collect me. I didn't want to leave without saying something to Quianna and briefly wondered if GOOD PUSSY already had me whipped.

I paused when I came back inside and saw two kids, that belonged to God knows who, standing in front of Mrs. P's sofa. They were pinching their noses and making disgusted but equally concerned faces.

When I stood over them, one five-year-old boy, whose name I didn't know, looked up at me with wide solemn eyes. "Uncle Sy, Nanna stink."

She did. What I first thought was gas had grown into a much stronger, lingering stench.

I would've celebrated to learn that the old lady had only suffered an embarrassing accident, but under that, my sensitive nose detected a subtler scent. Something five- and six-year-olds shouldn't be familiar with in a perfect world, but something smelled often enough in my chosen profession. I rolled her over, hoping to be wrong.

Her lids were half-closed, hiding the hazel, exposing only the whites of her eyes. Her mouth sagged open, but I felt no breath pass through it when I pressed my cheek to hers.

I grabbed her wrist, desperate for a pulse, knowing it was too late. Too late for anything the fam could do. Way too late for the paramedics we called on reflex.

Mrs. P had been gone for hours. Her body had already grown cold. I could smell death.

Chapter Seventy-four

For Quianna, tears came sporadically and in sudden bursts like those flash floods in the Gulf states. Throughout the day, her crying fits came in violent downpours, then vanished just as quickly, the redness in her eyes being the only traces of them having been. And during the calm between these storms, she brooded with a quiet rage that even the kids knew to avoid.

I was stingy with my own tears, not from lack of sentiment, just had few to spare. I'd already mourned. I had cried when Mrs. P first told me about the cancer in her room, and the night before in the motel bed with Quianna, some of that weeping had been for this inevitability. All the emotional shit had gotten purged. My well was dry.

The EMTs had pronounced Mrs. P dead right there in the living room. I had already known this, but everyone else had clung to the delusion. Mrs. P wasn't driven away from us in the rear of an ambulance, but a city coroner's van.

The family had just lost its rock. While I could never replace that, somebody had to stand temporarily in its place. I had no doubt that Quianna would eventually step up to become the matriarch they would all come to lean on, but right then—after losing her mother and brother in a three-month span—she needed her own crutch.

I saw Trayvion's effort to be strong in front of his friends, but I also knew the real purpose of his frequent trips to the bathroom, and why he always came out wiping his eyes.

So the task for leading the family through this fell to me by default, but the problem was that every minute I sat there offering my hand to hold and my shoulder to cry on only put the family in more danger. I'm a guard dog, not an emotional support animal.

It was five hours after we returned from the medical examiner's office, and I was deep in the throes of my addiction. Mrs. P had reminded me that I couldn't punch or kick bone cancer so I was fiending for an enemy I could put hands on. I was in the kitchen, seconds away from pulling Quianna to the side and telling her I had to go, when they kicked in our front door.

It was chaos for a few minutes: kids crying, women screaming, youngsters panicking, black-clad men with semi-autos forcing everyone to the floor. Street niggas would've just started blowing shit, but I could tell by their energy and all the barking orders these were the police. Six of them, all in black tactical gear.

They pushed Quianna to the linoleum, but I was calculating my chances. Four approached me, weapons raised, using the caution and respect that proved they were aware of my reputation.

The strap wasn't on me. It was probably for the best that I left the Herstal back on Monica. Even unarmed, I still would've acted up, but I was wearing the guilt from Nika. I would've did my thing right in that kitchen and most likely gotten another one of these babies shot in the process.

So I didn't resist when their gloved hands eased me down to my knees, then flattened me on my stomach.

I looked up from my awkward position to see Gamble and Bates looming over me like skyscrapers. I thought the sergeant was going to kick me in the face, but instead she motioned for the SWAT officers to pull me up.

Bates gave me a quick pat-down, and at feeling the object in my pocket, he pulled out the wallet that I stole off him. Bates sneered at me, used ASL to fingerspell "asshole." I smiled, knowing he learned that tidbit just for me.

Gamble looked to me tapping her watch to signify what we both knew. "You've been busy doing everything I told you not to do. I know you're what happened on Cascade."

I shrugged like I didn't know what the fuck she was talking about.

"You think I don't recognize whose truck that is out front? But for some reason, Dirty Red's not saying anything. Says they all had on ski masks, so he didn't see any faces."

I only shrugged again.

"Let's see if he still feels that way after he gets thirty years for the club shooting and for being a habitual drug trafficker."

I couldn't keep up my smug demeanor at hearing that. The slimy bitch was actually going to book the little nigga for selling her dope.

She took a step into me. "It was a mistake trying to push the same buttons on you that I used on others."

"You are under arrest for the murder of Darius Peterson." I thought Gamble was about to take me away, but the bitch hit me with a curveball. I looked just as sick as Quianna when Bates pulled her off the floor and began to read her Miranda rights. The kids all started to whine as the detective put cuffs on Quianna.

Trayvion went crazy, tussling and talking shit to the officer who held him. I had to give him a look that said, *Be cool.* Being restrained didn't mean that they would show restraint. I didn't want to see my godson's memorial spray-painted on the side of a building as he became the rallying cry for the next round of marches and protests.

Gamble said, "I told you before: it's easier not to care when it's just you."

As officers walked her out the door, Quianna threw me back a look like *What the fuck?* The one I returned said, *Don't worry, I'll do something.*

Even though it was clear from my expression I had no idea what.

Chapter Seventy-five

The kids were still blowing snot bubbles over Mrs. P when they had to watch their Auntie Q get dragged out in handcuffs. They didn't even complain when we sent them to bed long before their usual drop-off time. It was as if they were ready for this day to be over.

The adults didn't handle things much better, only there wasn't shit we could do legally to get Quianna back that night. If Gamble actually did book her, she wouldn't get in front of an arraignment judge until the next day.

But I didn't think this was a real arrest. Gamble had nothing on Quianna, not a damn thing that pointed to her killing her own brother. This was just a play to put pressure on me. I tested my theory when I had Trayvion's friend call every precinct we could find listed. No desk sergeant we could get a hold of claimed to have a Quianna Peterson in their system. This didn't necessarily mean she wasn't there, only that she hadn't been formally processed.

I had already planned to get Gamble off my ass. This shit with Quianna just pushed up my timeline.

But first I shot back to my motel room, borrowed my baby's rental, and dogged the clutch on the Davidson Freeway.

Next, I pulled up on Louie Boy's Baby Momma Number Six. At four-foot-nine, she barely measured to my stomach and looked annoyed to see me at her door. She answered it in some denim cutoffs, thick ass tatted up thighs, looking like a bite-sized snack.

Louie Boy was on the run, not answering his phone, and Number Six tried to play tough. She made me go goon. I didn't hurt her, just shook her up until she told me how to get in touch with Louie. I also squeezed for the details about her fling with Doc.

I exchanged texts with Louie Boy on my way back to Punchy's for Round Two. That fake shit about being The Man on Fenkell Avenue was the type of lie I could forgive. The problem was that he had lied to me about Doc.

I parked down the block from his house, concealed by nightfall, by five-percent tinted glass, and by the low-hanging limbs of a curbside maple. The Aston Martin DBS was still conspicuous in uppity-ass Sherwood Forest, but if I were in the Caprice or the Mark VIII, some nosy neighbor would have called the police on me within the first ten minutes.

I sat there for two hours thinking before I saw Punchy's headlights bend the opposite corner of the block. I was out the door and moving low along the cars parked on the street as the BMW slid smoothly into the driveway. I saw the silhouette of only one figure behind the wheel.

I crept on the side of his car, staying within the driver's blind spot. I quickly snatched open the door and jumped into the passenger seat, scaring the shit out of him.

Punchy's eyes went wide, and I covered his mouth to smother his surprised utterances. I drilled him three quick times in the short ribs.

I held up a fistful of the checking receipts I pulled from Doc's shoebox and then my phone with the first of my questions already preloaded. Punchy shook his head in response.

A little bit of time and money can make people forget where they came from. Back in the day, this muthafucka used to take so many ass-kickings in the hood, they started calling him Punching

Bag. I reminded my old friend of how he earned his nickname. Two more jabs to the same spot folded him around the pain, clutching his side. Bruised ribs were excruciatingly painful; I warned him that with a stronger shot, I could crack one and puncture his lung with it.

When I held up the receipts again, Punchy nodded to confirm what I already knew.

Back when he and Doc had that chance encounter at the casino a year before he died, Punchy had most likely done the same thing he had done on my first visit: brag about his come-up. Nobody was better than Doc at gaming an opportunity. Punchy was right that an all-cash business like vending machines was perfect for cleaning up dirty money. That night Doc had either sweet-talked or bullied Punchy into a partnership. All those payments Punchy had made to Doc's company, Deep Pockets Productions, had each been under ten thousand—the threshold amount to ring alarm bells with the feds.

The other item I had pulled from the shoebox was the leaflet that bore Councilman Henley's name for something called the Urban Renewal Project. When I pressed it to Punchy's face, he again gave a vigorous nod to confirm what I had been able to piece together on my own.

I didn't make the connection until I thought back to the first time I came through Sherwood and tied up his girl. The gun permit I found in her purse was registered to a Tyeisha HENLEY. For the past three days, I had been seeing that surname on billboards all over the city. This had triggered me to recall two separate conversations with Louie Boy. The first being how Punchy had fucked his way into a powerful family. The second one we had in Louie's Wraith when he told me this Councilman Henley was a lock to be the next mayor.

Then Gamble herself had added the frosting when she confessed that Doc was plugged into somebody major. Somebody major enough to have a crew of dirty cops on the payroll.

The part I didn't know was exactly what Doc had gotten involved in with the Henleys. But when I brought up the question on my phone, I noticed Punchy's frightened eyes kept darting from me to the back seat.

I peeked back there to see his eight-year-old daughter slumped in the seat behind his. She was deep in a sugar coma, probably induced by cake, ice cream, and half a dozen cups of punch. She had just come from a kids' birthday party—had fallen asleep with a gift bag in her lap, still wearing the party hat. She was too short for her head to clear the backrest of the seat, which was why I had thought Punchy was alone when I approached the Beemer.

Just as Gamble was teaching me, personal attachments were a liability in the game. Punchy shook his head and quietly begged me not to be the monster we both knew I was capable of.

I offered the cost of my mercy at a discounted price. I only charged the truth without omissions.

Chapter Seventy-six

Pain screwed his face into a tight grimace, and he occasionally hissed and groaned. This made it harder to read his lips in the BMW's darkened interior. Rather than have him cut on the light and possibly wake his daughter, I followed as well as I could.

According to Punchy, this whole thing had begun two years earlier in Washington, DC, when some mysterious lobbyist with long money and longer strings got congress to pass the Urban Renewal Project.

Punchy either whispered or silently mouthed: "Now these muthafuckas so slick, Sy, that they hide the shit inside some other shit. That way you ain't got Republicans and Democrats fighting over who get what, 'cause only a tiny handful even up on game."

Supposedly buried within a mountain of tedious legalese in some miscellaneous bill was hidden a stimulus that would grant seventeen billion dollars in federal aid to rebuild Detroit, Baltimore, and Philadelphia—three predominantly black cities overrun with crime and poverty. Punchy had used the word "gentrification," and my father had used it often to explain how white people would take over minority communities by making it too expensive to live there.

"They 'bout to build this bitch up to lure all the white folks back to the D, then push all the niggas out to the suburbs. You see what they already did downtown: casinos, hotels, and restaurants, new arenas for the all the sports teams. That was just the beginning."

Talking about the money seemed to ease Punchy's pain. He broke this next part down with the wide excited eyes of a child talking about Christmas. "And the gravy part is that the URP is strictly for the targeted cities, so the funds ain't even going through the state legislators. Seventeen divided by three mean that five-point-six billion in free money about to flow through this bitch!" Another nigga who assumed I couldn't do math. "The fed about to make it rain, and everybody who in-the-know twerking like a muthafucka."

With Detroit's history of civic corruption, it didn't take a genius to figure out that so much of that five-point-six billion was about to go for bribes, backdoor deals, and all types of shady shit. The Henleys were heavy hitters in commercial real estate with blood leading the city council. They were about to own a lot more office buildings, which meant a lot more lobbies and break rooms for Punchy's vending machines.

He explained: "The biggest hogs been lined up since Day One—shit, compared to them, Tyeisha's people just fighting over the scraps. The funds set to come through next month. But just like any game, you gotta pay to play. The buy-in ain't cheap: two million just to sit at the kiddie table."

Another big block just dropped into place like Tetris. Doc hadn't just used Punchy to launder his cash, but to get on the inside with the councilman. Doc then used that infamous gift of gab to get in on the Urban Renewal Project.

But Gamble was stuck on the outside looking in. It was why she had to call in a favor to take over Doc's investigation, and why she went through so much trouble to blackmail me. Her only interest in finding Doc's killer was that they most likely had the money.

Punchy confirmed it when I rightly guessed that the buy-in window was almost closed. This also helped to make sense of why Gamble only gave me three days. She was running out of time to get her ante up.

Tyeisha came outside through the side door, probably wondering why he was just sitting in the driveway. The moment her eyes fixed on me, I saw the panicked look of somebody ready to call the police.

I gave Punchy a warning glare that told him to check his bitch. He immediately jumped out the car and chilled her before she did something stupid.

As a sign of good faith, I allowed Tyeisha to take the girl. It was nerves as much as anger that caused her to fumble with the seat belts. She woke the sleeping princess and ushered her into the house, throwing evil glances back to me every few steps.

His daughter was safe and unharmed, but for quid pro quo I told Punchy I needed him to use the councilman to get an urgent message to Sergeant Gamble. I made him place that call right in front of me.

Chapter Seventy-seven

After leaving Punchy's, I went back to Monica and spent the rest of the evening at the old house, whipping something up in Mrs. P's kitchen. From there it hardly took five minutes using backstreets to get to the old Nature's Way factory. I arrived at ten-thirty, broke in through the loading door I used the day before, and spent another two hours getting ready.

I had a plan but not much faith in it. In my best-case scenario, I would still need to be saved and could only hope my unlikely partner came through. If he didn't, I was dead.

I texted Louie Boy to make sure he was in place. A few seconds later, my phone buzzed twice with no message: Louie's signal that he was outside and ready.

The center loading door to the docks that I entered by had been left open, high enough for a person to walk under. Another twenty minutes passed before a dark silhouette appeared in that space, black against the deep violet rectangle of the outside night. The six-foot shadow took tentative steps forward, the laser-like beam of an LED flashlight sweeping left to right. From my hiding spot, I watched Gamble walk about thirty feet into the factory, then stop. At her feet, I left another cheap corner-store phone with a three-part message: The first told her to put her gun on the ground and kick it away from her. The second was to keep her arms out at her sides.

I watched Gamble comply before I sprang out from behind the huge support column about ten feet to the left of her. I ran at her low and quick, my own flashlight strapped to my Benelli M4.

Her face appeared pale under the beam as she shielded her blue eyes. "Do you know how clichéd this is? The deal goes down in an abandoned warehouse. Tell me, are you gonna calmly walk away from the explosion as this whole place goes up behind you? In the biz, they call that the hero-shot."

I actually had something like that in mind. But I'm not a hero, and I promise she wasn't gonna like the twist I put on this ending.

She said, "My people know where I am and who I'm with. So if I accidently get my pretty face blown off by a twelve-gauge, something of equal value happens to the girl with the nice eyes."

I lowered my gun. We both knew I wasn't going to shoot her. At least not yet.

Where's Quianna?

She countered my texted inquiry, "Where's my money?"

It was someplace safe. I sent that to her phone and let her read it, then followed by asking about the video and any subsequent copies that she was supposed to bring for trade.

"Someplace safe," she parroted me, then shrugged innocently. "This reminds me of that scene in *Scarface* when Tony meets the Colombians at the motel. 'What? 'Choo want me to go out and come back in so we can start all over again; maine?'" I didn't know what she was imitating. I never saw the movie, so the reference was lost on me.

I asked another question: *Did Councilman Henley make you buy a building too so you would look like a legitimate business owner to get your cut of the stimulus?*

"If I were eligible for the stimulus, I would've never needed Darius." There was still a part to this I didn't quite understand.

Gamble laughed at seeing the curiosity in my eyes. "Would you like me to do you a favor and just lay out all the details of our evil plan while you secretly record me?" I wasn't the one she had to worry about recording her.

"I'm not the man in black, just a lowly civil servant who knows retiring on a cop's pension isn't going to cut it. I'm not the cripple who limps out the police station and then starts walking straight." I actually got that one. I did see *The Usual Suspects.*

I already knew Gamble wasn't the mastermind or stupid enough to talk me through the whole conspiracy. I just needed to distract her long enough for Louie Boy to deliver the package.

"Outside of Eastwood, there's only a short list of truly great actors who moved on to have the same success in the director's chair. You ever wonder why?"

Never. Not once.

"Because an actor is only responsible for his performance while the director is responsible for everyone's performance on the set. The director has to choreograph efforts, manage egos, and basically serve as the brain of the whole organism. She's the boss, and that requires a unique skillset."

I assumed her point was coming some time before Kwanzaa.

"Silence, this whole scene just proves you're not fit to direct. You're not the one who puts together schemes with a bunch of moving parts. You're more like a stuntman.

"That's why you've always been more comfortable with somebody else calling the shots. Tell the truth, isn't that what you miss most about Doc? He told you who to collect from or which competitors to shut down. He threw the stick, and you fetched. Only bosses are burdened with thinking. You're a goon—that's the part you're meant to play."

She saw something in my eyes that made her smirk. It was the opposite of the very same thing that swelled her with confidence even though I was the one with the gun. Maybe she knew she had touched upon one of my long-held insecurities.

Or maybe it was because I fell right into her trap.

Even in the darkness, I saw them coming out of my peripheral. Six shadows seemed to materialize like ghosts. They closed in on me from different directions with their weapons raised.

Chapter Seventy-eight

All that movie shit was just Gamble giving her crew time to get into position. I had told her to come alone. She had them sneak into the factory by different routes. The circle they formed around me tightened, and I could assume in the gloom they were demanding I drop my weapon.

I was an excellent shot, and the Benelli was about the finest tactical rapid-fire shotgun on the market. But I wasn't good enough to pump out six rounds in six different directions before I caught more than a few. I laid down the gun, but not my phone.

I recognized the sloppy-built dude with low sloping forehead and the big-nosed chick from the gas station, as well as the white boy with the buzz cut who was ice-grilling me on Monica. Square-ass Bates was there, looking as nervous as a virgin on prom night, along with two others I'd never seen. Big Nose scooped up my M4, while Buzz Cut pried the phone out my hand. Once he was sure I wasn't recording, he stomped my shit, ground it under his boot.

Gamble shook her head. "This was supposed to be the climax where we get to see all your father's training put to the test—I even found somebody special for you to play with. You'd whittle the advantage of my numbers until it was just down to you and me. A final faceoff.

"After all the thought I put into this, you just surrender like a little bitch?"

I just shrugged, let her see the disappointment was only hers.

"Do you know where my money is? Yes or no?"

I nodded, because I really did know. I pointed up above us. They scanned the catwalk with the flashlight beams until they found what I left up there. A small garbage bag, half full, was visible through the steel mesh flooring. It was situated in the middle of the longest bridge that spanned the entire production floor from north to south.

Gamble knew there was trickery on deck but was also hoping against hope that it wasn't. She wanted her share of the Urban Renewal funds too badly and couldn't take that risk.

"You say that's the money from the hotel. Where'd you find it? Who had it? And exactly how much is in the bag up there?"

I just looked at her like she was stupid for letting Buzz Cut break my phone. She eventually figured that out and gave me the burner phone I left the directions on for her when she first came in.

I had known she wouldn't come alone, but I didn't, either. I actually let her go on with that long speech about actors and directors because I had needed time to set up my own trap. I sent the message, then gave Gamble a sign she could understand. I held up my hand and curled down one finger after another until I got to my thumb. Zero.

For a few seconds, the sergeant and me just stared into each other's eyes. I glanced to the loading door after a few more seconds, then back to her.

She seemed amused by the confusion that started to cloud my expression. "Were you expecting something to happen? Like a homemade bomb going off under my car?"

When another figure stepped in through the loading door carrying a medium-sized duffel bag, I could tell by the walk that I was fucked. I didn't need him to step into the light to know that it was Louie Boy.

Another longtime friend had betrayed me.

Chapter Seventy-nine

Gamble said, "This is a classic tale of brains versus brawn, and you might've had a chance if you played to your strengths. But you tried to be a schemer and got out-schemed."

Louie Boy came into the circle of illumination created by their flashlights. This lame couldn't even look me in the eye. I could see in his sullen face he'd known this was coming since that first day we caught up in The Pastry Shop.

He dropped the bag at Gamble's feet as if happy to be rid of it, and they all gave it a wide berth. Louie held up the phone I had given him. "I w-was supposed to set it off w-w-with this."

Bates approached her. "Should we get somebody from the disposal team down here?"

Gamble glared at him as if that were the stupidest thing she'd ever heard. "Call the commissioner, everybody down at the First Precinct, and a few news cameras while you're at it.

"You just earned your way into my trust, so take this piece of advice: Don't say anything until you think on it first. Then run it by one of the others before saying it to me."

"Sykes, check it out." This must've been Buzz Cut's real name. I had already judged by the hair and swagger that he had a military background. And I could tell by how much confidence he showed stepping toward the package that he had some experience with explosives.

Louie Boy finally found enough courage to look at me. "It-it's not like what you th-think."

It was exactly like I thought.

"Two million in cash g-get you ten million in government f-funds. Tax-free. It w-w-was gone be enough for everybody to eat, but Doc got gr-greedy like he always do."

I just waved him off, wondering at what price did real men abandon their principles. And if they were willing to abandon them at any price, were they ever real men?

Buzz Cut knelt and slowly pulled back the zipper on the duffel bag to expose a simple trio of pipe bombs rigged to a remote detonator.

Gamble was talking her shit again. "I see all your moves coming before you make them. Only inattentive film watchers are ever surprised by the twist ending." I smirked because for once, this bitch was right.

Buzz Cut boldly pulled the entire package out the bag. "It's a fake!"

They all turned their attention back to me as if expecting to see surprise here. Of course I knew the bomb was a fake. It was just a harmless prop I put together using empty PVC pipes, wires, and an old solar calculator.

Gamble rubbed her chin, wrinkled her nose. "I'm trying to follow your train of thought here, Silence. Louis was supposed to place this dud under my car, and when my Camaro failed to explode, what was supposed to happen next? What was your point?"

This particular trap had never been about her. If I had wanted to, I could've blew up her Camaro from my phone. The decoy in the bag was just about helping me to expose a rat.

From the start, it never made sense to me that Gamble wouldn't scope out Louie Boy as the prime suspect for Doc's murder. Unless he was already on her leash. At some point, her or Doc told him about the URP, which was why Louie knew so much about the Henleys and city politics.

When I hit the send button on my phone, the one I gave him to detonate my fake package started to buzz. Louie Boy looked curiously at the text I had been waiting to send him: *Hey Shitty. H-H-Hope you can w-w-wipe with the left!*

The sound made all of them flinch. Louie Boy did more than flinch when the phone exploded in his hand.

He jumped up and down, spun in circles while fanning his arm. I was only able to stuff in the thin phone enough explosive to equal a M-80 firecracker. But this had been enough to blow off his pinky and ring fingers, leaving the thumb bent backwards with a tip hanging only by ligaments. Louie Boy tucked his mutilated hand against his side. His face made me think his howl was that of a wounded animal.

One of the no-names swept the phone from my hand while Big Nose, who was still wearing a cast on her wrist, clubbed me over the head with the Benelli.

"Cute. Real cute," Gamble admitted, only after staring cautiously at her own Galaxy.

"We should assume there's another incendiary device up in that bag," Sykes aka Buzz Cut advised. He was referring to what I'd left up on the catwalk.

"That's why he's going to go get it." Gamble announced. She made them pat me down to ensure that I didn't have another phone stashed on me somewhere. "And if there's anything in that bag except cash, shoot him in the head."

She assigned the task to Bates and the sloppy-built cop I fought at the gas station. Before Bates led me away, Gamble and Sloppy exchanged a glance that I knew the meaning of.

The duo walked me to the stairs that led up to the catwalk above. They had clearly learned their lesson from our previous encounters. Each detective had personal experience with the consequences of getting too close to me. They smartly gave me a berth of six feet.

As we climbed those switch-back stairs, Bates was three steps behind me with Sloppy three steps behind him. I could only hope dude had learned enough and was paying attention to my hands through those thick-ass glasses.

When we reached the top, Bates remained behind on the safety of the landing, while Sloppy-Built followed me out onto the wire-mesh catwalk. He kept about twenty feet behind me. If there was a real package in the plastic bag, he was clear just in case I decided to go suicide bomber, but he still had the range to shoot me if I acted up in some other way.

The footbridge had eight arachnid-like limbs that branched off the main aisle, which ran the length of the building. These lesser arms spread east to west, and after a few ninety-degree turns, terminated in small viewing platforms that permitted foremen to stand over every production station that had once been below. This gave the catwalk the appearance of a simple maze.

My stomach was doing somersaults. I wasn't entirely sure the rickety old structure would support our combined weight. When I climbed up earlier, it had taken all the courage in my reserve. I was suddenly and acutely aware of my two-seventy and the extra two-fifty or so my escort was carrying. I tiptoed, as if that could lighten me. The whole catwalk seemed to sway under my feet like a tension bridge in the wind.

I reached the bag, turned to him slowly with my arms out at my sides. Sloppy closed the distance to within ten feet but kept that buffer. The dark and distance made it hard to read lips, but the gestures he made with the Glock indicated that he wanted me to pick up the bag and empty the contents on the catwalk. He was in a shooter's stance, aiming with a two-handed grip, ready to make good on his sergeant's order.

I slowly reached down to grab the garbage bag and emptied it. The bundles of paper inside spilled onto the catwalk and over the side, where they drifted down to the circlet of corrupt cops waiting below. Something else slipped from the bag that I was quick enough to snatch while still in the air.

Around the same time, Sloppy-Built realized all that I had made rain was flyers to re-elect Councilman Corliss Henley: the mechanic to tune up the Motor City. Bates yelled something from behind that made the chunky detective turn backwards and fire a shot in his direction.

I took advantage of that distraction, struck off down one of the lesser arms of the catwalk. I did a running Superman leap off the edge.

Chapter Eighty

In hindsight, it wasn't Superman I was imitating, but Tarzan. About eight feet out from the platform hung an old rusted chain dangling from a large spool bolted to the ceiling. I imagined that the Nature's Way company had once used it to hoist the heavy machine parts of their bottling and labeling assembly.

First I had to dive over a four-foot handrail, but without actual superpowers, it was impossible to jump for height and distance at the same time. This physics lesson came to me as I soared briefly through the air, then started to sink with the chain still inches away from my outstretched hands. I was certain I was about to miss it and receive the crueler lesson that gravity had to teach me fifty feet below.

But my momentum carried me forward, even as I fell. I snagged the chain at about thirty-five feet and immediately called *Bullshit!* on every Tarzan movie I ever saw. That shit nearly tore my shoulder out of the socket. The rough, rusty links bit into my palms.

Sloppy-Built turned his gun back to me, looking like I'd just lost my damn mind. I had only put myself in a much more precarious position. Thirty-five feet up, hanging on for dear life, nothing to hide behind, and no weapon to defend myself. While everybody down below spotlighted me with their flashlights, Sloppy took aim to squeeze off what would've been a killshot.

That was when I hit the send button on the phone in the pocket of my sweats, the one I had stashed in the garbage bag with the Henley flyers.

Sykes had only been half-right when he warned that my real package was above, only not in the bag and not just one. Nine baby bundles, each one barely as strong as a single stick of dynamite. These were small-shaped charges that I'd placed on the suspension braces that tethered the catwalk to the ceiling. Synchronized or simultaneous explosions were a tricky thing to pull off. Thank the ancestors that all of the devices went off at roughly the same time.

Sloppy-Built was less than five feet away from one of the packages. When the brace snapped, that part of the catwalk teetered like a ship hit by a rogue wave. He was pitched overboard, only it wasn't cold ocean water waiting to catch him. I'd swear his body bounced five feet high before settling against the unforgiving cement.

The concussive effect of multiple explosions shook the building. This sent the chain hoist swinging wildly and me along with it.

My plan had been for the catwalk to come down all at once on Gamble and her crew. The problem was that I had underestimated the old building's structural integrity. Some of the suspension braces held. So instead, the system of overhead walkways only fell in sections, and some of those too slowly. This allowed the cops below to scramble like roaches.

In some places, wire-mesh chunks the size of trucks came down. I thought I saw Big Nose get crushed, but from my vantage point I couldn't be sure what happened to the rest. I was too busy spinning like one of those chicks at the club who danced hanging from those long silks.

The explosion not only sent a piece of shrapnel as thin as a pencil into my arm, the vibrations loosened the spool of chain connected to the ceiling. It unraveled, dropping your boy.

I didn't come down as fast as gravity would have brought me but still hard enough to put me flat on my back. I had to roll away before more heavy chain spilled down to crush me.

The fall knocked the wind out of me, and I knew my ankle was fucked-up even before I stood. I hobbled around the larger pieces of the catwalk that lay around me in ruined black metal. The rest still threatened me from above.

Big Nose lay faceup under a twelve-foot length of flooring, the crisscross grating of the wire mesh sliced into her body like a potato being cut into fries. I reclaimed my shotgun that had fallen a few feet away from her hand.

Not far from her, a second cop who I hadn't even bothered to label with a nickname was futilely crawling in place. His legs were pinned under one of the viewing platforms, so mangled it was clear he'd never use them again. He looked to me whimpering, probably begging me to help lift it or to put a bullet in his brain. I stepped over him in no mood to perform mercies.

The other no-name had tried to run before a portion of the handrail came down like a spear to skewer him. A pole, about the length needed for a street sign, entered through his neck and exited out his thigh, still with enough force to pierce the cement. He was a human shish kebab, dead while standing upright.

I must've still been dizzy from the fall. I didn't even realize I was being shot at until I spied dust kicking up at my feet.

Chapter Eighty-one

I bounced behind one of the load-bearing beams for cover. I looked around for the shooter until I caught a partial view of him. Buzz Cut was two beams away doing the same thing, concealing himself for cover. He raised a pistol and ripped two more shots at me.

A tactical shotgun was not the ideal choice in this situation. It was a piece of machinery made for up-close, messy work, not for a drawn-out fire fight sixty feet from your target. A legal M4 only carries five rounds, but this one was illegally modified to hold eight.

I pumped out two of them to provide suppression fire for my move. I tried to run but was slow on the bad ankle. He fired again while I was in the open, and I dipped behind a closer beam.

He was still posted behind the same beam, poking his head out just long enough to take a shot at me. If he was smart, he would've retreated as I advanced. Having only thirty feet between us improved my position and my aim.

The interior of the factory was too dark for me to catch the make of his pistol, but that advantage still went to him. He most likely had sixteen rounds to play with, that was if he didn't have an extended clip. My Benelli would run dry long before his.

I bet my life on another all-or-nothing gambit. I just charged him, emptying my shit as I came. The M4 was a rapid-fire pump that could spit five rounds in under two seconds, and the recoil was a bitch on my shoulder.

Buzz Cut had slotted himself into the socket of the I-beam, shells ringing off the steel all around him, too pinned down to fire back. My shotgun was done by the time I reached him, so I let it fall. It didn't matter, because by that point, I was close enough to put hands on him.

I grabbed his gun arm, twisted, and made him drop that. I tried to stun him with a throat shot, but he blocked me, hit me with a combo, then kicked my knee.

Buzz Cut looked at me like I'd just fucked up. This white boy clearly knew something and hadn't run because he had wanted this fight as much as me. I staggered a few feet back, making a new assessment of my opponent.

He said, "I was supposed to be in the car that night at the gas station, but something came up. Things would've been totally different if I was there."

I gave him a smirk that said, *Make me a believer.*

I attacked again, and he slowly did make me a believer, because I was on the losing end each time we traded blows. I had the height advantage, but his skills were sharper than mine, and not just because of my injuries. He was highly trained and more recently practiced.

Muay Thai, or Thai boxing, was different than regular kickboxing in that the latter focused strictly on the hands and feet as much as traditional boxing focused on the fists. Muay Thai was alone in that elbows, fists, knees, and feet, along with various clinches, were employed, causing an endless variety of strikes and defenses. In the military it was only taught in the most elite combat units. An ex-Army ranger had started me on it at five. Buzz

Cut had been in some type of special ops unit before becoming a cop.

He noticed from my side-to-side movement that my ankle was bad. He attacked from angles that forced me to put weight on it. He also made sure to tenderize it with low kicks from his steel-toed boot.

My shoulder hurt too much to jab with my right, and that made my punch combinations predictable. He caught my left, used it to pull me into a hip toss.

His jujitsu was just as clean, because he seamlessly took our fight to the ground. He still had my wrist, and I narrowly escaped an arm bar. This wasn't the UFC: no referee to stop the match when I tapped out. If I didn't break free, he would've snapped my shit at the elbow.

I rolled away, and we both scrambled to our feet; him a bit quicker than me. Buzz Cut caught me with a rising knee, but what really fucked me up was I stumbled backward and cracked the back of my head against the corner of the metal beam. That dazed me.

I was injured, and dude was nice, but I realized that wasn't the reason I was being outclassed. My mind was all over the place: Mrs. P, Quianna, little Nika. I had too many deaths and betrayals swirling around my mind. I couldn't calm that storm in the moment but did find that serene space within the eye of it. I remembered my breathing, centered myself.

When he attacked again, I anticipated rather than just responded. His moves were crisp, but I countered these, and after a while peeped his combination pattern. He liked to fake twice with the left, low-kick my shin, then shoot the real jab and follow with a straight right. We circled each other as I waited and watched.

And sure as shit, I could've set that Rolex Quianna gave me by it. Those two fakes came, and I got on his ass.

I stepped into the leg kick I knew was coming next, absorbed that pain, had to get in order to give. Blocked that left jab, then hit him with a four-piece, all kidney and rib shots. That folded him over. I clinched his neck, tried to break his nose with my knee, but he slipped away from me. Took a spinning back fist with him, though.

We engaged a few more times, but he found a much more disciplined fighter. I had adapted to his style better than he could adapt to mine. While I hadn't trained since I was seventeen, I had started much younger, which meant my technique was deeply ingrained. He still had to think on his moves and had a bad habit of leaning on prefabricated combinations rather than improvising. Because of this, he started losing those exchanges, first by a little, then by a lot.

In our last exchange, he caught another three-piece to the body before I went up top, a combo blow of the fist and elbow that rocked him. When he staggered back, I saw him making a new assessment of me.

If I had been looking closer, I would've also saw the mounting desperation. It wouldn't have surprised me when he dove for his gun.

I dove with him but grabbed and brought with me a length of the loose-hanging chain I used to play Tarzan. While Buzz Cut scrambled to get the gun, I scrambled to mount his back. I looped the chain around his neck and pulled until his legs started kicking like he was trying to swim away from a shark. I kept pulling for several minutes until they stopped.

His face was tinted purple with veiny bloodshot eyes bulging from his skull. I slumped on top of him, needed a few seconds to catch my breath. The Shango warrior in me quietly thanked the ancestors and my opponent for the best fight I'd ever had.

I used that respite for a quick body count. I had dropped the catwalk on three of them, and Sloppy-Built fell off the top. By my math, that left me with two and a possible. I scanned around, not seeing Gamble, her partner Bates, or Louie Boy.

My body was so beat the fuck up that it almost didn't answer my call to stand. I grabbed Buzz's Glock 19, checked the clip, then made my way towards the loading door with a walk that was half skip and half shuffle. My ankle had already swollen to the size of a grapefruit. My right shoulder was in its socket, but I definitely had torn ligaments. I had a chunk of steel the size of an ink pen stabbing me in my left arm. Plus my old bullet wound was hurting like hell again.

And I was still dazed from cracking my head against the pole, or else I would've thought to peek out before I dipped under the loading door. I stepped out onto the loading dock and right into another trap.

The first thing I saw was the headlights from Gamble's silver Camaro speeding off down the service street, leaving behind the unmarked Explorer her team had come in. This was parked behind the black-and-silver Wraith.

The second thing I saw was that Louie Boy was waiting for me on the other side of the loading door, draped in shadow. It happened so fast that I couldn't see what was in his good hand. He raised it a little quicker than I was able to raise my gun.

That was the last thing I saw.

Chapter Eighty-two

Something squirted into my face, and it felt like someone had put out cigars in my eyes. My nose burned, too, and it was almost impossible to breathe. I couldn't see shit, but the more I tried to rub my eyes, the worse they burned.

Then I got hit with something hard and wooden. Over the head and again across the back. I clamped my eyes shut, could only put my hands up in defense. Through blurry vision, I caught a brief glimpse of Louie Boy swinging one-handed with what could've been a two-by-four. When I tried to cover my head, I got hit across the ribs and then over the head when I tried to protect my ribs.

Panicked, I nearly forgot I had the gun and started swinging it around. I fired wildly. A few seconds passed without me getting whacked, and I started to think maybe I'd hit him. Then I felt myself get kicked in the back. I stumbled on the bad ankle and fell.

Not just to the ground but from a height. For an instant, the Earth disappeared from under me, and my feet went over my head. My body slapping hard against the concrete told me I'd just taken the seven-foot tumble off the edge of the loading dock.

The impact jarred me, and the Glock got away. I anxiously

groped the ground all around me, knowing that if Louie Boy found the gun first, I was done. I was on my stomach running my hands over the rough cement reading Braille. All I touched on were small rocks, broken glass, and a puddle of cool liquid I could only hope wasn't piss.

A kick to the midsection sent a jolt of pain through me and rolled me onto my side. That told me Louie was standing over me. Instinct told me he had the gun.

Keen sight and scent had always made up for my hearing, but I was blinded, and my sinuses burned. Not even a proud Shango warrior could overcome a deficit of three senses. I had gotten beat by a single blast of pepper spray.

I imagined Louie Boy standing over me with the gun aimed at my head, explaining why he had to do this—he was that type of nigga. He'd never been a killer, so he would need to justify this to both of us, as if I could actually hear him or cared to listen if I could.

I was trapped in a world with no sensation other than my own pains. Waiting for the end, wondering if I would even know when it happened.

I felt wetness spray my arm and assumed Louie spat on me—a petty but final *fuck you*. Then he tried to pull me up from my stomach to my knees, I guess to do it execution-style.

Mistake! Louie Boy made a critical blunder when he put his hands on me. I grabbed him, pulled him down to the ground, and rolled on top of him. I found and pinned his gun hand. I pressed my forearm into his throat and started squeezing the life out of him. Stupid muthafucka should've just shot me and got it over with. Another one who would pay for getting too close.

Strangling him took too long, and I thought about just snapping his neck instead, but there was something about this that felt off. Louie Boy wasn't fighting back, just frantically tapping my shoulder. The reason slowly dawned on me.

I kept the gun pinned with one hand just in case but ran the other over his face. Lucky for him, those big goofy-ass glasses hadn't come off during our tussle. I climbed off of Bates and let him help me to my feet, which was what he was trying to do when I felt him grab me.

It was still too painful to open my eyes for any longer than a split second, and even then, my own acidic tears reduced my vision to smudged photographs. I snapped enough of these to gather that the long dark blur at my feet was Louie Boy. Bates had killed him while Louie had stood over me, probably while my old friend was doing his monologue. That wetness I felt mist over me wasn't spit like I'd first thought but blood splatter from Louie's gunshot wound.

I gave Bates my key fob, and he guided me by the arm as I directed him to the Aston Martin I left parked out of sight on the other side of the factory. He helped me into the passenger seat. I felt us come to a jerky start as we pulled away.

While Bates drove in sporadic bursts of acceleration, then braked hard enough to throw me forward in my seat, sight returned to me slowly and in stages. I went from only being able to blink in quick, poorly developed photos to minutes later being able to hold my eyes open long enough for grainy three-second videos.

Bates put what felt like a small folded slip of paper in my hand. I had to squint hard and strain through the burning sensation to see it was the same note I had left in his wallet. I had written the words: *She knows you're a rat!!*

He had written just under it: *How did you know that Gamble had made me as IAB?*

The truth was that I didn't know. I just wrote that shit to sow some distrust between them. But Gamble had clearly figured out he was a mole for the Internal Affairs division—the cops that investigated dirty cops. Bates thanked me for saving his life up on the catwalk.

I saw the look Gamble gave Sloppy-Built as they led me away to get the money. That told me Bates was about to get killed right along with me then get put on my tab. His square ass had taught himself enough ASL to call me an asshole back at the house. As we climbed the stairs, I hoped that Bates was paying attention to my subtle hand movements. He had picked up enough sign language to heed the warning that I finger-spelled to him.

The department must've already suspected what Gamble was into. Bates was a new partner assigned to gather proof.

I only put together that I might have a potential ally in him outside of Mrs. P's house that night Nika got shot. When I manhandled Bates and threw him up against the car, I picked his pocket but also felt a tiny microphone strapped to his chest. He was wearing a wire. The enemy of my enemy . . .

I kept rubbing my eyes with my shirt until the muddled masses of light and shadow sharpened into the black post-midnight sky, the glare of headlights from the traffic surrounding us, the shining hood of the DBS. I was able to keep my eyes open for longer than a few seconds, even though it felt like peeling the scabs off two raw wounds each time I blinked.

I got annoyed by the way we were lurching forward and coming to these sudden stops. I borrowed Bates's phone to type a message: *What type of grown-ass man can't drive stick shift?* He started to make some lame excuse that I didn't feel like reading off his lips. I made fake-ass Norbit pull over, pushed him out the driver's seat before he burned out the clutch.

Driving a car this powerful at night with my vision only at about thirty percent definitely wasn't the safest thing. But it was our best chance of catching up with Gamble.

Chapter Eighty-three

Bates explained that a tracking device had already been placed on Gamble's car. So he had the advantage of knowing where she was going. According to him, GPS had her headed towards Metro Airport. I wanted that bitch too bad to ever let her skip off to some country with non-extradition.

On the freeway, I had the DBS Superleggera up to one-forty. I was hunched over the wheel squinting hard. Bates was nervous, kept asking me about my eyes. I gestured that I was straight even as I came dangerously close to getting us pinned under the trailer of a semi.

I think just to take his mind off my driving, Bates explained all the evidence he had accumulated against Gamble—even though having to read all this off his phone only helped to distract me from the road. He had secretly recorded hours of them discussing drugs they had stolen on raids and from the evidence room at the precinct, along with Gamble's connection to Councilman Henley. Trying to kill him had just been the cherry on top.

I eventually tuned him out to focus on my driving. My eyes still burned. My overall vision was improving but would suddenly regress, causing me to see the highway and other vehicles as indistinct shapes without sharp edges. I would then need a moment to blink the world back into clarity.

Those thick lenses must've given Bates telescopic vision, because he was pointing long before the smudge I glimpsed on the horizon took the form of a silver Camaro. I put the Aston's 5.2-liter V-12 to work and closed the distance to within a car length.

The Camaro ZL1 had motor, too—a supercharged V-8 running six hundred and fifty horsepower—but not a driver of equal skill. I figured the stud had chosen the car like her clothes to help defeminize herself, but in watching her drive, I could tell that she had never learned to tame the animal. She sloppily darted around the light sprinkling of traffic you would find on I-94 at one in the morning. Goofy-ass Bates cracked the window and started waving his badge in the air like that was supposed to make her pull over.

Gamble tried to shake me. She abruptly sliced across three lanes to catch the Merriman Road exit to Metro Airport. Then halfway up the off-ramp, she quickly cut back onto the freeway.

But Gamble wound up shaking herself more than me. She spent the next quarter mile swerving back and forth between two lanes as she fought to correct the wheel.

I sped up to give her bumper a love tap that sent her into a skid. The Camaro skated sideways over the berm, popped a tire, spun out, then stalled on the grassy embankment.

I needed about two hundred feet to brake. I backed up along the shoulder of the highway, and Bates was out the door before I could stop.

The driver's door on the Camaro was open, too. Gamble was on all fours, scrambling up the sloping embankment towards the service drive.

I kept backing along the shoulder, doing about sixty in REVERSE until I reached the Merriman exit that tripped her up. I shifted back into DRIVE and raced up the off-ramp.

On the surface street, I saw Gamble sprinting towards a Shell station with a gun in hand, while Bates's lagging ass was far behind, jogging like he was about to pass out. Under the pavilion, an older white dude filled up a gray F-150 pickup. When Gamble made a beeline for him, I already knew what she was on.

Mr. Justin Wilson, the dude whose credit card was renting the Aston Martin, was about to get an even bigger surprise on his monthly statement. I whipped into the gas station, laying on my horn to get the old man's attention. He and Gamble jumped out the way when I plowed into the pickup doing about forty. I buckled the nose of the exotic car and knocked the half-ton pickup back fifteen feet.

I sat behind the wheel, still stunned by the impact until the rear window shattered and bullets punched holes in the windshield. Gamble was in my rearview looking pissed. The muzzle flashes on her Glock 22 spoke silent death threats.

I dove out the driver's door, rolled to the other side of the pumps to keep some cover between us. On instinct, I reached to my waist only to realize I didn't have a gun.

The old dude was on the ground next to me still bitching about his truck. I snatched the old man to his feet, motioned for him to shut the fuck up and run.

He scrambled for the interior of the food mart. I followed, hobbled by my ankle, and caught the door right as the attendant hit the automatic locks. Bitch tried to trap me outside. I limped toward the register giving him a *What the fuck?* look. He returned one that said he didn't want trouble, mouthed something about me having to leave.

Gamble reached the doors, found them locked, then shot out the glass.

I ducked down and retreated deeper into the mini-store, hopeful for a restroom window or a rear exit I could escape through. The restrooms could only be accessed through a separate door on the other side of the building. No rear exit.

I saw Gamble flash her badge to calm the Chaldean in the plexiglass fish tank. Clearly she was making it seem like she was just doing her job, and I was the one on bullshit. So when the white cop murdered an unarmed black man, it would just be business as usual.

She began searching the aisles for me, the gun thrust out before her. I hid in the last one with the refrigerated beverages. I used the mirrors to keep track of her. I scanned the shelves. The closest thing to a weapon was a long plastic brush used to clear snow off of windshields.

I grabbed one and eased to the end of that aisle to crouch behind the potato chip display. Gamble was coming towards me, and I waited with my heart in my throat. Another situation where I had nothing but surprise as my ally.

But for some reason, I forgot that mirrors worked both ways. Gamble spotted my reflection before she turned into the freezer aisle, started firing right through the chip display.

I picked up the entire rack and charged behind it like a shield. I ran hard but was still too slow on the ankle. Gamble squeezed off a shot that made a family-sized bag of kettle-cooked Lay's explode right next to my face.

I rammed her with the metal display stand. The impact threw her back into the coolers. Her head shattered one of the glass doors, made cans of Diet Pepsi spill out to crack open against the floor. Gamble looked up to me, a gash on her forehead leaking blood down her face.

She tried to bring up the Glock again, but I smacked that arm with the snow brush. I sent her errant bullet to the floor, then twisted her wrist. When she dropped the gun, I kicked it away.

She said, "Another gas station. I guess there's some symmetry to that, but it's still a weak location for the climax. A shoot-out at the airport would've been so much more cinematic."

I couldn't deny that would've been a lot cooler, but this wasn't a movie. Things in real life rarely unfolded in a way to provide the most pleasing aesthetic. In real life, best friends betrayed you, innocent little girls got shot, and shit went down where it happened to go down.

I had spun Gamble around and coiled my arms around her neck when Bates appeared at the end of the aisle. He approached with his gun up but aimed at me. He barked for me to let her go, and I glared at him like, *Nigga please!*

Bates drew my attention to his lips. "Don't do it, man. She needs to answer for her crimes. Give me my suspect, and I promise I will find out who killed your friend."

This fool still didn't understand that wasn't the type of justice I dealt in.

He screamed that I owed him for saving my life, clearly forgetting that I saved his first.

"In three minutes, this place will be swarming with officers. If you let her go, you can walk away right now. I can get the girl released and get you the footage from the 76.

"But there's no place for the way you do things." His eyes became hard behind those magnifying lenses. "If you kill her, I swear by God that I will shoot you. Don't make me."

Without my phone, I had no way to explain that I wasn't a hero or an anti-hero. I am a goon. A man who doesn't use words but is extremely compelled to keep promises.

And I had promised Gamble she wouldn't like the twist I put on this ending.

So I twisted.

I snapped that bitch's neck right there in the beverage aisle. Let her body drop and dared Bates to shoot me.

Chapter Eighty-four

It should've been a dark day, one reflective of our collective mood. The rain should've fallen in a way that drew images of Noah and the flood. The sky should have been blanketed with violent black thunderheads producing lightning that flashed with apocalyptic fury. It should have appeared to the entire city that God himself was bitter and grieving.

To me, it felt like disrespect, or at least indifference, from the Man upstairs for it to be eighty-six and sunny. A few wispy cirrus clouds dusted the high atmosphere like a poorly wiped chalkboard, but other than those scattered streaks, the sky was in flawless imitation of Tarheel blue. It was a perfect day for picnics and parades, for family reunions on Belle Isle with barbeque and matching T-shirts.

Our family outing didn't involve a smoky grill or a festive game of young-versus-old volleyball. It was a generous turnout; more friends and supporters showed up than I knew she had. The day we laid sixty-three-year-old Dolores Peterson to rest was a dark one—fuck the weather!

The pastor at Triumph Church was a fifty-year-old ex-player in a ten-thousand-dollar suit and a long silky perm that made the salon rats jealous. He charged us the cost of two more suits to perform the eulogy and went overboard to make us feel like he earned every penny. This Katt Williams-looking muthafucka jumped around the pulpit for three hours, and I couldn't tell if he was doing standup comedy or throwing a concert—at one point, I thought he was going to pull a groupie up on stage to serenade her like Trey Songz.

And of course, all the old church ladies in the big hats loved it. It then became a competition between them to see who could out-grieve each other. They went from throwing up their arms in praise to rolling around in misery. A large woman in the fourth row eventually won when she pretended to faint and had to be carried out by four ushers. I suffered through the endless spectacle, and it was another of those moments when I was grateful for my handicap. I just watched it all wearing my permanent pair of noise-canceling headphones.

We took part in a thirty-two-car procession to the cemetery on 5 Mile Road. Since Mrs. P gave up her original resting place for Doc, we had to find her another. There was nothing available in close proximity to her son, so the two would be forever separated by one hundred and fifty yards of decaying strangers.

I thought I'd spent all my tears until the moment I watched that box sink into the earth. Just the finality of it got to me. Memories blurred my vision of the woman who accepted me into her home and taught me how to sign—my nigga-ass white Mama who talked shit, sipped Smirnoff, and smoked Newport 100s.

Quianna had been released the same night I snapped Gamble's neck, and she'd become the rock the family needed these past four days while making the arrangements. She stood next to me covered from neck to toe in black leather and Chanel. Quianna remained stoic as groundskeepers began to shovel dirt on the glossy mahogany casket. The big stylish wood-framed sunglasses had kept her face unreadable through the entire service, but she held onto my hand for much of it.

The only silver lining was that the same day we laid Mrs. P to rest, little Nika had opened her eyes. She was awake and responsive but far from a full recovery. Doctors had to remove one kidney and over a foot of large intestine. The next few months for her would be a gauntlet of follow-up surgeries.

I drove Quianna's Hellcat away from the cemetery. I waved Trayvion to the back seat but stopped the friend who seemed to be joined at his hip. I motioned for dude to catch a ride with somebody else. Some moments were just for the family.

They assumed we were headed back to the eastside house on Radom, where Pooh and everybody else were gathered for a small wake. Quianna and Trayvion both looked confused when I parked in rear of the Nature's Way factory. I pulled all the way through the yellow police tape that cordoned off the back dock where Louie Boy's body was found, and Doc's before him.

I'd been through too much and had no more patience to bullshit around or ease into it.

I texted Quianna: *Gamble arrested you never knowing how close she was to the truth.*

Chapter Eighty-five

I snatched Quianna's sunglasses off her face so I could read her eyes and so that she would know I wasn't playing some game. I hit the locks on the doors.

Her hazel eyes narrowed into angry slits. "You just watched me bury my mother fifteen minutes ago and you accusing me of killing my brother?"

That lick at the hotel had Doc and Louie Boy so convinced that one had betrayed the other. They never considered that a third party got down on them both.

Prime admitted that Quianna had been the only one to stay in touch during his falloff years, and whether by accident or not, he had most likely told her about the Holiday Inn, the same place they liked to count up when the three of them had the North Carolina plug. Louie Boy had thought those little dudes dressed in all black with the ski masks were Doc's Joy Road Boys. They weren't. In fact, they weren't boys at all.

Quianna pretended like she couldn't understand me, like she had the handicap. "You think me and the girls robbed my own brother?"

I know they did. I'm sure BANDS was getting decent money

from the trick parties and credit scams, but scooping old boy's Rolex showed me that Quianna wasn't above moving dirty.

In the end, it was her girl Lexy who slipped up in a moment of frustration and said something she wasn't supposed to. When Louie ran on us at the club, she called him a coward and hinted at him needing to change his drawers. Louie Boy had shit on himself when they put him facedown in the bathtub, and it wasn't something I could see him sharing with the world. The only other people who would know were the ones who held the guns on him.

I had to collar up Baby Momma Number Six to get her real confession. It wasn't Doc who got her to make the call that sent Louie Boy all over the city, just like she hadn't been seduced by Doc when they randomly bumped into each other at a club. Quianna had put that chick on her brother.

Number Six was actually the one who pulled Doc away from the room, which was why he was gone when Louie got back. While the stash was being hit, Doc was busy getting some head in the parking lot. This was the reason Doc suspected Louie Boy had set him up.

I peeped game when Number Six came to the door wearing the skimpy denim cutoffs. I texted Quianna: *You should've made sure she kept that BANDS logo on her thigh covered up.*

Quianna looked at me with half a sneer and half a smirk. I could tell that some part of her had been wanting to tell me this, had taken a certain measure of pride in it.

"Another thing I learned from my girl Tuesday: you could rob niggas, and if you do it right, they'll never suspect you. That's because men gone always underestimate females."

But what Quianna didn't realize was that she didn't just steal from Doc and Louie Boy. She had put a whole lot of shit in motion with their silent partners: dirty cops who were ready to kill, blackmail, and give out life sentences over their share of the money.

In response to this, she spat: "So what! Fuck that nigga Doc! Fuck him, Louie Boy, and the rest of 'em!

"And fuck Doc double! He buying bitches Escalades and new houses while his mother on the other side of town dying of cancer. What about paying a medical bill, bitch muthafucka? The only right thing Doc ever did was bring you home."

I'd seen Quianna pissed—I'd seen her beyond pissed—but never saw the amount of fury in her eyes that I saw right then. All that taking up for big brother had been done well enough to fool my lie detector. It was only in that moment I realized how deeply she despised Doc. It was a hatred that shouldn't exist between two members of any family, so seeing it between two members of my own was painful. Part of me was glad that Mrs. P had gone to her rest without knowing.

"I did that shit for you!" Quianna spoke this with such emphasis that I imagined it was a scream. "Everything them niggas eventually had was because of you. While you in there jailing, niggas out here riding Bentleys and shit, but can't put fifty dollars on your books. Doc, Louie Boy, Prime, even Punchy bitch ass—all them niggas owed you what I took and more. Not only was you supposed to get held down in the joint, you was supposed to get picked up in a limo full of naked bitches and get a duffel bag dropped at your feet."

Prime hadn't exaggerated when he said everything changed when I got down with the crew. Back in the day, I was new to the game but vaguely aware I played a key role in expanding their bag. Doc, Louie Boy, and Prime were hustlers who made respectable names for themselves in the hood, but being respected wasn't quite the same as being feared. I made them a factor. I couldn't quote an exact dollar amount on how much they profited off the work I put in, but I wasn't doing it for the money. At the time, I was just happy to be connected to something.

While Quianna was dead-on about how I aided their come-up, she was wrong about them owing me. The crew didn't owe me shit, and it was one of the most difficult lessons that a prisoner has to learn. He has to shake this idea that the streets owe him something. He mistakenly believes that getting locked up somehow martyrs him and puts family and friends in his debt, when in truth, it was his own choices that took his freedom, and in most cases, it was those same family and friends who were trying to influence him to make better choices. Inside I saw too many men sit and grow bitter over the thought of family members advancing in their absence, moving on to bigger and better lives while feeling like his share in that was being denied. Once he breaks the mentality that people owe him, only then he can appreciate what he does get for what it really is: a blessing.

I was in the middle of texting a summary of that personal philosophy to Quianna when I felt the muzzle of a pistol at the base of my skull.

Chapter Eighty-six

I had watched him get dressed, knew he had a pistol on him and didn't bother to take it. As much as it was expected, the cold kiss of steel against my warm skin still made me flinch.

When I first came home, I had thought the nervousness I felt in Trayvion was due to my reputation. He had actually been scared because he knew I was going to find Doc's murderer.

I raised my hands above my shoulders where Trayvion could see them from the back seat.

Quianna was turned in her seat, screaming at him to put the gun down. The fear for my life seemed genuine, but there wasn't shock or appall that my godson was prepared to kill me. While I was sure that she had known, too, still I needed to see Quianna's reaction to confirm it.

If Quianna wasn't there when it happened, Trayvion had called her right after, and she had helped him set up the scene. She had pulled off the perfect robbery, so she was convinced she could help her nephew pull off the perfect murder.

I saw the curiosity in Quianna as to how I might have deduced this. I honestly could've saved myself so much trouble if I'd only been paying closer attention. Both of them had been dropping small innocuous clues that didn't seem like much by themselves but told the story when pieced together.

I carried the biggest piece of evidence on me. For the sake of the gun at my head, I slowly pulled open the jacket to the black suit Quianna had bought me for the service. I directed her to grab what was folded, stuffed, and half-hanging from my inside breast pocket.

Trayvion didn't appreciate me having his orange notebook. He jammed the pistol against the back of my head forcefully.

Art in all its truest forms is cathartic, and a nineteen-year-old doesn't possess the emotional discipline to keep something so traumatic from weeding its way into his music. I had missed the hint that first day he rapped for me on the front porch. On its surface, that song "I Got the Juice" was just about overcoming his haters. But it was laced with shots at an absentee father, and a dark metaphor about what he'd done behind the Nature's Way building.

While Trayvion was asleep, I had spent the previous two nights going through his entire notebook. He never blatantly wrote about murder or gave incriminating details. It was mentioned subtly, never direct, and sprinkled throughout a dozen or so of his songs. In some places remorseful, in other places the deed was hinted at with a dark humor. It was camouflaged by the similes of a novice lyricist, only obvious to someone who knew the secret at its core.

Quianna cursed out Trayvion for being so reckless, but I gave a hand gesture that told her to chill. Let's keep the vibe nice and relaxed. I knew his hand was shaking, could feel the tremors through the gun.

I found Trayvion's eyes in the rearview mirror. They were red and leaking tears, mourning more than Mrs. P then; he wept for what he had done to his father, and probably for what he was about to do to me. I stared into his reflection until he felt my attention and stared back. In my eyes, there wasn't aggression, fear, or judgment.

"Everybody thought he was so helluva but the nigga wasn't SHIT!" He spat the last word like phlegm. "My mom dies, I come to live with him thinking he was finally gone be my dad. That nigga left Mrs. P and Quianna to raise me while he ran the streets fucking every bitch with a pulse. Ain't never made it to one of my birthday parties, but let some celebrity throw a White Party downtown. Then he go move with Darnia, think he take me with him?

"How he come through in a Maserati wearing a hundred bands in jewelry, but when I ask him for nine hundred dollars for some studio time, he can't do it?"

We were getting to the real shit now. The young brown face, so similar to that of his victim's, twisted in malice and appeared to age him ten years. He used his free hand to wipe an escaped tear. "Said he wouldn't waste a cent on my trash-ass rhymes. I was just another young nigga out here spitting about a life I ain't know nothing about. Said he don't endorse fake shit."

I shook my head because that sounded like Doc. But that harsh criticism may have only been to motivate Trayvion to go harder at his craft.

"That night he came over, I asked him to put me on with the bag, to let me prove it—I'd hustle up on the studio time myself and be street-certified. But the nigga just laughed at me, said I didn't have that in me. He put on Dirty Red and them Joy Road niggas though."

The connection between Doc and Dirty Red was another clue Trayvion had dropped. The day I gave Pooh the keys and sat on the Radom porch with him, Trayvion had looked nervously at the red Benz SUV because he knew who it belonged to.

In the end, Doc had been killed for his chain, just not the way I first suspected. Like too many of us, Doc had put his hustle over his seed. Adolescence brings unique challenges for a boy that requires a father's constant presence and guidance. First Doc ignores him as a son only to take another youngster under his wing and gives him all the time and attention his own son craves. For Trayvion, learning that Doc gave Dirty Red his D-chain and having to watch him floss in it on Instagram had been the last straw. It was as if Doc had literally passed his torch to a more worthy successor.

"You know even when I put the gun to his head he laughed. Said I didn't have it in me."

Promising to not make the same mistake, I gazed at him stone-faced through the mirror.

The only thing sadder than killing your own father for not believing in your dream was never realizing that he actually did. The brochures in the shoebox for music equipment had been a clue to Doc's plans for his URP money. The LLC that Punchy had paid checks to and that Doc had used to purchase the building, Deep Pockets Productions, had been a record label. In the articles of organization, Doc had named Trayvion as vice-president. I could only imagine Doc had brought his son here that night to show him how this rundown building was going to be their future headquarters. A two-million-dollar cash donation to Corliss Henley's re-election campaign would have netted a ten-million-dollar renewal grant, more than enough for renovations to build a world-class studio.

That was until his favorite auntie stole the buy-in money, essentially robbing them both. I decided that Quianna nor Trayvion never needed to know that part.

The question on my face right then was *Where do we go from here?*

Chapter Eighty-seven

Quianna wore the same quizzical expression as me. "After everything you learned, how can you sit here still loyal to that snake?"

It wasn't about loyalty anymore, at least not between me and Doc. Sending me to Darnia had been the first step in a clever path designed to keep me off of Trayvion's scent. She had used and manipulated me just like everybody else in my life. It was time to see if all of it was bullshit.

She asked, "So what you gone do?"

I drained all the emotion from my face. I just stared at her unblinking.

"Silence, you don't owe Doc shit, and Trayvion is family."

I just stared at her.

"Momma gone, Doc gone, and ain't nothing gone bring him back. All we got is us."

I didn't agree or disagree.

"We got the money and the cops been dealt with. You protected the family."

I still gave Quianna nothing and saw panic slowly rise in her sparkling hazel eyes. Behind me, I felt Trayvion grow more anxious.

"If Doc had been alive when you came home, he probably would've killed you."

I had considered that. Even though I never found proof, I was still convinced my boy had set me up to get a life sentence just so I wouldn't find out about Ja'Quezz. I didn't think he was above killing me.

But that wasn't the question I needed answered then.

I sat calmly, not moving. Quianna typically was so good at reading me, but this time I was a blank page. I gave nothing that hinted at my intentions either way. She was going to have to make a decision.

That much she understood. Her face flushed with anger, but there was sadness around her eyes. She spoke through a slow headshake: "Why is you making me do this?"

Because I had to know.

Trayvion said something from the back seat that I missed. I was too focused on Quianna. She barked at her nephew to shut up. It came from a part of her that resented Trayvion for what he'd done and probably always would. From the part where Li'l Quay-Quay still lay dormant, the girl with the beads and braids who had once looked up to her big brother.

"It's over, and we got everything. You got everything. You got me; you can have Lexy, too. Shit, having me means you got the whole damn BANDS Society. Can't you see that YOU the biggest winner in this?"

An attractive offer and the slightest nod of my head or curl of my lips into a smile would have been enough to satisfy her. Quianna could breathe a sigh of relief, and Trayvion could take the gun away from my head.

But I couldn't make it that easy for her as much as I wanted to. I had to know.

Her level of panic was reaching critical. She closed her eyes for a second, rubbed her temples as if getting a migraine, then looked back to me. "Okay Silence, what you want? Half the money? All of it?"

Another rare miss. Quianna should've known this was about something much deeper than money.

But I offered no clue. With my black suit and blank stare, I could've been the sexiest mannequin at the Ralph Lauren store.

She screamed, "Damn nigga say something!"

I never looked away from Quianna but could tell that Trayvion had relaxed somewhat. It was the ease that came over a person who had already made up their mind. I felt his hand tighten on the pistol. He was preparing to handle the recoil.

Even a warrior from the tribe of Shango had their limitations. Nothing I had learned in the church could save me this time. Only one person could.

Quianna knew it was coming, too. Her face was a stew pot of different emotions: fury, fear, sorrow, and shame. Tears moistened her eyes and made them shine. She didn't have to tell me this was my last chance. We both knew it. I waited for her decision.

It might have been two seconds, or it might have been two minutes—time can do weird shit in moments like this. I glanced to the rearview mirror and saw a killer's calm in Trayvion's young eyes. The gun no longer trembled. There was a separation between the desire to act and the will to do. That bridge was crossed. He had earlier made up his mind, but now he was ready.

Quianna stepped in probably an instant before he would have pulled that trigger. Trayvion looked at her confused when she ordered him to stop and demanded the gun.

The breath that exploded from my lungs could've filled a truck tire. I'd played a game of chicken far more dangerous than driving against traffic on Linwood Ave. Through it all, I was actually worried they could hear my heart booming in my chest.

Trayvion offered Quianna his gun, and I finally offered her a smile to let her know we were all good. I had learned what I needed to know. I was about to throw the Charger in gear, ready to take us home to where the rest of the family was eating and mourning.

I leaned in for a quick kiss, which Quianna gave me.

Then my baby shot me.

Chapter Eighty-eight

The pain didn't come on me right away. In the immediate aftermath, I didn't even realize what she'd done. I felt the thunderous vibration of the gun going off in the cramped car, then looked down to see blood pooling in my lap.

I turned to Quianna, thinking it had to be a mistake. Trayvion had carelessly passed her a pistol with the safety switched off and a round chambered, that the weapon must've discharged by accident.

In those beautiful hazel eyes that matched the color of sparkling cider, there was sadness, there was remorse, but there damn sure wasn't the shock or surprise of someone who'd just popped the man she loved by mistake. Cold calculation lived in those eyes. They were the eyes of someone studying a chess position and realizing mate in three but only if the knight is sacrificed.

It was only then that the pain knifed through me like something hot and menacing. I curled around my wound and used my hand to try to stop the bleeding.

Instead of helping me, my woman and godson threw open the driver's door, pushed me out the car onto the cold cement. Quianna scooted behind the wheel, and I watched from the ground as the Hellcat backed out of the docking port, turned right, then disappeared laterally down the service street. Quianna left me to bleed out in the same spot where her brother was left.

I got to my feet after two failed attempts but only made it to the street. I fell back on my hands and knees, imitated a three-legged dog as I crawled clutching my wound. I was no stranger to the sight of my own blood, but the amount I was leaving on the concrete shocked me.

I had no idea of where I was trying to make it to but didn't get fifteen feet like that before the pain tipped me over onto my side. I inched another two feet on my elbows and was done.

Blackness encroached on the edges of my vision. I just lay there thinking this is how the Shango warrior ends. Not brought down in some epic standoff with the police, not broke down in hand-to-hand combat by a superior fighter. Clipped by my own girl. I could picture T'wanda watching from the Other Side, laughing her ass off. Like I said, my father had taught me how to deal with every form of threat except for the most dangerous.

I curled up fetal, ready to leave the world the same way I'd come into it. Blood pooled around my body. I was going back into that dark place where my strange lover lived; I believed for good this time. My eyes closed to the sight of flashing lights.

I don't know how long it was from the moment I was shot until the ambulance arrived, just knew it felt quick, especially for an abandoned industrial district. I don't remember being loaded or any part of the drive. I vaguely remember going through the ER doors at Detroit Receiving. The warm embrace of blackness. A nurse standing over me with a friendly face. More blackness.

But for some reason, our affair wasn't meant to be, at least not yet. I didn't know how many hours had passed when I woke up in the ICU, wearing bandages and wires connecting me puppet-like to machines that monitored my vitals.

And my right wrist cuffed to the hospital bed.

This was exactly why I had carried that slug in my shoulder for so long, hoping to avoid this very scenario. Any person admitted into the hospital with a gunshot wound was reported to the police and detained for questioning.

Of course, in my own way, I told the two detectives who came to interview me to eat a dick. Somebody shot me; I didn't know who or why. They knew I was full of shit, but it didn't matter, because I was still stuck.

I finally met that parole officer I never bothered to go see. On my first day out, I was supposed to be in his office at the same time I was in Punchy's house tying up his girl. My no-call/no-show eventually caused him to issue a warrant for my arrest. So after all the murder and mayhem, in the end, I got booked for a parole violation.

I spent the next six days chained to the bed being babysat by two Wayne County sheriffs. Before the doctor who signed my discharge papers could cap his pen, I was transferred to the temporary detention center on Mound Road.

To my surprise, Detective—now Sergeant—Bates actually went to bat for me. He still wasn't happy about me killing Gamble, but the fat promotion helped to ease the pain. He couldn't detail my specific involvement in the case that made his career without losing his badge and getting me a thousand years. But he could vouch for me with my PO as a character witness.

It didn't get me sprung, but I did receive the equivalent of a wrist slap. Instead of me being sent back upstate to try my hand again with the parole board in another year, I was sentenced to forty-five days at the detention facility. I had been ready to die before going back to prison; while I wasn't happy, I couldn't complain too much about the result.

Prime pulled up on me once. I guess he and his boys had took that work and ran with it. He looked and spoke like the Prime I used to know—was over that feeling-sorry-for-himself shit. He bought me a sandwich and juice from the vending machines and put me up on his latest moves in a way that didn't seem like he was being fake.

Apparently Ja'Quezz was staying with him. Prime told me about T'wanda's funeral and did that in a way to say he knew I was responsible. I made no denials. His sister had to pay for her transgressions; in the end, even she had accepted this. I told my old friend with my glare that this would only be a problem if he made it one.

Dirty Red got cut loose on his charges after a few days. He put in two appearances that were primarily business meetings, still wearing a bandage on his left hand. Finalizing the deal we made on Mrs. P's porch became heated at some points. He still felt some type of way about his fingers, so I ain't trip when he didn't even buy me shit out the vending machines.

My third visitor was one I hardly expected. On my eighth day, I was in the weight pit squatting a light three ninety-five to rehab my injured leg when I received notice. I showered and put on a clean uniform, but they didn't escort me to the regular visiting room. Somebody had requested a non-contact visit, and I was led into a room where twelve booths had old grandma-style telephones hanging on the walls, plastic chairs fronting desks that were separated by a pane of one-inch tempered glass.

Quianna stood waiting for me in the last booth, even though we had the entire room to ourselves.

Chapter Eighty-nine

Quianna had changed her hair: jet black and draping her shoulders, straight and shiny as silk curtains. She wore a cream Balenciaga outfit that had the brand name printed on endless repeat in tiny diagonal stripes. She had on her lipstick and lashes. She looked so good that I knew my hard dick would disturb my sleep that night.

I didn't let any of this show on my face, though. I just waited for her to ease into the chair on her side of the glass before I followed suit.

The phones that hung to the right of each of us wouldn't be needed. I could read her lips just fine, and without a cell to text with, I was back to scribbling my thoughts on a four-by-six-inch flip pad that I carried everywhere in my shirt pocket.

For a while, the two of us just stared at each other until she finally mouthed: "Damn nigga, you can't get lined up in there?"

My head was covered with two weeks' worth of stubble. The facility had two inmate barbers on staff—one black, one white—but after seeing a few other dudes get their heads butchered, I decided I would thug it out for forty-five days and just let my shit nap up.

But there was no need to tell Quianna any of that. I just stared at her until she was ready to have a real conversation.

"Lexy said hey." She was still with the bullshit, so I made no response.

Lexy had been just another distraction. Quianna knew my weaknesses: a dark-skinned cutie with a colossal ass who just happened to know sign language was perfect bait. Too perfect to be coincidence. I believe Quianna's original plan had been to keep me swimming in so much BANDS pussy that I would never learn the truth. Only Lexy had wanted Quianna all to herself. She hadn't liked it but still played her role in Quianna's mind game. So fuck Lexy, too.

"Your leg okay?"

This was worth responding to. I scribbled in my sloppy block print: *Getting better.*

Quianna had probably figured that shooting me in the leg was the safest option. The problem was that her bullet had nicked the large femoral artery that runs through the upper thigh and nearly caused me to bleed out. And I would've, too, if it wasn't for the timely appearance of the ambulance, which of course was also her doing.

Luckily the bullet hadn't struck bone or done permanent nerve damage. I had needed crutches that first week after surgery. All that remained was a slight bob in my step that she probably noticed when the guards walked me in.

I could tell by the shift in her demeanor that the discussion was finally getting real.

"I didn't at first, but I get it now. In the car, you was testing me."

Bingo. The truth was that I'd figured out Quianna did the robbery even before we had our night at the motel. I loved her anyway. I never had any intentions of doing anything about what she and Trayvion did, but I had to see if she would really let him kill me. It was already proven I wasn't the smartest when it came to my dick and emotions. Considering how well Quianna had played the role of mastermind, I had needed proof that what she felt for me was real.

She made a show of moistening her lips. "You don't really think I was just faking? That fucking you was just part of the play?"

I had told myself to stay hard, but those cat eyes were fucking with me.

"Momma was the one who told you everything I done while you was inside, how I really felt. You think I could be so slimy as to recruit my mother and have her make up a whole story like that?" She asked this with a seductive smile.

I didn't feed into her weak attempt to soften my mood. While I knew the old lady wouldn't help run game on me, I still flashed a note to Quianna that said I thought she was capable of anything. She had helped to cover up her own brother's murder. Despite his confession in the car, the conspiracy theorist in me still wondered if Trayvion hadn't killed his father on her orders to make sure Doc never found out about the robbery. After all, if Trayvion had been in the back seat of Doc's Bentley that night, who was in the passenger seat?

Quianna was too good at reading me. She probably couldn't tell my exact train of thought but was able to gauge the overall theme. The smile faltered.

"If I could take back what happened in the car, I would. But baby, you scared me. I didn't know what you would do. I didn't know if your feelings for me was real. Plus you spent so many years with your head up Doc's ass that I—" The daggers I shot from my eyes diced the rest of that thought to pieces.

She paused for a moment, took time to script herself more carefully. "It ain't nothing I could do that would ever make you trust me now?"

She clearly didn't trust me, either. I waved my hands to draw her attention to our setting. We could've had a contact visit where we shared hugs, kisses, and sat next to each other with our fingers laced. She chose to put a wall of unbreakable glass between us.

Her gaze briefly dropped to the speckled tiles of vinyl composition, then bounced back to me. "So what are we supposed to do, Silence?"

I flipped to a fresh sheet and jotted something on my notepad, then held it up for her to read. The speed made my handwriting sloppier than usual. She needed a few seconds to decipher my hieroglyphs. She needed a few more to gauge my sincerity.

She frowned. "Why?"

I leaned back in my seat, let her read the answer in my face.

"Baby, I get it. You mad, you hurt, you feel like I was using you like everybody else."

We often do our best thinking in small quiet spaces, and with a little time to reflect, I realized I had used Doc as much as Quianna had used me. I'm a violent muthafucka, and the whole revenge thing just gave me a convenient excuse to do what I really wanted anyway. So for all the secrets and lies, I actually gave Quianna a pass.

If she had done this while still maintaining our brother/sister vibe, we'd be cool, but what I couldn't forgive was her giving me a sample of something not meant for me. Like fatherhood, love was an elusive prize I had convinced myself I could never have. She made me want it again, believe I could have it. That was a harsher wound than the one to my leg and would take a lot longer to heal.

She was still talking: "—know I fucked up, we both did, but we can get past this if you want us to." Quianna put her palm up against the plate of tempered glass and waited for me to mirror her from the other side.

And I swear on all the ancestors that I wanted to. I wanted to so bad that it hurt physically. I didn't just want to press my hand to hers, I wanted to touch her, wanted her body pressed to mine. I wanted her to feel like home again, like she did our first time at the motel.

But I had to leave her hanging. She pulled her hand down from the partition when the fact became obvious.

"Silence, I'm not leaving the city, and you not gone hurt me if I stay." That was in response to my last note. She made the declaration with a level of certainty that slowly eroded under the weight of my stare. "I love you, and you love me."

Both of us had already proven that we could hurt someone we love.

I reminded Quianna that she was a millionaire. She had the money and everything she made with the BANDS Society. I told her she needed to take Pooh, Trayvion, and all the kids and move to somewhere I would never find her. As of that date, she had a thirty-seven-day head-start, and I warned that she better be gone by the time I got out. I glared at her to show the lack of bullshit in my expression.

That made Quianna tear up. She began talking fast, trying to plead with me, but I looked down to my pad and scribbled my final note to her and slammed it palm flat against the glass. A one-word message with just three letters: *RUN!!*

I got up, turned my back on her, limped to the door, and banged for the CO. Quianna might've been pounding on the glass, might've been screaming my name. I didn't dare look back to see.

I returned to my cell and spent the next hour with my face buried in my pillow.

Chapter Ninety

Quianna only came to see me the one time. Prime never came back, and Dirty Red's second visit was only for finalizing the details of our new business arrangement. Nobody pulled up on me for weeks after that.

My strangest visit happened just three days before my release date.

I was watching Donald Glover host *Saturday Night Live*, reading his opening monologue via closed-caption, when a group of third-shift officers pulled me out my cell.

They said I needed to get dressed for a meeting with staff, and I looked at those fools like they were crazy. I wasn't new to this. What meeting would take place at eleven forty-five at night, fifteen minutes before lights out? No staff but custody and a few nurses working the infirmary would be at the facility this late on a weekend. I smelled bullshit, especially considering that six of the biggest COs they had were chosen as my escorts. I was leery as fuck but still slipped on my uniform and state-issued shoes.

The guards didn't cuff me, just walked me across the compound in a circle of gray and black. Six-on-one would be a hard hill to climb even if they were unarmed, but the Tasers and pepper spray on their belts gave me no win at all.

Even still, I was in fight-or-flight mode. Muscles tensed, walking on the tips of my feet, ready to scratch off at the first sign of trouble.

The administration building was a long two-story structure filled mostly with empty and unlit offices. While the rest of the prisoners were on their bunks for the midnight formal count, I was being led into the assistant deputy warden's office for God knows why.

I thought about Gamble and the cops I killed. How much pull did Councilman Henley have? Even while embroiled in his own legal battles, he still might be able to get me touched in prison.

ADW Addams was a mousy white lady, mid-fifties with thick glasses, who wore the same green skirt and black cardigan every day, as if it were her prison uniform. Her office was a windowless room on the first floor that was only twenty feet wide by fifteen long, stationed at the rear of the building near the segregation cells. A good place for a murder.

The man who waited in the office was neither one of the assistant deputies or the warden himself. He definitely wasn't Corliss Henley, whose indictment had his face all over the news. I'd never seen this older Rico Suave–looking brotha in his sixties who still had a head full of curly hair, slicked back and grayed at the temples. He matched my height but was lean as Prime in a fine gray pin-striped suit. I wasn't up on his brand of dress shoe, but they looked like something that would cost three months' rent in the hood.

The way this whole thing was set up had my paranoia on overdrive. I skewered him with my most intimidating frown that asked, *Who the fuck is you?*

Suave ignored me and gave the nod to the six officers standing on either side of me. Without question or comment, they filed out the room and closed the door on us.

No sooner than they left, he turned back to me and the grim

question I wore on my face. "It's better if we don't do names. You couldn't imagine the logistics it took to make this happen." He spoke the words slowly and carefully, clearly aware of my handicap.

I kept my game-face on, analyzed my opponent and options the way I was taught. While I got a killer's vibe from him, I liked my chances one-on-one; however, that still left the six officers waiting outside the door. I did a quick scan of the room looking for anything that could be used as a weapon.

He read my eyes. "It ain't that type of party, big man." He opened his blazer so that I could see he was unarmed. "Besides, if we wanted you dead, you would've been found hung in your cell that first night with a suicide note apologizing to Quianna, Trayvion, your boy Prime, even Mrs. P—God rest her soul."

He saw shock, then rage, tighten my features. "I'm afraid it is that type of party, though. You're not a talker, which is good. But do yourself a favor: listen." He took steps away from me, then turned back with a smirk after considering his last statement. "You know what I mean."

Suave walked to an adjoining door that was at the rear left corner of Addams's office. He passed through it at the same time a second suit walked in.

This was a clean-ass dark-skinned guy whose age was unreadable—he could've been anywhere from thirty-two to forty-five. His hair was cut close to bald; a neatly trimmed goatee framed his mouth and chin. He was a few inches shorter than me, not as bulky even though I could tell he was just as dedicated to his fitness. His suit was navy blue and from a more exclusive collection than what Quianna bought me from Ralph Lauren. His shirt was crispy white with diamond cufflinks. His cologne was subtle, just fragrant to me because of my sensitive nose.

But what wasn't so subtle was his aura. I can't explain in any way that makes sense, but he carried something in the room with him that just let you know he was somebody helluva without needing an introduction. It was his presence more than his clothes. Power just radiated off him and filled the deputy war-den's weak-ass office like static electricity. He had the vibe of someone who had shook Obama's hand while he was still in the White House, and probably made the president feel insecure.

"I apologize for the inconvenience of the time and place, but my schedule is tight and I'm still closely-scrutinized." He talked like a square, but I could tell there was hood in him. We were alone and I was uncuffed; he didn't seem the least bit threatened.

"Again, my bad. Is it more comfortable for you to read my lips, or do you prefer I sign?" He used ASL to say that the choice was mine and his hand formations were as crispy as his suit.

It didn't matter to me since I didn't have nothing to say to this nigga either way. I just continued to mug him, wondering what all this cloak-and-dagger shit was about.

He said, "I normally don't do this type of thing in person, but exceptional people deserve exceptional courtesy. The fact that I went through so much trouble to meet face-to-face is a token of the level of respect I have for you.

"And your father." That raised my eyebrows, and I suspected he knew it would.

I was slowly coming to the realization of who this mystery man was. And if he was who I suspected, I was totally and utterly fucked.

Chapter Ninety-one

"I met your pops once, even though he didn't really know who I was. I was very impressed by what he built out in Yakima." This muthafucka dropped that casually; it wasn't a boast. Just further proof that he was somebody powerful. Gamble had found out about the UOTA, but I'd never met an outsider who'd actually been to our compound.

"I appreciate that he's building soldiers, but I believe your father's endgame of using guerilla tactics to fight a race war is way too ambitious for his means. Still though, I donate considerable amounts of money and resources to the Temple of Alkebulan each year—more out of solidarity than expectation. He and I share a similar vision."

I was still hanging back by the entrance. When he made a gesture to offer me one of the two seats that fronted the desk, I crossed my arms defiantly. He nodded. It was a small victory that he conceded to me. He wasn't about to have a battle of wills with me, because he didn't have to. This was one of the few times I didn't feel the advantages of my size and training. Even though I had him by two inches and probably fifty pounds, he somehow felt bigger than me.

He leaned on the front of the desk before he spoke again. "The situation at the Tenth Precinct was being monitored from a distance by myself and other interested parties. While you deserve some praise for ridding the hood of a few dirty cops, you did interfere with something that I had already planned to resolve in a more discreet manner.

"Because of you, I lost containment of the situation, plus I lost someone who I had invested considerable time and money into. Do you have any idea of the billions you cost Detroit in city contracts? But more importantly, the amount you cost me personally?"

I wasn't too slow to connect the dots. Henley was supposed to be the next mayor but was facing life in prison because of his connection to Gamble. I'd heard through the grapevine that this caused Detroit to get cut out of their portion of the Urban Renewal Project. That slimy councilman had been in this dude's pocket, and he was pissed because I fucked up the whole play.

"Luckily, Philly and Baltimore are still good to go." Scratch that. He wasn't just the one pulling Henley's strings. This was the mysterious lobbyist who put the whole thing in motion.

He threw a quick glance to a Richard Mille that probably cost a million even though it didn't have a single stone. "I'm stationed out in Cali but was actually born and raised in the D. This community will always have special meaning to me. And now Detroit is going to miss out on a rare opportunity that would've revitalized it."

I signed: "You mean by pushing out all the blacks and letting the whites take it over." It only came out that way because ASL didn't have the words for niggas and honkies.

Dude looked at me like I was slow. "This had nothing to do with gentrification, just needed a few racist politicians to believe that in order to get my bill through. The URP was always for us, brotha. Five-point-six billion in tax-free grants earmarked for minority business owners in predominantly black cities. And all on the white man's dime."

I could've slapped myself. That was why Gamble had needed to partner up with Doc, then Louie Boy. Being Caucasian had meant she wasn't eligible on her own.

His look became stern, and that energy coming off him intensified until it raised the hairs on my neck and forearms. "It appears that I have you to thank for Sergeant Gamble, but the other greedy and reckless individuals involved like the Henleys will be dealt with accordingly."

It didn't take a GED to figure out what that meant. All the politicians and business leaders who had their hands in the URP pie were about to suffer a series of calamitous events: car accidents, drug overdoses, and unsolvable disappearances. Before he made it to trial, I figured that Corliss Henley would be found hung in his cell with a convenient note apologizing to all his loved ones—the same thing that Rico Suave-looking-ass nigga had threatened me with.

He continued, "However, I'm sure you and I can rectify things in a more civil manner. We are both honorable men, and as such, we both understand the character value in repaying a debt owed."

I used my fingers to say I didn't owe him shit. He used his superior talent and vocabulary to respectfully disagree. I saw in his dark-brown eyes that it really wasn't up for debate.

"Misfortune may have brought us together, but I believe our meeting to be serendipitous." I just frowned at him and the word I didn't understand.

"It took more than a few favors to keep you from going back upstate, plus get all copies of Gamble's video destroyed. And for the record, you can't just snap a white lady's neck in front of two witnesses and think that magically goes away." I had been thinking that Bates took care of the old man and the attendant at the Shell station.

He finished in a much sharper tone. "But don't get shit twisted nigga, I didn't do all this because I'm just friendly like that."

He read the question in my eyes. "Because Lutalo, you're a man with considerable talents. In the near future, my wife is going

370 • Zaire Crown

to experience certain difficulties that will bring her back to the city and in need of your assistance."

He went into his breast pocket and passed me a cheap flip-phone sheathed in a thin plastic slip. He had me remove it, then returned the sheath to his pocket.

This dude was slick, making sure I wouldn't have his finger-prints on the phone or the plastic he touched. As slick as the way he had played his entrance, making sure the guards had only seen his older partner.

He said, "Someone will be in touch."

Ninety percent of communication is nonverbal. Not speaking the threat gave it that much more gravity. He didn't have to warn me to keep the phone close or to make sure I followed the in-structions when the call came.

Just like he didn't have to tell me his name. It had been whis-pered in the hood for years as an urban legend, a mythical street king that most niggas didn't even think existed. This was the archvillain that Gamble had hinted at—the man in black who walks straight at the end. He was who Doc had aspired to be but couldn't have come close to even if he had lived.

We just stood face-to-face for a moment. He extended his fist to me, and I gave him dap.

I was probably the only man who had ever looked Sebastian Caine right in the eyes and didn't blink.

Chapter Ninety-two

Day Forty-Five.

I was up early that morning, again ready to sprint out the gate like a horse at the Belmont Stakes. My cell was empty. I didn't accumulate much property during my short stay and had nothing I wanted to take with me. Just the one thing I had to.

During the days that followed, my midnight meeting in the ADW's office had seemed like a strange dream. If I had been stupid enough to try to tell somebody, who would believe me? There would be no logbook he signed in, and even though there were cameras to cover every square foot of this facility, I was willing to bet there wasn't a single trace of video of him or the older guy with the slick hair. He had earned that moniker: The Invisible Man.

I packed the phone and allowed the sight and touch of it to confirm a bold reality: I was now in the pocket of about the most notorious muthafucka to ever play the game.

The officers came to take me up front at six-thirty a.m., and I was informed by the lady at the out-take desk that someone had dropped off an outfit for me. I offered a quiet thanks to whoever looked out. I stepped into the bathroom in state blues, stepped out swagged head-to-toe in green and red Gucci. The female CO at the desk hit me with a look that said I could get it.

By rule, I couldn't leave until eight o'clock, so I sat on the bench with an hour and a half to kill. I thought about how I had moved before and how these moves would be different. At first I pictured myself as a Ronin—a samurai with no master—and the fact that I thought I had needed a master showed how fucked-up I was in my thinking.

Mrs. P had given me some boss game that day when she told me to figure out what I enjoy doing, then make a hustle for it. I had known for a long time what I enjoy doing.

Whenever I had a choice to make between chilling with a woman or heading off into some gangsta shit, I always chose the drama. I had done it over and over with T'wanda back in the day, and I did the same thing with Quianna. It took that for me to finally realize this was the reason I wasn't built for relationships or being a father. The real reason I had to let Quianna go in that visiting room was not because she had hurt me, but because she would eventually get hurt by me. Connections were dangerous in the game I played. I would always make enemies, and the people I love would always be at risk as collateral damage, like Nika. I'm a goon. And even with all the risks, I still enjoyed being a goon more than anything else.

Now it was time to make a hustle for it. No more crews, no more tribes. From then on, I was no longer a Ronin: I was a mercenary.

I was escorted through the facility doors at 8:01. I noticed the stretched Lincoln Navigator parked in the prison lot but didn't give it a second thought until the driver followed, caught me walking southbound on Mound Road, and whipped up next to me.

I smelled the weed and alcohol before the back window rolled down. A pretty half-black/half-Asian face smiled at me and waved me to get in.

I climbed inside to LED lights, a mirrored partition, a turn-up already in progress. Despite the early hour, an empty rosé bottle rolled around the floor; Chun Li held another uncorked and half-drained. I looked over to the long bench seat to be greeted by three more smiling ladies with six naked titties bouncing free. We pulled off as Chun Li filled a champagne flute for me.

Even with my warning, part of me had still hoped the hazel-eyed girl would be there. Chun Li was able to see the disappointment in my face but wasn't as intuitive as Quianna when it came to my thoughts. She asked, "What's wrong, you ain't feeling the girls?"

I waved my hand to signify the selection was cool. All three were young—nineteen to twenty-two—and I guessed were new recruits, since I didn't recognize any of their faces. Two dark-skinned and one medium brown: all three met the BANDS Society's standard for beauty.

I still had my notepad. I scribbled a short question: *She still here?*

"Q keeping her new spot low-key." Chun Li's glare indicated she was up on the situation between me and her boss. "I don't know shit, and they don't either." She nodded to the girls.

Quianna wouldn't be stupid enough to send anybody I could squeeze for her location.

"She told me to give you this." Chun Li passed me another iPhone. I turned it on to find one message: *Welcome home. Hope we can talk soon.* It was anonymous, with no return number.

I cut the phone off, let it join the other in my pocket. I planned to have both checked for GPS or some other tracking app the first chance I got.

"Told me to give you this, too." Chun Li reached down for something at her feet. It landed with some weight when she dropped it in my lap.

I wondered why she was handing me a Paw Patrol bookbag like I'm a second-grader on his first day of school. I opened it and didn't find shit childish about what was inside.

The bag was crammed with cash stacks, too thick to fold and bundled in rubber bands. The bag was so stuffed I had to fight with the zipper. I wasn't about to pull any out to count up.

If Quianna got Louie Boy and Doc for three-point-eight million, minus what she had to split with the girls who helped her, and minus what she already had spent, I wondered what she had left. I wondered what percentage she felt fit to offer me. The bag was heavy as hell. If these were all hundreds, it could've easily been a million in there.

The smell coming off the cash confirmed what I knew about where Quianna had stashed the money. For my nose, the scent of dog food was strong but wouldn't affect how it spent.

That day she invited me upstairs for breakfast, not only did I notice that she kept her pantry locked with a deadbolt, I noticed the huge seventy-five-pound bag of Pedigree, even though she fed Chino a different brand. I had thought that was a lot of dog food for one puppy but put it out of my mind. Then when she moved over to Radom, I thought it was odd she would keep the same huge bag of dog food in her bedroom closet instead of the kitchen downstairs. She couldn't have one of the kids or Trayvion's friends stumble upon that by accident.

That sneaky little bitch. Thinking about her made me smile. My baby had said I was supposed to get picked up the first time in a limo full of strippers and get a duffel bag dropped at my feet. I was still in love. I didn't even deny the fact to myself.

I got off that sucker shit, focused on the things I had to do that day.

Like swing by Cascade to pick up some more money. The understanding I came to with Dirty Red was that I'd get Gamble off his ass, but in return, I demanded fifteen percent of the business, damages I'd collect on behalf of little Nika. In exchange for having me as a literal silent partner, the Joy Road Boys come under my protection. Which means I handle any and all beefs that come their way: civilians, rival gangs, even more dirty police. Whatever.

Next, I had memorized the driver's licenses of the two individuals I jacked for the cars that served me on my missions. I'd leave ten thousand in the mailbox of the young nigga I took Granny's New Yorker from, even though she was probably insured. I figured twenty stacks should make it right with Old School, since I had to pop him for the Buick.

I went to close the bookbag and put it away when Chun Li stopped me. "There's something else in there, too. One last gift Q wanted you to have." Her sly smile made me nervous.

There was a small pocket on the front of the bag that I unzipped slowly, as if I expected the thing to explode. Inside I found what looked like two glossy five-by-seven photographs. But these were black and shaded with gray lines and smudges. I didn't know what I was looking at, and I started to get irritated with Chun Li's stupid grin.

She finally took the picture and turned right side up what I had been looking at upside down. "That's the head right there." She traced the outline with her finger. "That's the body."

It was the sonogram of a seven-week-old fetus. I demanded another glass of rosé, sucked it down, and needed a refill.

Every time I had busted in Quianna, it felt like she was stealing a piece of my soul. When it comes to GOOD PUSSY, don't even think pull out. Plus the math added up.

I had thought the second sonogram was simply a duplicate of the first until Chun Li dropped the bomb that had me turning up the whole bottle.

Chun Li confirmed it with a nod. "She seven weeks, too. That shit you got must be potent. Congratulations. Daddy."

Quianna maybe, but Lexy no way. We only fucked without a rubber that one time at her house. I would need DNA to prove that one.

The more I thought, the more I started to believe this had been Quianna's plan all along. What if this was the real reason she had sent Lexy into my room that night? What if the too-small condom Lexy had for me was what made Quianna so pissed at her? At the club, Lexy had said Quianna was mad at her for not securing something; then I remembered that comment Lexy made at her house about already having one asshole baby daddy and not wanting another.

Quianna had set up the ultimate insurance policy. I had already proved by not killing T'wanda when I caught her cheating that I couldn't hurt a woman carrying my child. By the time I found out what Quianna had helped Trayvion do, it would be too late—she would be protected by my feelings for her and the seed growing in her belly. In her perfect world, me, her, and Lexy would be in a three-way relationship with them doubly protected and me locked down with two pairs of handcuffs. I had nothing to prove any of this, but I was back on my conspiracy shit.

My thoughts were so deep in the rabbit hole that I'd totally forgotten about Chun Li and the topless trio on the bench seat across from me. Chun Li had rolled a blunt, took a few hits, and was waiting for me. I absently pulled on it twice, then put it in rotation.

She gave the girls a nod, and two of them came to sit on either side of me while Chun Li got on her knees between my legs. She eased down my Gucci bottoms.

Chun Li jacked my beast to stiffen it, then smiled at me. "The Head Nurse is on call."

I watched the whole ten inches disappear in the mouth like a magic trick. Within seconds, she had taken my two baby mommas off my mind, had my eyes closed and me leaning back in my seat. I finally went to that place I watched her take the dude on the couch.

But the driver was going to have to make a quick stop at the store so I could grab some Magnum XLs. I wasn't busting in none of these bitches.

Epilogue

He was a coward-ass bitch.

In pressurized situations, people can tell you their life stories in an instant, with a gesture. He had been a sheltered child with no siblings who got everything he asked for from his upper-middle-class parents. He had never been in the streets, despite all the good gangsta shit he was selling. He was just a short muthafucka with a complex and a big mouth who was too used to getting his way. I didn't grow up with this dude. We had only met once and then briefly. His response to my presence told me everything I needed to know about his pedigree.

A real one would've tried to fight; a smart one would've tried to run. To come back to his dressing room after a sound check, to open the door and find me waiting on him, standing over three beaten and bleeding members of his security detail, would've made braver men than him run for their lives. Trust me, it had.

But he couldn't even move. He just stood there frozen at the sight of me like a deer trapped in the oncoming headlights of a semi.

I had spent the last seven months praying to the ancestors to catch this dude out in traffic or to bump into him at an event

somewhere. Then lucky me. Rick Ross comes to town for a concert at Little Caesars Arena and slides in a few local artists for his
opening acts.

As we stood facing each other in the doorway of his dressing
room, I waited for and hoped to see the exact moment when
recognition would brighten his eyes.

It didn't happen. The little rapper had probably disrespected
so many people that he'd completely forgotten about me and that
incident at the mall. Just totally wrote me off.

It didn't matter. I snatched his short ass in the room by his
chains and a fistful of shirt. I was happy to remind Brody Starrz
who I was.

For embarrassing Quianna in the food court, the cost had
been one broken bone. But that was before I fell in love and she
became my baby momma. The price was now going to be so
much more expensive.